Praise for Paul Cleave's
...estseller

...OUSE

"An inte......nish, I read *The Laughter-house* in one sitting. It'll have you up all night. Fantastic!"

—S. J. Watson, *New York Times* bestselling
author of *Before I Go to Sleep*

"This dark, gripping thriller, the latest in the Tate saga, is as hard-boiled as it gets. The surprise ending suspends all disbelief. Like a TV series that ends its season on a cliff-hanger, you won't want to wait until next year. This will leave the reader clamoring for the next book in the series."

—*Suspense Magazine*

"Piano wire–taut plotting, Tate's heart-wrenching losses and forlorn hopes, and Cleave's unusually perceptive gaze into the maw of a killer's madness make this a standout chapter in his detective's rocky road to redemption."

—*Publishers Weekly* (starred)

"In Cleave's third psycho-thriller, Theodore Tate is the quintessential flawed hero, a damaged soul hunting deviants in a forest of moral quandaries. . . . The novel is less a character study than a dissection of the need for, and cost of, revenge. . . . Cleave's horrific narrative takes no prisoners, with the bloody action relentlessly ricocheting around Christchurch at a pace that leaves the detectives near collapse. . . . An intense and bloody noir thriller, one often descending into a violent abyss reminiscent of Thomas Harris, creator of Hannibal Lecter."

—*Kirkus Reviews*

"A wonderful book . . . The final effect is that tingling in the neck hairs that tells us an artist is at work."

—*Booklist* (starred)

ALSO BY PAUL CLEAVE

Joe Victim
The Laughterhouse
Collecting Cooper
Blood Men
The Killing Hour
The Cleaner

PAUL CLEAVE

CEMETERY LAKE

A THRILLER

ATRIA PAPERBACK

New York London Toronto Sydney New Delhi

ATRIA PAPERBACK
A Division of Simon & Schuster, Inc.
1230 Avenue of the Americas
New York, NY 10020

This book is a work of fiction. Any references to historical events, real
people, or real places are used fictitiously. Other names, characters, places,
and events are products of the author's imagination, and any resemblance to
actual events or places or persons, living or dead, is entirely coincidental.

Copyright © 2008 by Paul Cleave
Originally published in 2008 by Random House New Zealand.

All rights reserved, including the right to reproduce this book
or portions thereof in any form whatsoever. For information
address Atria Books Subsidiary Rights Department,
1230 Avenue of the Americas, New York, NY 10020.

First Atria Paperback edition June 2013

ATRIA PAPERBACK and colophon are trademarks
of Simon & Schuster, Inc.

For information about special discounts for bulk purchases,
please contact Simon & Schuster Special Sales at 1-866-506-1949
or business@simonandschuster.com.

The Simon & Schuster Speakers Bureau can bring authors to your
live event. For more information or to book an event contact the
Simon & Schuster Speakers Bureau at 1-866-248-3049 or visit our
website at www.simonspeakers.com.

Manufactured in the United States of America

10 9 8 7 6 5 4 3 2 1

Library of Congress Cataloging-in-Publication Data

Cleave, Paul, date.
   Cemetery Lake : a thriller / by Paul Cleave. — First Atria Books trade
paperback edition.
      p. cm.
   1. Private investigators—New Zealand—Christchurch—Fiction.
2. Serial murder investigation—Fiction. 3. Suspense fiction.
4. Noir fiction. I. Title.
   PR9639.4.C54C46 2013
   823'.92—dc23   2012047800

ISBN 978-1-4516-7783-6
ISBN 978-1-4516-7786-7 (ebook)

To Joe—who got the ball rolling

PART 1

PART I

CHAPTER ONE

Blue fingernails.

They're what have me out here, standing in the cold wind, shivering. The blue fingernails aren't mine, but attached to somebody else—some dead guy I've never met before. The Christchurch sun that was burning my skin earlier this afternoon has gone. It's the sort of inconsistent weather I'm used to. An hour ago I was sweating. An hour ago I wanted to take the day off and head down to the beach. Now I'm glad I didn't. My own fingernails are probably turning blue, but I don't dare look.

I'm here because of a dead guy. Not the one in the ground in front of me, but one still down at the morgue. He's acting as casual as a guy can whose body has been snipped open and stitched back together like a rag doll. Casual for a guy who died from arsenic poisoning.

I tighten my coat, but it doesn't help against the cold wind.

I should have worn more clothes. Should have looked at the bright sun an hour ago and figured where the day was heading.

The cemetery lawn is long in some places, especially around the trees where the lawn mower doesn't hit, and it ripples out from me in all directions as though I'm the epicenter of a storm. In other places where foot traffic is heavy it's short and brown where the sun has burned all the moisture away. The nearby trees are thick oaks that creak loudly and drop acorns around the gravestones. They hit the cement markers, sounding like bones of the dead tapping out an SOS. The air is cold and clammy like a morgue.

I see the first drops of rain on the windshield of the digger before I feel them on my face. I turn my eyes to the horizon where gravestones covered in mold roll into the distance toward the city, death tallying up and heading into town. The wind picks up, the leaves of the oaks rustle as the branches let go of more acorns, and I flinch as one hits me in the neck. I reach up and grab it from my collar.

The digger engine revs loudly as the driver, an overweight guy whose frame bulges at the door, moves into place. He looks about as excited to be here as I am. He is pushing and pulling at an assortment of levers, his face rigid with concentration. The engine hiccups as he positions the digger next to the gravesite, then shudders and strains as the scoop bites into the hardened earth. It changes position, coming up and under, and fills with dirt. The cabin rotates and the dirt is piled onto a nearby tarpaulin. The cemetery caretaker is watching closely. He's a young guy struggling to light a cigarette against the strengthening wind, his hands shaking almost as much as his shoulders. The digger drops two more piles of dirt before the caretaker tucks the cigarettes back into his pocket, giving up. He gives me a look I can't quite identify, probably because he only manages to make eye contact for a split second before looking away. I'm hoping he doesn't come over to complain about evicting somebody from their final resting place, but he doesn't—just goes back to staring at the hollowed ground.

The vibrations of the digger force their way through my feet and into my body, making my legs tingle. The tree behind me can feel them too, because it fires more acorns into my neck. I step out of the shade and into the drizzle, nearly twisting my ankle on a few of the ropey roots from the oak that have pushed through the ground. There is a small lake only about fifteen meters away, about the size of an Olympic swimming pool. It's completely enclosed by the cemetery grounds, fed by an underground stream. It makes this cemetery a popular spot for death, but not for recreation. Some of the gravesites are close to it, and I wonder if the coffins are affected by moisture. I hope we're not about to dig up a box full of water.

The driver pauses to wipe his hand across his forehead, as if operating all of those levers is hot work in these cold conditions. His glove leaves a greasy mark on his skin. He looks out at the oak trees and areas of lush lawn, the still lake, and he's probably planning on being buried out here one day. Everybody thinks that when they see this spot. *Nice place to be buried. Nice and scenic. Restful.* Like it makes a difference. Like you're going to know if somebody comes along and chops down all the trees. Still, I guess if you have to be buried somewhere, this place beats out a lot of others I've seen.

A second flatbed truck sweeps its way between the gravestones. It has been pimped out with a wraparound red stripe and fluffy dice in the window, but it hasn't been cleaned in months and the rust spots around the edges of the doors and bumper have been ignored. It pulls up next to the gravesite. A bald guy in gray overalls climbs out from behind the steering wheel and tucks his hands into his pockets and watches the show. A younger guy climbs out the other side and starts playing with his cell phone. There isn't much more they can do while the pile of dirt grows higher and higher. I can see the raindrops plinking into the lake, tiny droplets jumping toward the heavens. I make my way over to its edge. Anything is better than watching the digger doing its job. I can still feel the vibrations. Small pieces of dirt are rolling down the bank of the lake and splashing into the water. Flax bushes and ferns and a few poplar trees are scattered around the lakeside. Tall reeds stick up near the banks, reaching for the sky. Broken branches and leaves have become waterlogged and jammed against the bank.

I turn back to the digger when I hear the scoop scrape across the coffin lid. It sounds like fingers running down a blackboard, and it makes me shiver more than the cold. The caretaker is shaking pretty hard now. He looks cold and pissed off. Until the moment the digger arrived, I thought he was going to chain himself to the gravestone to prevent the uprooting of one of his tenants. He had plenty to say about the moral implications of what we were doing. He acted as though we were digging up the coffin to put him inside.

The digger operator and the two guys from the flatbed pull on face masks that cover their noses and mouths, then drop into the grave. The overweight guy from the digger moves with the ease of somebody who has rehearsed this moment over and over. All three disappear from view, as if they have found a hidden entrance into another world. They spend some time hunched down, apparently figuring out the mechanics to get the chain attached between the coffin and digger. When the chain is secure the driver climbs back into place and the others climb out of the grave. He wipes his forehead again. Raising the dead is sweaty work.

The engine lurches as it takes the weight of the coffin. The flatbed truck starts up and backs a little closer. With the two machines violently shuddering, more dirt spills from the bank and slides into the water.

About five meters out into the lake, I see some bubbles rising to the surface, then a patch of mud. But there is something else there too. Something dark that looks like an oil patch.

There is a thud as the coffin is lowered onto the back of the truck. The springs grind downward from the weight. I can hear the three men talking quickly among themselves, having to nearly shout to be heard over the engines. The rain is getting heavier. The dark patch rising beneath the water breaks the surface. It looks like a giant black balloon. I've seen these giant black balloons before. You hope they're one thing, but they're always another.

"Hey, buddy, you might want to take a look at this," one of the men calls out.

But I'm too busy looking at something else.

"Hey? You listening?" The voice is closer now. "We've got something here you need to look at."

I glance up at the digger operator as he walks over to me. The caretaker is starting to walk over too. Both men look into the water and say nothing.

The black bubble isn't really a bubble, but the back of a jacket. It hangs in the water, and connected to it is a soccer ball–sized object. It has hair. And before I can answer, another shape bubbles to the surface, and then another, as the lake releases its hold on the past.

CHAPTER TWO

The case never made the news because it was never a case. It was a slice of life that happens every day, no matter how hard you try to prevent it. It made the back pages where the obituaries are listed, along with the John Smiths of this world who are beloved parents and grandparents and who will be sorely missed. It was a simple story of man-gets-old-and-dies. Read all about it.

It happened two years ago. Some people wake up every morning and read the obits while downing scrambled eggs and orange juice, looking for a name that jumps out from their past. It's a crazy way to kill a few minutes. It's like a morbid lottery, seeing whose number has come up, and I don't know whether these people find relief when they get to the end and don't find anybody they know or relief when they do. They're looking for a reason; they're looking for somebody, wanting to make a connection and to feel their own mortality.

Henry Martins. I pulled those stories from the newspaper database this morning just like I did two years ago, and read what people had to say about him when he died, which wasn't much. Then again, it's hard to sum up a person's life in five lines of six-point text. It's hard to say how much you're going to miss them. There were eleven entries for Henry over three days from family and friends. Nobody made my job easier by throwing a *Glad you're dead* in with their woeful sorrows, but each obituary read like the others: boring, emotionless. At least that's the way they come across when you don't know the guy.

Henry Martins's daughter came into the station a week after the old man was buried. She sat down in my office and told me her dad was murdered. I told her he wasn't. If he had been, the medical examiner would have stumbled across it. MEs are like that. It was easy to see she already had both feet firmly on the road of suspicion, and I told her I'd look into it. I did some checking. Henry Martins was a bank manager who left behind a lot of family and a lot of clients, but his occupation wasn't an opportunity for him to line his pockets with other people's money. I looked into his life as much as I could in the small amount of time I could allot for his daughter's "hunch," but nothing stood out as odd.

Two years later, and Henry Martins's coffin is behind me on chains as the wind increases in strength. And Henry Martins's wife is trying to avoid anybody with a badge now that her second husband has died, his blue fingernails the first indication that he was poisoned. Henry's daughter hasn't spoken to me because I'm no longer in the same position I was two years ago. It's easy to let my mind wander and think of things that might have been. I could have done more back then. I could have solved a murder, if that's what happened. Could have stopped another man from dying. The jury is still out on whether Mrs. Martins had bad luck or bad judgment when it came to men.

The rain gets heavier, creating a thousand tiny ripples on the surface of the water. The caretaker is backing away, keeping his eyes on the water. Slowly the elements seem to disappear—so do the voices, and the vibrations. All that is left are the three corpses floating ahead of me, each one a victim of something—a victim of age, foul play, bad luck, or maybe a victim of a cemetery's lack of real estate.

The three workers have all come over beside me. Their excited bursts of started but stilted observations have ended. We're standing, the four of us, in front of the water; three people are in it: it's like we're all pairing up for a social, but with one person left over. The occasion demands quiet, each of us unwilling to say anything to break the silence building between us. More dirt slides into and mixes with the water, turning it cloudy brown. One of the bodies sinks back out of view and disappears. The other two are drifting toward us, swimming without movement. I'm not about to jump in and pull them out. I'd do it, no doubt there, if the bodies were flailing about. But they're not. They're dead, have been for maybe a long time. The situation may seem urgent, but in reality it isn't. Both are face down, and both appear to be dressed, and not badly dressed either. They look as though they could be on their way to an event. A funeral or a wedding. Except for the ropes. There are pieces of green rope attached to the bodies.

The digger driver keeps squinting at the two corpses, as if his eyes are tricking him. The truck driver is standing with his mouth wide open and his hands on his hips, while his assistant keeps glancing at his watch as if this whole thing might push him into overtime.

"We need to haul them in," I say, even though both bodies are nudging against the bank now.

I had planned on staying dry today. I had planned on seeing one dead body. Now everything is up in the air.

"Why? They're not exactly going to go anywhere," the truck driver says.

"They might sink like the other one," I point out.

"What are we going to grab them with?"

"I don't know. Something," I say. "A branch, maybe. Or your hands."

"I'm not stopping you from using your hands," he says, and the other two nod quickly in agreement.

"Well, what about rope?" I ask. "You gotta have some of that, right?"

"That one there," the truck driver says, looking at the corpse closest to us, "already has some rope."

"Looks rotten. You gotta have something newer in the truck, right?" I ask, and we all look over at the truck just as we hear it start.

The caretaker is sitting in the cab.

"What the hell?" the driver asks. He starts to run over to it, but he isn't quick enough. The caretaker gets it into gear and pulls away fast. The coffin isn't secure. It starts to slide. It makes a grating sound, like heavy sandpaper dragged slowly against a floorboard. It hits the edge and starts to slide over it, then for a moment it looks like it's going to hang there, that it's going to defy gravity, but then momentum and physics kick in as the tipping point is reached and a moment later it goes crashing into the ground.

The driver keeps running after the truck even though the distance is growing. "Hey, come back here, come back here!"

"Where's he going?" the digger operator asks me, and I assume he means the caretaker and not the guy chasing him.

"Anywhere but here is my guess," I say, which is both extremely vague and extremely accurate. I pull my cell phone from my pocket. "You got some rope in the digger?"

"Yeah, hang on."

He wanders over to the digger. I phone the police station and get transferred to a detective I used to know. I tell him the situation. He tells me to sober up. Tells me of course there are going to be bodies out here in the cemetery. It takes a minute to persuade him the bodies are coming up from the depths of the lake. And another minute to convince him I'm not joking.

"And bring some divers," I say, before hanging up.

The digger operator has made it back. He hands me the rope. The truck driver is back too; he's swearing as his partner uses a cell phone to call their boss for someone to come and get them. I tie an arm-length branch around the end of the rope and make my way down the gently sloping bank, intending to throw the branch just past the nearest corpse to bring it closer, but it turns out the slippery grass beneath my feet has other ideas. One moment I'm on the bank. The next I'm in the water.

My feet are submerged in mud, the water up to my knees. Something grabs my ankle and I lever forward, my arms slapping the surface next to the corpse before I start sinking. I pull my legs from the mud, but there is nothing to stand on. This lake is a Goddamn death trap, and now I know why it's full of corpses. These people came to grieve for the dead and ended up joining them. The water is ice cold, locking up my chest and stomach and cramping my muscles. My eyes are open and the water is burning them. There is only darkness around me, compounded by the silence, and I can sense hands of the dead reaching to pull me deeper, wanting me to join them, wanting fresh blood.

Then suddenly I'm racing back to the surface, my hand tight around the rope that is pulling me up. I kick with my feet. Point my body upward. And a second later I'm right next to a bloated woman in a long white dress. It looks like a wedding dress. I push away from her, and the three men help me onto the bank. I sit down, gasping for air. Both my shoes are missing.

"Goddamn, buddy, you okay?"

The question sounds like it is coming from the other side of the lake, and I'm not sure which one of them asked it. Maybe all three of them in unison. I lean over my knees and start coughing. I feel like I'm choking. I'm shivering, I'm angry, but mostly I feel embarrassed. But none of the men are laughing. They're all leaning over me, looking concerned. With two floating corpses nearby, it's easy to understand why nothing here is a joke.

"There's something else you need to know," the digger operator says when I've stopped coughing enough to hear him. "I was trying to tell you before," he says, slipping that last part into the conversation as if each word is its own sentence, and his face screws up slightly as if each word has its own taste too, and none of them good. He makes it sound like whatever he has to say is going to be worse than what just happened, and I can think of only one thing that could possibly be.

"Yeah?"

"Marks. On top of the coffin," he says.

"How did I know you were going to say that?"

Now it's his turn to shrug. He doesn't come up with any suggestions of mind reading. "Thin lines," he says. "Like cuts. They look like shovel cuts," he says.

"From a shovel," I tell him. He gives me a funny look. I ignore it. My mind is running a little slow from the swim it just took. "You think this coffin has been dug up before?"

"I'm not just thinking it, I'm saying it. There are definitely marks on the coffin that nobody here caused. Shit, I wonder if she's empty."

She. Like a plane or a boat, because the coffin in a way is a vessel taking you somewhere.

We walk over to it. The coffin has survived the fall pretty well. There's a large crack running from the bottom corner along the side from the impact, but we can't see into it. I'm tempted to open her up, see what cargo she has or if she's been plundered, but the approaching sirens kill the idea.

I watch as the two police cars arrive, along with an ambulance and a pair of station wagons.

CHAPTER THREE

There is a natural progression to things. An evolution. First there is a fantasy. The fantasy belongs to some sadistic loser, a guy who eats and breathes and dreams with the sole desire to kill. Then comes the reality. A victim falls into his web, she is used, and the fantasy often doesn't live up to the reality. So there are more victims. The desire escalates. It starts with one a year, becomes two or three a year, then it's happening every other month. Or every month. Their bodies show up. The police are involved. They bring doctors and pathologists and technicians who can analyze fibers and blood samples and fingerprints. They create a profile to help catch the killer. Following them is the media. The media spins the killer's fantasy into gold. Death is a moneymaking industry. The undertakers, the coffin salesmen, the crystal-ball and palm readers, then eventually the digger operators and the private investigators: we're the next step in the progression, standing in the rain and watching as one travesty of justice reveals another.

I have shrugged out of my wet jacket and wet shirt, dried off using a towel an ambulance driver gave me, and pulled on a fresh windbreaker. My shoes are still sleeping with the fishes and my pants and underwear are soaking, but I'm safe from pneumonia. Nobody is paying me any attention as I sit on the floor of the ambulance with my legs hanging out, looking over the scene of, at this stage, an indeterminable crime.

The graveyard has been cordoned off. The two police cars have become twelve. The two station wagons have become six. There are roadblocks covering the main entrance, as though the police are preparing to fight back an upsurge of angry corpses. There are two tarpaulins lying across the ground; on each one rests a well-dressed but decomposing or decomposed body. A canvas tent has been erected over them, protecting them from the elements. Somebody has strung some yellow *Do not cross* tape around the tent. It keeps the corpses from going anywhere. There are men and women wearing nylon suits studying the bodies. Others are standing near the lake. They look like divers preparing for some deep-sea mission, only there are no divers here. Not yet, anyway. There are open suitcases containing tools and evidence beneath the tent. The rain is still falling and the long grass ripples with the wind. The digger has been taken away, and the coffin has been taken to the morgue.

I tighten my windbreaker and reach around for a second blanket. The inside of the ambulance is messy, as if it's sped over dozens of bumps on the way: God knows how the paramedics ever know where anything is. I wrap the blanket over my shoulders and let my teeth chatter as I watch the few detectives who have shown up. More will arrive soon. They always do. So far there hasn't been much for them to do other than look at two bodies and a lot of gravestones. They can't go canvassing the area because all the neighbors are dead. They have no one to question other than the caretaker, but the caretaker is off somewhere in a stolen truck.

The wind has picked up. Acorns are still falling, flicking off the tombstones and making small, metallic dinging noises as they hit the roofs of the vehicles. All this extra traffic, yet no other bodies have risen up from the watery depths of whatever Hell is down there. I glance over at the ambulance driver. He has nobody to save. He has nothing else to do than watch the show, bury his hands in his pockets, and keep me company. All of us are in that boat. He's probably just hanging around until he gets the call that somebody is dead or dying, blood and limbs scattered across the highway of life that he cleans up every day.

The buzzing of a media helicopter approaching from the north sounds like a mosquito. I touch the outside of my trouser pocket and run my finger over the bulge of the wristwatch I stole from one of the corpses after we pulled it from the water.

One of the medical examiners, a man in his early fifties who has been doing this for nearly half his life, comes out of the tent, looks around at the small crowd of people, spots me, and then heads over to a detective. They talk for a few minutes, all very casual—the relaxed conversation of two men who have delivered and received many conversations about death. By the time he comes over he is sighing, as though being in the same graveyard with me is such tiring work. His hands are thrust deep into his pockets. There are small drops of rain on his glasses. I stand up, but don't move away from the ambulance. I have a pretty good idea what the examiner is going to say. After all, I spent some time with those corpses. I saw how they were dressed.

"Well?" I ask, clenching my jaw to keep my teeth from chattering.

"You said there were three bodies?" the medical examiner says, and his tone is depressing, the kind of tone you wouldn't want to hear on a suicide hotline if you're calling and wanting to be told things are going to be okay.

"Yeah," I tell him.

"We've got two."

"The other one sank again."

"Yep. Bodies will do that. Bodies do lots of strange things."

He's right. He's seen it a lot over the years and so have I. "What else?"

"Schroder," he says, and he glances back at the detective he was talking to, the same detective I called, "said to throw you some basic facts, but nothing more. Just the same things he'll be giving those vultures out there when he releases a statement in an hour." He points to the edge of the cemetery where the media is no doubt congregating behind the police barriers.

"Come on, Sheldon, you can give me more than just the basics."

"Is that what you think?"

Suddenly I'm not so sure. One day everybody is your best friend; the next you're just a giant pain in the ass. "So, you're going to make me guess?"

"My guesses are supported by science," he says.

"Well, science away," I tell him.

"You saw the rope?"

I nod.

"I'd say they all had rope attached at one point," he says. "But not so much now."

"I don't follow," I say.

"You probably figured we're not dealing with homicides, right?"

I nod again. "The thought crossed my mind."

"At least not in any traditional sense," he says. "Probably not in any sense at all."

I stop nodding. "You want to clarify that?"

"Why? You think this is your case now?"

"I'm just curious," I tell him. "I'm allowed to be curious, aren't I? I'm the one who found these poor bastards."

"That doesn't make them yours."

"You think I want them?"

"You know what I mean." He looks back at the tent covering the corpses. The wind has got hold of one of the doors and is snapping it from side to side like a sail. An officer gets it under control and secures it. If the wind gets stronger out here things might start taking flight. "Okay, let me back up a bit here," he says. "First of all, the two bodies we've got—only one of them is intact."

"That's got to be one of two reasons, right?" I ask.

"Yeah. And it's the good one. Nobody tortured these people or cut them up—at least that's my preliminary finding. The worst body is simply coming apart from decomposition. He's missing everything below the pelvic girdle, and what is there is held together mostly by his clothes. Hard to tell how long he's been in the water, but it seems obvious that when we find the rest of him we're going to find more rope. Could be piles of bones stuck in the mud down there. The thing is, Tate, going by the woman we found, I'm pretty sure these people weren't killed and dumped in the lake. They were already dead. Dead and buried, I'd say," he says, and I think of the coffin with the shovel marks. "Don't know what originally killed them, but we'll get there. We'll get some time frames too."

I look past Sheldon to the grave markers all around us. There are a few things going through my mind. I'm thinking that somewhere out there is an undertaker or mortuary assistant saving money by reselling the same coffins to different families. Coffins are expensive. Use them once, dig them up, dump the bodies in the water, rinse down the woodwork, spray some air freshener in, and make it sparkle with a coat of furniture polish. Then it goes back on the market. Brand new again. None of those signs saying *As new, only one owner, elderly lady, low mileage*. One coffin could do dozens of people.

"You know you could buy a car for the same amount as a coffin?" the medical examiner muses.

"That's not it," I realize.

"What?"

"This isn't about reselling coffins," I say.

"What makes you so sure?"

One thing that makes me sure is the watch in my pocket. If it was about making money, that watch would never have gone into the water with its owner. But I can't tell him that. Instead I tell him an even better reason. "Why throw the bodies into the lake? Why not just throw them back into the ground? Or switch the coffins with budget ones? No, it's not about that. It's about something else."

"Yeah . . . maybe. I guess."

"I wonder how many more bodies are down there."

He shrugs. "We'll know soon enough."

If there are more bodies in the lake, the divers will find them. I'll be gone by then. It's unrealistic to think somebody will keep me informed—I'll learn the numbers from the papers. One thing I learned in the years before I left the police force is that life and death are all about numbers. People love statistics. Especially nasty ones.

"How old do you think this cemetery is?" I ask.

He shrugs. He wasn't expecting the question. "What? How the hell would I know that? Sixty, eighty years? I don't know."

"Well, the lake has always been here," I say. "It's not like they built the cemetery first and imported the lake to make it scenic. Which means this might not even be a crime scene. Except maybe one of criminal negligence."

"You want to elaborate?"

"It's not a stretch to imagine some poor management and attempts at utilizing space means some of these graves are too close to the water. Maybe some of the coffins have rotted from water damage and the bodies have been pulled into the lake, or there's an underground stream sucking some caskets along. Maybe they've floated up to the surface before, and the way the caretaker here dealt with it was to tie cinderblocks to them to hide them away."

Sheldon shakes his head. "Not in this case."

"You sure?" I ask, but I can tell he's sure.

"The woman makes me sure," he says. "She's been in the water only a couple of days. No time for your rotting-coffin theory. There are signs of mortician tricks that suggest she had a funeral, which is why I'm confident these people were once buried. In fact, she's the reason we're all here. She's the catalyst here—fat stores and gases brought her to the surface, and she brought the others up with her."

"She'd do that, even if she was embalmed?"

"She wasn't embalmed."

"I thought that . . ."

He starts nodding. "I know what you thought," he says. "You thought that everybody has to be embalmed, that it's law. But it's not. Embalming slows the decomposition for a few days so the body can be displayed—that's all it's for. It's optional."

"Can you tell if anything else has been done to the bodies?"

"Like what?"

"I don't know. It's not about reselling coffins and none of this is a result of nature, so these people were dug up for something, right? Have they been used for anything? Experimented on?"

"No way I can know that right now. But one thing I can tell you is one of the victims was wearing rings and a necklace. You can rule out grave robbery."

Grave robbery. I feel as though I've slipped back into a Sherlock Holmes novel. Holmes, of course, would find some logic in this. Often he would solve a case only by remembering something he read in some textbook ten years earlier, but in the end he'd get there, and he'd make it look easy. Looking around, I'm not sure if the evidence is here for anyone to deduce whether the person who did this was left or right handed, or worked as an apprentice shoemaker. Only Holmes would. He was one lucky bastard.

"Any way we can ID them?" I ask.

"We?"

"You know what I mean."

"We'll start with the woman. She should be simple. Then work backward."

I glance past the examiner toward the tent that shelters the dead and the wet. The wind chill seems to have dropped by around five degrees, and picked up an extra twenty-five kilometers an hour. The sides of the tent are billowing out. The blanket around me no longer feels warm.

"So how do . . . ?"

He raises his hand to stop me. "Look, Tate, your colleagues know what they're doing, and I've already told you more than I should have. Leave it to them."

He's right and wrong. Sure, they know what they're doing, but they're no longer my colleagues. I think about the watch in my pocket, hoping it will have one of those *To Doug, love Beryl* inscriptions on it. Then it's just a matter of finding a gravestone belonging to a Doug who was married to a Beryl. With luck, that gravestone is here. With luck, these people were given proper burials by proper priests under the proper conditions, and not autopsied and dressed up by some homicidal maniac in his basement.

A four-wheel drive pulls up next to the tent. Two guys climb out and walk around to the back of it. They each pull out a scuba tank, then reach further in for more gear.

"Look, Tate, I've told you what I can. It doesn't involve you, but if you think it does, then take it up with one of your old buddies. I have to get back to work."

I watch Sheldon as he moves back to the tent. The helicopter is still buzzing back and forth, the rotor blades sound like the beginnings of a deepening headache. I can imagine what the journalists are saying, what they're coming up with, and there is no doubt they're thriving on it. Bad things happening to good people always makes the greatest news.

CHAPTER FOUR

I hate cemeteries. I don't have a fear of them—it's not a pho-
bia like someone who is too scared to fly, but must fly anyhow.
I just don't like them. I can't really say they represent all that
is wrong with this world, because that wouldn't be a fair comment. Not logically. But I *feel* that way. I think it's because
they represent what happens to all the people in the world
who have been wronged, and even then they only speak for
the ones who are found. There are others out there in shallow
graves, in creeks and crevasses and oceans, or held down by
chains, who cannot be spoken for with gravestones, only by
the memories their loved ones have of them. Of course, that
isn't a fair statement either. That would be like assuming all of
the graves out here belong to victims of crime, and of course
only a few do. Most belong to people too old to live, too young
to have died, or simply too unlucky to keep living.

The rain is getting stronger and the sky is getting darker.

My cell phone rings every minute or so as I drive away and I'm lucky the thing still works after going in the drink. Salt water would have been a different story. As soon as I get past the gates I hit the blockade, where police cars are parked on angles across the road to prevent other people coming to mourn the dead, or to prevent the dead from escaping and mingling with the mourning. I weave my way through them into the media blockade. It's the circle of life out here. Vans and four-wheel drives with news-channel logos stenciled across the side and satellite dishes mounted on top are parked at haphazard angles, the rain no deterrent for the camera crews and reporters trying to look pretty in the drizzle. I manage to get past, pretending I can't hear the same questions yelled at me from every interviewer.

After them comes the first wave of get-home traffic that creates a blockade in the city at this time of the day. My wet jacket and shirt are in the back seat along with the borrowed windbreaker. I have the blanket draped over my seat so my clothes don't soak into the upholstery. With the heater blasting on full, moisture forms on the windshield that the air conditioner can't keep up with. Every half minute I have to wipe away the condensation with my palm. I turn on the radio. There's a Talking Heads song on. It suggests I know where I'm going, but that I don't know where I've been. I turn the radio off. Talking Heads has got it wrong in my case.

The first call I answer is from Detective Inspector Landry, asking me to head into the station to provide a formal statement. He probably figures he can do the world a favor by keeping me squirreled away for a few hours running over all the exact reasons that added up to my being in a cemetery with dead bodies that can't be accounted for. When I ask him if they've tracked down the caretaker, he tells me they'll inform me when they do, and we both know it's bullshit.

The next two calls are from reporters. I knew some of them would recognize me as I was driving away. Reporters are quick like that. I go further back than yesterday's news, and these guys have long memories. I hang up on their questions before they can finish asking them.

Then my mother calls me, telling me she saw me on TV sitting in the back of an ambulance and wanting to know what has happened to me. Clearly the police didn't have the cemetery as well cordoned off as they thought. I tell my mother that I fell into the lake, that was all, and that I still have all my limbs. She tells me to be careful, that I shouldn't go swimming with so many clothes, and that she and Dad are worried. Bridget, my wife, she points out, would be worried as well.

When I manage to hang up, the phone rings again and another reporter asks me whether I'm back on the city's payroll. I decide to switch my phone off, which is a pretty good decision considering the alternative of rolling down my window and throwing it into the elements.

I put both hands on the wheel and start thinking about the three bodies, wondering if there are more. I start spinning the possibilities around in my mind, but it isn't long before I have to concentrate less on the corpses and more on trying not to become one as the traffic becomes thick with SUVs blocking intersections.

My office is in town, situated in a complex with a hundred other offices, most of them belonging to law and insurance firms, from whom I get most of my business. Following cheating husbands for divorce settlements and photographing people scamming their insurance providers allows me to pay the rent, and occasionally I even get to eat. Now I'm digging up coffins and swimming with corpses and the pay is the same. I park in my space behind the building and, still shoeless and saturated, run inside to the elevators and ride eight stories closer to Heaven.

Because most of my clients are in the same building, and any other business I attract comes through phone calls and word of mouth, I come and go as I please, allowing my answering machine to be my secretary. I have enough computer skills to type up my own reports; I know how to file; and I know how to make coffee. A maid comes in once a month and drags a vacuum cleaner and a duster around, but the rest of the time I take care of the spic-and-spanning myself. Private eyes working out of dumpster offices, armed with fedoras and cigarettes, live only in the minds of scriptwriters these days. My office has nice art, nice plants, nice carpet, nice everything. In fact it's so nice it's a struggle to afford it.

I unlock my office door and switch on the light. The air is warm and has held the smell of this morning's coffee, probably because half of it got spilled across my desk by accident. The smell kicks my energy level up a few notches. The room itself is not large, and my desk takes up a quarter of it, backing onto a view of Christchurch that sometimes inspires me and sometimes depresses me. On the opposite side there's a whiteboard standing up on an easel that I often use to sketch ideas on in an attempt to connect the dots. The carpets and walls are mixtures of fawns and grays that sound like they are named after types of coffee. There are files stacked on my desk, a computer in the middle, and a bunch of memos I need to take care of.

I glance out at the city. It doesn't make me feel nostalgic enough to head back to ground level into the rain to see what I'm missing. I start playing with my cell phone. I turn it back on. It starts ringing. I pop the battery out and sit both pieces under the lamp to dry out.

I move into a small bathroom en suite and clean up. I have a spare outfit hanging on the back of the door, there for the day I fall into a lake of corpses or get shot in the chest. I get changed and ball the wet stuff into a bag, taking the watch I found out from my pocket first. Though perhaps *found* isn't as accurate as *stole*. It's an expensive Tag Heuer, an analog, and it's still working. Batteries in these things normally last around five years, and they're waterproof to two hundred meters. I look at the back: there is no inscription. But already a time frame is beginning to take shape.

My computer is a little slow and seems to take a minute longer to boot up for each year older it gets. I begin hunting through old news stories online, using search engines to narrow down my browsing, looking for any mention of coffins being reused to make money; but if it's happened in this country nobody has ever found out.

I run the caretaker's name through the same search engines and find other people with the same name doing other things in other parts of the world, covering occupations and religions and culture and crime. I find a link that takes me through to a newspaper story about the caretaker's father. He retired two years ago after forty years of graveyard service.

I use the online newspaper database of Christchurch City Libraries to go through the obituaries, seeing who died last week and who would fit the description of the woman from the water. I end up with four names, but can't narrow it down any further because the obituaries don't give descriptions or locations for the funerals. I wonder if Detective Schroder has already figured out an ID, and decide he probably has. Simple when you have the resources. He's probably circulating a photo of her body to morticians around the city; or, easier still, he's got the priest from the Catholic church at the cemetery to take a look. If they've identified her, then they'll be in the process of getting a court order to dig up the grave she was taken from. I look at my watch. It's after five thirty: everybody will be pushing into overtime, but it will get done today.

I put my phone back together and drop it into my pocket. It's a ten-minute drive from my office to the hospital, but it takes me thirty in the thick traffic and constant stream of red lights. Christchurch, during peak-hour traffic and bad weather, is always at its worst. I imagine most cities are. Cars are backed up and blocking intersections, and the gutters are starting to flow with rainwater. I have to take a detour when the flow of traffic is blocked by a bus that has driven into a set of traffic lights, squashing them beneath fifteen tons of metal and a few tons of commuters, putting the intersection out of commission. People are tooting at each other, but the rain stops them from winding down windows and yelling.

The hospital is a drab-looking building with no appeasing aesthetics and a design that would equally suit a prison. I park around the back, head to the side *Authorized Personnel Only* door, use the intercom, and, a moment later, get buzzed inside. I have to sign a log book and make idle conversation with a security guard while doing it. I'm starting to feel pretty cold again, and the idea of seeing the coffin and then having it opened in front of me isn't warming me back up. The elevator seems to take forever to arrive, making me wonder exactly where it's rising from. When the doors finally open, I ride it down to the basement.

The morgue is full of white tile and cold hard light. It's like an alien world down here. There are shapes beneath sheets and tools with sharp edges. The air feels colder than the lake. Cabinets are full of bottles and chemicals and silver instruments. Benches and gurneys and trays hold items designed to strip a body down to the basics.

The coffin looks older beneath the white lights, as if the car ride aged it by a quarter of a century. Plus it's more busted up than I first thought. There are cracks along the side, and the top is all dented in. The whole thing has been brushed down before being delivered, but it hasn't been cleaned. There is dirt and mud caked to the edges of it, and there are also signs of rust. It's resting on a knee-high table, which puts the lid of the coffin a little below chest height.

I tighten my hands in a failing effort to ward off the cold. My headache has become my sidekick; it beats away with varying tempos. I wish it would leave. I wish I could leave too. The smell of chemicals is balancing on a tightrope between being too overpowering and not overpowering enough to hide the smell of the dead. I can never remember the smell—all I can remember is my reaction—yet for those few minutes, whenever I used to come down here, I thought I'd never be able to forget it. The bodies aren't rotting, they're not decaying and stinking up the place, but the smell is here—the smell of old clothes and fresh bones and old things that can no longer be.

The lid on the coffin is still closed, and it's easy to imagine there ought to be a chain wrapped around it with one of those big old-fashioned padlocks attached. I can barely make out my smeared reflection in places, especially on the brass handles, my face broken up by pit marks made of rust. I run a finger across the shovel marks that the digger and truck drivers pointed out to me earlier. They're right in the middle of a long concave dent.

"She's been opened before," the medical examiner says, stepping out of her office and into the morgue behind me, and even though I knew she was there her appearance still startles me. "I wonder what's inside."

"Or what isn't inside," I say.

I put my hand out, expecting hers to be cold when she shakes it, but it isn't. "Good to see you, Tracey."

"What's it been, Tate? Two years? Three?"

"Two," I answer.

"Of course," she says. "I should have known that."

I smile at her and let go of her hand. I look her over without appearing to look her over. Though Tracey Walter must be my age, she looks ten years younger. Her black hair is pulled back and tied into a tight bun; her pale complexion is bone white in the morgue lights; her green eyes stare at me from behind a set of designer glasses. I think about the last time I saw her and know she's doing the same thing.

"Sure got busted up falling off that truck," I say, looking at the long cracks. "Caretaker was in a hell of a hurry."

"You've never seen an exhumed coffin before, have you?"

"Yeah? You can tell that?"

She smiles. "Movies don't show how much weight coffins are under once they're in the ground. Often it's enough to do serious damage. Part of this is from falling off the truck, but most of it will be from the pressure of being in the ground. Six feet deep means six feet of dirt piling up on top—like I said, that's a lot of pressure."

I start nodding. A lot of pressure. I hadn't thought of it like that before. "So, is there anything you need me to do?" I ask.

"Just sign this and you can go," she says.

"You're not going to open it while I'm here?"

"It was only your job to be at the cemetery, Tate. It was never meant to extend beyond that."

"Uh huh, but my job was to make sure Henry Martins

made it here, and those shovel marks on the coffin suggest otherwise."

She sighs, and I realize she knew all along she would never be putting up much of an argument.

"Put these on," she says, and hands me some gloves and a face mask. "The smell isn't going to be pretty. But you better not tell anybody you were here for this."

We shift a little closer to the coffin, and suddenly I don't want to see what's inside. This is a topsy-turvy world where corpses bubble up from lakes and coffins are full of empty answers. I pull on the latex gloves and slip the mask over my nose and mouth. If Henry Martins is inside, his fingernails may or may not be blue. If he isn't inside and the coffin is empty, then Martins is one of the bodies on the bank of the lake, or deep within its belly.

Tracey sprays some lubricant into the hinges before shifting a small crowbar into place and pushing down.

The coffin lid sticks because of simple physics. They were designed to take people into the ground, not to bring them back out and, like Tracey pointed out, the structure of this coffin has been altered with all that dirt pressing down on it for the last two years. I lean some weight onto the crowbar to help. It starts to groan, then creak; then it pops open. From inside, darkness escapes—along with it the smell of long-dead flesh that reaches through the pores on my mask and right up into my sinuses. I almost gag. Tracey lifts the lid the rest of the way open. I stand next to her and stare inside.

It isn't at all what either of us is expecting.

CHAPTER FIVE

Christchurch is broken. What didn't make sense five years ago makes sense now, not because our perspectives have changed, but simply because that's the way it is. All of us are locked into a belief of how this city should be, but it's slipping away from us, nobody able to keep a firm grasp as Christchurch slowly spirals into full panic mode. Pick up a newspaper and the headlines are all about the Christchurch Carver, a serial killer who has been terrorizing the city for the last few years. The police hate him, the media love him. He's a one-man money-making industry who is stretching the resources of the police—and the best they can do, it seems, is run ad campaigns on TV in an attempt to enlist new recruits. But the numbers don't add up. They can't, because the police can't keep up with the Carver, let alone the rising crime pandemic.

There are few solutions—but at least there are some, and that's where people like me come into the picture. Some of the smaller jobs get contracted out—the smaller things where a police presence isn't required—and in the beginning people complained. They no longer do.

So yesterday when one of the law firms on the next floor up contacted me with the job, it seemed like easy money. Crime fighting has come a long way since Batman and Robin: now it's all about the lawyers and, sometimes, even the law. And in this case nobody needed a cop to stand in the cold while a coffin got dug out of the ground. Cops were getting paid to get put to better uses. They were out there trying to stem the flow of violence, to push back the tides and fight the good fight. So I got paid to be there—a professional making sure the chain of evidence remained intact.

But nobody is paying me to be here in the morgue with a dead girl in another person's coffin.

And the police resources are about to get stretched even further.

I struggle to focus my thoughts. They cover a whole range of possibilities, as well as emotions. I feel sorrow and pain for whoever this woman is, and can't see any reason other than a bad one for her to be in this coffin. I'm thinking about hoaxes and jokes, and hoping like crazy this is one of them; and as much as I like to think there could have been an elaborate setup, I know it is much more than that. This is real. I shouldn't be looking at a woman, she shouldn't be dead, shouldn't be in a coffin that isn't hers—yet here she is, all laid out in front of me.

Tracey leans over the coffin. "This isn't Henry Martins," she says, not to be funny, not to state the obvious, but matter-of-factly, in a way that doesn't suggest the same disbelief I'm feeling, but that the cold part of her mind she must engage to do this job is now fully in control. Tracey's emotions have been locked away.

"She's decomposed, but not badly. Decomp comes down to temperature, soil, depth of the coffin, and how long she was exposed to the air before being put in here. No way to tell what age at this stage."

I'm hardly listening to her. My heart is racing hard as I look down at the body. There are areas where chunks of flesh have shrunken and dried, and other areas where it's completely disappeared. What she has looks like a shell, so that if I was to poke her with my finger she would turn to dust. The few patches of skin remaining are almost transparent, doing nothing to hide the storm cloud–colored bones that for the most part are exposed. Her face and eyes have gone, just dregs of dried-up skin and flesh and scalp hanging onto her skull. Her teeth look too large with nothing to hide them. Her hair is swept out fanlike beneath her body; it is long and dark brown and I imagine it was once well kept, that she liked to run her fingers through it, that it smelled of shampoos and conditioners, and it would brush against her lover's face as they held each other as one day became another. Her fingers are only bone; one rests across her chest, the other by her side. Resting between her palm and her thigh is a small diamond ring that in the light of the morgue refuses to sparkle. I figure it came loose when her fingers rotted away, and got shaken free when she fell off the back of the stolen truck.

Her clothes don't seem to line up right; her short dress is twisted and the buttons on her blouse are out of line, as if she dressed in a hurry or somebody else dressed her after she was dead. I dig my hand into my pocket and start playing with my car keys, wrapping them into my handkerchief over and over as my mind races.

Tracey looks up at me. "Are you okay? You look like you've seen a ghost."

I can feel sweat starting to slide down the side of my body. It has to be near freezing in here and I'm sweating.

"There were other people in the water, Tracey," I say, and the words are hard to form. "Maybe that means other girls, and if there are . . . Jesus, I screwed up."

"What are you talking about?"

"Two years ago. I should have dug Henry Martins up two years ago and we would have found this girl then. We would have known we were looking for a killer. We might have got him before he killed others."

Tracey looks at me, but doesn't know what to say. She can't tell me the world doesn't work that way, because we both know that it does. She doesn't say anybody could have made that same mistake. She doesn't try to tell me it isn't my fault. All that happens is that her shoulders sag a little and she looks away, unable to maintain eye contact with me.

But then she says "We don't know when the body was put in there, Theo. She might have only been there a year."

"I hope you're right," I tell her.

"You need to leave now, Theo."

"Come on, Tracey, there's got—"

"I'm serious," she says, looking up. "You wanted to know if Martins was inside—well, now you know. That was the deal. You can't look at this woman and think it's become your case. All you can do by being here now is compromise the investigation."

"You don't get it, do you?"

"What? That you could have made a difference two years ago? I know the case, and you're right. It could well be that you messed up and other girls have paid for it, but we don't know that yet, and won't until we know who this girl is and when she was put into this coffin. That aside, how many others are out there because you have taken bad people off the streets?"

"This isn't about checks and balances."

"I know that. Do you? And I know that you have to leave."

"You think that's what she'd want?" I ask, nodding toward the dead girl. "Or do you think she'd want as many people as she could get trying to find who did this to her?"

"Come on, Theo, it's time to go. I'll let you know if one of the bodies that turns up is Martins's."

"Yeah. Okay, do that," I say as she walks me to the corridor.

The moment we step into it, her cell phone rings. She shakes it open and starts talking. I pat down my pockets, then turn them inside out. I mouth the word *keys* to her and point back toward the morgue.

"Make it quick," she says, lowering the phone so the person on the other end can't hear.

I walk back into the morgue. I stare at the dead girl and I wonder what she looked like before Death crammed her into this coffin, taking everything away from her in one brutal insult. Looking at this cheap imitation of her makes me feel ill.

Tracey is finishing up her phone call when I rejoin her in the corridor.

"They've found the one that sank again, and another one," she says, slipping the phone into her jacket. "That's four in total."

"Any IDs?"

"They're close to ID'ing one of them."

"How'd she come up to the surface? The freshest one?"

"It was the cinder block," she says. "Looks like the rope was tied around it, but those cinder blocks can have sharp edges. The block landed against another block down there, and it damaged the rope. It cut through it partly. Gas buildup in the body was enough to break it. Look, you really have to leave."

"I get the feeling I'm going to be hearing that a lot over the next few days."

"Then do yourself a favor and drop this thing," she says, before turning away and heading back into the morgue.

CHAPTER SIX

The elevator is chilly, as if it sucked in most of the cold air when the doors opened. Outside it's only slightly warmer again. I think the sun could be melting the city into a pool of lava and I'd still feel this way after coming out of there.

It's still raining. Of course. On the way to my car I take the dead woman's diamond ring out of my pocket and begin to study it. There is an inscription on the inside, and I have to squint in the weak light of the parking garage to make it out. *Rachel & David forever.* It could have been a wedding ring. It reads like an adolescent inscription carved into a tree. The three stones are not diamonds, which could be why the ring was still by the woman's hand and not sitting in some pawnshop gathering dust. They're glass, cloudy-looking glass that for some reason seems to make the poignancy of what happened to her that much more awful. Somebody bought this for her; he couldn't afford real diamonds, but she didn't need real diamonds. Maybe they had a promise that when things got better, when the money started flowing from some plan he would one day hatch, he would buy for her any stone she wanted.

If Tracey spotted the ring, then pretty soon she's going to realize it's gone. The question is what she'll do about it. Call me? Or call somebody else about me? I should never have put her in that position.

This time when I get back to my office I slip in behind my computer and boot it up, studying the ring while I'm waiting. If the ring had been expensive, or custom made, it might have been easy to track down. I surf onto a secure missing-persons site accessible only to the police and social workers and a handful of private investigators. It only takes a few minutes to come up with a list of missing Rachels. I set the parameters of the search to go back two years, figuring she died after Henry Martins was buried.

I end up with two names, and one of them is from the same week Henry Martins died. Her name is Rachel Tyler and she was nineteen when she went missing. The second Rachel is ten years old and went missing two months ago and wasn't who I just looked at. The woman I was looking at in the coffin was Rachel Tyler. I'm sure of it. It's like a punch to the stomach. Two years—if it's her, then she was probably placed into that coffin not long after she went missing. It means two years ago I could have made a difference.

I print out Rachel Tyler's details. She was reported missing by her parents. I don't remember the case, and I guess that's because she was one of many girls believed to have run away. I also had a lot of other stuff going on two years ago. The reality is people in this country go missing every single day. Sometimes they turn up: they're broke and high and living in a single-room motel, having burned off all their cash in casinos betting on red instead of black. Sometimes they're being pimped out, forced into prostitution to pay back money for gambling or drugs or as a form of self-abuse. Other times they've left their wife or husband for somebody with a bigger bank account or a bigger house or a younger body. Other times they don't turn up at all.

The photograph of Rachel was taken at a moment of sourness, either faked or real, and it sure beats seeing a happy and outgoing girl holding ice creams or diplomas or helping the sick and elderly. She would be twenty-one now if somebody hadn't killed her, then jammed her into a coffin.

I study the photograph. Her brown hair is darker than when I saw it less than an hour ago; her blue eyes in the picture are bright and alive. I read through the file. The conclusion was that she ran away, that she fought with her parents or her boyfriend and couldn't take it anymore.

I look up Rachel's parents in the phone book and find that they are still at the same address. I wonder if they're still married and what kind of state they are in. I wonder how many nights they sit watching the door, waiting for her to stroll inside and tell them everything is going to be okay.

I slip the ring into a small plastic bag and drop it into my pocket. Then I look again at the watch I took from the body in the lake. I compare the time to my own. It's out by only a few minutes, but it could be the Tag Heuer is accurate and mine isn't. Its owner must have died in the same six-month period we're in now, between October and March, because the watch is set for daylight saving time. The date is out by fourteen days.

I grab a pen and start doing the addition. Every month an analog watch goes to thirty-one days, regardless of what month it is, and the user has to adjust it manually in the other five months when there are fewer. I work out that those five months would add up to seven days a year that the watch would be off by if it wasn't adjusted. That means this watch hasn't been touched in two years. So. It is now nearing the end of February. The guy who owned this watch was put in the ground sometime after the beginning of December and before the end of February two years ago.

I pick up the file with Henry Martins's details on it. He died on the ninth of January. Could be his.

I grab the phone. It takes half a minute for Detective Schroder to answer it.

"Come on, Tate, you know I can't answer any questions," he says when he hears my voice. "This has nothing to do with you. And soon it won't have anything to do with me either. I've got too much on my plate to chase after this one too."

"You're working the Carver case?"

"Trying to. Unless I retire. Which I might."

"One question. The body that floated up without the legs. Is that the oldest one?"

I hear him exhale loudly. "Look, Tate, seriously, I can't . . ."

"Just one question, that's all," I tell him.

"That's all?" he says. "Is that a promise?"

"For now," I tell him.

"The ME said it's hard to tell who went in first, but he'll figure it out. He said it looked like the two of them went into the water fairly close to each other. Why?"

"Can you let me know when he's told you?"

"No. Good-bye, Tate," he says, and hangs up.

I look at the watch. It's been on the wrist of a dead guy for two years, but not necessarily in the water for two years. It depends on how long he was in the ground before he went in the drink. Either way, it looks like two years is the outer perimeter of the time line.

I check the missing persons reports, but immediately the list of names coming up becomes too long, and there is no way to narrow it down until I know whether the killer had a type. Could be all the girls are similar ages, or have similar descriptions. Or it could be the other coffins don't have girls in them at all, but men.

I grab my dry cell phone and the printout of Rachel Tyler, and head back down to my car.

I've barely left the parking lot when I think better of my initial impulse. It's the wrong time of the day to show up at somebody's house to tell them their daughter is probably dead. Most people would think there never is a right time—but there is. It's the sort of thing you want to do earlier on so they can call friends and family who can come over to console them. Anyway, it may be Rachel's ring, but it doesn't mean it's her corpse.

I drive toward the edge of the city and park my car outside a florist that is open every weeknight until seven. I need to re-place this darkness with some light, yet the first thing I think about is how flowers and death have been mixed together over time as much as flowers and love.

"Hi ya, Theo." An extremely pretty girl with an easy manner smiles at me as I go in.

"How's it going, Michelle?" I do my best to smile back.

We make the usual chitchat, then she asks me if I'm after the usual. I tell her I am.

"Your wife must really love flowers," Michelle tells me, and I slowly nod.

Michelle picks out a bunch she thinks Bridget will like, wraps some cellophane around the stems, and hands them over. She writes down the amount in a small book behind the counter. At the end of the month, like every other month, she will send me a bill.

"Say hi to Bridget for me," she says, and her smile is infectious. Sometimes I think I could just watch this woman smile for ages.

I head back to my car and rest the flowers in the passenger seat, careful not to crush them. I glance at my watch. Bridget won't be in any hurry to see me, so I change my mind and decide maybe I can pay a visit to Rachel Tyler's family after all. I do a U-turn and drive back in the opposite direction, taking with me a bunch of already dying flowers and a whole lot of bad news.

CHAPTER SEVEN

Averageville. That's where the Tylers live. All the houses on the street are well kept, but there is nothing special, as if any one resident was too scared to make their house stand out above another. No huge homes with giant windows, no expensive cars parked outside, no Porsches or BMWs suggesting a world of big money and high debt. No beat-up cars sitting on blocks, no car parts scattered across dying lawns. Doctors and lawyers and drug dealers live elsewhere. This is typical living in suburbia, where robberies are high, but homicides are low. It's a pleasant place to live. Sure as hell beats some of the alternatives.

I slow down and glance at the mailboxes, getting an early idea how much further I have to drive. This wasn't my case when the bodies floated up. It wasn't my case when the caretaker took off. But it became my case the moment the coffin opened and Rachel Tyler's body made a suggestion that there are others out there who could still be alive if not for my mistake. I glance at the geranium cocktail next to me, and for a few seconds I think about my wife. I like to think that I know what she would want me to do, but I can't be sure. It's been a long time since she gave me any advice.

I step out into the light rain in front of a single-story house that was mass-produced back at the start of the townhouse era. Things are tidy, but a little run down. The garden has a few weeds; the lawn is a little long; the entire house looks a little tired.

The door is opened by a woman in her late forties, early fifties. She looks like she has been on edge for the last two years, expecting news at any moment. She is like the house—tidy, neat, but tired.

"Yes?"

"Mrs. Tyler?"

"Yes . . ."

I can tell she isn't sure whether I'm here to sell her encyclopedias or God, or whether I'm here to bolster or destroy her hopes for her missing daughter. Slowly I reach into my pocket and take out a business card. Her eyes widen and her mouth drops slightly as I hand it across, and when she reads it her mouth firms back up. She doesn't seem sure what to say. Doesn't seem to know whether to be happy or scared that I'm on her doorstep.

"My name is Theodore Tate," I say, "and I'm a private investigator."

"That's what the card says," she offers, without any sarcasm.

"Can I have a few minutes of your time?"

"Do you know where she is?" she asks, already sure of the reason for my visit.

"This is about Rachel," I say, "but not directly. Please, if we can step inside, I can tell you more."

She fights with the beginnings of a sentence; perhaps the struggle is with the hundreds of questions trying to come out at once, a hundred different ways in which to ask if her daughter is still alive. I bet she's rehearsed this moment time and time again, but the reality is crushing her, confusing her. She steps back and I move inside.

The hallway is warm and homey. There are dozens of photographs of Rachel on the walls, ranging over the nineteen years she spent in this world. There are pictures of her as a baby, her mother holding her tightly. The years have taken their toll on Mrs. Tyler. There are shots of Rachel next to a tricycle, in a sandbox, going down a slide. There is a man in some of them, holding Rachel's hand, or swinging her at the park, or helping her blow out a cake with eight candles on it. Rachel gets older. So do her parents. Fashions change and the three grow older, but the smiles are always there, keeping the parents young. One of these photos should have been with her missing persons report, but probably Mrs. Tyler couldn't part with any of them. I'm sure Rachel's bedroom will be just as she left it, the same posters on the walls, her favorite stuffed toys waiting for her on her bed, maybe even a stockpile of Christmas and birthday presents from missed occasions. It'll be like a time capsule.

Patricia Tyler leads me through to the lounge.

"Is your husband home?" I ask, praying she isn't going to tell me they are separated or, worse, that her husband has died from the pain of losing his daughter to a mystery, that he has spent the last six or eight or ten months in the ground.

"He's at work. He sometimes works late," she says, sounding sad about it. I can't imagine she ever sounds any other way. "Mostly, actually, these days. I should phone him, I guess. Should I?"

"If you'd like."

"What . . . what am I going to tell him?" she asks.

"Perhaps we should sit down for a few minutes first."

"Sure, okay, sure, I don't know where my manners are. Can I get you a drink? Tea? Coffee?" She starts to stand back up. "Anything, just name it." She's halfway out of the lounge when she pulls up short; then, fidgeting her hands, she slowly turns back to look at me. "I don't know what I'm doing," she says, and starts to cry.

She's not the only one who doesn't know what they're doing, and I suddenly wish I hadn't come. I feel the urge to hold her while she cries and an equally strong urge to turn and run back down the hallway and get the hell out of this street. I end up standing still.

"Please, just tell me why you're here," she asks.

I can no more easily tell this woman her child is dead than I could show her pictures of the corpse. I cannot tell her about Cemetery Lake, about a woman whose decayed remains look like they belong to Rachel. I can't mention the exhumation, can't detail my swim with the corpses, can't mention it's the same cemetery I almost buried my wife in two years ago after the accident. I reach into my pocket and produce the small plastic bag with Rachel's ring. She takes it without a word, then slowly sinks down into a chair opposite me. I sit down too. For a long time she says nothing.

"It turned up today in an investigation," I say, and she finally manages to pull her eyes away from it and look back up at me. "Do you recognize it? Does it belong to Rachel?"

"Where did you find it?" she asks. "Who had it?"

"Nobody had it on them," I lie, feeling bad and concerned with the way this is going. But of course what other way was there?

"But how, then?"

"Please, I need to ask you a few questions. The inscription, it says *Rachel & David forever.*"

"Was it David?" she asks, her voice raising. "Did he give you the ring?"

"No. Nobody had it. I found it."

"Where?" she asks, almost demanding now.

"Please, Mrs. Tyler, can you tell me about David?"

"How did you know to come here?"

"The inscription," I say, but then suddenly realize my mistake. The only reason I'd check missing persons would be if I believed the ring belonged to somebody who was dead. Mrs. Tyler, thank God, doesn't make the connection. "Please, tell me about David."

"David gave it to her for her birthday."

"Is David her boyfriend?" I ask, careful not to say *was*.

She nods. "I've already told the police all I know."

"But I'm not the police," I say, "and that means I can approach things differently."

She takes a few seconds with that, slowly nodding as she thinks it over. "You think she's dead, don't you," she says. It's not a question.

I think of the flowers in the passenger seat of my car, and I regret not driving out to see my wife first. I could have talked to her. Told her about my day. Told her how much I missed her. Could have held her hand and told her everything.

"I don't know," I say.

"Then what makes you think you can help her?"

It's interesting she has asked how I can help Rachel, and not her and her husband. *Interesting* isn't the word. It's *devastating*. This woman isn't just holding out for the possibility that her daughter is alive—she's holding on to the reality of it. But the question is more than that. It makes me think of exactly what I can do to help Rachel: nothing. Not now. I can't even help the others who have followed.

"I would imagine Rachel wants as many people helping her as she can get."

The point seems to hit home with her and she starts up again with the nodding, and then she starts up with telling me about her daughter. I realize I could be anybody in the world and she'd still be happy to speak about Rachel. She'd probably be the same way if I *had* been at the door selling encyclopedias or God. She talks for nearly twenty minutes and I don't interrupt her. I know what it's like to have lost somebody. I know what it is like to hold out hope. False hope is cruel, but perhaps not as cruel as no hope at all. It's a judgment only those who have been there can make.

"And David?" I ask, after she has told me what she can about Rachel's life, including in detail the days before she disappeared. "What can you tell me about him?"

"I thought he knew what happened," she says. "For those few weeks I was sure she was living with him. See, they were living together, but not really. All her things were here, are still here, but she wouldn't come home for days on end. When we didn't see her for a week we tried contacting her, then him, but he said he hadn't seen her. I thought he was lying, and that he was shielding her from us for something we must have done. But I knew, I knew something wasn't right. I don't know how, but I just knew. So Michael, my husband, called the police. We filed a missing persons report. We hadn't heard from her in nearly a week. It wasn't like her."

"What happened when the police spoke to David?"

"Nothing. They said they had no reason to believe he was lying. Still, I wasn't convinced. I would . . ." she starts, then takes a few seconds to gather her thoughts. She looks down at her feet. "I would go to his house at different times, but there was never any sign of her. I would knock on his door in the middle of the night. After a while I began to see that David was just as distraught as we were, and I started leaving him alone. I don't know if he really believes Rachel is still alive."

She looks back up. I nod sympathetically. Then I throw a couple of names at her: Bruce Alderman and Henry Martins. She shakes her head and tells me she's never heard of them, and asks me who they are. I tell her the names have come up, but I'm not sure where they fit into it, and that it may be unlikely they even do. She gives me a list of Rachel's friends, places she liked to go, photographs of her, people she worked with, David's address. She's giving it all some real serious thought, hoping for a connection, hoping she is going to mention a name that's the key to getting her daughter back.

She walks me to the door. She seems reluctant to let me go. I feel guilty I've deceived her, that I've given her more hope today than she had yesterday, and the guilt becomes a sickening feeling that makes the world sway a little as I make my way to the car. The police will identify Rachel Tyler. They will come here tomorrow or the next day, and they will tell Patricia that her daughter is dead. I can't stop it from happening. I can't prepare her for it.

It's getting close to eight o'clock and within the next twenty minutes it will be dark, the thick clouds bringing the night earlier than usual for this time of year. The flowers in the front seat still look fresh enough to keep on growing. I start my car and pull away, the small voice inside my head questioning what in the hell I am doing and the bigger voice, the one I use every day to justify my actions, telling me I have no idea.

CHAPTER EIGHT

Perception is a funny thing. Especially when you're dealing with luck. Somebody who survives a plane crash is considered lucky. Is he considered lucky to have even been on that flight? Or unlucky? Does the bad luck of being seated on a doomed flight cancel out the good luck of surviving? I don't get it that people are lucky to have lost only an arm.

My wife was lucky. That's what people say. An inch here or a second or two there, and things would have been different. I would have ended up burying her, and the flowers I keep buying would be going to a grave. Inches. Seconds. Luck. Good luck for her. Good luck for all. It doesn't add up. She wasn't lucky. Not at all. Wasn't lucky when the car plowed into her. She was lucky that her head hit the sidewalk at forty kilometers an hour and not fifty, but unlucky her head hit the sidewalk at forty and not twenty. Wasn't lucky when her legs were shattered, her ribs broken. Lucky to have lived, yes, but not lucky.

The nursing home is out of the city where suburbia kicks in and city noise dies away. It covers five hectares of land, with grounds scenic enough to be used for a wedding. The buildings are forty years old, gray brick with the occasional flare of polished oak windowsill—a combination of bad ideas or perhaps good ideas that didn't work. The driveway is long and shaded by giant trees that flourish in the summer and look like skeletons in the winter. I pull up outside the main office and for a few seconds try to imagine that this world hasn't gone mad.

The main doors are heavy and made from oak, as if to stop the weak from leaving or tempt the grieving to turn away. The nurse behind the reception desk smiles at me. Her dark red hair matches the sunset in the painting behind her.

"Hi, Theo. What have you done with the weather?"

I fake a smile of my own, the type anybody with social skills would apply when the weather suddenly becomes the topic of conversation. "Tomorrow I'm organizing sun. God owes me a favor."

She nods, maybe agreeing that yes He does. "Flowers for me this time?" she asks, like she always does, like she always will.

The nurses and doctors are always nice, always friendly, always professional, their questions and pleasantries always clichéd. The alternative is unthinkable. You'd ask how their day was going and they would tell you the truth and you'd never come back.

"Next time," I say, which is what I say every time. "How is she?"

"She's doing fine, Theo. But what about you? Is that you I saw on the news?"

"Yeah, it's been one of those crazy days." A fairly accurate summation, I feel. Not that all crazy days end up with somebody swimming in a lake full of corpses.

She nods. "Every day this city shows us a little more how things don't make sense."

"Sometimes I think Christchurch is broken," I say, "and nobody is ever going to fix it."

I walk down the corridor, passing empty seats and closed doors and a nurses' station that looks empty, but most likely isn't. The entire floor is speckled green linoleum, the sort that is easy to clean blood and vomit and shit off and will last two hundred years. The day is cold, but the air in here is comfortable. It's always comfortable, and so it ought to be. Some of the people in care here don't know how to complain, and some who do know simply don't have the ability anymore. There are more paintings with water and sunsets, peaceful scenes that are perhaps supposed to help calm the residents here before they move on from this world and into the next. There are pots full of artificial plants. And there are decorations for the people who come here who are on the verge of losing it.

I climb a flight of stairs, and halfway down another corridor I stop at Bridget's room. The door is open. She is sitting by the window, looking out at the misty rain and the trees and the lack of good weather that the nurses mention every time I arrive. She seems interested in all of it. I don't know whether she hears me come in. I close the door behind me. She keeps staring outside.

"Hey, babe, I've missed you," I say, but she doesn't answer.

I take yesterday's flowers out of the vase and put today's flowers in. She doesn't notice. She doesn't notice as I shuffle them around in an attempt to make them look nicer. I sit in the chair next to her and take her hand in mine. It's warm. It's always warm, no matter how cold the room gets. I'm glad for it, because it helps remind me my wife is still alive.

She occasionally blinks as I tell her about my day. There is no expression on her face as I run a brush through her hair, stroking it over and over, searching for the recognition that isn't there. She does not laugh when I tell her how I slipped into the water. She doesn't chide me for not telling Patricia Tyler that her daughter has been dead the entire time she has been missing. Other noises—the shuffling of patients, the squeaking of caster wheels—come from the care home, which, for the last few years, I have quietly nicknamed Death Haven. I'm not sure why I've come up with the name. I'm not sure whether thinking of it as Death Haven has made it more personal to me or less. Every day I have this romantic notion that I will come in here and Bridget will look up at me and smile. Every day. But she doesn't. I hold on to the hope, I have become attached to it sentimentally, in the same way Mrs. Tyler has become attached to the idea her daughter has run away and is living the perfect life in a perfect town and is so perfectly happy she just hasn't had the chance to call.

I keep talking until my throat is sore and I'm out of words. Bridget has remained in her catatonic state the entire time, happy in the world she is in, or perhaps sad; I wish I had a way of knowing. The window and the trees beyond hold for her the same fascination as they have done every day for the last two years. I feel exhausted, as I always do when I purge myself of the day's events. The silence in the room is peaceful, and in these quiet times I often think that I would be better off if I could be catatonic too, unknowing and unfeeling, and keeping Bridget company. I sit holding her hand for a few more minutes, then I stand, pulling her hand up slightly. She comes with me and steps toward the bed. Her actions are involuntary, her body just following the motions. She can move from the bed to the chair, and back again. Sometimes the staff will find her standing in the corridor, motionless, and twice she has made it down into the foyer. Guide a glass up to her lips and she can drink. Raise a fork to her mouth and she can eat. But she cannot fend for herself, cannot speak, cannot look at you with an expression that suggests she knows you are there. Everything is a thousand miles away, and her eyes are fixed on that point in the distance, continually searching, searching, but never finding.

She lies down. I kiss her on the side of her cool face—her hands are always warm, her cheeks always cool—then slowly make my way from her room. I don't turn back. I never do, not these days. I will see her tomorrow. And the day after that. And the day after.

Patricia Tyler isn't the only person in this city playing the waiting game. Or holding out hope.

Outside, the cold air feels like silk against my face. I stand next to my car for nearly five full minutes. I stand doing nothing as the rain dampens my jacket. I'm not even really sure whether I'm thinking about my wife or dead girls or bad luck and bad omens, all I'm really doing is getting wet and not caring too much about it. Finally I find the strength to drive away.

CHAPTER NINE

I turn my cell phone on and wait for it to ring, but it doesn't. Could mean people are getting killed elsewhere in the city and the reporters flocking there have forgotten about me. Could be the police know who put the bodies in the water and don't feel the need to let me know. Could be Tracey hasn't noticed the ring missing on the dead girl's finger and I'm sailing through trouble-free waters. Could be none of that. Might simply be a poor signal. Or that taking it for a swim has finally caught up with the inner components.

I go through the motions of changing gears and avoiding other cars before realizing I'm not heading home, or even to my office, but back to the cemetery where my day suddenly became interesting. Where there is death there is life—at least at the moment. Police cars are scattered across the landscape, but mostly localized by the lake. They are no longer guarding the entrance. I ignore them and head to the opposite side of the cemetery where the dead are still at peace.

I make the walk through the dark without need of a flashlight. It's a walk I could make with my eyes closed. The grass is wet and soon the bottoms of my pants and shoes are wet.

It's been a while since I last stood over my daughter's grave. After her funeral, I never wanted to come back. Seeing the smooth headstone with the brass plate carved with her name and the dates hurt too much. But it hurt even more staying away, and I ended up visiting her grave two or three times a week for the first year, and less often since then, and not at all in two months now. The doctors tell me they don't think Bridget knows that Emily is dead or even that Emily ever existed. I hope they're right—though I'm not sure what kind of person that makes me. Emily didn't have the good luck to become catatonic, but the bad luck to be killed: she had twice as many bones in her body broken as my wife; she hit the pavement just as hard, just as awkwardly, and just like that she was gone. No luck there at all, unless you count bad luck.

The tears don't come as much these days. The pain is part of who I am now. Getting rid of it would be like losing a limb.

There are flowers on her grave that have wilted and died, put there I imagine by either my parents or Bridget's parents. The coffin beneath the earth is child sized, and the mere fact there is a market for child-sized coffins in this world proves it's a messed-up one—and for the briefest moment I think about the condition the coffin is in, whether it's as dented and damaged as the one pulled out of the ground earlier today, or whether its smallness helped it withstand the weight of the earth above it. Then I wonder if she is even in there.

I don't bother to tell Emily about my day because she can't

hear me. Emily is dead, and none of the romanticized ideas I have at Death Haven reach out here.

I walk toward the lake and come to a stop near the police tape. It seems that every year the people who manufacture this stuff have to add another mile to the roll to keep up with the Christchurch crime rate. A good year for them means a bad year for the rest of us. The scene looks like an archaeological dig. There are more cranes and trucks than before. Strings of lights around the edges of the tents are glowing brightly as if a pageant is going on in the middle of it all—except that here the performers are women and men in different-colored overalls marching back and forth, cataloging death along with the different types of samples that come with it. There is a mound of dirt from another coffin that has been dug up. I thank God that Emily is buried far away from this scene, and then I curse Him for making me bury her in the first place. Then I think of the irony of that statement since I know there can't possibly be a God—or, if there is, that He abandoned this city a long time ago.

I'm about to duck under the tape when an officer who wasn't here earlier in the day approaches me and tells me in his sternest voice that I can walk no further.

"I just want to know how things are going," I say.

The officer gives me his practiced stone-cold glare, and tells me to read tomorrow's paper. I feel like hitting him.

"Has anybody spoken to the caretaker yet?" I ask him.

"Listen, mate, none of this is any of your business."

"I came to visit my daughter," I say, about to play the sympathy card. "Her grave is here."

His eyes narrow, and he looks like he is about to tell me that having a dead daughter doesn't give me a free invitation to go wherever the hell I please, but slowly he seems to become aware it's the type of comment I'd make him regret saying.

"I'm sorry, mate," he says, "but you've picked a bad time to come."

"Yeah, well, she picked a bad time to die."

He doesn't know what to say, so he says nothing, figuring this is best, and I figure he's right. I stay at the line of police tape, trying to make eye contact with anybody who will tell me anything, but there's too much going on for that to happen. The officer keeps looking at me like I'm a shoplifter. I feel his eyes on my back the entire way as I walk to my car. He's probably wondering if I'm for real.

The cemetery grounds are like a golf course, separated into many sections divided up by hedges and trees and bushes, and it's easy to get lost in here. The main road through it branches off to these different areas, and one of the bigger branches leads to the Catholic church, which sits left of the cemetery, back some forty meters from the road. A belt of trees forms a horseshoe barrier around its sides and back, so that if you're at the lake or even in other parts of the cemetery you might not even know it was there. This is the church that once held a ceremony for my dead little girl, but more recently gave me somewhere to serve the priest with an exhumation order for Henry Martins.

I park as close as I can to the huge oak doors that could pass entry to a fairy-tale giant and I walk up the stone steps. The wooden door on the right swings open easily and noiselessly. Inside the church the temperature seems to drop another degree with every step I take. Most of the lighting is coming from candles, with a few overhead lights dimly illuminating the chapel. There are dozens of pews, all of them empty except for one at the very front where a man is staring ahead, lost in thought, seemingly unaware or uncaring of my presence.

I walk down the aisle, letting my fingertips tap the pew

backs along the way. Left and right are tapestries of Jesus and stained glass windows of Jesus and paintings of Jesus. Somewhere around here there's probably a gift shop with coffee cups with a smiling Jesus. At the head of the church behind the altar is a large, wooden crucifix with a large, wooden Jesus carved onto it. Jesus doesn't seem to care that he's hanging on a slight angle, or that he's being promoted so heavily.

Before I reach the end of the aisle one of the boards beneath me creaks, and the priest turns suddenly. He steps out from the pew and smiles at me, but after a few seconds the smile falters, and I realize how hard it must be for him to maintain his composure under the strain not just of this day but of every day. Priests don't see the same violence that cops do, but they sure as hell hear about it—and worse. They're the ones trying to pick up the pieces of a broken family looking to blame more than just the man or the disease that took away their loved ones.

Two years ago he was there for me. Two years ago he tried to help me pick up the pieces of my life, only I didn't want his help. Not really. I wanted to pick up those pieces in my own way.

Father Stewart Julian, a man in his mid to late fifties who has been here for as long as I can remember, offers me his hand. He has a notepad in his other hand that he hasn't written a thing on, and a newspaper folded on the pew where he was sitting. His soft face, gray hair, and black eyebrows give him a kind look, but at the moment he looks tired. Still, I figure in his day, if Father Julian hadn't become a priest, he would've had women all over him.

"Awful day, Theo," he says, shaking his head, proving just how awful the day really is. "Just awful." His voice is low and easy to listen to, a voice well suited for the radio. "It's been

long and it's already late. You wouldn't believe how many
hours I've had to spend talking to police. Or to families of
those who have loved ones buried here. They keep calling,
Theo, scared that their mothers and fathers and sons and
daughters are being desecrated. Word has gotten out about
the bodies in the water, and people are thinking they might
be people who were buried here. The calls finally stopped an
hour ago, and since then I've been looking for a distraction."
He waves the notepad a little. "Have you seen this?" he asks,
and picks up the newspaper.

"Seen what?" I ask, pretty sure that the distraction was
a hundred miles away, because that's where Father Julian
seemed to be looking before he heard me.

"This," he says, and he points to the article.

"I've seen it." It's a newspaper article about the advertising
campaign for McClintoch spring water. Promotional bill-
boards have been erected across the country and advertising
spots taken out in newspapers. The ads say, *What would Jesus
drink?* and show Jesus turning wine into water with Mc-
Clintoch spring water labels on the bottles.

"I just don't understand," he says, shaking his head.

"Times are changing," I say, hoping my answer will apply
here. I like giving my priest vague answers, the same way he
used to give me vague answers. When my daughter was killed
and my wife lay in a state close to death, he'd tell me it was
part of God's plan. "Father, I was hoping you could help me
out."

"Helping you out, Theo, has led to a very long day."

I nod. Yes it has. "You'd rather have left things as they
were?"

"Well, no, of course not. But I think I need more notice
before I help you out so I can plan some holiday time."

We sit facing each other, mimicking each other's position with our elbows resting on the top of the pew. The pews are solid wood, worn a little around the edges, but they've held up over the years in the way that only expertly crafted furniture from sixty or seventy years ago can. Wooden Jesus is looking down at us, wooden nails in his wooden hands. He's holding up well too.

"It's been one heck of a day for me," he says. "For all of us. Sometimes I wonder . . ." He doesn't finish his sentence, just lets it trail off, making me think he's wondering lots of things, and I don't blame him. We're all wondering lots of things. Foremost he is probably wondering where God fits into all of this.

"You're starting to think retirement might be in the cards?"

His smile comes back for a few seconds—there are a few creases around the edges of his eyes—but then he sighs. "No, no, not yet. If I'm looking older than normal, it's the day. It's been a long one."

"For all of us, Father. What can you tell me about the caretaker who helped me this afternoon?"

He cocks his head a little and pushes his shoulders back for a few seconds as if ironing out a crick in his back. "Bruce? Bruce Alderman? Why are you asking?"

"I want to talk to him."

"Ah," he says, and slowly shakes his head. Suddenly he doesn't look as tired as he does sad. "You think he's responsible. Well, I can't tell you anything more than I've already told the police."

"And what did you tell them?" I ask.

"That Bruce is a good man," he says, "and this sort of depravity, well . . . it's simply beyond him."

It's been my experience that depravity isn't beyond as many

people as we'd like to think, and I'm pretty sure Father Julian doesn't need me to point that out to him.

I adjust my position on the pew. Well made doesn't mean comfortable. "Did you tell them where they could find Bruce?"

He shakes his head. "I didn't know."

"Guilt makes men run, Father."

His head goes from shaking to nodding. "So does fear, Theo. Nobody would like to see what he saw."

"But fear doesn't make them steal a truck and go into hiding."

He stops nodding. Now he just keeps his head perfectly still. "I wish I could simply ask for your trust in this, Theo. I can guarantee you, Bruce isn't a bad kid. And he couldn't have known those poor people were going to rise up from the lake."

"He knew what we were digging up."

"Of course he did. You had an exhumation order."

"No, it was more than that. He knew we were digging up something more."

"Something more?"

"The body we dug up wasn't Henry Martins's," I tell him.

"I saw the exhumation order, Theo. I'm sure that's who—"

"It wasn't Martins in the coffin," I tell him.

"But . . ." he says, and doesn't know how to continue. Not for about five seconds, and then he says, "So where is Henry Martins? Was . . . oh, oh no, he was one of the bodies in the water, wasn't he?"

"I don't know that," I tell him, "but it's likely."

"Then the coffin was empty?" he asks, in a tone of voice that suggests he's hoping his question comes with a *yes* attached to the end.

"No. It wasn't empty. It contained the body of a young woman by the name of Rachel Tyler."

The look of horror on his face settles in his features so heavily I'm worried they might set there. He doesn't look comfortable with it. In fact he looks downright sick. He reaches out and grabs the back of the pew, as if to stop himself from tipping off and falling into an abyss that is opening beneath him.

"She was murdered," I add. "And whether your caretaker did it or not, he certainly knows something. Please, Father, you have to help me."

He lets go of the pew, rubs his palm across the side of his face, then lifts both hands into the air as if the gesture can ward me off. "I . . . I wish I could help, but there's nothing I can say."

"Would you like me to bring you a photograph of Rachel? Show you what was done to her?"

The church seems to get colder as his horror turns to disgust, almost anger, and my stomach starts to knot. I wish I hadn't said that to him. He's too good a man to say shitty things to. This is the guy who got me through the hardest time of my life. This is the guy who would ring me every day after my daughter died and, when he couldn't get hold of me, he'd come around to my house to make sure I wasn't going to do anything stupid. Sometimes he'd bring me cooked meals. Sometimes he'd sit and have a beer with me. Ninety-five percent of those times we wouldn't talk about God or religion or the Big Plan. We'd just talk about life. We'd talk about my wife and my daughter.

Before I can apologize, he stands up and looks down at me, and he doesn't look angry, he looks disappointed, and that's far, far worse. "That sort of parlor trick is beneath you, Theo. If I could help you, I would, just as I helped you two years ago when you were lost."

"Please, sit back down," I tell him.

"You can't—"

"Rachel has nobody to speak for her. I need to do what I can," I tell him.

"She has God."

"God let her down."

He sits back down. He breathes out heavily. "You must have faith, Theo."

"Faith lets everybody down."

"People let themselves down."

I want to argue, but there is no argument a priest hasn't heard and isn't ready for. Their answers may not make sense, but they are a doctrine, there to be repeated over and over, as if the very repetition makes their case. I could take a photograph out of my wallet and show him my wife and my daughter, but of course Father Julian remembers them. He knew them before they were killed and after. I could ask him where God was during their accident, but Father Julian would have some dogmatic answer that God-loving and God-fearing people love to use—most likely the generic *God works in mysterious ways*, which I want to scream at every time I hear it.

"You're right," I concede, "and I shouldn't have said that about showing you a picture of Rachel. But you need to help me find your caretaker. He saw us digging up something that made him run."

"I still find that hard to believe," Father Julian says, but I'm starting to convince myself that the look on his face suggests it isn't that hard for him at all. "Unfortunately, Theo, as I keep saying, I don't know where he is."

"Start by telling me where he lives."

"The police have already been there and, to be honest, I'm not comfortable giving you information. You're not a cop anymore. This isn't your investigation."

"No, this has *become* my investigation. Two years ago I had an excuse to raise Henry Martins's coffin and I never did. That means . . ."

"I know what that means. You think that if there are other people out there in coffins they shouldn't be in, then you could have prevented it. Maybe this is true."

"It is true," I say, a little shocked at how quickly he has come to this conclusion.

"Two years ago," he repeats. "Exactly two years ago?"

"Pretty much," I tell him, knowing where he's about to go.

"Then you know you can't blame yourself," he says, but his eyes seem to betray his real feelings. "The accident—that was two years ago, correct? Was it the same time?"

"I still should have done more," I say. "But I lost my focus."

"You lost your family," he says. "And you lost control. This isn't your fault, Theo."

"There are going to be more girls out there in those coffins, Father. Three of them. I feel it. I can't make it right, but I also can't let it go."

He looks down at the floor as if there is some internal debate warring inside his head. That debate rages on for almost a minute. I don't interrupt him. When he looks up he seems to have aged a few years. He thinks this day is hard on him, but if I drove him to Rachel Tyler's house tomorrow to meet her parents he'd realize his day was easy in comparison.

"I suppose you could talk to his father," he says. "He may be able to offer you something."

I recall the article that I read about Sidney Alderman before I left my office for the morgue. The old man's retirement last year had made the newspaper, but it wasn't really news, it was just one of those human interest stories that are interesting to the people who knew Alderman and not to anyone else.

"Does he live nearby?"

"Closer than you can imagine," he says. "Promise me you'll be careful. Promise me you're looking for Bruce to question him, not punish him."

I shrug. "Punish him? I don't follow you."

Again Father Julian sighs, then slowly shakes his head. "Don't take the law into your own hands, Theo. Vengeance is God's, not yours—you know that. You know that better than anybody," he says.

He follows me to the church doors and gives me directions to where I can find Sidney Alderman. I thank him and he wishes me a good night, and again he tells me to be careful. I tell him I'm always careful.

He shakes my hand before he leaves, and when he takes his away I see that he is shaking. Then he disappears back through the doors. God's working day is still not over.

CHAPTER TEN

The rain has disappeared. For now. And the night has set in. I sit in the car with the heater going, trying to collect my thoughts, wondering why I'm chasing down Bruce the caretaker when I ought to be home chasing down some pizza with Jim the bourbon. I don't know, maybe it's just that my life isn't interesting enough to be at home getting drunk in front of reruns of bad comedies and reruns of bad news that happens every day. That's the problem with the news. The victims have different names, the presenters wear different outfits, but the stories are the same. Some of us put our hands up and say that's enough; we try to make a difference. When I was on the job we would arrest one killer and another would appear. It was like the sorcerer's apprentice Mickey Mouse cutting evil broomsticks in half, only to have each half grow whole and carry on doing whatever it was evil broomsticks did.

The inside of the windshield is fogging up, so I redirect the heater to take care of it. My reflection, slowly appearing on the warming glass, looks pale green from the dashboard lights. I take a small detour on the way out, heading back past the crime scene that was once a tranquil lake in the middle of a tranquil cemetery. The machinery is moving around—I can hear and see it—and I wonder what unlucky girl is being dug from the ground by a giant metal claw.

The cemetery road veers away from the machinery, from the lake, from my daughter, and toward more darkness and more trees and fewer gravestones, before taking me out onto the street. From there it's a thirty-second drive to Alderman's house, and most of that is taken up with hedge line views of the edge of the cemetery. There are only a few houses nearby. One is old and looks like it is ready to fall down; another looks brand new, as if it was built yesterday. I figure the houses in this area are, like many, slowly getting replaced. New replacing the old. The new then slowly becoming the old. Then the new becoming so old it becomes condemned. Hard to imagine, I guess, that any house becomes that way when it's getting built. But I suppose the same thing happens with people too. It's the cycle of life.

I strain to read the numbers on the mailboxes, but at last I park outside and walk up the driveway, the murky light from the streetlights detailing more of the house with every footstep. Warped siding and chipped concrete tiles, the windows smeared with grime, or cracked, the windowsills uneven. There is no garden, just grass and weeds and mud. The concrete foundation and steps leading up to the front door are flecked green with mildew, and it's the first time I've become aware that concrete can actually decay. There are no lights on inside. If a house could look as if it has cancer and is in its dying stages, then it's this one.

When I knock on the door the house creaks and I have the sudden fear it might topple over. Somebody inside yells for me to go away. I keep knocking, using the heel of my hand to keep the impact loud and annoying. Another thirty seconds go by. Then a minute.

"Jesus Christ, man, what the hell do you want?" The voice comes from behind my knocking.

It's turning into one of those long days when I'm not in the mood for personality clashes, so instead of telling him to open up the goddamn door before I kick it in, I grab a business card, identify myself, and tell him I have a few questions.

"I've had questions all day," he answers. "People only ever come to my door if they want something. I'm sick of people wanting something. How about what I want, huh? I want people to leave me the hell alone. Jesus, doesn't it look like I want to be alone? You see any invites?"

"It won't take long."

"No."

"That's a real shame," I say, "because it's cold out here. I'm going to have to keep myself warm somehow, and the best way to do that is to keep pounding on your door."

There is a small shudder as the door catches, then frees from the frame before swinging open.

The man confronting me is the man I saw pictured earlier this evening in the article about the retired caretaker. I reach out and offer Sidney Alderman my card, but he leaves me hanging.

"I know who you are," he says. "You're the cop who had to bury his daughter."

He spits the comment at me as though it's some kind of insult, and I'm unsure how to respond. The fact this man remembers me makes me shudder. Two years ago he covered

Emily's coffin with dirt. How the hell did he remember? The way he says it makes me want to hit him.

He grins, his aged face stretching dozens of wrinkles in dozens of directions. He has a few days' worth of gray stubble; his hair is disheveled, as are his clothes. He looks like he just spent a week in the desert. If I saw him two years ago I don't recall it. His eyes are unreadable in this light.

He smells of cheap beer and even cheaper vodka, and there is another smell there too, something I can't identify, but it makes me think of old men hanging out in hospitals and homes gathering a collection of old diseases.

"I'm looking for your son," I tell him.

"Only you're not a cop anymore, are you, Tate," he says.

"You don't have to be a cop in this world to want to look for somebody," I point out. "That's why they have phone books."

"Then let your Goddamn fingers do the walking," he says, and starts to close the door.

I stop it with my foot.

"What happened?" he asks. "You get sick of the dough-nuts?" He starts to laugh, then scratches at his belly as if he has just come up with a real humdinger. "No, they fired you, right? Why was that again?"

He keeps grinning at me. His teeth look like they haven't seen fluoride in years.

"Sure is a nice place you got here," I say—and hell, maybe the day isn't long enough after all, because here comes that personality clash. "You in the middle of renovating?"

"Yeah. It's a real palace," he answers, but his laughter doesn't have an ounce of humor in it. It's as though he's heard other people do it, maybe on TV or on the radio, and he's try-ing to imitate it. "Somebody died, right? Isn't that why they fired you?"

"Where's your son?" I ask him.

"Nobody knows," he says. "The police have been here all afternoon, right? They've gone through this place and asked me the same damn things over and over, and my answer didn't change for them and it ain't changing for you."

"Your boy is guilty of something. Things will go easier for him if he starts helping himself here," I say. "Tell me where he is and I can start to help him."

"You're a joke," he says, sneering for a few seconds and then grinning like the madman he's turning out to be. I feel sick knowing this is the man who covered my little girl's coffin with dirt. Sick he was anywhere near her.

"You can't hide him forever," I tell him.

"You finished?"

I think about Bruce Alderman and how he was behaving while we dug up the coffin, and I think about him driving away in the stolen truck with the coffin sliding off the back and hitting the ground. I think about how he has perhaps behaved his entire life. This man was his role model. Maybe the world should be thankful there were only four corpses found in the lake and not a hundred.

"You know, I am going to find him," I say, "only now it's going to be the hard way."

"I don't care about making your life easy."

"I'm not talking about hard for me," I say. "You should have given him up, Alderman."

Instead of getting angry Alderman starts to laugh again. "You're a cliché," he says. "And on top of that, you have no authority here." He composes himself immediately, as if the laugh was as fake as the concern he's displayed over the years filling in and digging out holes. "They never found him, did they?"

"What?"

"You know what I'm talking about."

I slip my business card back into my pocket. I'm glad he didn't take it. I don't want this guy touching my card; I don't like the idea that my name could be in print anywhere inside this house of the damned—worse, I don't like the idea of his fingers brushing against mine.

"I'll find your son," I promise.

"Ya think so?"

"I know so."

He shrugs, as if it doesn't bother him either way. Maybe it doesn't. Maybe he really doesn't care, and that's always been the problem for his son. Already I can see Bruce Alderman being found not guilty on a plea of insanity. With this man as his father, there isn't a jury in the world who would be unsympathetic.

"It's been a pleasure," I say, and I back away from the door, keeping my eyes on him. He stares at me as if he is trying to unlock some great mystery. The only mystery here is how somebody so antisocial can have worked these grounds for so many years. He closes the door.

I'm ashamed at myself, angry with him. I came here to interview the bastard yet the only thing I achieved was to let him crawl under my skin. And I can't take it out on either of us.

I reach the sidewalk, unlock the car, and swing the door open. And that's when it happens. I sense it immediately. It's a sprinkling of goose bumps that covers my arms and the back of my neck, and at first I think it's just a residual feeling that anybody leaving that house would get, but then something touches my back. I know it's a gun even though I've never felt one pushed there before.

"S-s-slowly," he says, "just move s-s-low-ly."

"Where?"

"Driver's s-seat. Climb in."

I do as Bruce Alderman says, trying to stay as calm as possible as he climbs into the seat behind me.

CHAPTER ELEVEN

Too much training and not enough experience. That's my problem. Plus the training never detailed anything like this. It was more a general thing, like a commonsense warning. If a gun is pointed at you in close proximity, stay calm. Try to talk your way out of it. It's advice I would've figured out even if I'd never learned it.

"D-d-don't try anything," Bruce says, so I don't. I don't fight for the gun. I don't open the door and try to run. Don't do any of this because it'd be pointless, unless the point was to get shot.

Instead I slowly adjust my body so I can turn my head and face him. The gun looks huge, but only because of the viewing angle and I'm not the one holding it. I wonder where he got it from. There are two hands on the handle. Both are shaking. A finger is wrapped around the trigger.

It strains my eyes to keep the barrel in focus, but I keep them strained. If Bruce Alderman wanted me dead, he'd have done it already, but I feel as though if I take my eyes off the barrel I'm going to die.

"What do you want?"

"I d-d-don't know," he says, and his answer is a problem. If he doesn't know, that means he has no plan, and that makes him far more dangerous, and it means maybe he is planning on shooting me. Maybe that's where his plan is taking him.

His hands keep shaking, the gun rising and falling with minute motions.

"You must want me for something," I say. "Probably to tell me something. Right? To tell me you had nothing to do with the dead girl we found?"

"Why were you t-talking to my f-f-father?" he asks.

"I was looking for you."

"You s-started this," Bruce says. "If it hadn't been for you, everything w-w-would be okay. It would be okay."

No, it wouldn't be okay. Hasn't been okay for Rachel Tyler for some time now. "Why is that?" I ask.

"What did my father say?"

"Your dad's a real affable guy. He had plenty to say."

He pushes himself back into the seat, but keeps the gun leveled at my head. "You think I k-k-killed those girls?"

I don't answer. I look at Sidney Alderman's house and wonder what he's doing right now. Could be Sidney knew his son was out here waiting for me and was putting on a show, his own little performance of misdirection. Could be he didn't know. It's not like they could have anticipated my coming here. Bruce must have been here all along, or he followed me from the church.

"Please, I-I . . . I need you to drive away from here."

I turn back toward him and stare at the gun barrel. "Drive? Where to?"

"I don't . . . I don't know."

"I'm not a taxi service. I'm not going to take you some-where where you can kill me in private. You want to do that, you do it here, and maybe your old man can help you dispose of my body. Or you might luck out and the cops will hear the gunshot. They're not that far away."

"Is that w-what you want?" he asks, pushing the gun for-ward a few more inches. "You think I w-won't do it? You think I've got something to lose by doing it?"

"I don't think that's your plan," I say, trying to sound calm, "and I don't think you're going to pull that trigger. You'd have done it already. You want to tell me something. Maybe you want to confess. Maybe you want to tell me all about it before putting a bullet in my chest." His hands start to shake a little more. I figure I'm only a few shakes away from getting the back of my head splashed on the windshield. "But you don't want that to happen here."

"Maybe you're wrong."

I think about my wife. If I'm wrong, I won't be seeing her again. If I'm wrong—and if I'm lucky—maybe I'll be seeing my daughter. Only problem is I don't believe in an afterlife. I think of Bridget, already alone and about to become even more so. Except that she'd stare out the window as my death made the newspapers and TV and she'd never feel the loss.

"So where do you want to go?" I ask him.

"Away from here. N-now."

I manage to shift my eyes from the barrel to his pale face. His features have sunken since the afternoon, as if the bubble of paranoia holding them in place is slowly deflating. His eyes dart nervously back and forth, unable to fix on any one thing for more than a fraction of a second, like he's hyped up on drugs. There are beads of sweat dangerously close to rolling into his reddened eyes. Behind him, further up the road, dead people are being found in other dead people's places. I look back at the gun, then at his eyes. Back and forth, back and forth, his eyes are looking for something—whether for help or for the demons that have chased him his entire life, who knows? Could be he's looking for his caretaker father to take care of this.

"Please," he repeats, more begging than demanding.

I turn around, and it's hard to keep looking ahead with the weight of the gun trying to pull my eyes back. I swing the car around, wondering if the old man is watching any of this from his filth-covered windows, or even if he can see through them. In the rearview mirror the house in the glow of my brake lights looks like it's set on Mars. I head past the cemetery, past the dozen or so people helping the dead and ignoring, for the time being, the living. I pass the large iron gates that look like they were sculpted two thousand years ago to guard some Greek mythological fortress. I pass the church parked back from the road. I'm not sure what Bruce Alderman's plans are, and I hope at least he knows. I pick a direction and stick to it.

We stop at the first intersection behind a beat-up pickup with a sun-faded bumper sticker on the back saying *Oral Me*. I look at him in the mirror. He looks scared. "Why don't you tell me what's going on."

The caretaker doesn't answer.

"I can help you."

"Help me?"

"You must want something," I tell him.

"Nobody can give me what I want."

"How do you know?" I ask.

"I know," he says. "It's impossible. Unless you can turn back time. Can you? Can you make the last ten years disappear?"

His stutter has gone and I suspect that's because we're away from the cemetery. Or, more accurately, away from his dad. He sounds like he did this afternoon when I spoke to him briefly before the digger came along and unearthed all these questions. He also sounds as if his question is genuine, as if he's holding out hope that maybe I can make the impossible happen. I hope it's not part of his plan.

"You're not the only one who wishes they could turn back time," I tell him. "All I can do is listen to what you have to say. And then I can give you some options. You want to tell me why you killed Rachel Tyler?"

"You know her name?" he says, instead of denying it like an innocent man would.

"I'm a quick learner."

"That's why you're looking for me," he says. "You think I killed those girls."

"You want me to think otherwise?"

He shakes his head. "I never killed anybody," he says.

"Uh huh. Is that why you were in such a hurry to leave this afternoon that you stole the truck? Is that why you've got a gun to my head? Doesn't seem like the path an innocent man would be taking."

"You don't know that," he says. "Can't know that. You'd be doing the same thing."

"I'm pretty sure I wouldn't be."

The intersection clears and we carry on, getting hooked into the flow of other traffic. We drive along in silence for a few seconds. I need him to stay calm.

"You have an office, right?" he asks.

"Why?"

"You must do. All PIs have offices."

"I don't know all the PIs in this world," I tell him. "Half

of them could be working out of their cars for all I know. Or their houses."

He pushes the barrel into my neck. He seems to be getting more and more confident. Only it's a sliding-scale type of confidence. He's more confident, perhaps, than a six-year-old girl walking through a cemetery on a dare. Not as confident as a guy holding up a bank.

"Will we be alone there?" he asks.

"Yes." I change lanes and start altering my course. "But the coffee isn't anything to write home about."

He doesn't offer any further conversation as we drive, and I decide against asking for any. I let him sit in silence, allowing him time to figure something out.

I turn into the parking lot behind my building, and I take my spot, which in the past I've had people towed out of. I look at him again in the mirror. "Now what?"

"Is there a security guard on duty?"

"This isn't a bank."

He stays out of reach as we walk to the back entrance, but comes in close when we get there. There's a swipe pad mounted on the wall—it's all very low-tech—and I slip a card through the reader. There's a mechanical sound of metal disengaging from metal, then I push the door open. He follows closely behind me, and my first opportunity of getting rid of him by slamming the door on his face is lost.

"How many floors?" he asks.

"How many floors what?"

"What floor are you on?"

"The eighth," I tell him.

"Let's take the stairs."

I've already pushed the button on the elevator and the doors have opened. "This is much quicker."

"Too confined," he says.

"You claustrophobic?"

"Where are they?"

"This way."

I lead him into the stairwell. It's cold and our footfalls echo as we take the stairs two at a time for the first four floors, then one at a time for the remainder. When we reach the eighth floor, we're both breathing heavily. We see nobody as we move down the corridor. There are potted plants full of crisp green leaves and no brown ones, oil paintings that don't represent anything, just colors and shapes thrown together in appealing ways.

We reach my office. I step in. Bruce reaches behind him and shuts the door.

"Sit down and keep your hands on the desk," he says.

I do as he asks, resting my palms on either side of the watch I took earlier. Bruce sits on the other side of the desk as if he were a client. He stares at the watch.

"You recognize it?" I ask him.

"How much do you know?" he asks.

"About what?"

"Don't be like this," he says, slapping one hand on the side of his chair while keeping the other on the gun. Steady now, as if all the nerves are gone. As if being away from the cemetery has cured him. As if over the last fifteen minutes all the confusion, all the fear, all the guilt have somehow lined up, found a way to get along, and formed a brilliant idea about what to do next.

"Okay, here's what I know," I say. "From the moment you found out we were digging up Henry Martins, you were nervous. You hung around despite that, but as soon as the bodies started coming up to the surface of the lake you bolted. Things were inevitable then. We were all on the same train ride. In the car a while ago you were surprised I'd identified the girl. Rachel Tyler. You asked if I thought you'd killed the girls. Not people, but girls. That means you already know that when the other bodies are identified, and the matching coffins dug up, there are going to be women in there. The only way you could know that is if you put them there."

He doesn't answer. Just stares at me, his hand shaking a little, his options racing behind his jittery eyes. I hope he's not coming back time and time again to the one where he pulls the trigger. Maybe that was his plan all along, and he's had it from the moment he climbed into my car. He partners up his free hand with the other one to steady the gun.

"What do you want from me, Bruce?" I lean back, keeping my arms out so my hands don't leave the table. "Just tell me."

"I need a cigarette," he says, and reaches into his pocket.

"I have a no-smoking rule in here," I say, and when he pulls his hand back from his pocket it's empty. He doesn't complain.

"I've never killed anybody," he says, after a few seconds of staring down at his shaking hands, one of which is wrapped tightly around the gun. "I know you think different, but it's the truth. I have proof. It's underneath my bed. I could take you there. You could talk to my father. He knows the truth."

"Uh huh."

"But you wouldn't let me take you there, would you?"

"No."

"You don't believe me at all, do you?"

I fight the temptation to shake my head. "Why don't you give me a few more details first?"

"There's no point. You'll never believe me. And I knew you wouldn't."

"Then why bring me back here? Why go through all of this?"

"I didn't have anything to do with them dying. Nothing. But I buried them—I had to. The girls, they deserved that. And now," he says, "now their ghosts will leave me alone, and you, you will take me seriously." My heart races as he twists the gun and jams the barrel beneath his chin. It's almost as frightening as having it pointed at me.

"Wait, wait," I say, and my instinct is to reach out to stop him, but I keep my hands flat on the table. "Listen to me, listen, Bruce."

He relaxes the gun for a moment, looking at me as if I must be an idiot not to understand him, but it's just enough of a moment to make me believe there's a chance neither of us has to die here. Not much of a chance, not long enough of a moment.

"Why did you take the bodies out of the graves? What did these girls deserve?"

For a moment he looks confused, as if he can't find the right words, then suddenly his face becomes calm and relaxed as some perfect clarity washes over him, and I know it's the clarity of a man who has made peace with his decision, and that there is nothing I can say or do to avoid his next step.

"For dignity," he says, "they deserved the dignity."

The gunshot rings in my ears. I smell cordite and burning flesh long after the pink mist settles, long after pieces of bone and brain are buried into the ceiling above him.

CHAPTER TWELVE

It's a life moment. One of those snapshots of time that never leave you, never seem to fade away. In fact it's the exact opposite—the colors, the imagery, the detail, they don't dilute, they grow stronger, clearer; the moment becomes more powerful over the years while others slowly disappear. The smell—the smell of cooking flesh, the coppery smell of blood, the gunpowder, the stench as his bowels let go, the sweat. The air tastes hot, it dries out my mouth and makes my tongue stick to its roof. All I hear is a ringing sound that seems as though it will never diminish, as if it too will only grow more powerful.

It's a life moment. I sit still, I stare ahead, I take it all in. I don't know if there are others in the building. Don't know if the gunshot has already been reported. Blood has formed thick splotches on the ceiling. They seem to hang there, motionless, unaffected by gravity. Bruce Alderman's body also seems to hang there, the hand still on the gun, the gun still pressed into his neck. The front of his shirt is clean, not a speck of blood on it. His hair is messed up, the bullet forming a volcano shape in the roof of his skull. And still he sits there, as I sit there, motionless, staring at each other, a life moment for me, a death moment for him. Time has paused, as if in a snapshot.

Then it begins again. His hand, still gripping the gun, falls away. It hits the top of his thigh, slides into the arm of the chair; the gun clicks against it and falls onto the carpet. His head drops down, his chin hits his chest; the gunshot hole in his skull is like an eye staring at me, the blood falling through it, giving the impression it's winking at me. Blood-matted hair falls into place and blocks the view. Blood pools on his shirt. It starts to pull away from the ceiling, droplets that form stalactites before breaking away and raining down. They pad softly into the carpet, make small thudding noises on the fronts of his legs, the back of his neck, the top of his head. It drops onto my shoulders, onto my arms, onto my hands that are still on the desk for him to see. He stays slumped there, this dead weight in my office chair, then slowly he tips forward, he gains momentum, then his forehead cracks heavily into the edge of the desk, jarring his head upright as his body falls, keeping him balanced for a moment longer, the back of his head almost touching his shoulders, his face exposed and his empty eyes staring at me, before he continues down to the ground where he lies in a clump that five seconds ago was a person but is a person no more. He lies on the gun, and still I sit here, watching, waiting: perhaps someone will come along and tell me that this is what I get for following up a line of questioning into an investigation that isn't even mine.

The pink mist slowly settles; the smell of the gunshot starts to fade, replaced by urine and shit; and the ringing in my ears slowly dulls to a shrilling noise.

I stand up slowly, as if any sudden movement might cause him to pick the gun back up and try prefixing his suicide with the word *murder*. I move around my desk to the body, careful not to step in any blood. I think of his last words. *They deserved the dignity.* He wanted me to take him seriously, and he succeeded. Only problem is I still don't believe he's innocent. Shooting himself in my office isn't the action required to prove innocence over guilt; if anything, it helps suggest insanity over sanity. I'd have told him this if I'd been given the chance.

I crouch down and put a hand on his shoulder. Without rolling him, barely without touching him, I go through his pockets.

There is a small envelope that has my name written on it, only he's spelled it wrong. In the bottom of the envelope is a small key. I'm about to sit it up on my desk when I see the blood mist has coated the surface. I fold the envelope in half and tuck it into my pocket. I go through the rest of his pockets. I find car keys and a wallet; I find tissues, two packets of antacids, a broken pencil, and one of my business cards. I leave them where they are.

I use my cell phone to call the police because my office phone is covered in blood. I ask for Detective Schroder, but get transferred through to Detective Inspector Landry. I'd rather not talk to him, but I'm not running high on options. I tell him the situation as if giving just any old police report. Before I finish I ask him to bring coffee.

"Jesus, Tate, this isn't my first homicide," he says.

"You mean suicide."

"Yeah. Whatever." He hangs up.

I sit on the ground out in the corridor, putting a cushion between me and the wall so as not to stain it with the blood splatter on my jacket, and lean back. I think of what Bruce told me. Why kill yourself if you're not admitting any guilt? How could anybody possibly believe he buried those girls, but had nothing to do with their deaths?

I pull the envelope out of my pocket. The key looks a little different from others I've seen, and I can't identify it. There are no marks on it, no numbers, no letters. It could be for a house, a lockbox, a safe, a boat—could be anything. It's just one more item that I've taken from somebody today. The ring is still in my pocket, and the wristwatch is still on my desk. I head back into my office and slip the watch into a plastic bag before dropping it into my pocket. This whole area is a crime scene now and I don't need awkward questions. I take out the key and put it onto my key ring so it looks like one of mine.

I'm still in my office when I hear them arriving. The elevator pings, the doors open, and half a dozen police, including Landry, spill into the corridor. Soon there will be others as they come to question and photograph and document and study. The cemetery crime scene was taken away from me, but this one is mine.

I stand by the doorway and watch. I have worked with most of these men and women in the past, but they look at me as if I'm a stranger. Their greetings are curt, and I am told to step into the corridor and wait.

CHAPTER THIRTEEN

The night drags on. My office is quarantined from me, and from the rest of the world, by yellow boundary tape with black lettering. Forensic guys dressed in white nylon overalls move slowly around inside, searching every square centimeter in case the vital clue is a microscopic one. Nobody asks to search me, but my hands are tested for gunshot residue and my jacket is taken from me because of the blood dust that has settled on it. I'm not concerned at all, because the evidence will show that the shooting happened exactly as I said it did. It can't go any other way. They can't come back to me tomorrow and say they've weighed it all up and their conclusion is I put the gun into his chin and pulled the trigger.

Still, it's a clear-cut case of suicide that can't be that clear because of the time they're taking to studying the angles and blood patterns. At least that's how it feels. They're taking this long to deal with it because they're dealing with me. They don't trust me the same way they trusted me when I was one of them. As an outsider I fall within the scope of their suspicions, and for this I only have myself to blame. I was a different man two years ago. A very different man.

Their questions begin to repeat after a while. The phrasing alters somewhat, but they're only variations of the same theme—one that fast gets tiring, and one which seems to suggest there is a degree of blame here that is mine. Only there isn't. I didn't force the caretaker into my car. Didn't force him to come back here. Didn't force him to shed brain and bone matter across my furniture.

In the end I'm told to go home. I'm not sure how happy I am to do that, but I'm not sure what the alternative is either. Hang around and watch, I guess, though there isn't much to watch. Just a bunch of guys doing the kind of tedious work that guys like me don't have the patience for. If it was daytime there'd be a crowd of onlookers tripping over each other to sneak a peek at the corpse, but I've already sneaked a peek, and more—I stole from it.

"One last thing," Landry calls out as I make my way to the stairwell.

I turn around, but keep my hand on the stairwell door. Landry isn't one of my biggest fans. There was a time when we were rather alike, but his life became his work while I did what I could to keep a balance. He's the same age as me, but he hasn't aged very well in the two years since I've seen him. He doesn't look good at all. He smells of cigarette smoke and coffee.

"What did you take?" he asks.

"What?"

"Off your desk. There are three clear spots. All that misted blood, except for three places. Two are from your hands.

Which is a good thing, because it shows where you were when he pulled the trigger. But there's something else. A much smaller patch."

"My keys."

"Doesn't look like you took keys."

"There was so much going on. I don't know. Maybe it was my phone."

"Didn't look like a phone. If I was to search you, I wouldn't find anything else?"

"What's your point, Landry?"

"No point. Just curious as to what would be important enough for you to steal from a crime scene."

"I'm not stealing anything, and anyway it's my office. Everything in there belongs to me."

"Not everything," he says, and he looks back toward my office where the body of Bruce Alderman is being carried out in a dark canvas bag.

Outside, it's drizzling again. It's almost two in the morning. My car is still damp inside, but at least there's no one in the back holding a gun. I drape one of the ambulance blankets over the driver's seat to protect it from any blood still on my clothes, then begin the drive home. The hookers and the homeless stare at me as I pass. I could be their salvation, their next meal, their next drink, their next score.

It's only a ten-minute drive home, but I'm almost falling asleep by the time I get there. My house isn't anything flashy, merely one of many placed slap-bang in the middle of suburbia. People live here, they spend their lives here, they make little people and pay big mortgages, and supposedly, *supposedly*, if they play by the rules then nothing bad happens to them. The problem is that tonight there is a van parked outside blocking the entranceway, so I can't just drive into the garage and walk into the house and ignore it. I pull up behind it and climb out, way too tired for any kind of confrontation. Immediately the doors to the van open. A spotlight comes on, a man with a camera resting on his shoulder circles around from my right, and a woman with shoulder-length hair appears on my left. The bright light accentuates her heavy makeup.

"No comment," I say before the cameraman can settle into a comfortable position and the reporter can push the microphone into my face. I'm way too tired for this bullshit.

"Casey Horwell," she says, "TVNZ news, just a few quick questions."

"No comment," I say, "and can you move your van? You're blocking my driveway."

"We have a report that Bruce Alderman, the suspect in the Burial Murders case, was killed tonight in your office."

I wonder how long it took them to come up with a name for the case—*the Burial Murders?*—or whether tomorrow somebody will have come up with a better one. Casey Horwell pushes the microphone closer to my face. I recognize her from the news. Her career took a slide a year ago when she released information she should never have had, along with her own spin on what it meant, and ultimately compromised an investigation. It resulted in an innocent man being found guilty in the court of public opinion for the rape of a young child. The night the segment aired, the man's house was burned down with him inside it. He survived with third-degree burns, but his girlfriend didn't. I guess tonight Horwell is trying to pick her career back up.

"No comment," I say.

"That's not going to get you far," she says.

"You need to move your van," I tell her, and I'm starting to get pissed off.

"Can you tell us about your involvement today?"

"No."

"You're no longer on the force," she says. "Why were you at the cemetery?"

My hands are in my pockets and I ball them into fists. "No comment."

"Bruce Alderman was killed four hours ago, and yet here you are, coming home," she says. "Why is that?"

I almost tell her that he wasn't killed, that he killed himself and there's a difference, a very big difference. Instead I say nothing.

"How is it you still get cases?" she asks. "Especially these types. I was led to believe everybody on the force hated you."

"Not everybody hates me," I tell her. "I'm sure they all hate you a whole lot more after you got that woman killed. At least I still have a few friends in the department," I say. "They do what they can to help."

She smiles and I'm not sure why. "Is there anything else you would like to add?"

"No."

"It's been a long day, I imagine," she says.

I relax the tension in my fists. "It has been."

"It's been a long day for everybody. I guess it must have been hard on you."

"Can you move your van now?"

"Of course. Thank you for your time, Detect . . . I mean, Mr. Tate."

The light on the camera switches off. Casey Horwell looks at me for a few more seconds, that same smile still on her face, then she turns away and climbs into the van. A few seconds later it pulls away. I get back into my car and park it in the driveway, too tired to put it in the garage.

My house has three bedrooms, but only one of them gets used. My daughter's bedroom is still set up as if one day she's going to return home, and I'm not exactly sure how healthy that is and I'm not exactly sure I care to know. If my wife were here maybe she'd have made a decision to change that, but she isn't. It's just like Patricia Tyler keeping a room for her daughter. Snapshots of time. It seems to be what life is about.

I jump in the shower to wash the blood and the confetti-sized pieces of the caretaker's skull off me. I climb out feeling more awake.

I put a CD on the stereo, grab a beer, and go out onto the deck, pushing play on my answering machine on the way. It's my mother. She's calling to see how the rest of my day went, and to ask about what happened. I make a mental note to call her tomorrow.

The night has warmed up a little, and I sit on the deck chair in the misty rain and stare up at the night, listening to the music as the beer helps calm my nerves. I'd sit out here sometimes with Bridget after Emily was asleep. It's sheltered from the wind when it's cold, but when the wind is warm it sweeps in from the opposite direction and onto the deck. I'd slowly drink a beer and she'd slowly drink a glass of wine and we'd talk about our day. I always felt as though I could tell her anything, but there were cases I couldn't bring home. They would stay in my mind, but I didn't want them in hers. They were a part of my life and I didn't want them to intrude on hers. We'd talk about our pasts and about our future; we had plans to move into a bigger house, we were debating whether to have more children. We would sit out here and laugh, we would make plans, we would argue.

The rain drifts away and the sky clears a little; a gap appears in the cloud cover, and for a moment there's a quarter moon up there; it throws around enough pale light so that when I look at my watch I can see the night is slipping further away. Emily's cat, a ginger tom named Daxter, comes through the sliding door and jumps up on my lap. He starts purring while I scratch him under his chin. He was only six months old when Emily died, and any question as to whether cats can remember people has been answered by the fact that the only place he ever sleeps is on her bed, and that sometimes he has the same look in his eyes my wife has—as if he's looking for something that isn't there anymore.

I finish the beer and head back inside. I refill Daxter's bowls with food and water, and he seems grateful enough. I walk past my daughter's bedroom, but don't go in. I think about Rachel Tyler, but I try hard not to think about what her final hour was like. I try to envision a scenario in which Bruce the dead caretaker is innocent, but can't seem to come up with much. Then I think about Casey Horwell, and can't help but wonder if there is any truth in what she said about everybody hating me.

Daxter is asleep on Emily's bed when I finally hit the sack. I lie in the darkness, thinking about my dead family and the man who made them that way. I wish that in this average house in this average street nothing bad had ever happened, but it's already too late.

CHAPTER FOURTEEN

I end up sleeping in, which isn't a good start to the case. When I flip open my cell phone I find that it has given up. The trip into the lake was worse for it than I thought. I shake it a bit and flex the casing, and I slip the battery in and out and try plugging it in, but nothing happens. I have no idea how many calls I've missed.

I drive through the city thinking that Christchurch and technology go together like drinking and driving: they don't mix well, but some still think it's a good idea. Everything here looks old, and for the most part it is. People living in the past have set historical values on buildings dating back over a hundred years, and have had them protected from the future. Investors can't come along and replace them with high-rises and apartment complexes. It's a cold-looking city made to look even colder in the dreary weather. Everything looks so damn archaic. Even the hookers look fifty years old. A glue sniffer on a mountain bike has a cardboard tube running from his mouth down to the plastic bag by the handlebars. He's multi-tasking. He's sniffing glue and riding on the sidewalk, and he can keep doing both without the distraction of lifting the bag to his face.

It's only eleven in the morning, yet I struggle to find a parking space at the shopping mall. I squeeze in next to a boy-racer Skyline that looks expensive and suggests the guy driving it has a job, though if he's here at the same time as me on a weekday then he probably doesn't, unless he's a private investigator. I head into a phone store and deal with a guy who seems more interested in staring across the mall at the hairdressers than he does at the phone I'm showing him. I look over at the hairdressers and can't blame him.

"It's cheaper to upgrade," he says, "than get this thing fixed. Plus it'll be away for a few weeks. What did you do to it, anyway?"

"It fell in the bath."

"Yeah—that'll do it. Anyway, this thing is obsolete."

"I bought it eighteen months ago."

"Yeah, like I said, it's obsolete."

He shows me a range of cell phones and I pick out one that looks like it shouldn't confuse me too much and will also be out of date in about a year. He sets it up so my old number will work on it, and warns me it could take between one and two hours to become active.

"Where do I recognize you from?" he asks, handing back my credit card.

I shrug. "Beats me."

He slowly shakes his head. "I'm sure I've seen you," he says.

I'm sure he has too—probably on TV yesterday when I was sitting in the back of an ambulance. We finish up and I let him get back to watching the hairdressers.

The police station is ten stories of concrete block and glass that was out of date around the same time it was built. I park out on the street and feed the meter before walking up the steps to the foyer. There isn't much going on at ground-floor level, just a few people waiting in line to make complaints. I sign in at a desk; the process is simple enough since I'm expected upstairs. I press the up button and a moment later the elevator arrives. I hit the button for the fourth floor, and the elevator comes to a stop on the first floor and I have company. A guy in overalls, thirtyish, carrying a bucket and mop.

"I'm the cleaner," he says, and he grins at me, showing me all his teeth. I smile back at him, and the elevator hits the fourth floor and the doors open. I step out, and the janitor follows. We walk a few paces before Carl Schroder sees us and comes over.

"Can I get you a coffee, Detective Schroder?" the janitor asks him.

"I'm fine, Joe. Thanks, though."

The cleaner walks away and I watch him go before turning back to Schroder. I've known Carl for many years. In another lifetime we worked the same cases as partners, dealt with the same problems. We used to be pretty good friends, but it's obvious he doesn't really want me here. He leads me over to a table to a bunch of forms and asks me to sign them. He tells me the crime scene has been released, and I ask him how the investigation is going, and he says it's going okay. He doesn't elaborate on that. Just says it's okay and nothing else, which means he either doesn't want to tell me or things are going badly.

"Sorry, Tate, I just don't have the time to give you any information. Finding those bodies, hell, you couldn't have picked a worse time."

"Who for? Them or you?"

He exhales heavily. "It's this fucking Carver case," he says, talking about the Christchurch Carver who, at this rate, seems will never be caught. "Man, it's like every step we take this guy is taking two steps. I don't know what the hell it is, but we're struggling. We're so understaffed, I don't know, we just need more man power. It's that simple."

"You offering me a job?"

"Good one, Tate. You're even funnier than I remember. Especially after last night's performance."

"What do you mean?" I ask.

"You're slipping. It looked bad, man, really bad. Friends in the department? Jesus, why'd you say that?"

"What are you . . ." But then it comes to me. I run my hand over my face and pinch my chin. "Shit."

"Yeah. You got that right."

"I haven't seen it, but I'm guessing she stitched me up, huh?"

"There's a copy if you wanna take a look. Media room's free."

The media room is big enough to hold four people if none of them is overweight, and its walls are lined with computers and monitors. News reports are kept as part of the database involved in ongoing cases; those that go to air are stored on hard drives. Schroder cues it up.

"It was on this morning," he says. "They played it at seven o'clock, eight, and nine. They're probably waiting till twelve to play it again if they don't have anything more."

I'm standing next to my car, coming forward to meet the reporters. From their perspective they couldn't have picked a better time to film me. From mine, they couldn't have picked a worse one. There is blood on my shirt and on my face, and pieces of what I guess might be bone or brain matter in my hair. My skin is pale and sallow and there are dark smudges beneath my eyes. I look like I might have been one of the finds in the coffins, and now I know where the phone guy recognized me from.

The reporter is talking to me, and I'm talking back, but you can't hear any of what I'm saying because the conversation has been muted. All you can hear is Casey Horwell's voice-over as they move from a shot of me outside my house to scenes of the graveyard. The shots go back and forth as she talks.

". . . used to be a detective for the Christchurch police, but for the last two years has been struggling as a private investigator. He offered to speak to us outside his house where he filled us in on some aspects of the case, but when we asked him why he was coming home and not being held in custody until the killing of Bruce Alderman was further investigated, he was unsure how to answer."

The interview is still showing me talking. But there are no words. Just the chitchat of me asking them to move their van, telling them I have no comments, and whatever else I said to get rid of them, but it looks like we're sharing an in-depth discussion. Then I disappear from the frame, and Casey Horwell is standing there, the only background is her van, and I bet they pulled over the moment they got around the next corner to film her.

"Two years ago the man linked to killing Theodore Tate's daughter disappeared and has never been seen again, and though the investigation is still open it appears nobody is making any effort to learn what really happened. The man's disappearance led to Detective Tate being dismissed from the police. Last night Bruce Alderman was violently killed inside Theodore Tate's office and again it looks like he is being dismissed. One can't help but wonder what forces are in place to allow a man like this to still be out on the streets instead of being held accountable for his actions. . . ."

The segment cuts back to me, still standing in front of my car. I know what's coming up before I hear it. It's the line. My line. And she has placed it perfectly.

"I still have a few friends in the department. They do what they can."

The segment stops and Schroder turns off the monitor.

"That was bullshit, Carl."

"You don't think I know that? Horwell's a classic case of somebody who threw away a promising career and is grabbing at straws trying to get it back. But you're slipping, Tate. Two years ago you'd never have made that mistake. And it doesn't matter what you said, she made you look guilty, man, just getting out of your car with all that blood on you—you looked like a monster. Can you imagine the shit that'd be raining down right now if you were still a cop?"

I can feel the anger building up inside. "I know, I know," I say, and Carl is the wrong person to be angry at. I'm the one who messed up. "But what was I to do? Just drive past and not even go home?"

He walks me back to the elevator. "That's exactly what you could have done. Did you even think of that?"

"You still on the case?" I ask.

"Landry's taking over. I'm still on the Carver."

"Has he identified the woman who was in the water?"

"Yeah. An elderly woman who died and was buried last week," he says.

"And the coffin? When you identified her, you pulled up the corresponding coffin, right? What was inside?"

"Why do I think you already know the answer to this?"

"Something Bruce Alderman said."

"Yeah. We got a girl who went missing six days ago."

"Six days ago? Who was she?"

"Oh, well, her name was . . . Oh, wait, hang on a second. You don't work here anymore, do you?"

"And there was a girl in Henry Martins's coffin too, wasn't there?"

He nods. "Come on, Tate, stop pretending you're only just figuring it out."

"You identify her yet?"

"Almost. We're taking what we know about the girl from last week and making the same assumption. We're figuring the girl in Henry Martins's coffin went missing around the same time he was buried."

"Seems like a safe assumption."

"Safe, but not confirmed."

"And the other two?"

"The other two are going to be damn difficult to identify, and it's not like we can just start digging up coffins for the hell of it."

The elevator arrives and the doors open. I don't move.

"We could have made a difference," I tell him.

"What?"

"Two years ago. Remember?"

He stares at me for a few seconds, no expression at all, no movement of his head, then slowly he starts to nod. "I know," he says.

"You're going to find more girls."

He says nothing. He already knows. I wonder if this is why he's telling me so much.

"We could have made a difference," I repeat.

As the doors of the elevator close, Schroder keeps standing where he is, staring at me.

Instead of driving to my office, I take a detour to the morgue. I figure if Tracey had noticed I'd stolen the ring she'd have called by now.

She's a little rushed off her feet and doesn't seem real glad to see me. Nor does Sheldon West, the ME I spoke to at the cemetery. But Tracey decides to accommodate me after I tell her things will be quicker for her if she helps me out rather than having me hanging around for the next two hours asking her the same questions over and over.

"You're a real pain in the ass," she tells me.

"You just need to spend more time with me, that's all. Get to know me a little better."

"Less time, Theo. That's why I'm agreeing to show you. Oh, and by the way, that was a nice job you did last night. You should try to get a job on TV."

"That's real funny."

She rolls Rachel Tyler out of a huge metal drawer and starts pointing things out as if she were Death showing a prospective client a neat way to die.

"It's hard to pinpoint a time of death, but it's around two years ago," she says, "which falls in with when Henry Martins was buried. I would have guessed that she was buried in his place, but the shovel marks on the coffin suggest he was in the ground first. However, I'd say she went into the coffin not long after he went into the ground. We're close to ID'ing her. Landry has a name; we're just waiting to confirm with dental records."

There's no point in telling Tracey I already know who it is. It'll only lead to awkward questions, and I'm going to be getting them as soon as Schroder makes a positive ID on the girl and speaks to her family. Yesterday Rachel Tyler's mother opened the door to hope. Today she'll be closing it.

"You know something, don't you," she says, her lips forming a thin scar as she stares at me.

"How did she die?"

"Who is she, Theo?"

"Somebody who was too young to die."

"Aren't they always?"

"I don't know. Maybe." I glance over at another table where a guy who looks as though he was around when those buildings started getting built a hundred years ago is lying. I wonder if he thought he was too young to die, or if he couldn't wait to get it over with. "But I'm going to help her. Can you tell me how she died?"

"Badly. But I'm guessing you knew that from the moment we opened up the coffin. Her hyoid bone was broken. She was strangled."

"Sexual assault?"

"Impossible to tell after such time."

"She was re-dressed after she died, right? What does that tell you?"

"It doesn't tell me anything. It only suggests."

"Dignity."

"What?"

"Something Bruce Alderman said to me last night. I'm still trying to figure it out."

Tracey shrugs. "That's beyond my scope, Theo."

I look down at Rachel Tyler with the huge Y-incision cut across her mummified body. She hasn't been stitched back together because what is left is mostly skeletal. She doesn't even look like a person anymore. Just a shell. A husk. Something you'd kick to the curb and throw out with the trash. If Bruce did this to her, then he got off lightly last night. I'd have done more than put a bullet in his head.

"Nothing else?" I ask.

"What else are you expecting?"

"I don't know," I admit. "Something helpful, I guess."

Tracey offers a small laugh and covers Rachel up. "Maybe we'd have had more luck if she had been found with something. I don't know—a piece of jewelry maybe. Perhaps even a ring."

She stares at me and I don't take the bait. "What about the other girl? Schroder said you've got another one."

"I'm not at liberty to say."

"She was strangled too, right?"

"Good luck, Theo. Part of me hopes you find who did this to her before the police do. Part of me wishes you wouldn't even try."

I pass the body of Bruce Alderman on the way out. It's lying naked on a slab of steel. There's a hole in the bottom of his chin and another in the top of his head. Once again I wonder where he got the gun from.

I hit the button on the elevator, and when the doors open Landry is standing there. His suit is ruffled up as if he slept in it, and he hasn't shaved since I saw him last night. Next to him is Sidney Alderman. Alderman looks pale; his eyes are darting back and forth as if he's searching for something, looking past me. But then he seems to focus, to figure out who he's looking at. He lunges forward, bringing with him the stench of alcohol.

"You fucker," he yells, jumping out of the elevator and taking a swing at my jaw, but I step back, and Landry grabs the back of Alderman's shirt and pulls him off balance. Alderman's fist crashes into the wall, and a moment later so does his face. "You killed my son!"

"That's enough," Landry shouts.

"He killed my boy!" Alderman pushes himself away from the wall, but only as far as Landry allows him. His knuckles are bleeding. "Why isn't he in jail? I saw the news, you son of a bitch, I saw what you did."

"I didn't kill your—"

"Tate, why don't you do us all a favor and get in the God-damn elevator," Landry says.

"You murderer!" Alderman yells. Then, much more quietly, "Why do you keep letting him get away with it?"

The shouting has brought both of the medical examiners into the corridor. Sheldon looks bothered, as if the violence is about to escalate and include him in it. Tracey looks disappointed.

"Get in the elevator, Tate," Landry repeats.

"You're a dead man," Alderman yells again as the doors start to close. "You hear me? A dead—"

I'm not sure whether I actually hear the rest, or whether my mind just fills in the blank.

The drive to my office I spend in Alderman's shoes, and I have a bad feeling that I'd be coming to the same conclusions he has. I told him things were going to be hard for his son. That same night his boy ends up dead. And the following morning I'm all over the news, looking like a damn killer. I'm going to have to keep looking over my shoulder. I'm sure of it.

Back at the office, I'm greeted by the onlookers who missed out on last night's show and try to supplement their lack of daily drama by staring at me as I walk up the corridor. They ask me questions. They look deflated that I'm not still covered in blood. There is police-scene tape across my door. I screw it up into a ball, carry it inside, and shut the door on my audience. All I can think about is how many of these people have seen the news and, thanks to a desperate reporter using desperate tactics to be noticed, now believe I pulled the trigger.

The office stinks and makes me feel a little ill. I lay a

bathroom towel and some newspapers over my chair before sitting down. I tear up a tissue, wad it up, and stuff it into my nose. I plug in my cell phone, but it's still not connected, so I wipe down the office phone with some wet tissues until it's clean enough to use. I phone my insurance company. It turns out I have life insurance, house insurance, contents and car insurance, but not the kind of insurance that allows for this. If a pipe had busted or the carpet caught fire, the insurance company would play ball. But when it comes to messy suicide, they don't want to know. When I hang up I look through the phone book for a number for a company I've never had to call, but that I've seen perform over the years. The cleaning crew promise to come out today. They'll replace what they can't clean, which will include the office chairs.

When I get off the phone I look over the chair Bruce Alderman was sitting on, then slowly I stand up and peer over the desk, as if I'm still expecting to see him lying there. All that's there is a lot of blood. I sit back down and go through the phone book. The first number I dial is for the wrong Martinses, but the second one I get right and Laura Martins answers the phone.

I explain who I am, and Henry Martins's daughter remembers me.

"So now you think differently," she says, "and another man is dead. That witch killed them," she says, referring to her stepmother. "And the only thing on the news is these people who floated up in the water and the dead caretaker. What about my father? Why doesn't he get a mention?"

"They're keeping the names out of the media for the moment," I say. "They have to, until they identify everybody."

"Why my dad?" she asks. "Why choose him to take out and throw in the water? Why not somebody else?"

"It was just a random choice. The day the girl was murdered probably coincided with your father's burial."

"So it's random? Just one of those things? Like a bad statistic?"

There isn't any answer that will satisfy her, so I don't offer one. Instead I push on. "Your father, did he own a watch?"

"Yes."

"Was he buried with it?"

"I . . . I'm not sure. Maybe. I don't really know."

"Okay. Can you remember what kind of watch it was?"

"Not really. It was old, though."

"Old?"

"Yeah. He's had it my entire life. Is it weird that I can't remember if he had it when he was buried?"

I run some names past her, but she doesn't recognize any of them. Then I thank her for her time. The Tag Heuer didn't belong to Henry Martins, because it is ten years old at the most. I switch my computer on and go through the file I was creating yesterday, tapping at the keyboard tentatively and barely touching the mouse because they have blood splatter on them. I head back onto the missing persons website and look for young women who went missing two years ago. Rachel Tyler's name comes up again, and so do four others. I read the files. One of them was found two months later. The others have never shown up. I look at the photos. One of the girls was seventeen, another was thirty-two. Could be both are in the ground in the cemetery. The seventeen-year-old, Julie Thomas, definitely shares some characteristics with Rachel Tyler. Similar height, similar age, long blond hair, both good-looking. Most serial killers have a type. Looks like I've found it, but to make sure I check for the reports of women who went missing six days earlier. There is only one. Jessica

Shanks was twenty-four years old and was reported missing by her husband the day she didn't come home from work. I read through the details. The file hasn't been reported as being closed, but I imagine sometime within the next twenty-four hours the update will have been made.

I print out the photos, one for each of the girls. I set them side by side on the floor since I can't use my desk. Rachel Tyler, Julie Thomas, and Jessica Shanks. Without a doubt, the killer had a type. Somewhere in this database is another young woman to complete the set.

I print out the files, and then I power down my computer and unplug it all. I remove the tissue from my nose, then carry the computer down to my car: I don't want it to get damaged by the cleaning crew, and I'm not sure when I'll be back. Until all the blood is gone I'll work out of my house.

When all the gear is loaded into my car, I return for the whiteboard, which I wipe down with more wet tissues. I also grab my cell phone. It has one bar showing on the power scale—I should've bought a car charger too. I leave the easel behind and carry the whiteboard to my car, nodding at the people who ask me questions on the way and ignoring their requests to stay and hang out a while to catch them up on all the gory details.

CHAPTER FIFTEEN

David the boyfriend lives in a house that is almost as run down as Sidney the retired caretaker's. The place hasn't seen as much in the way of paint over the last few years as it has rust and spiders. The guttering has corroded away, the windows are covered in grime, the siding warped and unwelcoming. It's in the middle of dozens of others, each one in need of a handyman's touch or a wrecking ball. I can't figure out how David still lives here. I can't figure out how anybody could live here longer than a week. But maybe he likes it and it's a simple case of me not getting it. Perhaps this is the stereotypical pop-culture way to live. Derelict is the new black. Grunge is in, being broke is in, making sure the house you live in looks like crap is in. He doesn't own the place, but rents it, like all the other students in this area, which means he slips easily into the day-to-day routine of not giving a damn about the condition of the property, and the owners know one day they're going to bulldoze or burn it down anyway and don't care as long as the rent is paid. This isn't suburbia; most of the people living around here are university students struggling to survive. Rachel Tyler was a student. I can't imagine her staying here for more than a few days before returning home to grab a few things or a good night's sleep or the chance to step out of a shower cleaner than when she stepped in.

A young guy with studs in his ears and lips and nose opens the door. He must have real fun going through the security foreplay before boarding a plane. He's squinting because the cloudy glare is too bright for him. His T-shirt reads *The truth is down there* with an arrow pointed to his crotch. All of a sudden, the last thing I want to know is the truth.

"David Harding?" I ask.

"No, dude, he's not here."

"Where is he?"

The guy shrugs. "Studying, I think. Or sleeping."

"Sleeping?"

"Yeah, man, you know, that thing you do in the morning after being out all night."

"I thought people slept in the night," I tell him.

"What planet are you from?" he asks.

"An older one. Does he sleep here?"

"Yeah, man."

"So if he's sleeping, could it be that he's sleeping here right now?"

He seems to think about it. "It could, I suppose."

"Then how about you put that university education of yours to some good use and figure it out for me."

"Whatever, bro," he says, then turns and walks up the hallway, grabbing the wall twice as he goes to make sure neither it nor he falls down.

I take a couple of steps inside, figuring Stud-Face here is happy for me to do so, but simply forgot to extend the invite. It's colder inside than out—probably an all-year-round feature of these houses. The air is damp and the carpet, wallpaper, and furniture could do with a permanent dehumidifier. There are posters on the walls, but no photographs of friends or family. I can hear mumbling from the other end of the house, but can't decipher it. It sounds like hangover talk.

I keep walking. The hallway takes me into a kitchen straight out of the start of last century, and with rotting food lying around that could be from the same era. The kitchen bench has a Formica top patterned with yellow flowers and strewed with the remnants of fast-food packets. The coffee pot is hot. I pour a cup just as Studly comes through. He doesn't seem surprised at all that I've invaded his house and made myself at home. I figure it's a student thing.

"He's tired," Studly says, summing up the hangover in an ambitious lie.

"He's this way?" I ask, heading out of the kitchen and back into the hallway.

"Dude, I said he's tired," Studly says, louder this time. "He doesn't want to talk."

I turn around and stare at him, and there's something in the way I look at him that makes him decide he doesn't seem to mind anymore whether I go and wake David or not, as long as I'm not bugging him. He shrugs and goes about riffling through the fridge for something that could be food.

David Harding's bedroom is dark and smells worse than the rest of the house. I turn the light on, but it doesn't really help much. On the floor is a double mattress with no base. It looks like it's had a dozen people jumping up and down on it. David doesn't look up. He has his head buried in a pillow.

I crouch down next to him. "David."

"Go away," he says.

"I need to ask you some questions."

"I don't care."

There are clothes scattered across the floor, pages from work assignments and textbooks piled on the desk and chair. Food wrappers and crumbs cover the carpet. I open the curtains and let in some light. He groans a little. I roll him over, and for the first time he takes a look at me. His hair is sticking straight up around the back and the left-hand side from where the pillow has crushed it. There's gunk in the corners of his eyes. His skin is pale, suggesting he doesn't get out much. There is something that looks familiar about him, and I put it down to the possibility I might have seen his picture in the papers when Rachel disappeared. He looks lost, the kind of lost only somebody in their twenties looks when they're still at university racking up the degrees with no idea of what they really want to do in life.

"Drink this," I say, handing him the cup.

"Go away," he says, not taking it.

"It's hot," I say, "and you don't want to risk me spilling it all over you."

He sits up and takes it. "What the hell do you want?"

"To talk to you about Rachel."

"Let me guess—her mom asked you to come here, right?" he says. "She still thinks I killed her."

"I'm working for Rachel, not for her mother. Did you kill her?"

He looks ready to throw the coffee at me. "Get the hell out of my room."

"I found her body."

He stares at me for a few seconds without moving. Then

he sits up straighter and tightens his grip on the coffee mug. "She's dead?"

It's such a simple question. There is no emotion there, just a look of complete surprise, his mouth slightly open and his eyes slightly wider. No tears, no anger, no frustration. Just acceptance. Acceptance of a question I think he's been asking himself over and over—the big *What if. What if she's still alive? What if she isn't?* And finally the answer.

"She was found yesterday," I tell him.

He shakes his head. I'm sure he doesn't think I'm making this up, but he shakes it anyway, as if he can ward off the bad news. "Are you sure?"

I hand him the ring. He sits the coffee on the floor so he can look at it. He turns it over and reads the inscription. Then he slips it onto the tip of his finger and slowly spins it around, studying it from every degree.

"I gave her this," he says. "It wasn't long before she disappeared. I promised her that when we graduated I'd take her away from here and we'd never come back." He smiles, then gives a short, half-second laugh that sounds more like a grunt. "It feels like a lifetime ago."

"She hated it here? Why?"

"I don't think she really did," he says. "I guess that's the thing about this city, right? You can love and hate it at the same time. I think she just felt claustrophobic here, you know? She wanted to see the rest of the world, and I was going to show it to her. Doesn't every young person want the same thing? Where did you find her?"

"She was buried in a cemetery."

He frowns, then commits to screwing his face up instead, as if he's just bitten into something rotten and something dead. "Huh?"

"She had been put into somebody else's coffin."

His head is slowly shaking. "I don't get what you're saying. She was buried?"

The emotion is coming now. His hands are shaking a little, and his eyes are starting to glisten over, just as I've seen it dozens of other times in those who have lost loved ones.

"We were exhuming a body," I say. "The person we thought we were digging up was missing. Rachel was there instead."

The still shaking head. He's hearing what I'm telling him, but it's a struggle for him to process. Of course it is. He's hearing that the girl he loved was murdered and stuffed into somebody else's coffin. "Who were you digging up?"

"A guy called Henry Martins. Ring a bell?"

And still his head is shaking. "Why would it?"

"He was a bank manager. You sure you've never heard of him?"

Finally his head becomes still. "Does it look like I've ever needed a bank manager? How'd she die? Was she buried alive? Oh, Jesus, don't tell me that."

"I'm not sure," I say, which is not actually telling him anything.

"You're not sure?" he asks. "Did you see her?"

"Yes."

"How'd she look?"

"She was still wearing the ring," I say, which isn't quite true.

"How'd she look?" he repeats.

"She's been dead two years, David. That's how she looked."

He runs both his hands through his hair. "This isn't right," he says. He throws back the blankets and stands up. He's wearing a pair of boxer shorts, and his body is pasty white. He pulls on a pair of jeans. The ring is still on his finger.

"It never is. Tell me what happened," I say.

"What?"

"When you last saw her, tell me what happened."

"Nothing happened. It was just a non-moment. I can't even remember," he says.

"Sure you can. Everybody remembers the last moments."

David's moment turned out to be like any other. He had dinner with her. They ate fast food while they studied. They went to bed together, though he tells me the house was tidier back then. They woke up together; he headed for class and she went to find some breakfast. It was a slice-of-life moment that has probably been playing over and over in his head for the last two years. He'll have been thinking about all the factors that had to come together for this to have happened. He could have skipped class. His class could have been at a different time. Or hers could have been. They could have had breakfast together. They could have had dinner separately the night before. Any link in the chain could have been broken and the result would be that they'd still be together.

The reality is, of course, they could have broken up or he could have got her pregnant and left her for a life of less responsibility, or she could have cheated on him. Young love can lead anywhere. But it never should have led to this. He says he didn't even know she was missing, that he figured she'd gone home that night and hadn't called.

"Was she having any problems?" I ask.

"No. None that she told me about."

"Anybody giving her a hard time? Hanging around? Anything at all out of the ordinary?"

"You don't think I've been asked these questions? Man, I've been over this with so many other people, and I've been over it with myself every single day. I loved her. I still do."

I nod. "Okay. Where'd she go for breakfast?"

"She ate at a university café. You guys already know that."

I don't feel the need to correct his impression that I must be a cop. "Humor me."

He starts pacing the room. "She was spotted in there. She left around ten thirty. She ate bacon and eggs smothered in tomato sauce. I never figured out how she could eat that combination. Then she left. And that's all anybody knows."

"Was she supposed to meet anybody?"

He shakes his head. "She was going to class."

"Was she seeing anybody?"

He stops pacing the room. He stares at me. It's similar to the look I gave the cop in the cemetery last night. "What, like having an affair?"

"Was she?" I ask.

"Rachel would never have done that."

"Would you?"

"Hell no. I loved her!"

"So you can't think of anywhere else she might've gone."

"I don't know, man. If I did, I'd tell you. I'd have told you two years ago."

"Okay, okay. Who else can I ask?"

"What?"

"She has to have had a best friend, right? Who would she talk to when she was complaining about you?"

"She didn't complain."

"Then you must've been the perfect boyfriend."

"Alicia North. They'd go shopping all the time and they'd complain about men. Rachel said she did it more for Alicia than for herself. But Alicia didn't see her that day. I think Rachel did it because she loved shopping. It was kind of annoying. She used to make all these damn impulse buys."

"Where does Alicia live?"

He starts pacing the room again. "I don't know," he says. "I haven't spoken to her since."

"Ever heard of a woman called Julie Thomas?"

"Julie Thomas? I don't know. Is she a student here?"

"No."

"I don't think I've heard of her."

"You sure?"

"Yeah," he says. "Why?"

"She went missing around the same time as Rachel. What about Jessica Shanks?"

"She go missing too?" he asks.

"You heard of her?"

He shakes his head.

"What about Bruce Alderman?" I ask.

"Alderman? Umm . . . no, I don't think so. Should I have?"

"I don't know."

"Did he kill Rachel?"

"I'm not sure."

"Can't you interrogate him or something?"

"He's dead. He shot himself last night. But he said he didn't do it."

He stops pacing. "What? He shot himself? I . . . umm . . . Do you believe him? That he didn't do it?"

"Enough to keep looking into it," I tell him.

"Her mom thinks it was me."

"I know."

"I didn't do it."

I look into his eyes. There is sorrow there—I recognize it and I feel it—and though he doesn't know it, that sorrow is a bond between us. He isn't acting. His pain is real. Real enough that if I put him in the room with the man who killed Rachel, he would become a completely new man. He would cross a line that he could not turn back from, and it wouldn't bother him. He'd cross it again and again if he could.

"I know."

"And that Harry dude," he says, "what happened to him?"

"Henry Martins. We're not sure exactly. Look, David, don't try to get back to sleep. The cops are going to be here soon. Just tell them what you know."

He looks confused. "You're not a cop?"

I hand him my card and take the ring back off him. "I used to be, but that was a long time ago."

CHAPTER SIXTEEN

There are no police cars parked outside the Tyler house. They've either been and gone or are on their way. There is, though, a car parked up the driveway that wasn't there last night. Probably the husband. He'd have got the call seconds after I left last night and rushed home. He didn't put the car away. Didn't get up this morning to go and move it. He's waiting inside with his wife, waiting for the news. Waiting to hear about his dead daughter.

I check my phone. It has one bar of battery life, three bars of signal, but it still hasn't been connected to the network.

The door is opened before I get to it. Patricia Tyler's wearing the same clothes she had on yesterday. She probably slept in them. Or hasn't slept at all.

"Something's happening, isn't it," she says.

"Yes," I tell her. There's no way around it.

"We're finding out today, aren't we?"

"Yes."

"Did you know yesterday? When you came to my house, when I let you inside. Did you know my daughter was dead?"

"I suspected."

"Yet you said nothing."

"I'm sorry."

"You're sorry," she says, and her voice is calm and even, tired-sounding. "They called fifteen minutes ago. They didn't say anything, but I could tell. They're on their way to speak to us."

There is nothing I can say to make her feel any better, so I say nothing. I wait her out, knowing she hasn't finished, but also knowing I can't wait too long—the police are going to be here soon.

"You're sorry," she says, "yet you came in anyway. You made me believe there was a chance my daughter was still alive."

I didn't make her believe anything. I could have shown up with her daughter's hand in a plastic bag along with the ring and she'd still have held out hope. I think she's still holding out for it now. "Can I come in?"

"I don't think so."

"A man killed himself in my office," I say. "It was last night. He put a gun to his head and told me he had nothing to do with what happened to Rachel, and then he pulled the trigger."

She doesn't look shocked. Doesn't look satisfied. She just looks tired, as if anything and everything is too much for her now. "I saw you on the news," she says. "It didn't make you look good. Do you think he killed Rachel? Did you kill him for what he did to her?"

"I didn't kill him," I tell her. "And I don't know if he's the one who hurt Rachel. You can never have justice for what happened, but finding who did this is as close to it as you can get. But if he was telling the truth, then there is still somebody out there who has to pay. That's why I'm here. For Rachel's sake."

"For Rachel's sake," she repeats, and there is no inflection in her voice, and I can't get a read on her reason for repeating it. "That reporter," she goes on. "She said your daughter was killed. So you know. And maybe that pain we share will take you further than the police. Maybe it will make you fight harder for Rachel."

"It will," I tell her.

"You promise?"

"Yes."

She leads me through to the lounge. Her husband, an overweight guy with gray hair and dark shadows beneath his eyes, stands up from the couch, seems about to shake my hand, then pulls it back as if the contact will taint the news he's about to get.

"Were you the one who found her?" he asks.

"Yes."

"How . . ." He looks down, studies the carpet for a few moments as if it's going to save him from something, then carries on without looking back up. "How'd she look?"

It's the same question the boyfriend asked. They want to hear that she looked at peace, that she still looked good for a girl who was murdered two years ago. Only she didn't look good. She looked like she died hard.

"Like she was asleep," I say, hoping they'll believe the lie, hoping that when they plead with the detectives to see her body they won't be allowed to.

"It's hard to believe she's really dead," he says, looking back up. His face is rigid, void of hope. Except for his eyes. His eyes are haunting. I have to look away. "It ought to be easier," he adds. "You'd think two years would have prepared us for this."

He probably knows exactly how many days it's been. I think of my wife and daughter, and I think about what the last two years have prepared me for. Fate came along and destroyed the Tyler family, and a week later it destroyed mine.

"People keep saying that time heals all wounds," he says. "They say we should get on with our lives. Like we're just supposed to forget all about Rachel. Like we're supposed to give up on wondering. Give up on our hope. They don't get it. They think it's like losing a puppy or misplacing car keys. They talk without experience; they offer advice, thinking they know what we need to hear, sure that the best thing for us is simply to move on."

"But you know all of that, don't you," Patricia Tyler says.

"Why are you here?" her husband asks.

"For Rachel."

"Shame you weren't there for her two years ago," he says.

"Michael . . ." his wife says.

"I'm sorry," he says. "It's just that, well . . ." He doesn't finish. He sits back down on the couch and starts to look around the room as though he's misplaced something.

"I've spoken to David," I tell them.

"You spoke to *David*?" Patricia says.

"He said that Rachel liked to shop."

Patricia looks to her husband. They stare at each other, the kind of look a couple shares when trying to decide whether to let the rest of the world in on the big secret. It's an innocent statement, which I'm sure will have an innocent answer, but they're both looking for a different question and answer here—they're wanting the answers to what happened to their daughter. They're trying to figure out how her shopping got her killed.

"Sure, she shopped," she says.

"Did Rachel use a credit card?"

"The Goddamn bank sent us a bill," Michael Tyler says. "They told us if we didn't pay it they were going to get the debt collectors onto us. We explained Rachel had gone missing. Hell, it was in the news, so they already knew. Only they didn't care. Their argument was nobody had any proof of what happened to Rachel and they shouldn't end up footing the bill."

"It was awful." Patricia Tyler's tears start to come now. For a few moments she does nothing to try to stop them, just lets them roll down her face as if she hasn't noticed them. Then she raises a handkerchief and tries to dab them away, but they keep on coming. "Can you imagine that? Our daughter is missing, possibly dead—or, as it turns out, she was. Or is."

"Both, actually," her husband interjects, and he looks close to tears too, and he shrugs a little, as if unsure why he made the comment. I know the moment I leave they will fall into an embrace neither of them will ever want to break.

"And those heartless thugs at the bank register us with a debt collection agency," Patricia says, "and we had to pay it. Can you believe that?"

"Do you have that last credit card statement?"

"We have everything," she says.

"Can I see it?"

"Why?" she asks.

"It might tell me where Rachel was that day, or in the days before."

"The police already have a copy of it," she says. "It didn't lead them anywhere."

"But it might lead me somewhere."

She doesn't argue the point. She just walks out of the room, leaving me and her husband alone in uncomfortable silence until she returns with the bill, which takes her two minutes. I keep waiting to hear the sound of a car pulling into the driveway. If Landry catches me here, he's going to be truly pissed off. She hands me the bank statement. I scroll down. Clothes, CDs, more clothes. Gas.

"These are all standard places she went?" I ask.

"They're on all of her bills," Patricia says.

"Where was her car found?"

"At the university," Michael says. "It was where she always parked it."

"And the florist?" I ask, stopping my finger next to the purchase she made a week before she disappeared.

"She bought flowers for her grandmother," Patricia says.

"Anything else here stand out?" I ask.

"Nothing," she says.

"Okay. Can I take this with me?"

"Don't lose it," she says.

She walks me to the door. Michael Tyler stands up, seems about to join us, but sits back down. The hallway is warm and there seem to be more pictures of Rachel hanging up than there were when I was here last night, as if the Tylers thought they could use them to keep the bad news at bay.

"The man last night. The reporter said his name was Bruce Alderman. You haven't said it, but you think he's innocent, don't you? That's why you're here."

I think of the look in Bruce's eyes before he pulled the trigger. I think of the key in his pocket with my name on the envelope. "I don't think he did it," I admit.

"Will you find who did?"

"I'll try. I promise."

I'm halfway down the walkway when it strikes me. I turn

back around and Patricia is still standing there watching me, watching the person who two years after her daughter went missing came along and told them all was lost. "The flowers for her grandmother. Was there an occasion?"

"My mother died a week before Rachel disappeared. It was one of the reasons the police thought she'd run away. Rachel and my mom were close. For the first few years my mother helped raise Rachel. The police assumed she was depressed and needed to get away. She bought flowers to take out to the cemetery for the funeral."

"Which cemetery?"

"Woodland Estates."

Woodland Estates. The cemetery with the lake. The cemetery with my daughter.

The cemetery where Rachel Tyler was found.

CHAPTER SEVENTEEN

It's a connection that was there two years ago, but nobody was looking for it. Nobody even knew to look for it. Why would they? No way could they have known Rachel Tyler was going to be found one day buried in a cemetery. No way could they have known that going to her grandmother's funeral would send her into the scope of her killer. Is that what happened?

My cell phone rings, which is good news for me, since it means it's up and running. I look at the display, but don't recognize the number.

"Hello?"

"What are you doing fucking with my investigation?"

"Who is this?" I ask, even though I already know.

"Who the hell do you think? You visited the Tylers."

"Look, Landry, I was . . ." But I don't know how to finish.

"Jesus, Tate, what the hell are you playing at here? You're going to seriously mess things up for us."

"I know what I'm doing," I tell him.

"If you knew what you were doing you'd still be carrying a badge. You're going to mess things up, and if it wasn't Bruce Alderman who killed those girls, that means we've still got a serious investigation on our hands. Which means there's going to be a trial once we catch the guy, and suddenly we're going to have to explain your actions at the trial. How's that going to make you look? Or us? You think any defense lawyer worth more than ten cents isn't going to be able to shred our case apart because you've fucked up all our evidence? Sidney Alderman is sure you killed his son. Come on, Tate, you gotta be more careful. You can't let this bullshit happen."

"I didn't kill him."

"I know that. We all know it," he says. "But not Alderman. He's sure you pulled the trigger. You might want to watch your back."

"It was an empty threat," I say, not believing it.

"Maybe. I'd still watch it anyway. He's building up some Dutch courage."

"What do you mean?"

"He went straight from the morgue to a bar," he says. "He's drinking himself into a state, and I don't know whether it's a better or a worse one."

"Let me guess. You gave him a lift?"

"That's a shitty question, Tate. I'm trying to help you out here."

"Okay. Okay, I get the point."

"I don't think you do," he says, "because somehow you got her ring."

"What?"

"Rachel Tyler. You got her ring. You showed it to her parents."

"Bruce gave it to me."

"Bullshit. You had it yesterday afternoon. How'd you get it? You steal it out of the coffin? Where are you right now?"

I was outside the cemetery about thirty seconds ago, but now that I know Sidney Alderman isn't home, I'll give his house a visit instead. "I'm at home."

"No you're not. I'm at your house and you're not here."

"Good one, Landry. I'm standing in my driveway and you're nowhere around."

I'm pretty sure we both know the other one is bluffing.

"Stay out of my case, Tate. Your name comes up one more time, and I'm going to take some action. Got that? You could do time here, man. You're compromising things. You stole evidence, which, by the way, I want back."

"Okay, I'll . . ."

But he's already hung up. I step out of my car and look up and down the street, suddenly worried that Landry might be watching me after all. There's no sign of anybody. He was right about one thing, though. My name is about to come back up in about twenty minutes when he goes and talks to David. Things, like he said, are fucked up.

I knock on the door and nobody answers. So I move from window to window, peering inside, but since even sunlight can't seem to penetrate the grime there isn't much chance I can see anything. A guy like Sidney Alderman would come out and tell me to go to hell if he knew I was looking through his windows. That means he definitely isn't here. I try the back door. It's locked. So is the front. I get out the key Bruce left for me and try both doors, but it doesn't fit. It's not even close to fitting.

There are still plenty of ways to get inside, and I opt for the less subtle approach of kicking in the back door. It opens easily enough, bouncing back off the wall and almost closing again, stopped only by the busted-up jamb. The cops will know who did it. But if I'm right about things, it won't matter. They'll be glad I did it.

The first thing I can smell is alcohol. I move up the hallway. The carpet is worn and the floorboards beneath it groan. There are three bedrooms, one messy, one tidy, and one completely empty—not a single piece of furniture or poster on the wall. Of the two in use, the tidy one is tidy only in comparison to the messy one, and the way things are all slightly out of whack in there suggests the police have been rummaging around looking for something and one of the Aldermans has rummaged around putting things back. I figure whatever evidence Bruce had hidden under his bed is now sitting on a desk somewhere in the police station.

The kitchen is swamped with dirty dishes and empty beer cans. In the lounge there are bottles and cans on every available horizontal plane. Sidney Alderman had a hard night. The arms of the lounge suite have been ripped up at the front, suggesting the presence of a cat, but there is no food bowl around, so maybe it got sick of the living arrangements and moved out. I'm surprised, though, to see photo albums scattered across a coffee table—Alderman didn't seem the type to get hung up on family moments. I pull on a pair of latex gloves before opening the cover on the top one. Color photographs of happier times are arranged neatly in the pages. A man, a woman, a child. The Alderman nuclear family. They all look happy. Smiles, relaxed, candid moments, posed photos for birthdays and Christmas. Sidney Alderman is a different man here, the type of man who back then was mostly likeable.

I keep going. I already have a feeling about what is coming up. The man and woman and child start to get older. They grow. They still look happy. I recognize the house in the background of some of these shots. Summer photos. Winter photos. Snapshots from school plays and school sports. I move from one album to another. The house is neat and tidy and looks welcoming. It looks well maintained. Fresh paint, clean windows, no broken roof tiles.

Fashions change. The eighties become the nineties. Some of the furniture is updated. The carpet in one photo is that awful orange and brown Axminster stuff from the late sixties and becomes that awful, flecked, pale green stuff from the early eighties. The TV is updated. A cat appears in some of the pictures, a black thing with a swath of white fur around its neck.

The parents get older, and the kid gets taller and starts taking on the features of the man I met and saw die yesterday. Sidney Alderman looks like a happy man. Looks happy in the holiday photographs. Beaches and boats and fishing lines. Ugly shirts and bad haircuts and boxy-looking cars with poor fuel consumption. The house stays the same. The smiles stay the same. On to the next photo album. More holiday snaps.

Then Alderman's wife is no longer around. The smiles are forced and thin, and the gaps in time between photos start to extend. No more holidays. No more happy moments. Just forced moments. Like birthdays and Christmases that nobody wants to be at. The wife doesn't come back, and the decaying state of the house in the photographs suggests she isn't going to. The years pass with only a few moments caught on film, but nothing heartwarming—the participants are going through the motions, they're drawing on the memories of how these events ought to be, drawing on them so they can remember how to smile. At the back of the photo album is a collection of newspaper clippings.

My cell phone rings and breaks my focus. It's another number I don't recognize. I answer it, but nobody speaks back. I don't say anything either. There's a slight hissing sound that every cell phone in the country must get, the kind of hissing that can never fool you into thinking you're talking on a landline.

Then, after ten or twenty seconds, a voice comes on the line. "You took away my son." The words are slow and solid, as if each is its own sentence, as if he's struggling to say them and has to concentrate really hard. "You took away my son," he repeats when I don't answer him.

I look down at the albums and the empty booze bottles. Alderman found out last night that his son was dead. There's no way in the world the police decided not to inform him immediately. No way they figured it was the sort of thing they could put off until they swung by this morning to take him to the morgue. It's got to be why these photo albums are out. I remember doing the same thing, and even now I sometimes still do it. I wonder if over the last few hours he's come to the conclusion that I'm to blame for everything—for his wife leaving him, for his house wearing down, for his son killing himself, and for his son burying others.

"I wanted to help him. I didn't want him dead. But I didn't kill him. He killed himself. That was his choice and I had nothing to do with it."

"You killed him."

"I didn't kill him."

"You killed him because you're a killer," he says. "It's in your nature. You said last night you were going to find him. You said if I helped you, you'd go easier on him, but I didn't help you so you went hard. You went as hard on him as you could."

"He killed himself out of guilt," I say. "You knew what he was doing."

"He wasn't doing anything."

"How many are out there?" I ask.

He returns to saying what he says best. "You killed him."

"How many others? Is it just the four?"

"The police are lying to protect you, just like they protected you two years ago, just like the reporter said."

"You don't even know what you're talking about," I tell him.

"I saw him this morning. He was laid out on a piece of steel. He was broken. He wasn't my boy anymore. It wasn't Bruce. It was some *thing* with its head all busted up. You jammed that gun into him and pulled the trigger."

"You know I didn't do that."

"Don't tell me what I know," he yells. "You don't have the right to tell me what I know! He was my boy! My boy! And you killed him."

"He killed himself."

"I've always thought about what you did," he says, "and I always wished I had the courage to do the same thing."

"What?"

"When Lucy died. It was the same thing, you know. But I did nothing. I let it eat me up all these years and I did nothing. But not this time."

I unfold the newspaper clippings. They're not big articles, because it wasn't a big enough story to hit the front page. Just like with my family. They're small stories jammed in the back pages with the opinions and reviews and the who-gives-a-damn sections of the paper. Alderman's wife, Lucy, was killed by a learner driver who was still mixing up the difference between yielding and not yielding. There's a quote: "She just came out of nowhere." It's similar to my own story, but not that similar. Though maybe enough that there could have been a bond between Alderman and me. His wife went shopping for groceries and lost her life because of an accident. It was a run-of-the-mill routine: you climb into your car and an hour later you're cut out of it. No malice. No intent. Just bad luck combining for everybody involved. A left turn instead of a right, ten seconds earlier or ten seconds later: any of those, and she'd still be alive. Similar in some ways to my own story. Different in others. My wife and daughter weren't driving. They were walking. It wasn't a learner driver who hit them, but an experienced one. He was experienced in a lot of areas. Mostly proficient in drinking more than he was in driving. He had a criminal record a mile long. He was a repeat offender. He would be pulled over and fined. His car and his license would be taken off him and he would get them back. It became a routine. He just kept on going back out on the roads, and the world just kept on letting him. When the fines increased, it didn't matter. He just kept on paying them, racking up his mortgage account with drunk-driving conviction payouts. There wasn't anything the criminal system was prepared to do about it except take a collective breath each time to see if this would be the one when he killed somebody. Nobody cared. As long as he paid his fines, he was a source of income. He was revenue. He was good for the country.

The connection between Alderman's wife and my own is a strong one in some ways, but not in others. We both lost our own lives the day we lost parts of our family. He spiraled into an abyss that he is still in now. I have an abyss of my own. I figure if Alderman had done something all those years ago, maybe he would be a different man. But like he said, he did nothing. I figure if I'd done nothing, I'd be a different man too.

Better men? We could be. Or we could be worse.

"You took the law into your own hands," he says. "You

did it after the accident, and you did it again last night. You killed my son. You killed him for doing nothing. Ten years ago, when Lucy died, I did nothing. Not this time. This time *you* are going to pay. Your wife is going to pay. And this time your friends in the department can't do a damn thing to help you."

The temperature in this impossibly cold house drops even further. It's like somebody has just strapped a block of ice onto my back. I can feel the weight of it pushing me down. I tighten my grip on the phone. The air is thick and damp and tastes like sour sweat, and all the words in the newspaper article seem to swirl around as if the ink is wet and running.

"You better be kidding right now, you son of a bitch."

"You think the police are kidding and my son isn't really dead? What do you think, Tate?"

"My wife has nothing to do with this."

"How can you be so stupid as to think bad things don't happen all the time to innocent people? You know that first hand. You experienced it last night when you killed my boy. You experienced it two years ago. And you're experiencing it right now."

The phone goes dead. I look at the display. The battery hasn't gone flat. Alderman has hung up.

I dial him back. He doesn't answer.

I hit the driveway running. I reach the car and the tires shriek a little and leave some rubber behind. I speed past the cemetery where a patrol car is just entering the gates. The driver looks back over his shoulder, but he doesn't turn around and try to pull me over. The cemetery and the patrol car quickly get smaller in my mirror. I call the nursing home where my wife lives—if *live* is an appropriate word. She *resides*, maybe, not *lives*. A nurse I've spoken to only a few times answers the phone. I ask for Nurse Hamilton. A moment later she comes on the line.

"Theo? What can I help you with?"

"It's Bridget."

"What about her?"

"I think she's in danger," I say, and I hold the phone between my ear and neck so I can change gear. "I need you to go and check on her."

"Danger? What kind of danger?"

"Can you just check to make sure she's okay? Then stay with her until I get there."

"But . . ."

"Please, I'm on my way. Just go and check on her."

"Fine, but I can tell you now there aren't any problems. We provide excellent care, as you know, and—"

"I'll stay on the line," I say, hoping it will hurry her up. It does.

I continue to speed. I wish I had my car from two years ago with the siren installed. I wish I could flash and sound it at the surrounding traffic to get them the hell out of the way.

I hit three green lights in a row; I run through two oranges. And I slow down for a red before accelerating between cars to a chorus of blasting horns.

Nurse Hamilton comes back. I hear her pick up the phone, but she doesn't say anything. It's as though she's on the other end of the line composing her thoughts. Trying to figure what she needs to say. Figuring it because there's a problem.

"Carol?"

"Bridget is in her room," she says.

"Are you sure?"

"Of course I'm sure," she says.

"Is somebody with her right now?"

"We have very adequate staff here, Mr. Tate," she says, speaking formally, as if giving testimony to a jury.

"That's not why I'm calling. Look, it's hard to explain, but I'm almost there. Please just do me the favor of staying with her until I arrive."

"Very well, Theo. We'll—"

I don't hear the end because the phone cuts out. I look at the display and watch it going through the motions of powering down. I try to revive it so I can call Landry or Schroder, but the battery is completely drained.

I get to the nursing home ten minutes later. The day has cleared up even more, bits of blue sky threatening to grow as the afternoon moves on. I look around at the other cars, trying to figure if one of them is out of place, but I don't even know what Alderman would be driving.

Inside, I rush past the nurses' station. The woman at the desk recognizes me as the guy who rang not long ago and gives me the sort of look that suggests I've ruined her afternoon.

Bridget is sitting in front of the window the same as any other day. Being here in the early afternoon is no different than being here in the early evening. She's not watching TV. Not getting up and taking a shower or doing a crossword puzzle. Her world is twenty-four seven and there are no breaks. I rush to her and hug her and she doesn't hug back, but that's okay.

"This is all very out of the ordinary," Carol Hamilton says.

I pull back and hold Bridget's hand. "Has anybody come here to visit her?"

"Nobody who hasn't visited before."

"What about somebody else? Anybody unknown show up to visit, anybody at all?"

"What is your point, Theo?"

My point is simple for me, though perhaps not for her. Still, I decide to give it a go.

I explain the conversation I had with Alderman, touching only on a few of the points, and even then only briefly. She takes it all in stride, as I figure only a cop or a nursing-home professional could—both have seen way too much to be surprised anymore. In the end she points out that nothing bad has happened, therefore the man who threatened Bridget must have been lying, must have been making a desperate attempt to upset me because of his son. The care home is a top-rate facility, she reminds me, and they let nothing happen to their charges. She does make a concession about being more vigilant, and tells me to call the police. I tell her that I will.

She leaves me alone with Bridget. I don't want to leave her here. Not anymore. I want to be able to take her with me, but where to? Back to my house? How would I even begin to look after her? No. She's safer here.

Carol comes back. "There's a phone call for you. You can take it in the office."

I follow her back downstairs.

"Hello?"

"How did it feel, huh?" Alderman asks. "To think she was dead? To think I had done something to her? That's how I feel, you bastard. You killed my son, so for me the feeling is always there. It's going to stay the same. I wanted you to know how it was going to feel. I wanted you to imagine the loss. And not the same loss you suffered two years ago. But the kind of loss that's deliberate, the kind of loss you can only experience when one human being goes out of his way to kill someone you love. Hurts, doesn't it? But I just did you a big favor and left your wife out of it. It wasn't her fault. I still want to make you suffer though. I want your pain permanent. And you still have another family member who won't care what I do to her."

"What are you talking about?"

"You took my son," he says. "You still owe me."

He hangs up.

I hand the phone back to the nurse, extending my arm without really seeing her. The desk, the paintings, the window into the office behind her—they all seem to lose detail and disappear.

"Theo?"

I know Carol is speaking to me, but I don't look at her. The phone has gone from my hand, but I'm still holding out my arm ramrod straight.

"Theo?"

She touches my shoulder and the contact seems to work. I look at her and she starts to say something, but I don't wait to hear what it is. I cover the foyer with large strides and the heavy door weighs nothing as I pull it open.

I make the drive back to the cemetery in about the same amount of time I made it from the cemetery to the nursing home. People toot at me and give me the finger. I race through intersections and run red lights when there are gaps in traffic. When I reach the cemetery I have this hollow feeling in my stomach, similar to the one that was there the day my daughter died. It's a feeling that grows worse when I bring the car to a stop. I run toward Emily's grave, though the pile of dirt next to it already tells me what I'm going to find. All these cops out here and nobody stopped Alderman from desecrating her grave. But why would they? They were never there to protect her from dying. Just as I wasn't there. And in this case it simply would have looked from a distance as if Alderman was doing his job. Just digging a hole. Just moving on with life after losing his son—if they even saw him at all. And looking toward the lake, I can already tell they couldn't. There was no way.

I stand at the edge of the grave. I know now there were two reasons Alderman threatened my wife. The first was to scare me. The second was to send me away from the cemetery. That means he was watching me all along. He was waiting.

My little girl's coffin is down there. The lid is open and Emily is gone.

CHAPTER EIGHTEEN

All the oxygen is sucked out of me. I stare down at the coffin with the silk linings and soft pillow, and the world outside of the grave fades away and goes black. There are crumbs of dirt where my daughter should have been. The brass handles have pitted, the glossy sheen of the wood long since gone. There are cracks and dents in the wood. My first reaction is to climb down and make sure with my hands as well as my eyes that Emily isn't in there. My second reaction is to scream. Instead I fall back to the third reaction, the one I had two years ago when I got the call about the accident. I drop to my knees and start to weep and try to convince myself this isn't really happening.

It should be simple to know which is worse—my wife missing or my daughter—but suddenly I don't know. Suddenly they both seem as bad as each other. I guess the worse of the two is the one that is happening. I've dealt with a lot over the years, but never somebody's dead child being stolen from a graveyard. Kidnapped. I don't even know if that's the term for it.

I have no real idea what to do. No real direction to take. A dead child is every parent's worst nightmare. What is it when all the nightmares come true?

I have lost Emily. Again.

Two years ago it had been on a Tuesday. Tuesdays are a nothing day. People don't make great plans for a Tuesday. They don't get married. Don't leave for holiday. They don't organize housewarmings. But the fact is one in seven people dies on a Tuesday. One in seven is born. What better day to lose your family? Is there a worse day? That Tuesday should have been like the others. I kissed my daughter and my wife on the way out the door, and the next time I saw them Emily was lying on a metal slab with a sheet tucked up to her neck so I could see her face. Bridget was in a world between life and death, hooked up to machinery and surrounded by doctors.

Hours earlier they had gone out to see a movie. It was two o'clock in the afternoon, and Disney was entertaining my seven-year-old daughter on the big screen with animals that could talk and evade capture and do taxes and everything else clever animals can do. It was school vacation. My wife was a teacher, so it was vacation for her too. At quarter to four the movie ended and my wife walked my daughter outside along with dozens of other parents and children. They walked around the shopping complex sidewalk toward her car. It was ten to four, and already Quentin James was drunk. It was ten to four in the middle of the afternoon, and Quentin James was behind the wheel of his dark blue SUV, which he had paid a four-hundred-dollar fine to get back that morning. He had no driver's license, but that didn't stop him from paying the fine; it didn't stop the courts from handing over the keys. I can only imagine how it happened—bits of imagery I added together with details from eyewitnesses. The SUV swerving through the parking lot. The SUV jumping the curb onto the sidewalk. My wife and daughter hearing it, both of them turning toward the sound. Emily's tiny hand tight inside my wife's grip. The look on Bridget's face as she realized there was nothing they could do, that the SUV was going to knock them around like rag dolls.

She pushed Emily out of the way. That's what they tell me. She did what any mother would do and tried to save her daughter. Only it wasn't enough. The four-wheel drive slammed into them both; it knocked my wife onto the hood, it rolled my daughter beneath the wheels, and it broke them. It broke my little girl up inside beyond repair. It did the same to my wife. It did the same to me. And to my parents.

And still Quentin kept driving. He would tell me two weeks later, when I took him away to a small corner of the world, that he couldn't even remember running into them. He told me that it wasn't him, not really, but the man he became when the booze took over. Therefore I had the wrong man. He was sick, he said, and it was the sick Quentin who ran over and killed my daughter. The Quentin pleading for his life in front of me wasn't the man who had killed my girl, at least according to the sober Quentin, but that didn't matter to me. It was the bullshit plea of a weak and cowardly drunk during one of his few sober moments. He said he couldn't remember running them over, but that didn't matter either. I could. And so could witnesses. They told me the impact sounded dull, like heavy suitcases being dropped on the pavement from a second-story window. They told me my wife rolled across the hood of the SUV and was thrown hard onto the concrete.

They told me my little girl tumbled and bounced beneath the chassis until she was spat out the end, ejected from between the wheels all twisted and bloody. They tell me my wife and daughter ended up in the same place, side by side on the street. Quentin kept on driving.

Quentin James was caught within an hour. His four-wheel drive with the grille on the front that was never once used off road in the four years he owned it was impounded. It was kept as evidence. He was charged with manslaughter and reckless driving, but he should have been charged with murder. I never figured that one out. The guy chose to drive drunk. He chose to do it every single damn day of his adult life. That means it didn't come down to fate or bad luck, but down to a conscious choice. That and statistics. It came down to mathematics. It means it had to happen. Put a drunk guy out on the roads every day and he's bound to kill somebody. Has to happen, the same way if you keep flipping a coin it has to come up tails at some point.

So for me, manslaughter didn't cut it. Didn't come close. He got released on bail and he tried to get his car back, but for the first time ever they wouldn't let him have it. They couldn't—because people were outraged by the accident. They were angry at the system that allowed him to keep going free. So this time the courts weren't giving his car back, not at least until the trial was over. It was as though the judge finally figured out that giving this guy his car back was like handing Jack the Ripper a scalpel, that in this case it couldn't all be about revenue gathering. This time James would do time. That was for sure. They'd lock him away for two years in a cell that was a hell of a lot bigger than the coffin my daughter got locked in.

But everything worked out different. Quentin James never

went to jail. My daughter is no longer in her resting place. The world has gone topsy-turvy and I don't know what to do. I'm kneeling in the grass next to a mound of dirt and an empty coffin. Sidney Alderman has come along and dug up her grave in the same way his son dug up others. He has dug up and torn the stitches from the memories, and the pain of losing my daughter is as strong as it was the day Quentin James stole her from me. James is no longer around to direct my anger toward, but Alderman is, and I'm going to find the son of a bitch.

I stand up. I turn my back on the grave of my little girl. The sky has cleared even more and it looks like it could actually turn into a pretty good day. As good as it can get, weather wise. As bad as it can get in every other way. I start my car and drive to Alderman's house. I'm tempted to drive right into it, just hit the sucker at a hundred kilometers an hour and shred the siding and plasterboard to pieces. Instead I bring the car to a fast stop up his driveway, skidding the shingle out in all directions and creating a thin cloud of dirt that drifts past the front of the car and toward the house. I get out and slam the door, wishing I had access to the gun the caretaker's son used on himself. All I have access to is my anger—it should be enough. I think in the end anger will beat out sorrow on any given day. Even on a Tuesday.

CHAPTER NINETEEN

The house still smells of alcohol and the air is damp. The furniture bugs me in a way that furniture shouldn't be able to do. I want to set fire to the place. Pour gasoline all over the walls and floors and the clawed-up lounge suite and turn the whole fucking lot to ash. Preferably with Sidney Alderman in here. Preferably with him gagged and tied and very aware of what is going on.

Only he isn't here. He's off somewhere with my daughter doing God knows what. Burying her somewhere, I guess. Or dumping her in another lake or a river or an ocean.

The photo albums have all disappeared. It tells me Alderman knew I was here and was figuring I'd come back. I start looking through the house again. I go through his drawers and his cupboards, but I don't find anything useful, because anything useful the police will already have found. I pull everything apart. I dump files and trash and books on the floor as I go, but there's nothing. I push everything aside roughly, making a mess, enjoying the process of damage. It's not enough to take away any of the pain, but for the short term it will have to do.

I head back out to my car and grab the charger for my cell phone. I plug it into a socket next to Alderman's toaster and watch as my phone starts to power up. I leave it charging while I check the bedrooms. Bruce Alderman said the proof was under his bed, but he may as well have said that a year ago. The two bedrooms in use have completely distinct personalities. It's obvious to see which one belongs to the old man and which to the son. The father's bedroom has wedding pictures up on the wall. It has underwear scattered across the floor. It has a busted-up clock radio lying on a pile of old newspapers. There are booze bottles stacked along the windowsills. The curtains are grimy and old. The bed hasn't been made; the pillow case is blackened in the middle from sweat and dirt and whatever product the old man once ran through his hair. The loss of his wife was so hard on the guy that he never recovered. He lost control of his own life, and ten years later he's still losing control.

I walk into Bruce's room. It's like walking into a cheap motel room that prides itself on doing the best with what it has. The bed has been made. Books are stacked almost neatly on the bedside table. Three pairs of shoes are lined up beneath the window. Sneakers, dress shoes, work shoes. I look under the bed. Whatever evidence was there has gone. I check the closet and go through the pockets of whatever is hanging there. Then the drawers. I'm not tidier than the police. I pull the drawers all the way out and check beneath them for any taped-up envelopes or photographs he has hidden there. But there's nothing. I pick up and riffle through the books. Nothing falls out of them. I check the titles on the spines. He read a mixture of fantasy and sci-fi, but there doesn't appear to be any serial killer novels or FBI handbooks about how to avoid getting caught. There are shoeboxes stacked in his wardrobe that are full of mostly junk—a Rubik's cube, small plastic Smurfs, old coins, even some old shoes.

I check under the bed again, just in case, but there's nothing there at all. Just dust. Which doesn't make sense. People always squirrel crap away under their beds. Bruce Alderman has nothing, except the thick dust, and there are no clean patches where items have been removed. I drag the bed out from the wall.

The corner of the carpet is easy to pull up, because it's been pulled up before. Plenty of times, I'm guessing, which is why he never stored anything under the bed, because then he would have had to drag stuff out and stack it up and then unstack it and push everything back, all of that to gain access to his secret hiding place. There are four A4-sized envelopes side by side under the carpet, each one very thin. I pull the carpet all the way back, but there is nothing else.

I spill the contents of the first envelope onto the bed. I open the other three. They're all the same. Different articles cut from different newspapers, nearly twenty of them covering the different women. A separate envelope for each of the four girls. The dates begin two years ago and end two days ago. There are articles for the three girls I've identified, and for the fourth one I haven't. Her name is Jennifer Bowen. I now know all four names.

Four women missing from Christchurch, but the world kept on spinning. Nobody took a moment to figure out what in the hell was going on. Four women from four different backgrounds, all of them young—born within five years of each other—and no one made the connection. They didn't make it because they didn't want to. The articles are full of suggestions. The girls were wayward. They were runaways. The articles about Rachel Tyler suggest she fought with her boyfriend. They hint that the boyfriend could have been responsible. They mention the dead grandmother and lead a path for the reader to believe she could have run away because she was upset. They suggest lots of things and confirm nothing, just throwing out ideas in the hope that if they cast a wide enough net they might cover something correctly.

I slide all the articles from all of the envelopes into the one. They don't do much to back Bruce Alderman's claim that he didn't kill these women. All four of them could have died in here. And Emily? Did Bruce's father bring Emily back here before driving her away? Did he carry her corpse and rest her on the couch while he packed some things together? No. He would have dumped her in the trunk of his car. He wouldn't have been careful about it.

I take my phone and step outside. The lake, the church, the land of the dead—none of it can be seen from anywhere on this property, not unless I was to take the ladder out of the shed and climb up on the roof or scale the fence. I do the latter.

The property backs onto the cemetery. The police, the excavations, the canvas tents, and crime scene techies—these things don't reach Alderman's house. I can't imagine what it would have been like to grow up in a house where the view over your back fence was of trees and granite headstones. Surely it had to be disturbing. Surely it couldn't have been healthy. I wonder if this environment is what made Bruce Alderman a sick man. Whether it made Sidney Alderman a sick man. Or whether it was the loss of their mother and wife that made them so.

CHAPTER TWENTY

I'm half expecting to find my house has been set on fire when I get home. Or the windows broken. Or, at the very least, to have *murderer* spray-painted across the garage door and fence. I pull into the driveway, stand next to my car, and stare up and down the street. I'm looking for Sidney Alderman, but he isn't here. Nobody is. Not even Casey Horwell. All of my neighbors are off doing whatever it is that neighbors do. Mow lawns. Pull weeds. Cook food and watch TV. None of them are trying to figure out where their dead children are. I'm careful as I make my way inside. I had a gun pulled on me last night, and hours later a microphone, and I'm not eager to make either mistake twice.

I plug my cell phone back into the charger, then I bring the computer in from the car and set it up on the dining-room table. Bridget would not be pleased. I use the Christchurch Libraries' database of newspapers to find more articles related to the ones Bruce clipped. I take on board as much as I can from them, and from the missing persons reports, and as much as I can about their lives and about their deaths—not that any of the articles say they are dead. But they sure read as though the journalists were all betting heavily on it. I print out a photo of the fourth girl, then line the pictures up in a row. Their killer certainly had a fondness for a specific type of girl.

I spend two hours reading all about the missing, and it's hard, because my mind keeps returning to Alderman and Emily.

I search the obituaries for the weeks prior to the girls' deaths, looking for the same last names to see if there was a reason for any or all of them to attend a funeral. I come up with nothing. It's not a busted lead at this stage because it could be they still went to funerals of people outside their families, or family members with different last names. The only way to know for sure is to start making some phone calls, but right now talking to these dead girls' families is the last thing I feel like doing.

I set the whiteboard up, propping it up on a chair and leaning the top against a wall. I've got nothing but a permanent marker to draw with, but go ahead anyway, starting with a time line. I figure that Henry Martins would have been buried two days after he died. If I add those days on to the date of his death, it matches up nicely. Henry died on a Tuesday and was buried on a Thursday. Rachel was last seen Thursday morning, and was reported missing by her parents the following Tuesday. But then I add the other missing girls to the time line, and find that the dates between disappearances are not that even. The first two girls went missing within a month of each other, then there was another eighteen months until the third went missing, and the last was less than a week ago. It doesn't suggest that the murderer is escalating or slowing, and I'm not sure what that in itself suggests. Guys like this tend to start killing more often as the need overtakes the desire. Or there is something in their life that triggers the impulse to kill. I look at the time line and wonder what made this guy kill at these particular moments. Was it simply that the right type of girl came into his localized view of the world? Or did he go hunting for women to fit his type? There has to be more to it—I write *Prison?* on the board, wondering if the killer could have been in jail for eighteen months. It's common for serial killers to get arrested for an unrelated crime.

I go through the obituaries again, hunting out those who died in the days leading up to the girls' disappearances. Four of these people are no longer in their coffins, and are lying on morgue tables in different stages of decay, their bodies water-logged and bloated or decayed.

I look at the time line. I think about Emily. I think about Bruce Alderman and about his father. Then I think about where I was two years ago and the difference I could have made. That was my chance to save these girls. Maybe Landry was right, and I am fucking everything up. I don't know. All I know is that I have to find Emily.

My cell phone finally has a full charge. I go through the memory of incoming calls, put Landry's number into the address book, and then dial his phone. He picks it up after half a ring.

"I was about to call you," he says. "Your name just keeps on popping up. You need to stay the hell away from my investigation."

"I can help."

"Help? You seen the news lately?"

"Look, that isn't . . ."

"I don't mean that screwup you made last night. I mean the new one you've got on your hands today," he says.

"I haven't heard. What have I done now?"

"You must've really pissed off this Horwell chick at some point. What'd you do, sleep with her?" he asks.

"Yeah, good one, Landry."

"Turns out when people don't like you, they really don't like you. I guess I'm starting to see why."

"There a point here?" I ask him.

"She interviewed Alderman this morning. Had to be sometime after he hit the bar, but looking at him it couldn't have been long after. Didn't seem to have many drinks under his belt."

"And?"

"And it wasn't good. It's like she saw this fire burning inside him and just started throwing on more fuel. Hadn't been for all those angles and splatter trajectories, even I'd be thinking you were guilty. Anyway whatever anger he had about you before, you can double it and double that again. Just keep an eye out. And do us all a favor, huh? Stay indoors and turn off your phone until we get this thing nailed down. When it goes to court, we're going to be looking at some defense lawyer pointing the finger at you and saying—"

"Yeah—we covered this already."

"Then why don't I feel assured?"

I look down at the photographs and the newspaper clippings. "Look, Landry, I got something for you. You want to hear it or not?"

"That depends on how you got what you got. Is this going to backfire? If you've got anything and you've obtained it illegally, I don't want to know about it, right? Otherwise it'll blow up in our faces."

"Okay."

He doesn't say anything and I don't add anything else, and he reads my silence accurately.

"You're unbelievable, Tate."

"You want the names of the other girls or not?"

"Do me a favor and don't tell me. There's a hotline for information. Ring it anonymously and give it to them, okay? Call from a pay phone or something. Anything you give me from an illegal search is poison. Come on, Tate, you know that."

"I'm no longer a cop. Those same rules don't apply."

"Yeah, and this serial killer's defense lawyer you don't want me to keep reminding you about is going to—"

"Right," I say, interrupting him. "No problem. So you don't want my help."

"Help? Is that what you think you've been doing? I gotta go. Make sure you—"

"I got something else."

"You're going to give me a heart attack, Tate."

"Look, this is something good. It's something you can say you came up with on your own, so you don't have to—"

"Come on, I know how to do my Goddamn job."

"Rachel Tyler," I say, "before she died she visited Woodland Estates. Her grandmother died. It's the same cemetery." Landry doesn't answer. I can tell he hadn't made this connection. I press on. "I think the others might have been there too. I think that's the connection. That's what drew them to the killer."

"You got anything to back that up?" he asks.

"Not yet. But I'm—"

"No *buts*, Tate. You're off this thing. Go ahead and make that call to the hotline, give us those names. Do it now."

He hangs up without me telling him Alderman has my daughter. And that's okay—I want to deal with Alderman myself.

The phone call I'm going to make will take most of their legwork out of play. It'll mean the contents of the other two coffins are no longer up for grabs. But that call can wait. First I'm going to find Sidney Alderman and do what it takes to get my daughter back, and that's something I don't need Landry's help for.

CHAPTER TWENTY-ONE

The church is bathed in sunlight on one side and shade on the other, the two halves separated by a thin line like good and evil. It looks like there's probably a difference of twenty degrees between the two. The stained-glass windows look dull and fogged up with age. The concrete brick around the edges of the shady side has speckles of mold. The gardens have low-key and low-maintenance shrubs spaced out about a meter apart. There aren't any weeds, but that'll probably change now that Bruce is gone.

Mine is the only car out front, and there's nobody inside the church either. Except, of course, for Father Julian, who appears from a side door to the right of the altar when I'm about halfway up the aisle. Maybe I passed through a motion detector. Maybe he's been hanging out all day for the chance to trap some soul into a conversation about God. But the way he moves toward me makes me think he's been waiting for me to show up.

"You're here," he says gravely.

"We need to talk."

"You're right. We do." He looks paler than yesterday, as if a chunk of his faith has slipped away during the night. Or been stolen. "We need to talk about Bruce. Though to be honest I don't know if I can. I don't think I can talk to you."

"Father Julian, please, you have to—"

"I don't know, Theo," he says, glancing at the large envelope in my hand. Some of the color is coming back to his face, and the look in his eyes suggests it's coming back on waves of anger. "I remember what it was like for you two years ago."

"It's not like that now."

"Do you remember I used to come around to your house?" he asks.

"Of course I remember. But this isn't like that other time."

"Perhaps not for you, but perhaps it's like that for me. Bruce was . . . well, Bruce was like a son to me. What you've done—"

"I didn't kill him."

His expression doesn't change. He looks as if he was prepared to hear me say that, and equally prepared to dismiss it. He looks like a man struggling to stay in control. "This is not the time or especially the place for your lies."

"I didn't touch him."

He shakes his head. "You lost your way, Theo. You lost your God. You lost your faith."

"I lost my family," I tell him. "You used to think that was part of God's plan. If you were right, then what happened last night was also part of His plan."

"You're trying to be smart," he says. "After all that you've done."

"I didn't do anything," I tell him, putting my hands up in a warding-off gesture, the *There's nothing up my sleeve* sign.

"No? I know what you're capable of. The man that killed your daughter, do you remember what happened after he disappeared?"

"I remember you stopped coming around," I tell him.

"I tried to help you," he tells me. "But you didn't want it. I tried to stop you from heading down a path, but you wouldn't be stopped. And this is where it has brought you, this path, this path where innocent men die. Innocent men like Bruce."

"I didn't touch him," I say, "and I sure as hell don't hurt innocent men."

"Oh, you didn't touch him, did you?" he says, his voice getting louder now, and I realize it's the first time I've ever heard him yell. First time I've heard anybody in a church yell. "Then how in the hell did he end up dead!"

"He shot himself. There was nothing I could do."

"You sure found yourself able to do something two years ago."

"That was completely different." Now I'm the one getting close to yelling. "And you know that. You damn well know that."

"I told you that Bruce was a good boy," he says, his arms going out to his sides and his hands flicking forward, as if trying to discard something sticky from his fingertips. "I told you he had nothing to do with those girls dying. I told you! Why couldn't you have listened? You've shown so much trust in me in the past, why couldn't you have shown it now?"

"Goddamn it, Father Julian," I yell, and the words don't make him step back—in fact he takes a small step forward. He looks like he wants to hit me. "I didn't kill him! Why the hell don't you pick up the phone and make a call and speak to anybody down at the station or at the morgue and ask them what happened? They'll tell you."

"You mean your friends?"

"Come on, you can't believe that bullshit you saw on TV," I tell him.

He nods. He concedes the point. "He was a good boy," he says, much quieter now.

"Maybe he was. Part of me certainly believes he was. So instead of getting angry at me, why don't you stay angry at whoever did this. How about you give me a hand here and help me clear his name? Bruce told me he was innocent, that he buried the bodies, but that he didn't kill those girls. How about you help me, or are you too caught up with those assumptions of yours?"

He looks at me for what feels like a long time, as if inside somewhere he's searching himself for the right thing to do. The time it takes him suggests he's either searching real hard or he's slipping on just what the right thing is these days.

"I'll listen to you, Theo, just one more time. Then you have to promise me you'll never come back here."

"Once you hear what I have to say, you won't ask me to—"

He shakes his head and cuts me off. "Promise me," he says. "Under the eyes of God, inside His church, promise me you'll never come back here."

I make the promise. It's easy to make when you don't believe in God or His church.

"My office," he says. "We'll talk there."

I follow him through the side door. The corridor is dimly lit, and we pass other doors and plenty of drafts—churches are full of drafts. He leads me into a small, dusty office that is cluttered with old-looking books and mismatched furniture. He takes a seat behind his desk. The sun has arced around in the sky and is shining directly on him. It makes his face look whiter, almost glowing. Like a halo. The dust particles floating in the air are all a bright white. The light makes the stubble on his face look patchy, and it takes some of the anger out of his eyes and makes them look tired. There's a crucifix hanging on the wall behind him. Jesus has a downcast look about him, as if he's bored by it all, as if he's seen every church office there is to see and after two thousand years of it he's about had his fill of churches. The entire office looks as though every night somebody sneaks in here and alters everything slightly. It's the same way my place looks when I can't figure out where I left my wallet or keys. I sit down opposite him.

"If I'd helped you last night, maybe . . ." Father Julian hesitates. "Well, who knows?"

"I didn't kill him."

Father Julian sighs. "What do you want from me, Theo? Did you come for somebody to forgive you? Because you've come to the wrong place."

"Did you know that Bruce owned a gun?"

"He didn't."

"It sure looked like he did."

"Is that supposed to be funny?"

"No. But think about it. If I was going to kill him, why would I take him back to my office? You think I'd shoot him in front of my desk so the whole world would know about it?"

"I . . . I suppose not. I don't know. I don't know what to think. All I know is what you're capable of. All I know is that you think it's your job to protect the world from bad people, and I know you don't have the right to judge who those people are."

"That's right," I say. "You do know what I'm capable of. So you know that if I'd wanted to kill Bruce, I'd have taken him somewhere else. Nobody would ever have found him."

His jaw tightens and his eyes narrow slightly, and the look he gives me is the kind of look I never want to be given again.

It's one of disgust and disappointment. Finally he leans back in his chair and forms a steeple with his hands, touching his fingertips to his chin. He looks like he's praying. Jesus looks down on him, but doesn't seem to be listening.

"Come on," I say. "You don't have to like it, but it's a good point."

He nods. "What else did Bruce tell you? Did he know who killed the girls?"

"He didn't say. He just said to talk to his father. The only person I can think of who Bruce Alderman would be burying those girls for is his father."

"You think Sidney killed them?"

"It's possible."

"So what do you want from me? To tell you about Bruce? I've already told you, he was a good kid. There is one more thing, though, and I want you to think deeply on this. Yesterday he was alive, and today he isn't."

I don't answer him. I just let him have his say, knowing the sooner he gets everything off his chest, the sooner I can get on with things, and the sooner I can get my little girl back into the ground. The world is definitely fucked up when the goal of the day is to bury your daughter.

"What happened after Bruce's mother died? What happened to Sidney?"

"What?" He looks shocked.

"His mother. Ten years ago, when she died, what were things like?"

He breathes out heavily, reinforcing just how much of an ordeal it is to have me here. "It was the same thing, I guess. It was like one day he was alive, the next day he wasn't. Though it wasn't even really that. It's not like he was dead. He just became . . . lost. They both did."

"And?"

"And what?" he asks. "People become lost when that kind of thing happens. Come on, Theo, of all people you don't need an explanation on that. Sometimes people never re-cover, or they recover in the wrong way. And some people are lost in a way you can't ever put your finger on."

I think of Sidney Alderman digging up my dead daughter. I can safely say I could put my finger on dozens of different reasons why the old man is more screwed up than he is lost. "Did either of them ever give you a confession?"

"Come on, Theo, you know I can't answer that."

"There were four of them in that lake, Father. So far the police have identified only two. Soon they'll know all four."

"Four girls," he says. "What a waste of young lives."

"Well, now's your opportunity. . . ." I stop talking when sud-denly it hits me. Father Julian's anger can't all be directed at me. It must also be directed at himself. He's been holding out on me. "Yesterday," I say, talking a little slower now, "yester-day I said there could be others in the coffins, but I never said they were all girls. Or that they were young."

He starts to say something—probably to protest that some-how he heard or that he guessed—but he gives up the pretense and says nothing.

"You knew!" I say. "You fucking knew!"

"Theo!" he yells, banging his fist down on the table. "Enough! How dare you use—"

"How dare *I*?" Now it's my turn to bang my fist down on the table. "How dare *you*! You knew all along and did nothing? You did nothing? How can that be?"

He doesn't answer, and the silence that falls between us then is unexpected, as if we're both too aware that what we say next may damage irrevocably whatever relationship we have. But perhaps that has already happened. Perhaps everything went to hell two years ago when he thought he could save me from the path he says I went down.

"What was I to do, Theo?" he asks, almost in a whisper now, and the question seems genuine, as if he really wants me to come up with other options when there are none. "You know the rules. You can argue them and you can hate them and you can rant and rave about the injustice of it all, but you know, Theo, you know the deal."

"One of the Aldermans confessed to you. One of them killed those girls!"

"That's not what I said, and that's not what happened!"

I stand up and open the envelope and tip it up in the same manner I did when I found it. The articles spill out in the same way. I brush my hand over them, fanning them out like a deck of cards. Father Julian's eyes are pulled to them.

"You already knew the girls were in there. You knew they were dead."

"Sit back down, Theo."

"These are the girls we could have saved. What was it you said to me yesterday when I told you why this case was important to me? You said it wasn't my fault. You were right and you were wrong. See, I thought it was completely my fault. But not now. Now I share that burden with you."

He reaches out and touches the articles, picking some of them up. I watch his eyes, but they don't scan over any of the words. The more he shifts the clippings around, the more dust floats up in the air. I'm not sure what he's looking for. None of the disappearances made the front pages. There are no huge headlines or bylines. Maybe if one of them had been a rock star or the mayor's daughter, things would have been different. Though that's about to change. Tomorrow Rachel

Tyler is going to be all over the news. And the other girls too. People other than their friends and family are going to care. People are going to look at the names and faces and wonder how the hell their city became a breeding ground for the kind of violence needed to take these young women away, and for the kind of ignorance to let it happen without asking why.

"You're the one who said I went down a path, Father. Tell me, what path have you taken? By protecting bad people you're betraying the innocent."

"It's so easy for you, isn't it, Theo? It always has been. Guys like you think they can just come in here and get what they want." I'm not sure what he means by *guys like me*. "You have these great expectations that all you have to do is ask and I'll break the confessional seal and tell all. You don't think it hurts? Huh? You don't think that hearing all the poison coming from these people takes its toll? Don't you think I want to be able to pick up the phone and make the world a better place?"

"Then why don't you? These girls, you could have saved them."

"At what cost? You still don't get it, do you? You think if this was just about me I wouldn't do it? If it was just a matter of getting fired and losing my church, I'd pull the pin for the greater good. But this isn't about me, Theo. It's not about you either. It's not about those girls out there. It's about God. About our faith. It's about not breaking one of the oldest rules in the church."

There are so many angles from which to attack his argument, but for what point? He's right and I'm right and we both know it. And there's nothing we can do. He has to stand by his beliefs, and I have to stand by my anger with him for not having done something to prevent all of this.

"That's how you knew Bruce was innocent. He wasn't the one who confessed."

"We can't go down this road."

"What road?"

"The one where you start twisting all the boundaries, where you ask who didn't confess so you can narrow down your suspect pool." He runs both hands through his hair, then wipes them down the front of his cassock.

"I think I've already narrowed it down," I say, and I start to scoop the articles back up.

"It wasn't Sidney Alderman."

"Then who?"

"If I could break that rule and start telling, then what about you? You think you'd be a free man right now?"

Part of me wants to lean forward and pick him up by his collar and shake him until all that I need from him falls from that locked vault inside of him where he keeps secrets. Another part is thankful. He won't give up these secrets, and he'll never give up mine either.

"You're letting a murderer get away." There is no conviction behind my words. It's a last-ditch effort, and one that I don't expect to get me anywhere.

He seems to know this. "It haunts me."

If I tell him what Sidney Alderman has done to my daughter, will it change his views? I don't think it will. The priest's ideas about what Sidney Alderman is like are all outdated. He built up a friendship with the guy thirty or forty years ago, and that's how he still sees him. I wonder what it would take—whether there is a limit to how much pain there is—for Father Julian to accept that his faith and his convictions simply aren't worth it. Is there a number? A dozen dead girls? A hundred?

"Sidney Alderman. Tell me where he is."

"I don't know."

"Did he kill those girls?"

"I want you to go now, Theo. And I want you to remember your promise."

"But you can tell me about him, right? You can at least give me some history there."

"Sidney Alderman is a very sad man, Theo. Like you, he has lost his family. Surely you remember how you felt the day Emily died. Surely you can empathize."

Of course I remember. But I didn't go around digging up graves. "What happened to him two years ago?"

"I don't follow."

I finish putting the articles into the envelope. One of them said he retired two years ago. Is that enough? People become killers when there is a trigger. When there's a defining moment that makes somebody snap. I figure it's more likely Sidney Alderman would've snapped ten years ago when his wife died, not two years ago when he retired.

"Somebody has to pay for this," I say.

"Somebody already has."

"But not the right person." I tuck the end of the envelope back into itself. "The police are close. All of this, it's unraveling. You had your chance to help, but you didn't take it. This was your chance for redemption, Father."

"Don't do anything stupid, Theo. Bruce Alderman, he was a good man. And Sidney—well, inside he is a good man too, and one who right now is attending to his son. Respect that. Let him mourn, and let the police deal with him."

I walk to the door and Father Julian doesn't get up. He doesn't make any attempt to follow me.

"I can't do that," I say.

He shakes his head, but doesn't offer any more words of wisdom. I leave him in his office and I walk back past the pictures of Jesus and his buddies. I wonder what they would think of the priest's decision to keep the secrets shared with him to himself, whether they'd agree with his convictions or whether they'd tell him he was a fool. I wonder if right now Father Julian is praying for guidance.

At the front of the church is an alcove in which a registry— thick and divided up into sections, the covers leather with gold script across them—rests on a pedestal. It's sorted alphabetically, and those sections are broken down chronologically. I go through the pages, looking for more connections between the girls and the times they went missing. I can't find anything. There's also a large reference map pinned on the wall; it has the cemetery divided up into numbered sections like a street map. It's all I need to find my next two locations.

The first one is a grave. It's close to the back of the houses further up the street, about as far away from the church and the lake to the east as it can get while still being within the boundaries of the cemetery. I drive as close as I can before getting out and walking. There is a pathway that leads through some more trees, and suddenly I'm in an area of the cemetery that feels isolated. I figure Alderman won't be back anytime soon, so he's not about to drive past my car and see that I'm here. I figure he's sitting in a bar somewhere getting drunk, or he's driving around, trying to work out where exactly to put my daughter. Or he's parked up on the side of the road, coming to his senses, wondering what in the hell he's doing. Maybe getting ready to bite down on a bullet. Like father like son. Only that's not a real possibility. Ten years ago, maybe, Alderman might have been the kind of guy to question his actions. But not now.

The day's getting brighter. Getting warmer. But I still feel cold inside. I walk around the gravestones, each one a story, each one a memory. Some good, some bad. These people all influenced other people's lives. They made differences. They met other people and paired up and made babies while they made futures together. Some died of old age. Others of disease. The messages on the gravestones are all similar. They're sentiments, they're statements, they're final messages left to the world in the hope they will never be forgotten.

The one I want is tidy—no weeds, no long grass—but there are no flowers there either. I stand in front of it for about a minute before heading back to my car.

The second location is a large shed at the far northeast corner of the cemetery. It's separated from the cemetery first by a wooden fence, then by a line of poplars. It's about the same size as my house, but there are no inner walls or partitions. It's full of garden tools and sacks of grass seed and plant seed. There's a tractor and a ride-on lawn mower and a digger. The tools that were needed yesterday to exhume Henry Martins were here all along, parked in a row. Instead contractors came and used their own equipment, and I wonder how different things would be now if they hadn't. I take a look at the place, but nothing stands out—there are so many possible murder weapons in here, it'd take a week to examine each of them. This shed could be a crime scene.

There is a stack of cinder blocks beneath one of the benches. Hanging up on a nail near the window is a coil of green rope. I reach up and roll it between my fingers. It's made up of hundreds of individual strands of what looks like hemp. It's the same stuff that was connected to the bodies, and would have swelled when it got wet. Thousands of people in this city probably use it.

I walk over to the digger. There is fresh dirt on the teeth of the scoop. Sidney Alderman used it to bring my little girl up into the light. He probably laid her in the giant claw and drove her back here in it. I move around the shed, looking in every shadow, behind every item, pushing aside anything that could possibly hide the body of my daughter, and after ten minutes it's obvious she isn't here. I look back at the tools and the rope and this shed could easily be the place where four young women met their deaths. I stand in the center and slowly turn around, covering each angle with my eyes. Two wheelbarrows. Pieces of plywood. Buckets. Boot prints with chunks of dirt, bits and pieces of wood, tarps, ropes, work-benches. A horrible place to die. The air is musty, and I can smell oil and grass clippings. There are cobwebs and stains and warped boards and cracks in the glass. There are patches of rust in the roof and plastic buckets set below to catch the rain. There are shelves full of mechanical parts—levers, cogs, engine bits, most of them rusted.

I climb into the digger and start it up. The seat is uncom-fortable, and has sharp splits in the vinyl where the foam bleeds through and looks like snow. I pull up a lever to slide the seat back. I've never driven one of these machines be-fore, but the simplicity of the levers and pedals makes it easy enough after a few minutes' practice. The digger vibrates as I roll forward. It bounces up and down with every small dip in the shingle road. The wheels leave deep imprints in the wet lawn. A set of imprints head off toward the area where Emily was buried. I make a fresh set as I drive to the grave I stood in front of twenty minutes ago.

Getting my daughter back is the priority, and anything that happens in between I'll put down to God's will. That ought to keep Father Julian happy.

CHAPTER TWENTY-TWO

There is an abyss. Those it waits for can stand on the precipice, some live there, and then there are those who sink into the depths as if attached to cinder blocks. I'm not sure where I stand, and that might be one of the problems with the abyss— you never really know if you can keep dropping lower. That's what the last two years have been like. I slid into the abyss, and what I saw down there frightened me; since then, I've been doing what I can to pull myself away. Perhaps, though, all I've been doing is staying at the same depth, just waiting for one more moment to sink me lower.

I think that moment is here. I don't know. I hope the fact I'm indulging in some self-evaluation means I'm aware of the slide, just as an insane man can't be insane if he is wondering if he is. A man who thinks he has sunk as far as he can perhaps hasn't sunk that far at all. The problem is, when you're sinking and not looking for a life preserver to pull you back, then perhaps you really are gone.

I try making another call, but Sidney doesn't answer. His phone is switched on, because it goes to voice mail after five rings. He's probably sitting there staring at it. He's got my dead daughter in the back of his car and that means he's going to ignore my calls. He's got his own dead son whom he has to start making arrangements for lying on a slab of steel in a cold morgue with a sheet draped over him. He has to start picking out coffins and flowers and headstone engravers. He has to pick out a suit for his son, and a funeral home, and he has to let people know so they can show up. He's got a lot on his mind. But he has to figure out first what he's going to do with Emily. And he's worrying about what I'm going to do to him.

I close my eyes. I question what I'm doing, but not enough to stop doing it. I send him a text.

I want my daughter back and you're going to give her to me. We're going to make a trade. Trust me, it's a trade you'll be willing to make.

I'm sitting in the digger underneath one of the bluest skies this summer. I'm parked back by the shed. It feels like I'm melting out here. It's taken me the best part of two hours to do what I figure would have been a twenty- or thirty-minute job for one of the Alderman duo. Nobody came over to investigate the sound. Cemeteries don't get a lot of foot traffic in the middle of the week, and I've had this area all to myself.

The phone starts to ring. I flip it open.

"Fuck you," he says. "You murdered my boy, and you think you have something to trade?" His words are slurred, and I realize he has crawled back into whatever bar he dragged himself out of to take my daughter away.

"I didn't kill your son."

"He's dead, ain't he?"

"Bring back my daughter and we'll talk about it."

"What?"

"You heard me," I say. "I want to make a trade."

"Trade? You have nothing that I want."

"That's what I thought at first. Until I started playing your game. The digger wasn't that hard to use. I got the hang of it in the end."

"Where are you?" he asks.

"I'm where you were ten years ago," I say, and I hang up.

A few seconds later the phone rings again. I switch it off.

There's a faucet outside the shed and I'm thirsty, but I don't want my lips to touch anything that Sidney Alderman's lips might have touched. I climb down from the digger and step into the shade. I start going through the tools. Gardening equipment, mostly, but some carpentry stuff as well. Could be that twenty years ago and in a different life, Alderman had a hobby. Maybe he and his son would hang out in the shed and make wooden stools or birdhouses, and they'd shoot the breeze with small talk about angles and miter cuts and joints. There are power tools for every occasion too. I ignore them all and pick up a shovel.

I carry the shovel back to the grave rather than taking the digger. I rest beneath a tree that shelters me from the sun. I try not to think about the last twenty-four hours that have led me here, then I realize it's actually the last two years that have done it. I wonder if the man I was back then would ever have thought of pulling the sort of crap he's able to do now. I hope not, then I figure that if I was going to hope for anything it'd be that the last two years never happened.

That immediately leads me to start thinking about Quentin

James. I have had two lives—the one before meeting James, and the one after—and I have been two separate people. Father Julian would say there was Theodore Tate with his family, and then there was Theodore Tate who went down a path he shouldn't have taken.

The same could be said of Quentin James. There was Sober Quentin and Drunk Quentin. There was probably a third Quentin too. One who recognized the change, but one who was kept quiet with beer and sports TV and mortgage payments. There is a third Tate—one who can't say no to whatever the hell it is that I'm doing now. I felt so many things when Quentin told me he was sorry, but pity wasn't one of them. I don't feel it now either.

It takes Alderman thirty minutes. The sun is a little lower, but no less hot. The beat-up SUV comes along the road, the sun glinting off the windshield, which is the only clean surface on the vehicle. The vehicle sways left and right as he struggles to control it.

I don't move. He parks as close as he can get, and when the door opens he steps out and pauses, looking around for what I can only guess is me. He doesn't see me. He has to pass through the section of trees where I'm sitting, but still he doesn't see me. He approaches the grave slowly, swaying slightly as he walks, as if the world is dropping away from beneath him with every footstep. Me, I'd have been running. He reaches it and he stands at the edge and he looks down and he does nothing. Just looks into the earth and sways, staring, just staring, until finally he climbs in.

I move toward him. The angle increases the closer I get, allowing me first to see the opposite edge of the grave, then Alderman's head, and then the rest of him. He's in there trying to pry up the edge of his wife's coffin, but it's difficult because all of his weight is on the lid. My shadow moves across the casket and he notices it. He looks up, having to twist his body to do it, which is a little awkward for him. He's straddling the coffin like a horse, except he can't get his legs over the sides. He's looking up into the sun and has to hold a hand up to shade his eyes.

"You fucker," he says.

"Where is she?"

He gets to his feet and has to reach out to steady himself against the dark walls. I show him the shovel.

"You think I'm afraid of you?" he asks. "You think I haven't been waiting for something like this?"

I smack him in the side of the face with the shovel—not hard, but hard enough for him to fall back, his legs coming up and his head bouncing into the coffin.

"Jesus," he says, touching his face. He leans to his side and spits out some blood, then wipes his hand across his mouth. "Fuck."

"Where did you put her?"

"Fuck you," he says. "Is my wife in here? Is she, you piece of shit?"

"She's there, and unless you want to join her you're going to tell me where you put my daughter."

"Your daughter? How about you tell me where my son is? Or have you forgotten? He's down at the fucking morgue!" The words forced from his mouth are surrounded by booze and spittle. "Yeah, he's getting cut to pieces with fucking bolt cutters and blades, and you know what? You want to know the fucking punch line? You put him there!"

There's no point in arguing. No point in telling him over and over that I did not shoot his son. Casey Horwell has already convinced him otherwise. "My daughter. Where is she?"

"You shot my boy."

"Tell me!"

"You'll never find her."

"Goddamn you," I say, and raise the shovel as if I'm about to hit him again. He flinches away, and I take a step back. "Goddamn it," I repeat, and I throw the shovel at him. I throw it hard. The shovel head hits him in the shoulder and bounces onto the coffin lid. Alderman falls back and braces himself against the wall. He starts massaging the impact point on his body.

I curl my hands into fists; I'm shaking, and I'm not really sure exactly where this anger is going to take me. The bottom of the abyss is waiting.

Alderman picks up the shovel and uses it to get to his feet. He reaches for the edge of the grave. I figure he must be drunk, because he puts his hands over the edge as if he thinks he can pull himself out and not have anybody try to stop him. I squeeze my foot down on his fingers. He pulls them back, raking the skin off the back of his hand. He looks up at me as if he's the victim here, as if he's done nothing wrong. There is a patch of blood starting to spread on the shoulder of his shirt and now on his hand.

"The girls, what happened?" I ask.

"What girls?"

"What girls do you think I'm talking about?"

He shrugs, but he knows. "I had nothing to do with them. And nor did Bruce."

"He buried them. He admitted to that. Did he kill them?"

"Fuck you," he says.

"Or did you kill them?" I ask.

"This is bullshit. All you've done is kill my son and you don't even know why."

"How about you explain it to me?"

"You're asking the wrong man," he says.

"Who should I be asking?"

"Who the hell do you think? Your pal Father Julian. Go ask him all about it."

"What does that mean?"

"I'm not saying another word until you let me out of here."

I back away from the grave.

"Where are you going?" Alderman calls out.

I don't answer him. I walk over to his SUV. It's dusty and there are several rusting stone chips across the front of it. The driver's door is open and there is a *ding, ding* sound coming from the dashboard—his keys are still in it. I pop open the back door. My daughter is sprawled out in the back beneath a dark blue tarp, her hair all matted and limp, her favorite dress in better condition than her body. Her little body has been ravaged by decomposition. I lean against the SUV and I keep my eyes downcast, fighting the nausea, not wanting to look at her face because much of it has gone. It has rotted away, leaving a mask of such horror that all I want to do is scream. She should be in school right now. Should be two years older. Should be nine years old and looking forward to going home and getting her homework out of the way so she can spend time doing what nine-year-old girls do—which is what, I don't know, but I should have been finding out. This world is so fucked up that it's starting to make me think what Bruce Alderman did last night isn't such a bad option.

I close the door. I walk back to the grave. Alderman is still making his way out of it. He's struggling because the dynamics are difficult for him. He's drunk, his body can't perform as well as a younger man's could, his shoulder hurts and his fingers hurt, and he's having difficulty getting up over the edge. He needs to be taller or stronger or younger or sober, or he needs a ladder. He looks up at me.

"You son of a bitch," I say.

"So I was wrong. So you did find her."

"It's time you gave me some answers," I say, and I reach down and grab a handful of his hair in one hand and the front of his shirt in the other. I pull him up hard, wanting it to hurt, and he grunts as his body is dragged over the edge of the grave.

"Ah, fuck, slow down, damn it," he says, but I have no intention of slowing down.

"I didn't kill your son," I say, and I keep pulling him upward.

He braces both his hands over my hands to relieve the pain that must be flooding through the top of his head. I can hear scalp and hair beginning to tear. When he's out far enough, he gets his knees on the ground and stops trying to hold on to my arms. Instead he twists his head, pulls down on my hand, and clamps his teeth over my thumb.

"Shit," I say, and I pull back my hand, but it's no good. He's biting hard, trying to sever the thumb.

I can't crash my knee into his chin because it'll push his teeth all the way through. Instead I let go of him and hit him. His head moves, making his teeth rip at my thumb like a great white shark sawing through its prey by shaking its head. So I push forward. We both stumble, and a moment later we're falling through the air.

And back into the grave.

CHAPTER TWENTY-THREE

Mostly I land on Sidney Alderman. My elbow crashes into the coffin and my thumb is jarred from his mouth. My knee hits the wall, but the rest of me lands against the old man so the impact is cushioned. Alderman isn't so lucky. He doesn't have anybody to land on. Just his wife, except that her years of offering any support are over. So he lands hard up against the wood with the shovel beneath him—harder, I imagine, than if he were falling in there by himself. Because I'm falling with him, there's my weight and there's momentum and the laws of physics, and they all add up very badly for Sidney Alderman. His head bounces into the edge of the coffin.

I push myself up, bracing my hands against the dirt walls and the coffin. Blood is pouring from my thumb. The edges of the bite have peeled upward, revealing bright pink flesh. I reach into my pocket for my handkerchief and wrap it tightly around the wound. It doesn't hurt, but I figure in about twenty seconds it's going to be killing me. I get to my knees and shake Alderman a little. There is no response, so I shake him harder. When he doesn't stir, I take the next step and search for what I'm beginning to fear, putting my fingers against his neck. Blood starts to leak onto the coffin. The lid is curved slightly, so the blood doesn't pool; it runs down the sides and gets caught in a thin cosmetic groove running around the edge of the lid. Drop after drop and it starts building up; it climbs up over the groove and soaks into the dirt.

There is no pulse.

I start to roll Alderman over, but stop halfway when I see the damage. The tip of the shovel is buried into his neck, its angle making it point toward his brain. His head sags as I move him, and the handle of the shovel rotates. His eyes are open, but they're not seeing a thing. I let him go, and he slumps back against the coffin. My hands are covered in his blood. I stare at them for a few seconds, then wipe them on the walls of the grave, then stare at them some more, before shifting my body as far away as I can from Alderman, which isn't far. I wipe my hands across the wet earth once more and clean them off on my shirt. All the time I keep staring at Alderman as if he's going to sit up and tell me not to worry, that these things happen, that it could've happened to anybody.

Jesus.

I climb out of the grave. It's a lot easier for me than it was for Alderman because I'm working with a whole different set of dynamics. I lie on the lawn, staring up at the sky that is just as blue as it was when I was sitting in the digger, digging up the grave.

Jesus.

I get up and start staring at Sidney Alderman from different angles that don't improve the situation. I try thinking about

Emily, looking over at the SUV that is hidden by the trees, knowing she's in the back, hoping her presence will make things seem better than they are. Hoping to justify Alderman's death by thinking he deserved it. I try this, but it doesn't work. It should. But it doesn't. He deserved the chance to tell me everything he knew about the dead girls, and those dead girls deserved that too. I think about Casey Horwell and I wonder how she'd react if I called her and told her where her story had led. I figure she'd be thrilled—it'd give her the airtime she is desperate to get.

I walk over to the trees so I can see both the grave and the SUV. I look from one to the other. Is there a next step? I figure there is. There always is. I have, in fact, two first steps to choose from—the problem is each one heads in a different direction.

The first one requires me to reach into my pocket for my cell phone and call the police. Only I don't. They'll say I wanted this to happen. They'll say Alderman pushed me too far, and that I reacted. Only they'll say I had time to calm down, because there were several hours in between Alderman taking Emily out of the ground and me putting him in it. Hours in which I dug up his wife's grave, spoke to the priest, and continued the investigation. So they'll say I didn't snap. They'll say it had to be premeditated, because I had plenty of opportunities to go to the police, but I didn't. They'll say I knew what was happening, that I looked into the abyss and dived right in.

I go with the other direction.

I climb back into the grave and roll Sidney Alderman over. His blood is now pooling on each side of the coffin. I tug at the shovel, but at first it doesn't move. It's caught on something inside his body. I shift it from side to side, loosening it like removing a tooth, and it comes away with the squelching sound of pulling your foot out of mud. I toss it out onto the grass and climb back out.

I walk to the other side of the trees and scan the graveyard. There isn't a soul in sight. I walk back and start to scoop dirt on top of Alderman. It hits him heavily: some pieces stay where they hit, others roll down his side and into the blood. The sound can't be mistaken for anything other than dirt against flesh. I drop the shovel. There are black crumbs of soil stuck on the end of it, glued there by Sidney Alderman's blood. I make my way back to the shed and return with the digger. I can only take the road so far before I have to drive over and around other graves and around trees to reach the plot, and when I get there it doesn't take as long to fill the grave as it took to empty it. When I'm done I drive the digger back and I stand in the shed, trying to keep my feet under me as the world sways. Another Tate has just been added to my collection of personalities. Each one more messed up than the other. Leading me where?

A tightness spreads across my chest, and suddenly the shed seems way too small, the walls cramping in, the ceiling lowering down. I get outside only to find that the whole world doesn't seem big enough anymore.

The clouds are back, the sun completely gone now. Dusk is here, and it's a little hard to make out the scenery. I find the SUV and drive to my daughter's grave. There I sit until a few nearby mourners leave the area. Then I carry her gently, scared she'll fall apart, scared that I'm going to fall apart. I rest her on the ground, then climb six feet closer to the Hell that I've proven again I'm destined for. I reach out and scoop her up, then lay her down. She doesn't look like Emily. She may be wearing the same dress, have the same hair, but everything else is different. It's different in a way I don't want to think about. I tuck her hair away from what face she has left and stroke it behind what ears she has left. I close the lid, not wanting to spend any more time with her, but at the same time I want to spend all night here, holding her hand.

I use the same shovel that killed Sidney Alderman to bury her. It seems right that I do it this way, and I relish the pain that courses from my thumb and up through my entire arm. It takes me an hour, and when I'm done my shirt is covered in dirt and is damp all over, and the day is dark and the makeshift bandage on my thumb even darker. I throw the shovel in the back of the SUV. The vehicle is covered in my fingerprints. My own car is still here. I'm a murderer, and if I'm not careful the world is soon about to know.

I drive back to the shed. I find some turpentine and soak some rags in it, then I go around wiping down every surface I've come into contact with. I drive to Alderman's house and park up the driveway and I do the same thing there. I wipe down the SUV and I carry the shovel back to my own car. When I leave, nobody follows me. Nobody seems to care.

I drive to the nursing home. The staff at the home doesn't appear thrilled to see me. Carol Hamilton has gone for the day, and nobody else asks me what in the hell I was on about this morning. Nobody asks why I look like shit, my clothes messed up, my skin black with dirt, why I have a filthy hand-kerchief on my thumb. I spend an hour with my wife, and now more than ever I need something from her—a squeeze from her hand, or her eyes to focus on me and not past me—but she can offer me none of this. I don't fill her in on anything that's happened. I stare out the same window she stares out, and I see the same things, and this is the closest I have felt to her in two years. Part of me envies her world.

When I get home I use a saw to cut the shovel into half a dozen pieces. I wipe each of them down, but I know I'll need to do more than that—will have to dispose of them where they'll never be found. I climb into the shower then, and watch the dirt and blood wash away, though I still feel covered in it. I remove the handkerchief from my thumb and rinse the wound, which continues to bleed weakly. It needs stitches, but I'm not going to get them. I bandage it and make some dinner, but I can't eat. I turn on the TV, but can't understand what the news anchors are even talking about. I grab a beer and sit out on the deck and stare at a piece of concrete we left exposed five years ago when we built the deck. The cement was wet and we carved our names into it so they could never be washed away. Daxter comes out and jumps up on my lap, but only stays a few seconds before jumping back down. I stare at the names in the cement as I finish my beer, and then I stare at the ceiling of my bedroom while looking for sleep. I think of Quentin James and the Alderman family and the four dead girls I've never met. I have robbed their families of any closure, because the man who could help me is dead. Any hopes they had for answers I took down into the abyss with me.

CHAPTER TWENTY-FOUR

At four in the morning I give up on sleep and sit at the table drinking coffee. I keep going over what I've just done, as if by picturing each detail there might still be the chance to go back and change it.

Two years ago, after I spoke to Quentin James, I slept like the dead. I got home and made some dinner, I watched some TV, and an hour after midnight I went to bed. It was a new day and I was a new man, and when I slipped between the sheets I closed my eyes and pictured my family and I fell asleep. There were no nightmares. No questions. No guilt. I remember waiting for the guilt. I went and spoke to Father Julian and confessed my sins and waited for it to kick in, but it didn't. I slept like a baby that night.

But not this time.

I drive back to the cemetery. The night is cold and daylight is still a few hours away. On the way I throw yesterday's clothes into a dumpster, just as hundreds of guilty men before me have done. At the gravesite where Rachel Tyler was dug up I stand next to the corner of the lake and I think about the choices that have made me who I am. Then I realize they were choices made for me. Quentin James started me down this road. He gave me no option but to drive him out to the middle of nowhere and leave him behind. What else could I have done? Let him serve his time in jail so he could kill again when they set him free? Fuck those people who think that alcoholism is a disease. Cancer is a disease. Tell people with cancer that alcoholism is a disease and see what their views are. It's all about choice. People choose to drink. They don't choose to get leukemia. So James had only himself to blame. He chose to keep drinking. He could have chosen to stop. Could have chosen to get help. He chose the path I took him down.

I kick a clump of dirt into the water and watch it disappear. Do I have limits? Do I kill the next person I suspect is a murderer? Hell, what about the next time I have to stand in line somewhere and I get sick of waiting? Gun down those ahead of me? Shoot the guy servicing my car because he tries to stiff me on the bill?

The crime scene still has tape fluttering in the breeze. It isn't really a crime scene. It's more of a depraved scene, where the dead were replaced by a different dead. The digging equipment has gone. The tents have been taken down. The grass has been trampled flat. The circus that came to town has left. I stare out at the lake. I wonder how deep it goes, and how it was down there in the water for the divers. I go over the last two days, trying to filter everything until the answers are clear, but if there are any answers I keep missing them.

When I move away from the water, I don't look back. I

reach the caretaker's grave and I stand next to the turned-over dirt, and I listen to the wind and the early morning and I listen for a voice coming from beneath my feet. There is none. I drive to the church. I leave my car running and walk up to the big doors and start banging on them, breaking the promise I made to Father Julian that I'd never return. There is no response, so I walk around the side and start banging on a much smaller door.

Father Julian yells at me to hang on. A few moments later the door unlocks, then swings open. He is wearing a pair of faded pajamas and a robe. His hair is stuck up on one side.

"Theo. What are you doing here? Do you know what time it is?"

"You have to help me," I tell him.

"Help you? I've done enough of that lately."

"Please, this is important. Sidney Alderman, was it him?"

"I can't . . ."

I reach out and grab hold of his arm, and rest my other hand on his shoulder. I grip him tightly and pull him forward so our faces are almost touching. "Was he the one?"

"Theo—"

"If he was, you don't have to tell me. You wouldn't be breaking the confessional seal," I say, and I can hear the desperation in my voice. "But if he isn't, if he didn't confess, you can tell me. God won't care about that."

"What have you done, Theo? What have you done?"

"Tell me."

He looks into my eyes, because at this distance there is no alternative. Slowly he then starts to shake his head. "Go home, Theo."

"Not until you tell me."

He reaches beneath my grip and pushes me in the chest.

I stumble back and don't fall down, but I feel like I've fallen anyway. Back into the abyss.

"Bruce buried those girls for somebody," I say. "Was it his father?"

"This has gone on long enough."

"Was it for you, Father?" I ask, unsure where the question is coming from. "Did you kill those girls? Was Bruce burying them for you? Sidney said to ask you about it. He said you knew a lot more than you were saying. How deeply are you involved? Did you kill those girls? Or are you just happy to protect the man who did?"

"Get out of here, Theo. Get the hell out of here or I'm calling the police. I mean it."

He takes a step back and slams the door.

I stand in the same spot for half a minute, wondering if the exchange really happened the way I recall it—whether Father Julian had Bruce bury those girls—and questioning what insanity has come over me to think such a thing.

I'm sure he watches me from somewhere inside the church as I make my way back around to the car. I feel dizzy, and I feel sick, and my stomach feels hollow, as if I haven't eaten in months. I climb into my car, and I drive away from the graveyard, certain now that the man I killed was certainly one sick son of a bitch, but he was also innocent of murder. I drive away, thinking how much right now I could really do with a drink.

PART II

PART II

CHAPTER TWENTY-FIVE

The city is white and cold and full of long shadows. The air is like ice. The heater is strong enough so only the edges of my windshield have frosted over, but not strong enough to stop the middle of it from fogging. There are circular smear marks from where I've wiped it with my hand. My drink seems to be keeping the cold at bay much more effectively than the heater.

It's June now and Winter has arrived. The grass has become crisp with frost and cracks like glass underfoot. The shadows of the cement markers are longer than they were two months ago when I fell into the lake. At the moment the air is deathly still. The trees are motionless, caught in a snapshot. Nothing out here is moving. The church looks uninviting, as if the desperately cold temperature inside has convinced even God to move out. But it's not completely empty. Father Julian is in there. Somewhere.

I take another sip. My throat burns. I shiver.

The clock on my dashboard is off by an hour because I never got around to changing it when daylight saving ended back in April. It says nine a.m., and I know that means I have to add an hour or perhaps subtract one—I can't remember which. Not that it matters.

I watch the police car in the rearview mirror as it rolls to a stop behind me, the gravel twisting and grating beneath the wheels. Nothing happens for about thirty seconds as the occupants wait in the warmth. Then the doors open. The two men approach. I roll down the window just enough to speak through. The winter morning seizes on the moment and floods the car with such savage cold air that every joint in my body starts to ache.

"Morning, Tate," the taller of the men says, using just the right tone to suggest he's ready to haul my ass down to the cinder-block hotel. His words form tiny pools of fog in the air.

"I thought it was afternoon."

"You can't be here."

"My daughter is buried here," I say. "That gives me the right."

"No it doesn't."

"This is public property."

"There's a restraining order against you, Tate," he says. "You know that. You can't come within one hundred meters of Father Julian."

"I'm not within a hundred meters of him."

"Yes you are."

"I don't see him," I say.

"That's because he's inside."

"But it would've been illegal for me to go to check, don't you think?"

"What I think is that you're doing your best to get arrested."

"Then you need better thoughts. Shit like that will only bring you down."

He nods, but he's no longer looking at me, he's looking at what's in my hand. "Is that what I think it is?" He's looking at my Styrofoam coffee cup that doesn't have coffee in it.

"Don't know. It depends on what you're thinking. You're a whole lot more negative than I gave you credit for."

He looks over at his partner, then back down at me. "Jesus, Tate, it's a bit early to be drinking, isn't it?"

"It's happy hour somewhere in the world."

"Then coming with us isn't really going to set you back."

They open the door for me and I step outside. My breath forms clouds in the air. The gravel crunches beneath my feet, tiny pieces of frost snapping between them, and the trees that were ever so still while I was sitting down seem to lunge toward me as I walk. The officers escort me to the back of their car and I have to reach out and grab hold of it to stop from falling over. Then they take the bourbon off me. Hell, what next? First I lose my family, now I lose my ability to drink?

The police car is warmer than my own, and the view somewhat better since the windshield isn't iced over. The drive doesn't include any conversation, and I pass the time by looking down at my feet and telling myself not to be sick since the car seems to be swaying all over the place. At the station we ride up an elevator that seems to move way too fast and I have to grab a wall. Then the men march me past dozens of sets of curious eyes. I don't meet any of them; I just glance at their looks of disappointment before reaching an interrogation room.

They sit me down in front of a desk that in another life I used to sit on the other side of. They close the door and I stand back up only to find that it's locked. I walk around for a bit before deciding I might as well sit back down. I know the procedure. I know they're going to make me wait before sending somebody in. I need to use the bathroom, and if they wait too long I have no reservations about pissing in the corner. Why should I? If I can kill people, I can do anything.

It takes forty minutes before Detective Inspector Landry comes in. He's carrying only one cup of coffee that I know isn't for me, and a folder that he sits on the desk, but keeps closed. He looks like he hasn't slept in about a week, and there are dark smudges beneath his eyes. He still smells of cigarette smoke and coffee. He looks stressed. He's been a busy man with all the rest of the bullshit that's been going on in the city while he's been trying to figure out how those bodies got in the water. Other murders, other cases.

He sits down and stares at me. "Explain this obsession to me once again?" he asks.

"It's not an obsession. Am I free to leave?"

"What do you think? You violated a restraining order. You were in an automobile, behind the wheel, while under the influence."

"I haven't been given a breath test."

"You want to take one?" he asks.

"What would be the point? I wasn't driving."

"But I could argue that you drove there drunk. Or were about to leave drunk. Your keys were in the ignition."

"You could argue that, and I could argue that you're an asshole."

"Fuck it, Tate, why the hell don't you try to help yourself here? Huh? Why don't you capitalize on the fact that right at this moment I'm the best friend you have in this city."

"And why's that?"

"Because you made the call and gave us the names of the other two girls. That got us started."

"That was two months ago," I say. It was the same day I contacted Alicia North, the best friend of Rachel's that David had told me about. Alicia North hadn't heard of Father Julian, hadn't heard of Bruce or Sidney Alderman, hadn't heard of anything at all that could have helped me. It was also the same day I started cracking lots of seals on lots of bottles of alcohol in order to push the visuals I was having of a lifeless Sidney Alderman into the back of my mind. It was the first day after I had killed him.

"Yeah, it was two months ago, but I'm a giving guy and right now I'm giving you some goodwill. See, the way we've been seeing it, Sidney Alderman did a runner the same day you told me you had the names of the girls and a day before somebody rang the hotline with the anonymous information. Since then there haven't been any more missing girls."

"So I'm in your good books and Alderman is in your bad books. Fine. You going to let me go?"

"The problem," he says, and he makes a face when he sips at his coffee, "is Father Julian. Somehow he fits into all of this, and that's a problem. For us, for him, and for you. If you thought the case was over, you'd be at home right now. You wouldn't be following Julian. And if you believed Alderman was guilty, you'd be out there looking for him."

"Now you're the one who seems obsessed."

"Strange that Alderman didn't wait to see his son buried. He didn't take his car. He didn't pack any clothes. That adds up badly, Tate, and I keep coming to the conclusion that you know something about that. How many times have we pulled you in here now?"

"If you've got a point, just make it."

"How about you take this chance to explain things to me, and maybe I can start to figure out what in the hell is happening to you. You're more drunk each time we drag you in. This is the third time since the restraining order was issued a week ago. Anybody else and they'd be kept in custody. They'd be facing time. There ain't going to be any favors if we bring you in for a fourth. Come on, man, you know sending an ex-cop into prison isn't going to be pretty."

"Can I go now?" I ask.

"No. Tell me about Father Julian."

"What about him?"

"You're practically camping outside his church in your car most nights. That booze is fucking up your brain because you can't figure out what a restraining order means. He says you're stalking him, and that's exactly what you're doing." He takes another sip of coffee, puts it down, and leans forward. "Unless I'm missing something here, it looks like you want to end up in jail. Is that it?"

I shrug as if I don't care, but the truth is I don't want to end up in jail. If I wanted that, I'd tell him all about Sidney Alderman and where they could find him.

"So what is it about him that makes you want to sit outside his church watching?" he asks.

I try to maintain eye contact with him, but say nothing.

"Come on, Tate, give yourself a chance," he says. "We're through playing games. Next time we bring you in here, you're staying. You get my point?"

"You've said it twice. I got it each time."

"Yet here you are," he says.

"Look, I've got nothing else to say."

"Well, the opposite goes for Father Julian. He has plenty to say about you."

"I doubt that."

"Why's that? You think anything you've said to him is covered by priest-parishioner confidentiality? You're right—to a point. He says anything you've told him he can't share. But what he can share is his concern. He said two months ago you went in there and asked him to help you find Bruce Alderman. We all know where that led, right? Next thing we know Bruce Alderman shows up in your office dead."

"Look, Landry, he didn't show up dead, okay? It's not like he shot himself before walking into my office."

"The following day you go see Father Julian again, this time asking for help in finding Sidney Alderman. It's the same day you call me telling me you know who the missing girls are. Father Julian said that if he knew where Sidney was, he'd tell him to stay clear of you. Why do you think he'd say that?"

I look down at my thumb and the deep scarring from the bite that Sidney Alderman took. Sometimes it still hurts.

"You think Father Julian is guilty of something?" he asks.

"What would he be guilty of?" I ask.

"I don't know. You tell me. You think he killed those girls?"

"This is bullshit," I say.

"He knows something about you, something he wouldn't tell me. But I'm figuring it out," he says, and he runs his hand across the cover of the folder he brought into the room with him. The folder is thick, and the pages between its covers could be blank for all I know, though Landry wants me to believe they're full of circumstantial facts that any moment are going to line up in the right order for him to arrest me for something.

I say nothing.

Landry fills in the silence. "See, it's just a matter of connecting the dots. Yours are easy, because it's a simple time line. The last two years, Tate, you've had a lot happen. The accident with your family. I sympathize with you—nobody should lose what you've lost."

I still say nothing. I don't want to help Landry get to wherever he is leading.

"What do you think ever happened to Quentin James?" he asks.

"I don't know."

"You seem calm about that, Tate. Me, I'd be angry as hell. I don't think I'd have resigned myself to the fact that he got away. I'd be jumping up and down and phoning the police and phoning the media and I'd be out there looking for him. I'd be annoying the hell out of everyone—asking questions, putting pressure on anybody I could to make finding Quentin James a priority. But not you."

"Maybe he'll show up one day and justice can be served."

"If it hasn't been already. It's hard to go missing for that long, especially in this country. Then two months ago things change again. People die. They go missing. And what happens? You start drinking. You start showing up at the church drunk. You harass Father Julian. You hound him with questions. A week ago he files a restraining order against you and you just ignore it. Want to know what I think?"

"Not unless you're going to charge me with something. Otherwise, I'm leaving."

I stand up. The interrogation room sways a little. I reach down and grab the desk.

"Sit back down, Tate, before you pass out."

"Charge me or I'm getting a lawyer."

"You violated a restraining order," he says. "That means we can charge you."

"Then do it. You think I care?"

"You know, I don't really think you do. And that's the problem." Landry gets up. He picks up the folder and his coffee, and he walks to the door. He juggles them so he can manage the handle. "I can see I'm wasting my time here. But let me warn you, don't go back to the church. You go any-where near Father Julian and I'm going to have you arrested. There's going to be no more of this bullshit, right? No more of us feeling bad at the shit you've had to go through, no more of the people here feeling sorry for you and searching inside themselves to still care. You're falling apart, and any loyalty you built up here is rapidly dissipating. You want to stay out of jail? Then you need to take a good, long, hard look at yourself and figure out what's wrong. You get me?"

I get him.

"And for Christ's sake, Tate, go home and take a shower. You smell like a brewery."

CHAPTER TWENTY-SIX

I sit back down and wait for a few minutes, thinking about what he's said, trying to decide whether the police could help me if I told them the truth, or whether they would crucify me. When I get up, I have to hold on to the desk again while I get my balance. In that time I come to the conclusion that Landry doesn't have any idea what he's talking about—none of these people do—and that they should just leave me the hell alone.

From every cubicle and every corner of the fourth floor somebody is staring at me. I make my way to the elevator. Two years ago I was part of this atmosphere. I was one of the team, doing what I could to try to repair the broken bits of this city, to fight back the tides of surging violence in what was, and still is, a losing battle. Then things changed. The world changed. I handed in my resignation because I knew the department was going to ask for it. I didn't want to stay and didn't know what I was going to do once I left. The day

I walked out of here, I had people coming up to me and patting me on the shoulder or shaking my hand and telling me that whatever happened to the missing Quentin James was something he deserved. Nobody came right out and said they knew I had killed him, because nobody knew and, more importantly, they didn't want to know. They all had suspicions, and they were all on my side, but if any proof had come along they'd have locked me up without remorse.

Now these same people stare at me. Nobody approaches. They look me up and down; they study my wrinkled clothes and my unshaven face, and they wonder what shitty thing could happen in their lives to turn them into me. They're wondering just how far away I am from drinking myself to death, whether the booze will get me or whether I'll end up sucking back the barrel of a shotgun. Hell, we're all wondering the same damn thing. I feel like shouting out to them that I don't care anymore, and that I don't want their pity.

I reach the elevator and before the doors can close Landry slips through. He has a packet of cigarettes in his hand.

The elevator starts its descent. I can feel it in my stomach, as if we're falling at a hundred kilometers an hour. I hold on to the wall. Whatever conversation Landry is planning has to be short.

"I know you killed them," he says. "Alderman and James."

He turns toward me and lightly pushes me against the back of the elevator. He holds his palm on my chest and keeps his arm straight, as if holding back a bad smell.

"This Quentin James asshole, I don't care that you killed him. Hell, it's one thing we have in common, because sometimes, sometimes, I think I'm capable of doing the same thing. But that's the difference, right? I haven't had to cross the line because I haven't lost what you've lost. And who knows?

Maybe any one of us here would've done the same thing. This job, Tate, it's a mission—but now you're on the wrong side of it. See, we could forgive you with Quentin James. But not anymore. Whatever you're doing now, it's my job to find out. It's not because I hate you, you know that. It's because it's part of the mission. You would have understood that once. You might be willing to let your world fall apart, but think of your wife. Are you really that prepared to let her waste away—"

I push him away and take a swing at him. He ducks, pushes my arm in the direction it's going, and slams me into the adjoining mirrored wall. My face presses up against it and the view isn't good. There are red, razor-thin lines running through my eyes, tying my pain to the surface for all to see. My breath forms a misty patch on the mirror.

"You done?" he asks.

"I'm done."

The doors open and he lets me go. I walk out and he follows. He taps his cigarettes in his hands and walks off in a different direction. I do my best to hold a straight line, but it's impossible. I use the ground-floor toilet before heading outside.

The cold air makes me feel sick, just as almost everything seems to now. The chill stirs up fragments of the conversations with Landry. The bourbon floating in my system doesn't keep any of them at bay. I hail a taxi, and when I'm home I hover in the hallway in case I have to dash into the toilet to throw up. Then I stagger down to my bed. I crash on top of it and fall asleep for the rest of the morning and into the middle of the afternoon.

CHAPTER TWENTY-SEVEN

There's nothing like waking late in the day with a hangover. It's something every cop goes through at some point. Perhaps the difference between a good cop and a bad cop is the frequency. Though even that may not be true. Good cops often drink lots just to help them get through it. And I'm not a cop anymore anyway.

My bedroom is a mess. I can't remember the last time I made the bed, and I'm not even sure what the point of it would be. Socks, underwear, shirts, and more socks and underwear cover the floor. In the kitchen there are bourbon bottles and pizza boxes all over the counter. There are glasses everywhere and smells coming from cupboards I haven't opened in a long time. It's just like the Alderman house. I pour a glass of water and gulp down a pair of painkillers. I should probably eat, but never seem to have any appetite—though the number of pizza boxes suggests differently. I open the fridge on the off chance that might change, but when I see what's in there I reckon I'll probably never eat again. I make some coffee, then take a shower. It's been a while since I used a washing machine or an iron, and I don't see any point in breaking a tradition that seems to be working. I grab some clothes from the top of one of the hampers, figuring they'll smell less than the ones at the bottom, and definitely less than the ones I just slept half the day in. I dig my hands into the hamper and pull up the clothes from the bottom, recycling them to the top where they'll air out more.

The dining table has a stack of unopened bills. Bills for power, for the phone, for the mortgage, and for my wife. Most of Bridget's bills are covered by insurance, but not everything. There's even an outstanding bill from the florist. The rent on my office has expired—or, more accurately, I stopped paying it, and a message left on my machine says the lease is being terminated. I think after what happened the last night I was there they were quick to kick me out. The industrial cleaners came out to give me a quote, but I wasn't there to see it. They tried contacting me for a bit, but then gave up. I don't even know what in the hell happened. There's probably a bill in here to tell me.

I don't have the money to pay for another taxi—I'm not even sure how I paid to get home from the station. The small amount of cash left in my wallet already has a designated purpose. I don't have a lot of options.

It takes me over an hour to walk to the cemetery, by which time the day is fading and my hands and feet are almost numb. The church looks dark and gloomy. Mine is the only car parked out front. I'm violating the boundaries of the restraining order even approaching it, but that's just one more thing I couldn't really give a damn about.

Just as I get the car started, a van pulls up behind me, blocking me in so that I can't go anywhere. It's a similar view to the one I had this morning, except it isn't two policemen who wander over, but a reporter and a cameraman. I recognize Casey Horwell immediately. She pulls down on the front of her suit jacket to try to get her breasts looking a little better than they are, and it occurs to me that if she can't get a miracle like that in a church parking lot she's never going to get it.

"Just a few questions," she says, knocking on my window. Her voice is muffled behind the glass.

"No comment," I say back.

I don't know what to do. I can't drive anywhere, and I can't talk to these people, and I can't just sit here hiding, because that makes me look guilty or stupid or both. The only alternative is to open the door and climb out. Which I do. Then I think there was another alternative, but it involved pushing Casey Horwell over into the gravel and stealing the cameraman's camera. Instead, I try my best to put on a blank face and use it to look into the camera.

And I say nothing.

"You're back here at the cemetery where it all began," she says, and I wonder how she knew I would be here—a tip-off or a lucky guess. Maybe luck didn't have anything to do with it. Just logic.

I don't respond.

"Which is strange, because it's now on public record you have had a restraining order filed against you. You were picked up this morning violating it, and instead of being thrown in jail, the friends you so proudly have in the department let you out, and what's worse is they bring you right back here so you can get your car."

I let her carry on, not bothering to correct her mistake on

how I got here. The last thing she wants me to do is to say absolutely nothing and give her dead air. She starts to scramble, trying to keep up.

"Would you care to comment on the disappearance of Sidney Alderman?"

I don't answer her.

"Because my source tells me that you're involved with his disappearance."

Still nothing.

"What do you think Father Julian's involvement is in all of this? How long will you keep stalking him? And how far do you think you will take it?"

Her questions are suggestive, but I don't answer them. I'm sure that on camera I look tired and hungover and every bit the murderer she wants me to be. But there's no way I'm going to say anything to her.

Finally she gives up. "That's a wrap," she says, and drags her finger across her throat. The cameraman lowers his camera. The light switches off.

"Who's your source?" I ask.

"Didn't think you were talking," she says.

"Who?"

"You don't seriously think I'm going to tell you that?"

"You can't, can you, because there is no source," I say. "You keep pissing people off, Horwell, and it's going to catch up to you."

"And you'll take care of that? It's what you do, isn't it?"

I climb back into my car. She walks with the cameraman back to the van and I think I hear her saying there's enough time to do something with the piece tonight. Great. That means I'll be making the ten o'clock news. Just when my parents are likely to be watching.

The van pulls away and I wait until the lights disappear before driving off in the same direction, heading for the nursing home. I don't want to spend any more time with the dead. I'm aware of the irony, of course—sitting with Bridget is hardly like spending time with the living. But Bridget doesn't seem to mind the way I look or that my clothes are covered with stains that were once food related. She doesn't care that I no longer show up with flowers. She lets me hold her hand while I stare out the window at the same useless view she's been staring at for twenty-six months now. I don't talk to her. What would I say? That I spent the first third of the day drunk, the second third asleep, and I'm planning on repeating one of those thirds for the rest of it?

The darker it grows outside, the more our reflections start to solidify in the window. If the accident hadn't taken her away from me, would she still love me? Would the last four weeks of my life have turned her away? Or would she have saved me?

When I get outside I look up to see her sitting by the window, staring out. I give her a wave, and allow a flutter of hope that she might wave back. She doesn't even move.

I stop at a bottle store on the way back to the cemetery. The pull of both these places is so strong I'm unable to drive anywhere else. The store is small and cold and full of bright colors and shiny bottles that suggest drinking ought to be a lot more fun than it is. The guy behind the counter doesn't recognize me—I've been using different stores over the two months, which I guess means that part of me doesn't want to be found out as a drunk by strangers. I use the last of my cash, emptying out my wallet and dropping the loose change into my pocket.

I park by the tree line near the caretaker's grave. I open the fresh bottle of bourbon. I intend to let the remainder of the day slide by without me breaking any laws other than being too close to Father Julian. I wonder too, though without much hope, whether the cold might just come and take me in the night.

CHAPTER TWENTY-EIGHT

Around midnight I wake up covered in fog. It clings to me with cold, misty fingers. When I stand up I find that the fog is only at ground level, about waist high. I can't see my legs. Or my drink. I kneel back down and have to use my hands to find the bourbon. The bottle is on its side. I stand back up and check it out. Most of it has gone, seeped into the ground. Maybe the caretaker can enjoy it.

My head starts pounding and I reach into my pocket for painkillers. You learn a few tricks when the drinking turns from a habit into a way of life. I wash them down with more booze and for a moment consider taking all of them, given how long they'll take to kick in. Then I stagger to my car and scrape my credit card across the windshield to clear the ice—it's the only thing it's good for these days. I turn the heater on full and start the car, but keep the lights off and wait for things to warm up before rolling through the fog. I kill the engine at the edge of the parking lot and take another swig from the bottle. Things are obviously turning my way—otherwise all of the bourbon would have poured out while I was asleep.

The church is still dark and the living quarters around the back are out of view. I sit in the car with the heater on, sipping more bourbon to summon up the courage, all too aware there was once a day when I didn't need bourbon fuel to find my strength.

I need to talk to Father Julian. I can convince him to tell me the truth.

I get out of the car. I close the door quietly and walk slowly toward the church. My upper body looks like it is floating on top of the fog. The quarter moon is forming weak shadows, making pale reflections dance off the stained glass windows, making the images move, making them look like they are watching me. My toes are numb and painful, and my legs are getting wet from the fog. I'm almost around to the side of the church when I trip on what feels like rock. I go down hard, bracing my fall with my hands. There's a fierce stinging in my palms from the stones that have cut through my skin.

I roll onto my back and stare up at the sky, but all I can see is the fog that has wrapped around my body. It's like being inside a cloud. I reach up as if to punch a hole to look through, but it makes no impression.

I'm lying there, picking away at the stones in my palms, when the sound of the church door opening and then closing makes me go completely still. I stay flat and roll my head toward the sound, but can't see anything. I can feel the moisture from the ground cooling the hot blood on my hands. I have to sit up to see through the top layer of the fog.

A figure moves along the wall of the church, keeping in the shadows. I stay calm, knowing there's no way Father Julian can see me. Suddenly I feel something sparking away inside of me, something that has been numb since I killed Sidney Alderman. It's a mixture of hope and curiosity. The ground seems to sway as I stand back up and begin to follow Father Julian. He passes my car, keeping a wide berth, finding safety in the darkness of the church, and then moving into the trees that line the path to the road. Had I still been in the car I would never have known he was there. He's deliberately trying to hide from me.

Julian crosses the road to where his car is parked and starts to work the key into the lock. I turn back and race to my own car, then wait until I hear Julian's starting before I start mine. Out on the road I see that he is about three blocks ahead of me. The fog that had attached itself to the cemetery and church has just as strong a grip out here, only the streetlights make it look thinner. Julian turns left. I turn my lights on and begin to follow him. I can just make out his taillights through the fog about two blocks away.

The occasional car comes toward us. Julian drives around the cemetery, then turns toward town. He starts to drive faster and I do the same, knowing if he gets too far ahead I'll lose him as soon as another set of taillights appears. He races through the intersection and I follow suit. I close the distance until there's only half a block between us. He isn't making any evasive maneuvers, but that doesn't mean he hasn't figured out I'm following him. And it's quite clear that if he parked out on the road and snuck past my car he didn't want me to know where he was going. I think about where he might be going that he doesn't want me to know about. Is he meeting somebody? Is he going to meet the person who killed those girls? To counsel him? To try to make him confess?

The lights ahead turn orange. Julian makes it through. I put my foot down, gaining on him a little more quickly than I would have liked, though I'm pretty sure he's not going to . . .

Only I don't make it all the way through the intersection.

The car emerges out of the fog like a train. I turn my head toward it, toward the twin headlights barreling down on me. I lift my hands up to cover my face as the car slams into me, the shrieking sound of metal loud enough to make my ears bleed.

For a few moments there is nothing but madness as I scramble to gain control of the car, but it's impossible. There is another explosion of sound as I come to a stop. The world slowly darkens around me. It darkens, it disappears, and then there is nothing.

CHAPTER TWENTY-NINE

Alcohol and burning metal. That's all I can smell. The windshield has shattered into thousands of tiny diamonds. The engine has stalled, the front of the car has folded around the lamppost. The hood has twisted and bent up into a V, and from beneath it plumes of steam are rising and mixing into the fog. More steam is coming through the air vents into the car. The stereo is going. The heater is going. There is a high-pitched ringing in my ears. The lamppost is on an angle. Its fluorescent light has busted and sparks are slowly raining down on the car. I can taste blood and bourbon. There is a pain in my leg. My chest. There is pain everywhere. I tilt my head back and there is pain there too. I close my eyes and wait for it all to disappear. It doesn't.

My neck hurts when I move, but I manage to unclip my seat belt. The door is buckled and there is safety glass all over my lap. There are chips of paint on my hands, cracks in the dashboard, and sharp pieces of plastic sticking up. One of my fingernails has lifted up and bent all the way back, a few threads of skin the only things stopping it from touching my knuckle. Before thinking too much about it, I wipe it backward across my leg so that the strands of skin stretch and break and the nail sticks to my pants and stays there. The door won't budge, so I try to climb over the passenger seat. It is then that the floodgates open and pain wracks my body, one knee jamming into the hand brake, the other into the mostly empty bottle of bourbon that has somehow jumped from the car floor and onto the seat in the crash. It is all I can do not to cry out as I push open the door and stumble out to the road. My feet skid on stones and glass and I fall onto my knees.

The world is caught in the grips of an earthquake, but I'm the only one feeling it. I get up and balance myself by holding on to the side of the car. There is a shooting pain rolling up and down my leg. The glow from the traffic lights changes color as one set goes red and the other green. Glass grates beneath my feet as I move, pieces of it cutting into the soles of my shoes. There is blood on my shirt and pants and more of it flowing down the side of my face. I reach up and pull away fingers covered in blood. Only one of my eyes is focusing.

I look back into the car at the empty bottle of bourbon, and I understand instantly that its contents have brought me to this. I lean in and grab it. I adjust it in my grip, wrapping my fingers tight around the neck, and then I pitch it into the distance. It disappears into the night.

I look up at Jesus who is looking down at me from above the hovering fog. His eyes are open and his mouth is in a tight smile. He is looking into me, but he is not admonishing me. He is too busy. His hands are wrapped around a bottle of McClintoch spring water. The bourbon bottle crashes and the sound brings the world into focus. It tones down the ringing in my ears and allows a flood of other sounds to pour in. I look away from the billboard and wipe smoke and blood from my eyes and I move away from my car to draw in clean air.

The abyss gets deeper.

The path Father Julian told me I'm heading down takes an even worse turn.

A woman is screaming. It's a high-pitched note that threatens to break the windshields of other cars pulling over. Ahead of me a four-door sedan has spun around in the intersection. The front of it is completely caved in. Clouds of steam surround it so I can't tell if anybody is inside. The screaming is coming from a woman who has pulled over and has probably thought her entire life that she would take action in a moment like this and is quickly finding she can't. She has opened her car door, stood up, but hasn't gone any further. Another car is starting to pull over.

I reach the wreck first. I push my arms into the steam and touch metal, pushing myself close enough to see inside. There's a woman in there, slumped over the wheel. She looks young. Like me, she had no air bag. I try opening the driver's door, but it's jammed. The woman's eyes are open; they are rolled into the back of her head and her jaw is pushed forward, either broken or locked, and there is a steady stream of blood coming from the left side of her mouth. I pat down my pockets and find my cell phone, but can only stare at it in my hand.

"Out of the way, buddy," a man says, reaching past me. He tries the driver's door too, then moves around to the passenger side. He opens it. It screeches loudly. He looks over at me. "You gonna use that thing?"

I look down at my cell phone. It has survived the crash, but still I can only stare at it.

I have just become the very thing I hate the most. I have become Quentin James: full-time drunk and part-time killer.

CHAPTER THIRTY

They want to take me to the police station, but my injuries re-
quire otherwise. I sit in the back of an ambulance and nobody
talks to me. A paramedic tends to my wounds, but he doesn't
really seem to be putting any energy into it. Like everybody
else he'll be wishing I was the one who was dead.

After a while a policeman takes a statement from me. He
doesn't know who I am. Doesn't know my history. I tell him
what happened. He tells me that witness reports indicate that
I ran a red light. That it had been red for at least two seconds
before I hit the intersection. He asks if I've been drinking.
I tell him I have because he's going to test me anyway. He
pulls out a Breathalyzer and makes me say my name into it, as
though he's giving me an interview and the Breathalyzer is a
microphone. He looks at the numbers then writes them down.
I know what they're telling him. I'm way over the limit even
though I feel sober. Killing a woman will do that to you.

At the hospital I'm put up in an emergency ward with dozens of other people. My bed has a curtain drawn around it. The cut in my leg is stitched up and bandaged and I'm told it will leave a scar. There are other cuts over my body too, other scars. The finger with the missing fingernail is cleaned, wrapped in gauze, and bandaged. There is a cut at the top of my forehead, which gets stitched. Blood is cleaned off my face. Safety glass is plucked out of my knees. My scraped-up palms with tiny pieces of shingle in them are cleaned.

When the nurse is all done fixing me up she pushes past the curtain and Landry pushes his way in. He is expressionless, as if he can't be bothered being angry with me anymore. It's worse.

"Of all the people to be drunk and driving," he says.

"I don't need the lecture."

"What were you thinking, Tate?"

I shake my head. Who the hell knows? "I don't know."

"I tried to warn you."

"I know."

"Don't you have anything else you can say?"

"I . . . I don't know. I wish I did." I feel so numb. So numb.

"The girl's in a coma," he says. "It's serious. Four broken ribs, a punctured lung, and her jaw was dislocated. You're lucky she's not dead."

I'm lucky.

My heart starts to flutter. "I . . . I thought she was dead."

She's lucky.

Luck.

"I know," he says. "Only nobody felt like telling you."

I'm too angry at myself to direct any of it toward him. "She's going to be okay?"

"You better pray, Tate. You better pray."

Nobody comes to see how I'm doing over the next hour,

and nobody has made the effort to feed me any painkillers, though the throbbing in my head and from all the wounds is becoming unbearable. Nobody cares about that. They all care about the woman I hurt, and so they should. I want to go and see her. I want to speak to her family and tell them how sorry I am. I can't, of course. I'd simply be making myself the punching bag for their anger.

Eventually two officers come to get me. They don't cuff me. With a bare minimum of words and gestures they escort me out to a police car. I sit in the back for the short drive to the station. They don't put me in an interrogation room. Instead they escort me to the drunk tank full of other people who've made similar fuckups tonight.

I find a small piece of real estate I can call my own, a piece of bench between one guy already passed out and another guy on his way to passing out. I take my jacket off and ball it up so I can lie down and rest it behind my head. I've never been in jail before—not one I couldn't freely leave at any time—and even this is only a waiting room for the real thing. The smell is overpowering and the moans coming from the other drunks irritating. The floor is covered in piss and the toilet looks about as bad as toilets can possibly get. The cream cinder-block walls spread a chill into the room.

I stay awake all night. Occasionally our numbers go up, and in the end we all make it through to the morning. As they lead me from the cell I think about Bridget and Emily and what they would think of me now. I remember having the same thought yesterday.

I'm led through to the same interrogation room I sat in yesterday. Everybody looks at me on the way. Yesterday it was with pity. Today it's contempt.

CHAPTER THIRTY-ONE

"Driving under the influence. Reckless driving. You're in some real trouble," Landry says. He's wearing the same clothes as last night. They're all wrinkled up, which means he probably slept in them. He looks even more tired than the last time I saw him.

"How's the girl?"

"Stable."

Stable. Better than I ever thought she'd be. But nowhere near what I want her to be. "Is she going to make it?"

"Maybe you should have been concerned with other people's safety before getting behind the wheel drunk."

"Is she going to make it?" I ask again.

"I don't know. Probably."

"Probably? Don't you care?"

"I care, you son of a bitch." Landry bangs his fist down on

the table. "I'm the only one in this room who does, and what you did last night proves that."

I look away. I have no answer to that.

"What in the hell were you doing?" he asks.

"Nothing."

"You're doing nothing at that time in the morning? Come on, Tate. You were at the church again."

"No, I wasn't."

"In fact you were. I saw you there. Lots of people did. See, it was on TV. That reporter of yours showed it. She did a great job of it, showing you right outside the church breaking your restraining order."

"I was getting my car."

"You were breaking the law."

"Come on, Landry, you could probably see me climbing into the damn thing. And I left straightaway."

"Then what? You go back a few hours later and decide to watch Father Julian? What's the big plan here, Tate? Are you that desperate to kill yourself?"

I wonder if Father Julian heard the crash. I wonder if he looked in his rearview mirror and decided he had more important things to take care of. "What's going to happen now?"

"Two things. We're going to talk to Father Julian. We're going to ask him if you were there last night, and if he says you were, you know what happens: we're going to take his word for it. We're going to ask him once and let him think about it, and if he says yes we're not even going to ask him if he's sure about it. You get my point?"

"I get it."

"But first you're going to be charged with DUI. You'll be escorted down to court later this morning. I'm going to do you a favor and let you wait here rather than back down in the cells. But it's the last favor I'm ever going to do for you."

He leaves me alone. I rest my head in my arms and manage to get two hours of sleep before the same two guys who brought me upstairs take me out to a patrol car and drive me to the courts. The day is wet and cold and gray. The drive is depressing. We make no conversation and the driver has the window cranked down halfway so the cold air keeps blasting me. I watch the world go by, feeling so disconnected from it I'm not sure if I'll ever make it back.

I'm kept in the holding cells with a whole bunch of people whose futures are about to be determined by the same people about to determine mine. My headache hurts and so do the wounds. I'm given a court-appointed lawyer who doesn't introduce himself so I don't get his name, and he talks low and quickly to me in the two minutes we have before my arraignment.

In court I stand in the dock with my head down and listen to the charges. I know how it all works. This is the same thing that happened to Quentin James. The judge sets bail and says that if it can't be paid they will hold me. I can't pay the bail. I'm taken back to the cells, the plan being that sometime in the middle of the afternoon I'll be transferred to prison. I need a drink.

The holding cells are full of people who have done shitty things too, some worse than me, others not as bad, but we're the dregs of society. We all sit on benches and keep ourselves to ourselves. The entire place smells like urine. I don't know how much time passes before one of the court security officers opens up the holding cell and tells me to follow him—all I know is that the next step in the chain isn't going to be any prettier than this one.

"Your bail's been made," he says, surprising me.

"Made? Who by?"

"Your lawyer."

I slow down my walking and almost come to a stop. He glances back at me and tells me to keep up.

"I don't even know my lawyer," I tell him.

"Yeah, well, it's not the same guy," the officer says, shrugging. "You got a new lawyer now. Means you might have a chance at a real legal defense."

We go through a few doors and I'm asked to sign some forms. Before I can, a guy in an expensive-looking suit comes to greet me. The suit is so sharp it's hard to believe he'd dare sit down for fear of it wrinkling, but it isn't as sharp as his smile.

"Theo," he says, stepping forward and pumping my hand so vigorously it's suspicious. "Glad to finally meet you."

"Glad?"

"Well, of course the circumstances are awkward," he says. "Not dire, but with your past they shouldn't be anything we can't handle."

He introduces himself as Donovan Green. He stands over my shoulder as I sign the series of forms in front of me. The officers hand me over my wallet and my watch and my phone. The phone is dead.

Green walks me outside toward a black BMW in the far corner of the parking lot between a high concrete wall and a dark blue SUV with tinted windows and mud splashed up the sides. The day is cool and the breeze makes the exposed grazes on my body sting. I pick up the pace a little to get to his car faster.

"Who hired you?" I ask.

He doesn't slow down. Just keeps on walking like a man on a mission. "You mean you don't know?"

"I have my suspicions," I answer, but truthfully I don't have any idea.

"You still have friends in the department," he says, and the line is starting to sound all too familiar.

"I wouldn't have thought so," I tell him. "Listen, thanks for bailing me out, and I appreciate all you're going to do for me, but all I want right now is to go to the hospital."

He doesn't pause. Just keeps walking. "The hospital? Injuries hurting, huh?"

"I want to see the woman I hurt."

He slows down. He comes to a stop and turns toward me, his back now to his car. "I don't understand," he says. "You want to see her?"

"It's not that hard to understand," I tell him. "I want to see how she's doing. I'm the reason she's in there."

"I'm well aware of why she's in there," he says, a little too harshly. "Look, Theo, it's just not a good idea."

"I need to see her."

He shrugs, like he no longer cares, but he also keeps staring at me. Hard. "Okay," he says. "It's your idea. I don't agree with it, but let's go."

We reach his car. It turns out it's the dark SUV and not the BMW. He puts his briefcase down while he digs into his pocket for his keys. He checks one, then the other, and I know how the routine goes when you can never find them.

"Must be in the briefcase," he says, and he pops it open. "Yep, here we go." He unarms the car and the doors pop open. "Hop on in," he says.

I climb inside. The interior is comfortable and warm. A small fantasy plays out in my mind, and in this fantasy I climb into the backseat and lie down and get a few hours of sleep. Green plays around with his briefcase before opening his door. Then he leans in. He's pointing something at me.

"Whoa, wait a . . ."

But it's all I can say before he pulls the trigger. My body jerks back, my head cracks into the window beside me, and the world goes black.

CHAPTER THIRTY-TWO

The blackout lasts only a moment. I come to and the pain in my head from the impact helps to numb the pain flowing through my body, but only for a few more seconds. The two catch up and the electricity raging along my spine from the Taser gun takes over. Tiny dots have flown out from the Taser, they're confetti-like and all have serial numbers on them; they're part of the design so the police can track where they've been fired and by whom. Of course that's no good if the Taser has been stolen or bought illegally. Green says something, but I can't hear him. Two barbs are buried into my chest, delivering hundreds or even thousands of volts. He turns the gun off, but there's no relief. He rips the barbs out. The pain drops, but I still can't move. Blood drips from the barbs onto my shirt. He wraps the cords around the unit and drops it into his briefcase. Then he moves into the seat behind me, pops my seat so I'm leaning back, and drags me into the back of the SUV. It's like my fantasy is going to come true after all.

He takes some plastic ziplock ties from his briefcase, rolls me onto my front, and a moment later I can hear the little notches clicking into place. I can't fight him. All I can do is stare ahead in whichever direction he leaves me facing. He moves back to the front. The engine starts, and we roll forward. I try to sit up, but can't, though some feeling is begging to return. The tinted windows mean nobody can see in. I can't speak and don't know what I'd ask if I could.

I can hear other cars. I can hear people talking on the street. The hustle and bustle of city life. But my lawyer doesn't say a word. He's still on that mission he looked like he was on when striding across the parking lot. I can smell upholstery and sweat. I can taste blood. My arms and legs are tingling. I can tighten my fists and wiggle my toes. The cramp in my muscles starts to relax. I try to struggle against the plastic ties, but it's no good. They dig into my wrists and ankles.

"Where are we going?" I ask, the words coming out smoother than I would have thought.

"You tried to kill my daughter."

So my words may be smooth, but his words don't make sense. "What?"

"My daughter, you asshole. You ran into her last night and now she might die."

I don't answer him. I think about Quentin James, I think about how what I did last night was just like what he did to my family. I think about how the transition from Theodore Tate's life into Quentin James's is complete. "I'm sorry," I tell him.

"Shut up," he says.

"Where are you taking me?" I ask.

"I said shut up!" he shouts, and he pulls over and reaches toward me.

Christ, there's a needle in his hand.

"You struggle and it's only going to be worse," he says, and he's right because I do struggle and it does get worse. The needle breaks off in my arm before he can push any of the fluid into me. "Bastard," he yells, then he starts clubbing me in the head with something, I don't know what, and everything goes dim as the darkness rushes back.

CHAPTER THIRTY-THREE

I have no idea where we are. In the woods, somewhere. He must have carried me here from the SUV. Or more likely dragged me, since the backs of my shoes have a buildup of mud and leaves on them. The surroundings remind me of where I was two years ago when I was the one holding the gun and not the one under the barrel of it. I am lying on my side, the wet dirt cold against my body. There are hundreds of trees and ferns and rocks, and there is a light rain. My cell phone is in a dozen pieces on the ground ahead of me.

The world comes into sharper focus and that's a problem, because in the center of my view is my lawyer. He's no longer wearing the suit. The gun looks like a nine millimeter. I figure it's loaded to the max and this guy looks like he's in the mood to prove it.

He notices me staring at the gun, then he turns it in his hand and looks at the side of it, as if he's seeing it for the first time.

"It's amazing what you can get for a few thousand dollars when you're motivated enough," he says, and I can tell from the look of him and where we are that he is, without a doubt, extremely motivated. "All you need is to be prepared to spend a few hours in the worst part of town. Guns, Tasers—there's no limit when you've got the cash. And the desire."

My hands are still bound behind me. I tuck my legs beneath me and manage to get onto my knees. The Taser pain is gone, but not the pain from the beating the guy gave me to knock me out. I have to blink heavily every few seconds just to keep things from going fuzzy, and it's a struggle to stay balanced. The broken needle is still in my arm. Blood is running down my face. It's getting dark. Must be around four o'clock. Maybe five. Or maybe it's not getting dark at all, and it's just my brain shutting down.

"What do you want?" I ask, though I already know.

"What do you think I want?"

I think about what he said in the car. About his daughter. "It was an accident. I'm sorry."

"Ah huh. You think being sorry negates all of this?" he asks. "You think if she dies your sorries will help me sleep at night?"

I close my eyes while he talks to me. His words are very similar to the ones I said to Quentin James, only for him I didn't use a *What if* because Emily was already dead. I wasn't waiting on more information on which to base my decision. Nothing was going to change. One difference is I didn't bind Quentin with plastic ties. I held him at gunpoint and made him walk. I made him carry a shovel because I wanted him to know how it felt to be a victim. I wanted him to know that the feeling he had, that he was about to die, was the same feeling I'd had every day since the accident and what I would feel every day for the rest of my life. Hell, for me it was worse.

I already had died, and it was because of him. Father Julian used to come around to my house and we'd talk about that feeling, and I knew the only way to feel any better was to make the man who had done this pay. I couldn't tell Julian that, but I suspect he knew. That day in the woods Quentin James prayed for a God who wouldn't show up. I made James dig a grave, and all along he cried and told me it was an accident, he told me he wished he could change time, he told me it was Quentin James the drinker who had killed my daughter and not the man holding the shovel. The man holding the shovel was going to get better. He was going to seek help. He would go to jail and he would live with what he had done, and he would get better.

I'm a different person when it happens, he'd told me. *I'm no longer me.*

But I didn't care; my wife was no longer what she had been, and my daughter was no longer alive, and therefore I was no longer me too. I watched as the sweat began to expand in circles from his armpits over his shirt, even though it was cold out. Dirt was sticking to his face, to his hands; he rolled up his sleeves and dirt began to stick there too. I told him it was too late, that it didn't matter what he said now, that being sorry wasn't going to change the past and wouldn't prevent the future. He cried. He begged for his life. He tried to make me change my mind, but it didn't matter. I was never going to let his justifications and sick excuses stop what was coming, and I'd made that decision before heading out there. I had to. I had to. It was the only way to go through with it, and the only way to save others from him.

Now my perspective is changing. Maybe the same damn thing that got me here is the same thing that happened to him. I never looked into his history. Never learned whether his family had died, never learned what drove him to drinking. There was way too much anger for that. He stood in the grave and he cried as I leveled the pistol at him. He told me he was sorry, and I told him that was enough, that I didn't want to hear any more, that it was time to take responsibility. Through all his fear there must have been some hope I was going to let him go. I was hoping he would accept it, that he would shut up and make peace with his maker and just accept it. But he didn't.

Quentin James was still begging for his life when I shot him in the head. It didn't feel as good as I thought it would. I imagine it didn't hurt as much as he feared. One moment he was staring down the barrel of my gun, the next moment he was slumped in the dirt.

I shuffled his body so it was nice and snug in the grave he'd dug, and then I buried him. I walked away without giving him a prayer or spitting on his grave. There was just a smooth transition between shoveling dirt and then turning away. A smooth transition between going from father to killer. I carried the shovel back to my car, drove away, and have never been back.

Unless I'm back here now. These could be the same woods.

"It was an accident," I repeat.

My lawyer is nodding. "You had a daughter," he says. "It's all over the news now. How the hell can you, of all people, drive while completely tanked?"

It's a good question. One with a complicated answer. One that involves me accidentally killing a man who dug up my dead daughter. One that involves a priest who once tried to help me, and is now hiding the truth from me. I don't tell him any of this. Instead I say, "There's no shovel."

"What?"

"There's no shovel," I repeat. "You should have made me bring a shovel."

"What for?"

"What do you think?"

He nods. He's figured it out. "You think I care whether I bury you or not? You think I care whether you're ever found?"

"You should," I tell him.

"Yeah? Why's that?"

"Because you're going to throw away your life," I tell him. "I deserve what I get, but you don't deserve to be punished."

He takes a small step back. I'd rather he come forward. I'd rather he was pointing the gun at my head. Rather he did us both a favor and got this over with.

"What?" he asks.

I look from the barrel and into his eyes. "Just pull the trigger."

"I'm going to."

"Yeah, you're saying it, but you're still talking about it," I say. "Look, for what it's worth, I'm sorry. But if you're waiting for me to beg for my life, I'm not going to. You might want that, but it'll only make it harder. It'll haunt you. The fact is you'll shoot me and you'll discover it wasn't satisfying. You'll feel nothing. At least that's how it was for me."

"What do you mean?"

"Could be different for you," I say. "Your daughter's alive, right? Rather than being with her, you decided to come out here and be with me. You've got your priorities wrong. You could have brought me out here anytime." There's a wedding ring on his finger. "Your wife and daughter, they need you now."

"Shut up," he says. "Don't tell me what my family needs."

"What's her name?"

"What?"

"Your daughter," I say. "Her name. I don't know anything about her."

"You don't deserve to know it."

"Maybe you're right," I tell him. "But I feel if you're going to kill me I think I ought to know her name."

"Fuck you."

"Just pull the trigger."

"What's your hurry?" he asks.

"I don't know," I say, and it's true. "I really don't know."

"You don't think I'm going to do it, do you?"

"What do you want me to say?" I ask. "You want me to say something that will sway your decision? How about this? Your daughter could have died, but she didn't. She's fighting for her life and she's still with you. Does that make a difference? Of course it does. You'd have to be stupid not to recognize it. Do I deserve to die for that? That's up to you. Me, I'm at that stage where it doesn't matter either way."

He says nothing for a few seconds. None of the anger has disappeared from his features. In fact he looks even angrier. "How dare you."

"What?"

"How dare you kneel there and act like a Goddamn martyr," he says. "How dare you act like you're the one who's the victim, like you're the one having a bad day. Don't you get it? Don't you get what you almost did?"

"Of course I do."

"Yeah, you're good at taking responsibility, right? But all you're doing is trying to mess up my reasons for bringing you out here. Why don't you just shut up, huh? Shut up and let me decide for myself what I'm going to do," he says. "This is my life we're talking about. My sixteen-year-old daughter you tried to kill. How dare you kneel there acting as if you don't care whether you live or die. Show some respect and at least beg for your life, right? Make me feel something. Make me want to hate you even more, make me want to hate what I'm doing."

"I'm sorry about your daughter," I tell him. "I really am."

"Emma," he says. "Her name is Emma."

"My daughter's name is Emily," I say, as if she's still alive. At first I'm not sure why I say it, but then it comes to me. I want to live. I don't want to die out here. I want the chance to make things right.

"Emma. Emily," he says. He doesn't expand on the thought, but he's really thinking about it. Thinking hard. Maybe drawing some parallels between the two names.

"I still have a wife," I add. "Her name is Bridget."

"I know. And I'm sorry about what happened to your daughter," he says, "but that makes what you did even worse. Don't you get that? It doesn't make me sympathize with you, it only makes me angrier."

"And so it should."

"There you go again," he says. "You're trying to diminish the moment."

"Are you really a lawyer?"

"What?"

"You talk like one," I tell him.

"I'm a divorce lawyer."

"And when you came to the prison, you gave them your name, right?"

"I had to so I could bail you out. But they don't know I'm the one who brought you out here."

"You don't think they'll figure it out? You don't think they'll work out that the lawyer, who they'll soon realize is the father of the girl I hurt, was the last person to have seen me? It'll take them all of about thirty seconds to figure out. And you went into town and bought yourself some black-market weapons. That shows premeditation. That's bad for you."

He thinks about it for a few seconds. "Fuck," he says.

"See, you're being driven by emotion, not logic. You should have known that. It's a pretty simple equation, and you looked right over it. Don't do this. Don't throw away your life."

He takes a step forward. He keeps the gun pointing at my face. But the cold and the nerves are too much for him to control, and his hand is shaking badly. His breathing is ragged. He's fighting with the same decision I had back when the roles were reversed, only it was a decision I didn't fight with. I was comfortable holding a gun. I just aimed and fired.

"I'm going to do it," he says.

"You've got no argument from me."

"Shut up, damn it. Let me think."

I stay on my knees and I force myself to keep looking at the gun, and it terrifies me. His face is taut with pain, his mouth forms a grimace as he runs through the scenarios in his mind. One, he walks away with blood on his hands; the other, he walks away feeling a little unsatisfied. I decide against giving him any more advice. He's a big boy. He can make up his own mind. As I wait, the sounds of the forest fill in the silence. Birds, mostly. The breeze shifting branches around. A falling pinecone cracks against a fallen branch somewhere.

It takes him a minute. It's painful to watch. Painful to stare at the gun as it rises and falls slightly as his arm shakes. The entire time I keep thinking he's going to pull the trigger, or accidently pull it. In the end he takes a step back. Then another. But he keeps the gun pointing at me.

"If she dies," he says, "we're coming back out here."

He backs away, turns, and then I am alone.

CHAPTER THIRTY-FOUR

I lie on my side and bring my knees to my chest and squirm around to bring my hands up under my feet. It doesn't work. I roll around, but the plastic ties are securing my wrists, and there isn't enough room to stretch my arms all the way around. I get back to my knees and sit down, stretch my legs out, and start rubbing them back and forth across a mossy rock. The moss scrapes away and exposes an edge for me to saw against. It takes only about a minute for the binding to snap through. I do the same with my wrists, then pull the syringe needle out of my arm. I toss it on the ground next to my busted cell phone.

I head in the same direction as the lawyer. My clothes are damp and cold. Donovan Green, if that's his real name, may not have finished me off with a bullet, but that doesn't mean I'm getting out of here alive. Unless I can rub some bandages together and make a fire, I'm going to freeze to death out here. The trees and ferns brush at me, scraping my hands and snagging my clothes. Small grazes lead to cuts and then to bleeding. My head is still throbbing, and my chest is sore from the Taser barbs. My hand hurts the most: the finger with the ripped-off nail feels as if it's on fire.

The lawyer has left a path, and for a moment I wonder if Father Julian would suggest this is the path I created two years ago, the path in which there can be no redemption. I keep my eyes on the ground and follow the twin lines that have been cut into the dirt by my dragging feet. I figure he would have parked nearby, not wanting to drag me far in these conditions, and a moment later I hear a car pass by. I pick up the pace and break through some trees and onto a road. Red taillights are disappearing in the distance.

The mud has had a snowball effect on my shoes, and I kick and scrape them against a tree to break it off. With no other options, I dig my hands into my pockets and start walking. No other cars come past as I walk in the same direction as the one I saw. I still don't even know where I am. My teeth are chattering and every minute or so my body gives an involuntary spasm that lasts a couple of seconds. Quentin James would have had a similar walk if I'd have let him, except his would have been in nicer conditions. I brought him out on a sunny day, a warm day, as sure as hell a nicer day to die than today.

I reach an intersection and a couple of cars go by. I wipe my sleeve at my face to clean away some blood. I start to have an idea where I am. Nobody pulls over to offer me a lift, and I don't put my bite-scarred thumb out to ask for one.

The road heads toward the city and, eventually, toward home. It'd be a fifteen-minute trip if I was driving. Walking, it's going to take me a few hours. At least. If I was driving I'd be doing eighty kilometers an hour out here. I figure at the very least I deserve to be walking. At the very least I'm lucky to be alive. And there's that word again. *Luck*.

The day becomes evening and the evening is dark. The rain begins again. It gets heavy for a while and washes the mud and dirt down my body before lessening to a drizzle. My joints grow increasingly numb. My feet feel like slabs of ice. The walk is a sobering end to a day and to a way of life.

It's almost midnight when I get home. I don't have my keys and I hadn't even thought about them until now. They're in my car, and my car is in an impound lot somewhere, or maybe a wrecker's yard. I sit down on the front step and lean against the door. I'm exhausted. The soles of my shoes have small stones and slivers of glass buried into the tread. I feel like I could fall asleep here. I feel like I want to cry.

I rest for a few minutes before getting up and walking through to the backyard. I grab a rag and a roll of duct tape from the garden shed, wrap the rag around a small rock, put the tape across the window to muffle the sound, then smash the glass.

While the shower warms up I find a bottle of bourbon and sit down in the living room. I wonder what Quentin James would have done had I let him walk home. Would he have taken a drink? I figure he'd have needed one. Would he have kept on drinking until one day he killed again? I carry the bottle into the kitchen. I grab a glass. I fill it to the brim and then I pour the rest of the bottle down the sink. I scour the house for more bottles. There are plenty of them, a few with just enough in them to make me feel warm if I allowed it. I tip them all down the sink, and then I drop every single empty in a recycling bin outside. I head back inside and stare at the one glass I filled.

I strip out of my clothes and throw them into the washing machine. The shower is still going, steam flooding into the hallway. I walk around the house, picking up other clothes I've worn over the last few months and I stuff as much as I can into the machine. I set it going. I stand in the kitchen with only a towel wrapped around me. I stare at the drink. I put my hand on the glass. It's cold and smooth. Just one more drink and then I'm done. That's all.

I have it halfway up to my lips when knocking comes from the front door. I set the glass back onto the counter. I head down the hallway. A red and blue light is arcing through the windows and lighting the walls. There are two possibilities. One I can live with. It means one of my neighbors made a call because they heard somebody breaking in. The second one means Emma, the sixteen-year-old girl I hurt last night, has died. Maybe I poured away all that bourbon too soon. I have the urge to run back to the kitchen and grab that last drink.

Instead I head to the door. I'm as nervous as hell when I open it. It's Landry.

"You're going to have to come with us, Tate," he says, ruling out possibility number one.

"She's dead, isn't she," I say.

"What? No, no, it's not about that."

"Then what?"

"Just get dressed, Tate," he says. "We'll talk about it at the station."

"Talk about what?"

"I said we'll talk about it at the station."

"I'm not going anywhere with you unless you tell me what this is about," I tell him.

He sighs. "It's about Father Julian."

"What? Look, this is bullshit. I haven't been near him all day."

"You're coming with us."

"It's true. I've been in jail half the damn day, and I spent the other half with my lawyer. He can vouch for me."

"Tate, it's simple. Don't stand there and pretend you don't know."

"Don't know what?"

He sighs again, this time much deeper, and this time he slowly shakes his head to stress just how tiring he is finding me. "Come on, do you really want to play this game?"

"Humor me."

"Okay, fine. We went to speak to Father Julian this afternoon. You remember Father Julian, right? He's the man you've been stalking? Well, we were going to ask him if you were there last night on account of the fact we're pretty sure you were. And I'm sure he would have said yes."

"Would have?"

"See, that's the problem, Tate. He's dead. Somebody murdered him last night. And right now my money is on that somebody being you."

CHAPTER THIRTY-FIVE

I try to figure out what he's saying. I don't even know when last night was. Technically it's just been; it's after midnight now. But he doesn't mean today. He means yesterday. Technically. He's talking about twenty-four hours ago. A lot has happened since then. It feels like two days have passed since I followed Father Julian from the church, but it's only been one. Hell, it's probably only a few minutes either side of that.

"What?"

"You're going to need to come with us, Tate," he says.

I look down at my towel. I look at my dirty feet and the lines of blood on my chest. "I didn't have anything to do with it."

Landry looks me up and down. "No?"

"No."

"You're saying even though he had a restraining order against you, even though you were picked up at the church the morning of the day he died breaking that order, even though you were caught on film there yesterday evening, and even though you crashed your car, drunk, a few minutes from the church around the same time Father Julian died, that you had nothing to do with it?"

I don't bother answering. It's hard to defend yourself when you're wearing only a towel. But I figure Landry or one of his buddies must have been dropping by the house on and off all day since I was signed out of the courthouse in the afternoon. That means Julian wasn't found till around then at the earliest. Any earlier and I'd never have been released.

"Put on some clothes, Tate. You're coming with us."

"I'm calling my lawyer." I think of Donovan Green, but can't really imagine him being happy to take my call.

"Get him to meet you at the station."

I have nothing to put on except a pair of shorts and a T-shirt that have been building up dust in the corner of the bedroom. Everything else is in the washing machine. I throw on a jacket and my running sneakers. We step outside. It's cold. I can see faces in neighboring windows.

I'm put in the back of the car and driven away, and this time I'm handcuffed. Landry stays behind with some others to go through my house. At the station I'm reacquainted with the interrogation room. They lock me in, and the call I get to make to my lawyer isn't brought up again, but that's okay. I haven't been having a good day with lawyers. I rest my head on my arms and close my eyes, knowing I'm going to be waiting here a while.

Landry comes in an hour later, and he has Schroder with him. That means one of them is going to be my friend while the other puts on the pressure. I already know who will play which role, and I figure they know I'll know that too. They set up a video camera and point it so it covers all three of us. I can hear it recording. Schroder sits opposite me and Landry stands. It's pretty cold in here, especially as I'm dressed for summer.

Schroder sits a folder on the table and opens the cover. There are photographs of Father Julian in there. His head has been beaten in, blood all over his face and neck. His clothing is disheveled. One eye is open, but the other is closed because of the way his face is pressing against the floor. He doesn't look like he died easy. Not like I could have earlier on today out in the woods. His open eye has a tiny pool of blood in it. Schroder starts to lay the photos out on the table. There is a close-up of Father Julian's mouth. His lips are open; his teeth are exposed and bloody. Behind them is a deep darkness.

"Some ground rules first," Schroder says. "You know how this goes, you've been on this side of the table, so we're not going to try and play you," he says, trying to play me. "We're just gonna lay out the facts and you're gonna get to state your case. That sound good to you?"

I shrug. "Sure. What about my lawyer? You think it'll sound good to him?"

"You can have a lawyer if you want one. We're not going to feed you that bullshit line about only guilty men wanting them," he says, which is his way of feeding me the line anyway.

"Let's just get this over with then."

He slides a piece of paper over to me. "Just sign this," he says.

I don't read it over. I just check a few of the words to make sure it's the same form I used to slide over the table to people. It's a waiver, saying I'm happy to talk without a lawyer present.

"What's the problem?" Landry asks. "You decided maybe you've got something you don't want to share with us?"

I sign the form. The alternative is to phone Donovan Green and get him down here.

The form disappears back into the folder. The photographs of Father Julian remain.

"The message is clear," Landry says.

"What message?"

He looks at Schroder and shrugs, as if he really can't believe what he just heard. Schroder lays out a few more photographs.

"You didn't want him to talk," Schroder says. "And you wanted to leave him a message. That's why you cut out his tongue."

"Hang on a second," I say, leaning forward.

"Why are you in such a mess?" Landry asks. "You're covered in blood. In dirt. What have you been doing? You've been burying something?"

"I was in an accident last night."

"And you were cleaned up. All the clothes you were wearing today are in your washing machine. They all have blood on them too?" Schroder asks.

"You'd have been better off dumping them, Tate," Landry says. "All those years busting people for this same kind of shit, I'd have thought you'd have learned more."

"When the hell did you make it a law that a man can't start cleaning up after himself?"

"The way you've been lately," Landry says, leaning against the wall, "we've all thought it was a law you'd made."

I look at their positions. One sitting. One standing. One my friend, the other my enemy. The acting is going to be a stretch for only one of these men. Soon Landry will pace behind me, in and out of view, then he'll lean over me. The game they said they wouldn't play they're already playing. They have to. They don't know how to do it any other way.

"Why don't you tell us about Julian?" Schroder asks. "Why were you following him?"

"I haven't been following him, and I certainly didn't do this to him. First of all, if I was trying to leave a message by cutting out his tongue, the only person that message could be for would be you guys, right? It'd be stupid of me to have done that."

"Listen to him," Landry says, looking at Schroder, but really talking to me. "He thinks there's some sense in all of this."

"I didn't kill him."

"Try selling us another story," Landry says. "Nobody in this room has any false pretenses about what you're capable of, Tate. We know you're the reason nobody has heard from Quentin James in two years."

"Look, Tate, cut us some slack here, okay?" Schroder says. "You know how it works. You can sit there all night stonewalling us, but in the end we'll learn what we need to from you. Why don't you save us all some time?"

I look at the photos of the dead priest. There are eight of them. "Why? So you can pin this bullshit on me?"

"If you didn't kill him, then what's the problem?" Schroder asks. "The evidence will prove that."

"Depends on how you're going to look at the evidence," I say. "Seems to me you're already looking at it and don't have a clue how to read it properly."

"We're wasting our time," Landry says. "I say we lock him up and tell his fellow prisoners he used to be a cop. Let them loosen him up."

"Yeah, good one, Landry."

"Why were you following him?" Schroder asks.

"Like I said, I wasn't following him."

Schroder presses on. "What were you doing before the accident?"

"I wasn't following him."

"We need to show him a few things," Schroder says, then he stands up and walks out of the room. Landry doesn't fill the empty seat. He pushes his hands against the top of it and leans forward.

"You used to be one of us," he says. "What in the hell happened?"

"What do you think?"

Before he can answer, Schroder steps back in. He has a cardboard box full of plastic bags. I can't tell how many there are as they all blend into one. He starts laying them out on the table.

"The watch," he says, "used to belong to Gerald Weiss. He was buried with it two years ago. So how is it you've come to own it?"

"I found it."

"There are two ways you could have got it," Landry says. "Either you stole it off a dead man when you were in the water, or you stole it off a dead man when you were pulling him out of his coffin."

"Even you're doing a shitty job of trying to believe that," I say, and Landry looks pissed off. "You're trying too hard here. And one day that's going to come back and kick you in the ass. You're going to try too damn hard, and people are going to suffer for it."

"You're either a thief or a killer," Landry says firmly, as if they are one in the same. "I think that's why you were so damn keen to help out with the exhumation of Henry Martins. You knew who was going to be in there. You wanted to try and control the situation. But the problem was the corpses, right? They floated up. If they hadn't, we'd never have known about the others."

"Look, cut the routine or I'm gonna change my mind and ask for my lawyer."

Schroder slides over another bag. It has the newspaper articles I found in Alderman's bedroom. "You've been holding back on us," he says, adding the printouts I made when sketching out the time lines of obituaries and the missing girls. "You knew long before us who was in the ground."

"That's because I used to do this too," I say, and it's true. I used to do this, and between the times I did and the times I haven't nothing really has changed. Violent acts are still a huge part of this city, as are the gray skies and the rain waiting at the threshold of every cooling hour. Bad things happening to good people. There are kids in this city being born, being loved, growing up into the choices that make them good or bad. There are kids out there without any chance at all. Some will become good, some will become evil, some are born and tossed into dumpsters. I was part of the world that tried to correct all of that, the world that tried to keep some of it in check. But somewhere along the way I lost track of it all. I fell into the abyss.

"Nobody seems to have forgotten that as much as you, Tate," Schroder says. "You're nothing like the man you used to be. You used to be a real stand-up guy. And now you've got a DUI hanging over your head; we've got you for theft, for stalking, and you're looking real good for murder."

"Without any evidence you can't hold me here without charging me. That means I'm here on my own merits. That means I'm free to get up and leave."

"No, you're not free until I say you're free," Schroder says. "We've got a techie going through your computer files. You've been following Father Julian since the day Sidney Alderman went missing. And these newspaper articles. How is it some of them are originals? To me, that suggests they were cut out as the girls went missing. How'd you get them?"

"Bruce Alderman gave them to me. He left them in my car when we drove to my office."

Schroder slides another plastic bag over. It has a small envelope inside with my name written across it. There are bloody smudges across it. For a brief moment I'm back in my office, the smell of burning metal and blood in the air, a pink mist creating a cloud over the caretaker's head that has just been distended by a bullet.

"What was in here?" Schroder asks. "The articles? See, the articles aren't folded up, and they'd need to have been folded to fit in this envelope."

"I can't remember."

"We found writing samples at the church," Schroder says. "This is Bruce Alderman's handwriting."

"So?"

"So what else have you stolen?" Landry asks.

"I haven't stolen anything. That envelope has my name on it, so whatever was in there was mine."

"He wrote you a letter? A confession? A suicide note?" Schroder asks.

"No."

"Thought you couldn't remember what was in there?"

"I can't."

"But you can remember what wasn't in there."

"Memory is a funny thing."

"Cut the crap, Tate," Landry says.

"It was the watch, okay?" I say, and it sounds believable enough. "Alderman had the watch. I don't know how he got it, and when he gave it to me I didn't know who it belonged to."

"Bullshit," Landry says.

"Then you ought to shut up until you can prove otherwise."

"Out of all the people in this city, why'd he come and see you?" Schroder asks.

I shrug. "I don't know. I think it was because I was the face he connected to what was going on. I was the one who found the bodies. I was the one who came along with the exhumation order and started all of this."

"You kept things from us," Schroder says. "You stole evidence that would have helped us piece things together quicker. That ring you took from Rachel Tyler—let's not forget you took the ring from Rachel Tyler. The time line would have changed. We'd probably have caught the person who started all of this."

It's true. But the moment that coffin opened and I saw a dead girl, I had no choice. There were other dead girls because of me, because of a decision I failed to make correctly two years earlier. How could I not take the ring? It led to suicide. It led me to murder. It led me to drunk driving and to being taken into the middle of nowhere where I should have been left.

"All these innocent girls," Schroder says, spreading out the articles, one bag for each girl. "Do you even care?"

"Of course I do."

"He doesn't," Landry says, "otherwise he'd be helping us."

"You've turned one of your rooms into an office," Schroder says. "Into a command post."

"You're charging me with that too?"

"Just tell us, damn it," Schroder says, getting angry now. "You were following Father Julian for a reason. What do you think he did? You think he killed Sidney Alderman?" He leans back in his chair. "No, I don't think that's it," he continues. "You wouldn't be following him for that. You wouldn't care about one angry old retired caretaker getting taken out. So there's more to it. You were following him because you think he had something to do with the dead girls. Your office is dedicated to that case, and to Father Julian. You have pictures and articles pinned up all over the walls. You think the two go hand in hand. We were looking at Sidney Alderman as a possibility. And more so after he disappeared. We thought he ran. But not you. You kept looking at Father Julian. He was on our radar simply because everybody connected to the graveyard was on it. Only Alderman made a bigger blip, and when he disappeared his blip overshadowed everybody else's. So we kept looking for him. It's as though you knew something. It's as though you gave up looking for Sidney Alderman because you didn't think there was a point. Either you thought he was innocent or you thought he would never show up again. It's just like two years ago with Quentin James. Which is it?"

"You tell me."

"You think Julian killed those girls," Schroder says. "We'll know soon whether your thoughts have any foundation. In the meantime, tell us what happened to Sidney Alderman."

"I don't know."

"But you knew to stop looking for him," Landry says. "Why did you focus on Father Julian?"

"I wasn't focusing on him."

"Why did you kill him?" he asks.

"I didn't."

"This is going nowhere," he says. "Show him the weapon," he says to Schroder.

"The weapon?" I ask, immediately confused.

A smirk appears on Landry's face. "The weapon, Sherlock. Like I said earlier, you really learned nothing from your years on the force. We searched your house, remember? What, did you think we wouldn't find it?"

Schroder lifts the last plastic bag from the box and puts it on the table. Inside is my hammer from home. It's covered in blood. And I already know it's going to belong to Father Julian.

CHAPTER THIRTY-SIX

"You've been following him for two months," Schroder says. I keep staring at the hammer. My hammer. My hammer and Father Julian's blood. I have this weird thought that maybe I got so drunk I picked up that hammer, drove to the church, and beat him to death. Only there's no amount of bourbon in the world that would make me do that. Unless I thought he was guilty of something. Is that what happened? No. Of course not. But a small part of me is scared that maybe I'm capable of more when I'm drunk than when I'm sober.

"You think he's guilty of murder," Schroder says, carrying on. "You were parked outside his church every day before the restraining order, and some days since. And you want us to believe you had nothing to do with his death." He puts the murder weapon down slowly, as if carefully balancing a cup of water filled to the brim, which, suddenly, reminds me of the glass of bourbon sitting on my kitchen counter. He puts it in the center of the table so we're all within reaching distance. Maybe he's hoping I'm going to make a break for it. I'm sure Landry is. He's hoping this can all end right now.

"Where did you find it?" I ask.

"Where you left it," Landry answers.

"I want my lawyer now."

"Yeah, guilty people always do," Landry says to Schroder before turning back to me. "Come on, Tate, you know how it goes. You've seen it before and you used to hate it too."

"Hate what?"

"When the perp keeps on denying it even after we've got so much evidence against him," Landry says. "It's pathetic. And in your case it's downright embarrassing."

"You've got nothing," I say.

"Nothing? Are you kidding me?"

"Tell us again why you were following him," Schroder says. "Come on, Tate. If he was guilty, then let us help you. I mean, hell, if it turns out he killed those girls, we'll probably end up giving you a medal," he says, which is the biggest lie anybody has said inside this room. "Just tell us what happened. We're all on the same team here."

"I didn't kill him," I say, but my teammates don't believe me. I want a drink.

"Give us a few minutes alone," Schroder says, and Landry looks angry, but I know it's an act. I know they've cued up their conversation before coming in here and this is the point where Schroder becomes my friend. Landry shakes his head, then walks out without saying anything else. It's part of their game.

Schroder leans forward. He gives me a sympathetic smile. An *I know how you're feeling* look, but he doesn't know how I'm feeling. He never will. "You have to give me something here, Tate, or I can't help you."

I figure it's best if I play the game too. But before I do, I decide to give him something. "Father Julian knew who killed those girls."

"What?"

"He told me he knew. And Bruce Alderman, he buried them. He told me that."

He leans further forward. "What? Why the hell didn't you tell us that?"

I explain to Schroder my conversations with the priest, detailing my pleas for Julian to tell me who had done it, even touching on the frustration I felt. I can see Schroder wondering how far he'd have pushed it if he'd known that Father Julian had been confessed to. I tell him about Bruce Alderman and what he said about dignity before elegantly blowing his brains out.

It takes me ten minutes to tell him, and he goes through a different range of emotions, starting with anger and ending with much deeper anger. When I'm done he sits there staring at me. He's no longer leaning forward, as if trying to protect himself from what he would do to me if I were in range of his fists. "You should have told us," he says, his voice low and firm. "We could have convinced Julian."

"I doubt that."

"We could have done something, Tate," he says, his voice raising. "Anything! But instead you let two months slide by and now it's too late. That's why you were outside his church, right? You weren't following Father Julian. You were watching to see who came to see him! You were waiting in case the killer showed up, only you didn't know who the hell you were looking for!"

"I had to do something."

He bangs his hand down on the table. Hard. The noise bounces around the small room. "You fucked up," he says.

"I know."

"And now Father Julian is dead. And you're in a world full of shit."

"It's an abyss."

"What?"

"Come on, Carl, you know me. You've known me for nearly twenty years."

"Which is why this is hard for me too," he says, but I'm pretty sure it's harder for me. "We found the hammer in your garage."

"And that's why you're going to let me leave." It's time to play the game.

"What?"

"You've got nothing to hold me here," I tell him. He looks down at the hammer in such a way as to suggest maybe I've forgotten it's there. But I haven't. "You found it in my garage."

"Yes."

"Okay, well, first of all you don't even know if it's my hammer."

"That's not the . . ."

"Second," I say, and I hold up my hand and start counting off my points. "You're going to print it and find my prints aren't on it. You're going to think a guy who used to be a homicide detective was dumb enough to clean off his fingerprints, but not the blood, was dumb enough to keep the weapon, was dumb enough to leave it in his garage for anybody to find."

"Not dumb, but drunk," he says.

"And that's exactly my point."

"What?"

"Three," I say, counting off another point with my fingers. "And this one is the kicker. This is the reason I'm about to get up and walk out of here."

Schroder slumps slightly in his chair. Not much, but enough to show he knows what's coming.

"The time line," I say. "See, we know the time line, Carl, but the problem is the guy who planted the hammer there didn't."

Schroder says nothing. He knew I'd figure it out, but was hoping it wouldn't be this quickly. Or he was hoping to rattle me enough that I'd give him something more, maybe tell him about Sidney Alderman.

"You think he died around midnight," I say, not because he told me, but because that's when I saw the person leaving the church, the person who I thought was the priest. Only it wasn't the priest, it was the man who killed him. The killer knew my car was there, but he didn't see me because I was covered in ground fog. He probably figured I was passed out drunk in the front seat because that's what I was used to doing. He stayed in the shadows where he thought he was out of sight.

"But I didn't make it home. Only the killer couldn't have known that. He drove to my house and replaced the hammer he had stolen to kill the priest. He didn't know I was following him. What he couldn't know was that I would be involved in an accident. Your boys came and locked me up. My car was towed away, and after you found Julian was dead, you would have had it re-towed, this time as evidence in a murder investigation. You had it brought here and every inch of it has been gone over. No blood from Father Julian and, more importantly, no hammer, right? And it's not like it got logged along with my wallet and cell phone. I didn't have it on me. And you would have searched the area of the crash, would have searched the roads between the graveyard and the accident. You found nothing. Until tonight. So how'd I put it there?"

"You could have dumped the hammer, picked it back up tonight. Maybe that's why you're covered in dirt."

"Why would I dump the hammer? I couldn't know I was going to crash. What would be the point of dumping it, just to come back tonight to retrieve it and hide it in my garage?"

Schroder says nothing.

"Then the whole tongue thing. Like I said earlier, why the hell would I cut it out? Because I didn't want him talking? That's the sort of message you want to leave when there are others who can still talk, right? A gang thing. But not in this case. This time it was designed to make me look guiltier. It would look like I was pissed at him for talking to you guys and complaining that I was following him."

He starts tapping a pen against the table in a slow, rhythmic pace. Then he leans forward and starts packing up the photographs.

"So you know I didn't kill him, but you haul me down here anyway," I say.

"Come on, Tate, you know how it is."

He's right. I do know. There are two things that bug me. The first is, why plant the hammer in my garage and not the tongue?

"Somebody still killed him," Schroder says.

"Uh huh."

"You can help us out there."

"You shouldn't have jerked me around, Carl. You should have just asked for my help."

"Hey, don't go playing the victim here, Tate. You almost killed a woman last night. Hell, maybe you still did—last I heard she was stable, but that don't mean shit and you know it. Father Julian had to file a restraining order against you and you kept breaking it. You were there the night he died. You're involved, Tate. Julian died, and if you'd been up front two months ago maybe he'd still be alive now. Sidney Alderman is nowhere to be seen and you're acting like he's dead. Same goes for Quentin James. You need to start giving me some answers. Look, you know that by keeping these from us," he says as he touches the bags with the jewelry and the articles, "you slowed down our investigation. Things would be different. We might have looked further. We might not have pinned all our beliefs on Alderman. Fuck, Tate, we needed this one. There's been so much shit lately with the Carver case, and that's just the tip. You'd know that if you gave a shit, or if you read a newspaper." He pauses, takes a pencil out of his shirt pocket, rolls it across his fingers, then snaps it in half. "Look, you get the point. We needed something to work out, not just for the victims and for their families, but for us. People don't have faith in the police anymore, Tate, and it's hard to blame them. That could have all changed, but you held back on us."

"Was I in the news today?" I ask.

"Did you even hear anything I just said?"

"The papers, Carl. Was I in them? The accident?"

"Not the papers, no," he says. "The accident was too late for that. But you've been on the news all day."

"Since this morning?"

"That's what *all day* means."

"Then why the hell aren't you asking yourself the obvious question?"

"Which is?"

"Why would the guy who planted the hammer in my garage not take it back out after seeing the news? He must have known being in jail would clear me."

I can tell from his expression that Schroder hadn't thought of it. "Maybe he didn't see the news," he says.

"Come on, Carl, you know just as well as I do that these guys always read the papers and watch the news."

He taps one half of the broken pencil against the table. "This is going to be a long night," he says. "We're going to get this sorted."

"Then I'd better make myself comfortable," I answer, and I lean back in my chair.

CHAPTER THIRTY-SEVEN

Schroder was right and wrong. Right that it was going to be a long night. Wrong about us getting it sorted. Landry showed up on cue, but their routine at trying to shake something loose from me was ruined by the murder weapon. It was planted, they both knew it, and that was the problem. They'd have had a better chance if they hadn't found it. They held me long enough to go over the same questions and until they were satisfied the people going through my house had searched enough for, what I imagine, was evidence of what really happened to Sidney Alderman, evidence of what I suspected Father Julian was up to—only there was no evidence there. I could tell Landry was itching to keep me locked up, and that Schroder was tempted to go along with it, but in the end they had nothing to hold me on. Even the blood and dirt on my body I explained away as a bad fall while I was out walking trying to clear my head. Nobody bought it, but it didn't matter.

When we're done I'm escorted to the elevator by both Landry and Schroder.

"This isn't over," Landry says, and he's right—it isn't over. Somebody killed Father Julian, and that same somebody tried to send me to jail for it. I suspect that same somebody will be the man who killed those girls. I'm going to find that somebody.

When I get to the ground floor there are two officers there waiting for me. I follow them outside and I climb into the back of their car and none of us make any kind of conversation as they drive me home. We drive through the city. I stare out at the nightlife, people driving to or from work, to or from bars, to or from something better or something worse.

They drop me off in my driveway. They back away and this time there are no faces pressed up against neighboring windows to see what I'm up to. My house is locked up and I still don't have my keys, so I go inside using the same busted window as before. Schroder never mentioned the window, and I guess maybe he figured out why it had been busted. My house isn't any tidier since the police have scoured their way through it. The articles and pictures from the bedroom I'd set up as an office have all gone. All that are left are pinholes in the walls. The computer is gone, my notes are gone, even the whiteboard has been taken. Landry will trawl though everything and he'll get me back in to answer more questions—maybe even later on today. But there is nothing in any of those notes about Sidney Alderman. Nothing about Quentin James.

I make some coffee, and the caffeine wakes me enough to realize I'm so tired I don't even know what my next step should be. The coffee tastes good, but not good enough to consider making another. I stare at the glass on the counter, which is still full of bourbon. I think about tipping it down the sink, then I think about tipping it down my throat, and I don't do either. I head down to the bedroom. Everything is messy. The mattress has been tipped up and thrown back on the base. All the drawers have been pulled out. The wardrobe has been opened and everything inside pulled out.

I head down to the laundry and check the washing machine. At some point the wash cycle stopped. The clothes I put in there are all done. There are bloodstains on some of them from the accident and from the trip into the woods, but those bloodstains are mine.

I take a quick shower. It feels like the best shower I've ever had, but I'm too tired to really appreciate it. Daxter stands in the bathroom and watches me as I dry off. When I'm done I feed him and he seems appreciative.

It's almost six in the morning before I climb into bed. I reckon Landry and Schroder will probably be going through the same motions. I start to set the alarm, but in the end I can't decide what time to set it for, so I switch it off. I bury my head into the pillows and try to get to sleep.

CHAPTER THIRTY-EIGHT

The house is full of warm colors and my neighbor's face is frozen with cold emotion.

"What do you want to borrow my phone for, Theo?" she asks.

"Because mine isn't working."

"You think the police bugged it? They could have. They were there all night. That was one stupid thing you did," she says.

"I know."

"After you losing your little girl and everything. Real stupid."

"Can I borrow your phone or not?"

Mrs. Adams stares at me for a few seconds without saying anything, and I can tell she's really debating the issue. She doesn't want me inside her house. This woman who looks like everybody's grandmother and who brought cooked dinners to my house at least once a week for almost a year after Emily died. This woman who I would occasionally find weeding my garden or trimming some bushes because I'd been too tired or too busy or too lazy to do it. There was always a wave and a smile and a good word that things would be okay, that Emily was with God, that everything would be okay.

"I don't know," she says. "You could have killed her."

"That wasn't my intention," I say, as if that could possibly excuse it. Just like it wasn't Quentin James's intention to kill my daughter.

Mrs. Adams doesn't pick up on the comment, and instead stands aside. "Don't take too long," she says.

She stays a step behind me as I make my way through her house, as if suddenly she thinks I'm not only a drunk driver, but also about to steal one of the thousand knickknacks covering the tables and countertops. "Phone book?" I ask.

She sighs, and I have the impression that if she'd known in the beginning I was going to be this much trouble she wouldn't have let me in. She rummages through a kitchen drawer and pulls out the white pages.

I call the hospital and ask after the condition of Emma Green. It turns out that's the girl's real last name—Donovan Green wasn't faking it after all. The nurse tells me she can only give information out to a family member.

"Can you just tell me if she's doing okay?" I ask.

"When are you guys going to learn you can't just keep chewing up our time with questions all day long?" she asks.

"What guys?"

"Reporters," she says, almost spitting the word out before hanging up. My guess is that if she knew who I was it would only have been worse.

I make my second call, this one to the morgue.

"It's Tate."

"Tate? My God, I heard about what happened. Are you doing okay?" Tracey asks. She's the first person to have done so, and it feels kind of nice.

"Doing okay? I guess that depends on your definition," I tell her. "Listen, I need to ask if you can help me out on a few things."

There's a few moments of silence, and I'm about to ask if she's still there when she speaks up. "Tate, I'm sorry about everything that's happened," she says, "but you know I can't help you on anything. Not just because of the last few days, but you stole that dead girl's ring right out of my morgue. I had Landry down here asking me about it this morning and I didn't know what to tell him."

"I'm sorry I had to put you through that."

"Yeah, well, I'm sorry too," she says, and I can picture her slowly shaking her head. "Because now I'm the one who's getting a reprimand. This could end up being serious. For all I know, I could get suspended. Or worse. I gotta go."

"Listen, Tracey, please, it's important."

"I can't."

"It's the girl," I say, "that's all."

"What?"

"I need to know how she's doing. The hospital won't tell me."

"I don't know how she's doing," she says.

"But you can find out, right?"

"You're really pushing it, Tate."

"Please. It's important."

She goes quiet again. This time I know she's still there. I just wait her out. "Call me back in five minutes," she says.

"I gotta come down there anyway. Put my name on the list. I'll see you in a few hours."

"Look, I can't just—"

"Thanks, Tracey. I'll see you soon." I hang up before she can object.

Mrs. Adams doesn't seem too impressed that I'm taking up so much of her time. Scattered across the kitchen are baking ingredients that must all have come together to form whatever fantastic-smelling thing is turning brown in the oven.

I make another call. My mother answers, slightly out of breath, as if she's just run in from the yard.

"I've been trying to call," she says. "Your cell phone isn't switched on."

"I lost it."

"And your home phone is disconnected."

"I forgot to pay the bill."

"Is it true what the papers are saying?" she asks. "Please, Theo, please don't tell me you did what they're saying you did."

"I haven't seen the papers," I tell her, "but yes, it's true. I'm sorry."

"I should have done more," she says.

"What?"

"This is my fault," she says. "I should have seen what was happening to you ever since the accident. But don't worry, we're here to help you now."

"It's not your fault. Anyway the reason I'm calling is—"

"Of course it's my fault," she says. "Your father and me failed you. We must have. I'm so sorry," she says, which makes me feel even worse.

"Listen, Mom, it's not like that. I'll explain it better when I see you, but for now I want to ask if I can borrow a car."

"A car?"

"Dad hardly uses his, right? And you two can share yours while I'm using it."

"What's wrong with yours? Oh," she says, figuring it out. "I don't know if it's a good idea."

"I'm not going to wreck it, Mom."

"I don't . . ."

"I'm okay now," I tell her. "I promise. And I need this, okay? I need you guys to trust me."

"Of course we trust you. But . . . but won't they have taken your license off you?"

"They went easy on me because of my history," I say, which is a complete lie. My license has been taken off me. If I get caught driving I'll be heading straight back to jail. There'll be fines. It's the Quentin James factor.

"I'll bring it over to you," Mom says. "I'm sure Dad won't mind."

We both know that he will. I hang up the phone and hand the white pages back to Mrs. Adams.

"I wouldn't be trusting you," she says, then she offers me one of the muffins she's just baked, as if some grandmotherly gene inside her can't prevent her from reaching out. I grab one before she can change her mind, figuring it's the healthiest thing I've eaten in weeks.

"You know, Theo, I don't mean to sound hard on you, not after everything that's happened, so please, don't take this the wrong way, but it's never too late to pull yourself together. We're always next door if you need some help along the way."

I thank her for the use of her phone and for the muffin. She gives me another one to take home with me. If more people were as forgiving and as helpful, maybe we could cut away some of the cancer that has set into the bones of this city.

It'll take my mother an hour to get here with the car, so I kill some time by going to buy a newspaper. I keep thinking people will notice me, that they'll know who I am and what I have done, but nobody pays me any attention because my photo isn't in the paper, only my name. The guy at the shop knows me, though, because I've been coming here for years. He looks at me, looks down at the front page, and looks at me again. He seems to search for something to say, and I think all his angry one-liners trip over each other and he ends up saying nothing. He even gives me the right amount of change. I get back home and read the article. It's all about the accident. About me. It doesn't paint a pretty picture. I read the article about Father Julian, but it doesn't reveal anything I don't already know. At least my name isn't mentioned here—yet.

I switch on the TV and watch a couple of minutes of the morning news. Father Julian's murder is the headline, and it looks like it's going to be a busy day for the media. Casey Horwell gives a report. She talks about the murder weapon being found and she says where, offering my name as if she knew all along what I was capable of, her smirk suggesting she could see this coming even if the police couldn't. I wonder how in the hell she found out where the weapon was found and who her source is. She talks about Father Julian's tongue being removed. I get angry just looking at her, and have to turn the TV off or risk throwing the remote at it.

I start to tidy the house and do some more laundry. Then I spend a few minutes in my daughter's bedroom. The police came through here last night, but they haven't messed it up, just left things slightly askew. It reminds me of Father Julian's office, the way everything is where it should be, but only just. The police here showed some respect. They searched this room and found nothing except a lonely shrine and evidence of an even lonelier parent. Daxter looks up at me from the bed. He follows me back down the house and I fill up his food bowl.

Six months ago I had a spare bedroom that seemed to be a magnet for all the crap in my life that I couldn't seem to fit anywhere else in the house or garage. These days it's an office—or at least was until last night. I sit down at the desk and drag a pad out from the drawer. I start writing down the names and the dates of the women who were killed. I start compiling as many of the notes as I can remember, but the last eight weeks have been a haze of alcohol, of guilt, of anger at the priest and at myself, and the small details have all slipped away, drowned beneath an ocean of self-resentment. I do the best I can with the details I remember, and I start to create another time line.

Just before my mother arrives, I head into the kitchen and pick up the glass of bourbon still waiting for me on the counter. I can't bring myself to throw it out. I don't know why. I put it into the fridge, then hide it at the back. When my mother arrives she looks around the house, unable to stop herself from commenting about the mess, the smell, the stuffy air, the broken window. She looks me over. The gash in my head has closed back up, but it isn't pretty. The bruises on my face she attributes to the accident, the same way Schroder and Landry did. There is a huge bruise running down the side of my neck, and she can't see the bruise across my chest from the seat belt. I have cuts all over my hands; the end of the finger bandage is stained with blood.

My mom is in her late sixties, but thinks she is in her forties and that I'm still nine years old. Her hair isn't quite as gray as my neighbor's, and her glasses aren't quite as big—but I figure in ten years they'll be a match.

"You need to go to a doctor," she says.

"I'm fine. I've already been checked over."

"Doesn't look like they did a good job."

She starts to tidy up. I tell her not to bother, but the only thing she doesn't bother to do is listen to my requests. Mom tells me how disappointed Bridget would be if she knew what was happening, not just about the drunk driving, but also the way I've been treating myself lately. I keep saying *I know* over and over, but she doesn't seem to get tired of hearing it. After nearly an hour she lets me drive her back home and I keep the car.

"I'm also strapped for cash," I say, "and I need a new phone. I hate asking, but can you help me out here?"

"There's already some in the glove box," she says. "We worry about you, Theo. More than you think. Are you going to come in and say hello to your father?"

"I don't know. I guess that depends on how disapproving he is that I'm borrowing his car."

"Then you'd best be on your way," she says, grinning at me. She leans over then and gives me a hug, and for the briefest of moments I feel like everything is going to be okay.

When I get to the library I open the glove box and find an envelope with a thousand dollars in cash. She must have dropped into a bank on the way. She knew I didn't forget to pay the phone bill, that I didn't pay it because I haven't worked in weeks. I suddenly feel like turning around and giving it all back—the money and the car—because I don't deserve anybody to worry about me. But I don't. There are too many dead girls, too many dead caretakers, and a dead priest all pressing me forward. Plus somebody out there tried to frame me for murder.

The library is warm and quiet. Plenty of people who live

in different worlds from me are sitting down reading about worlds similar to the one I'm falling into. I find the newspaper sections on the computer and print out all the articles that mention the missing girls. There are the ones I got from beneath Bruce Alderman's bed, plus the stories that have been in the papers since the girls were discovered. I spend the rest of the afternoon rereading these stories and printing them out. I print out the stories about Bruce Alderman's suicide and about his father's disappearance too. I end up with a stack of paper dedicated to the dead almost a centimeter thick.

I leave the library and hit five o'clock traffic. SUVs are blocking views at intersections, and not for the first time I figure they're the reason everybody in this world is going nuts. It sure as hell was my reason. I look at the money my parents gave me, and the math is simple—there's enough here for me to drink my way out of this and every other problem for the next few weeks. I could go into a bar—there are several en route—and things would be okay again, at least for a little while.

WWJD?

What would James do? I figure Quentin James would have pulled over. He'd have slipped inside and let five minutes turn into ten, ten into an hour, an hour into a night. Or maybe if I'd let him live things would be different now. Perhaps he'd have found redemption, or God, or something that would have kept him out of those bars. I don't know, and thinking about James kills any desire to go inside. I drive past them all and don't look back.

CHAPTER THIRTY-NINE

On the way to the morgue I stop in at the store where I bought my last cell phone. It feels like a long time ago. Much longer than eight weeks. I spend a hundred and fifty bucks on a cell phone that has more features than even Gene Roddenberry could have dreamed of. I ask to get my number transferred over and am told it'll take an hour or two.

There's a security officer sitting behind a desk at the entrance to the morgue. I give him my details and he checks my name on the list. He gives me a visitor's pass and I attach it to the front of my shirt. He seems friendly enough, which I suppose must mean he hasn't spent any time reading the papers or watching the news. The guy probably gets a big enough dose of reality working the morgue.

As I head down the corridor the temperature drops with every footstep. I go through the large, plastic doors that separate the corridor and offices from the freezer, where all the work is done. It's been two months since I was last here. Before that it was two years. It means my visits are becoming more frequent.

"Hi, Tate," Tracey says, moving over toward me from the large sets of drawers in which are stored the other people unlucky enough to be here at six o'clock on a Friday night. "You just caught me."

She looks different. Her hair is a little frazzled. She looks paler and tired, more worn down, as though both life and death are starting to get on top of her.

"It's been a rough week," she says, as if acknowledging my thoughts.

"Yeah. Tell me about it."

There are empty metal tables with sheets and tools, but no bodies.

"I could really use a drink," she says, then pauses, recognizing her mistake. "Sorry, Tate, that was a bit insensitive."

"Yeah, so is drinking and driving. How is she?"

"She's doing okay. She's pretty banged up, but she's out of the woods. The head trauma was the problem—there was some internal swelling, but the pressure's been relieved. She's going to have some tough months ahead of her, but it could have been worse, right? You know that more than anybody."

You know that more than anybody. How many people have said that to me over the last twenty-four hours? "So . . . she'll get back to a hundred percent?"

"That's what they're saying."

I move from foot to foot, trying to get some warmth back into them. My finger with the missing nail is throbbing. The bandage is dark gray and filthy-looking, and hasn't been changed.

"Does it hurt?" she asks.

"It's okay."

"Let me re-dress it for you while we're talking."

I follow her through to the office and sit down. She drags her chair around, pulls on some latex gloves, and takes the old bandage off my finger. The gauze has caught a little, blood and pus having set on the outside of it.

"Have you worked on the priest yet?" I ask.

"Come on, Theo, you know I can't share any of that with you."

"It's important."

"I think you're forgetting that I'm still pissed at you for stealing Rachel Tyler's ring."

"I'm sorry about that."

"Oh, well that covers everything then, doesn't it? As long as you're sorry." She pulls the gauze away, ripping off the scab.

"Aw, Tracey." I pull my hand back.

She drops the gauze into a bin. "I go to bat for you by never mentioning it, and suddenly Landry's down here this morning asking me about it. Now I'm the one who's gonna get crapped on."

"Let me make it up to you," I say.

"Give me your hand."

"No."

"Come on, Theo, grow up. Give me your damn hand."

I reach back over and she starts to clean the wound.

"Look," I say, "I think I'm entitled to some information here. After all, I'm the one they accused of killing him."

"If anything, that entitles you to absolutely no information at all. When was the last time you let a suspect walk down here and ask whatever he wanted about the crime?"

"This is different."

"Not to me," she says. "Not to anybody. You shouldn't even

be here." She cuts off some fresh gauze and places it over my fingertip. Then she adds some padding. "Goddamn it, Tate, if there was somebody as qualified to take over, I'd probably already have been suspended."

"They know I didn't do it. Did Landry tell you that?"

"Yeah. He did. But that still doesn't change anything."

I look over my shoulder at the drawers through the office window. One of them contains Father Julian. Two nights ago I came close to occupying another one. The throbbing in my finger grows stronger, and Tracey starts to bandage it.

"It changes it for me, right? Think of it from my perspective. The cops know and I know that somebody killed Father Julian and tried to pin that on me. I think that means I have a stake in this investigation. I think that it means I deserve to be told as much as possible so I can try to defend myself."

"Defend yourself against what? They already know you're innocent."

"Come on, Tracey. You know the score. You know three of those girls would still be alive if I'd done my job properly two years ago. I want this guy off the street."

She tapes off the bandage and leans back. "People who you want off the street are never heard from again, Theo. I'm sorry, but I can't give you anything."

"Was the hammer the cause of death?"

"It's getting late. I've got a family to get home to."

"Come on, give me something here. Bruce Alderman, his father, now the priest—they're dead for a reason. And this person who planted the hammer in my house is probably the same person who killed all those girls."

"Sidney Alderman is dead? How do you know that?" she asks.

"I'm guessing, but it makes sense, right? Everything is related."

"Not everything," Tracey says.

"What do you mean?"

She sighs, and her shoulders slump as if she's sick and tired of talking to a ten-year-old.

"Please, just drop it," she says.

"Would you? Come on, Tracey, name me one detective you know who wouldn't be trying to do the same thing."

"The problem is you're not a detective, Theo. Not anymore."

"I know, but—"

"Look, one thing, okay? I'm going to tell you one thing, then I want you to leave."

"Okay."

"And you can't come back. You promise?"

I've heard that line before. "What is it?"

She sighs. "Okay, Theo, I tell you this and then you leave. Sidney and Bruce Alderman. They're not related. Sidney Alderman is not Bruce Alderman's father."

CHAPTER FORTY

I pin the photocopies of the newspaper articles up on the wall in my office and stare at the spot where my computer used to be until knocking at the front door breaks me out of the fugue. I think about ignoring it, but it just keeps going. I head into the hallway and swing the door open. Carl Schroder is there holding two pizza boxes in his arms. Suddenly he really is my best friend.

"Thought you might do with some food," he says.

"I'm in the middle of cooking something."

"I looked in that fridge of yours, Tate. What in the hell could you possibly be cooking?" He braces the pizzas in one hand, a bottle of Coke under his arm. He reaches into his pocket and pulls out my keys. "Might make it easier for you getting in and out. Saves breaking more windows."

"Seriously, Carl, this isn't a good time for me," I say, taking my keys off him. The small key I got from Bruce Alderman is still attached to them.

"Spare me the bullshit. This place hasn't had any food in it for a long time. Except for this kind. You've got enough pizza boxes stacked in your kitchen to build a fort."

My stomach starts to growl and my mouth waters.

"I was going to bring beer," he says, reaching under his arm and grabbing the Coke, "but something told me that was a bad idea."

"You're a real funny guy."

We move through to the dining room. I grab some plates and a couple of glasses. The pizza has a range of different types of meat on it, so between that and the Coke I reckon I'll get the nutritional value I need for the day.

"So why are you here?" I ask him.

"Look, Tate, Landry can be a real asshole, but that doesn't mean he doesn't have a point."

"Which is?"

"The fact you've become a real mess."

"I'm in the process of changing that," I tell him.

He looks around the room, absorbing the comment. "I guess you are."

"That's what life-changing moments will do to you."

"And what was that?" he asks.

"What do you think?"

"The accident," he says, and he's right—it was the accident more than it was being taken into the woods, or being framed for murder.

"It's kind of ironic," he adds.

I know what he's getting at. He's saying that if it hadn't been for me driving through that intersection and hitting that car, I would now be in jail. I'd have been arrested for murder. He's saying that picking up the bottle and getting hammered was the only thing that kept the frame job on me from being complete. It all comes back to that word: *luck*.

"Did you really think I did it?" I ask.

"Sure we did. Until the weapon showed up. That threw a wrench in the works. Or a hammer, I guess, in this case. It messed everything up. So you were lucky."

"I shouldn't have needed to be lucky. I didn't kill the guy and that should have been enough."

"Come on, you know sometimes that isn't enough," he says, which is a really depressing thought.

"So why are you here?" I ask. "Other than to make sure I'm eating okay?"

"How long's it been since we hung out, Tate?"

"Probably around the same time you stopped calling me. Hell, it was the same time everybody stopped. If I remember correctly, it was around when Emily died."

"That had nothing to do with it."

"Then what was it?"

"It was Quentin James," he says. "Nobody believes he ran. We all know you killed him. But without a body, without any proof . . ."

"I didn't kill him."

"Hey, I'd have killed him. Any one of us would have—and that's why none of us looked real hard into finding him. It just sucked that it had to be you. And none of us wanted to hear you say it. What would have happened if over a few beers one night you told me what you'd done? What then? No, none of us could call you, Tate. It was the only way. It was safer. And not just for you, for us. It may not have been what you wanted, but it's the way it had to play out. It was the way you made it play out."

I don't answer him. I'm not sure if he's made a valid point

or whether he's just made up an excuse that sounds believable. I guess if I were in his situation I'd have done the same thing.

We sit in silence for a few minutes, eating our pizza and getting through our Cokes. The Coke tastes different without bourbon added to it.

"Tell me something," I say, finishing one slice and getting ready to start another. "Bruce Alderman. Did you ever look at him for the murders?"

"We looked at everybody."

"Yeah, but how much did you look at him?" I ask.

"Not as much as his father."

"Which father?" I ask.

"If you're trying to get at something, Tate, just spell it out."

"I didn't mean his priest."

He sets down his pizza. "Who told you?"

"That Bruce and Sidney weren't related? I've known from the beginning. Do you know who the real father is?"

He picks up his slice and starts back in on it. "Tracey told you, that's what I think. Probably recently too. Maybe today. No way you could have known from the beginning."

"How'd you figure it out?" I ask.

"Probably the same way you did. You want to share first?"

"Come on, Carl. You wouldn't have come around unless you had something for me."

"And you need to stop reading things into situations that aren't there. I don't have anything for you. I came around to check in on you."

"I appreciate that," I say, "but come on, just give me that one thing. You know we screwed up two years ago. You know we could have stopped this, and three more girls would still be alive for it. I can't let it go."

He sets his pizza back down. "I'm surprised it took you this long to play that card," he says.

I don't answer. I just wait him out and he carries on.

Like I said, we were looking at everybody, right? A case this big, all those girls—we're gonna run all the DNA we can get hold of. Absolutely we're gonna do that."

"And Alderman agreed to that?"

"No, he didn't agree. He didn't even know. He came down to identify his son's body. When he took a swing at you, he hit the wall, right? That gave us his blood. We threw it into the database we were building."

"And?"

"And the results are still out on DNA. Come on, Tate, this shit still takes a couple of months to get back to us. Nothing has changed there. But we'll know any day now. Blood tests proved the two Aldermans weren't biologically related."

"Why'd you test?"

"Like I said, all that stuff just gets done, right?"

"What about Father Julian? You checking to see if his DNA shows up anywhere it shouldn't?"

"How did I know you were going to ask that?"

"Well?"

"You've had plenty of opportunities to tell us about Father Julian, Tate. You kept refusing. But, like I say, we're still waiting for DNA results."

"Father Julian was Bruce's real father, wasn't he?"

"What makes you say that?"

I think about what Father Julian said about Bruce being like a son to him. "A hunch."

"Don't know. It's quicker to disprove parenting through blood comparisons, which we've done. But it's going to take longer to confirm. We'll know soon."

"How soon?"

"We'll know when we know. That's just the way it is."

I wish testing were as quick as it is on TV. It's not. It's about eight weeks of sitting around waiting while the specimens are sent out, tested, retested, and sent back. Like Schroder says, it'll be any day now.

"You're going to compare the DNA you've been collecting against the samples found at the crime scene in the church?" I ask.

"Gee, why didn't we think of that? I didn't realize the impact of you leaving the force."

"Yeah, good one, Carl."

"You fucked up," Schroder says.

"What?"

"This whole thing. You fucked up. And it's only a matter of time until we find Sidney Alderman."

"When you do, can you ask him about Father Julian? Maybe he knows something."

"Yeah, I'll make sure I do that. I'll wrap his hands around a crystal ball. See if that'll help the conversation. It sure has to be better than this." He swallows the last of his drink, then stands up.

I walk him to the door.

On the step he turns around and faces me. "You know his wife died in an accident, right?"

He knows I do. I found the article online and printed off a copy. It was pinned to my wall with all the others.

"What of it?"

"With everything that's going on, some bright spark had the idea that maybe there was something more to her death."

"You're kidding," I say, suddenly worried about where this is going.

"Nope. It's bullshit, right? It's a stupid idea. But the decision has come down from the top. One of those dot the *i*'s and cross the *t*'s that's going to cost time and money and get no result. The upshot is we're digging her up on Monday."

My stomach lurches upward, and I'm worried the motion is strong enough to knock me off my feet. My future flashes in front of my eyes. It starts with me throwing up all over myself. Then it skips forward to another exhumation that goes horribly wrong. It's two-for-one Monday at the cemetery—it's not just one Alderman being dug up, but two. Then it ends with handcuffs and another ride in a police car, interrogations and trials, then jail time. Lots and lots of jail time.

"Don't you need something more to be able to do that?" I ask.

"The gun Bruce shot himself with," he says, ignoring my question. "Do you know where he got it?"

"I always wondered," I say, and the visions are still happening. Two dead Aldermans and me in jail getting the shit kicked out of me by two guys I arrested years earlier.

"It belonged to his father," Schroder says. "I mean it belonged to Sidney Alderman."

"And?" I ask, not sure where he's going with this.

"And Alderman bought that gun years ago. He bought it the same week his wife died. About two days before she suddenly jumped out in front of a car by accident. Hell of a coincidence, don't you think?"

"You think he bought the gun to kill his wife and pushed her in front of a car instead?"

He shrugs. "I'm not saying anything," he says. "But you remember what happened last time we started digging up bodies? I'm telling you, Tate, it's going to be a long week. And take some advice—get yourself a good lawyer, man. These drunk-driving charges aren't going to disappear, friends in the department or not. You're going to be doing some time. Get yourself sorted, start jogging—you've put on what, three, four kilos in the last month? Get your life back on track. Do anything else but this case, man. I know we could have made a difference two years ago, but you have to let it go and let the rest of us take care of it."

His cell phone starts to ring.

"Hang on, Tate." He talks quickly into it, then hangs up. "I gotta go," he says, and rushes to his car.

All I can do is watch him as he speeds out of the street, and all I can think about is what they are going to find buried in the dirt when they exhume Sidney Alderman's wife on Monday.

CHAPTER FORTY-ONE

For the longest time I can't move. My breathing becomes shallow and I start to sweat. The house is cold and the air slightly damp because of the busted window in the lounge. There is a restricting pain in my chest. On Monday they are going to find Sidney Alderman buried on top of the coffin of his wife. He's going to look like he died hard. There'll be plenty of evidence that I'm the one who killed him. It won't be like Quentin James, where they knew I did it, but didn't try looking too hard to prove anything. This time they'll make an effort because the man I killed was innocent.

I walk outside to the garage and find a piece of plywood and some nails; of course, I have no hammer. I use a drill and some screws to hold the plywood over the busted window. The work helps to calm me, at least for a few minutes. When the last screw is buried, I start to go through my options, and the one that keeps coming up is that I ought to call Carl Schroder and tell him to come back here. We could sit down and he could listen to my sins.

I sit down at the table and eat some more pizza, staring blankly at the wall, the act of eating a mechanical one that has no enjoyment. I need to start making the most of good food, since I won't be seeing any for another ten years. On the other hand, Schroder was right. I should be joining a gym. Or at least running. Doing something. I reach down and grab a handful of stomach. Two months ago I was lean. Now I'm not. I reach up and find extra padding around my neck and jaw that shouldn't be there either.

I finish off the pizza and drink the rest of the Coke. Daxter comes wandering down the hall, probably hoping I kept him some pizza. I give him his usual and he seems placated by it. I head to bed and set my alarm clock. I slide it to the far end of the bedside table to kill the risk of my reaching out and slapping the snooze button while still in some dreamlike state. I stare at the dark ceiling and the dark walls and I think about Sidney Alderman and the expression that will be on his face. This strange image comes to me, of where they dig him up and there is still one more breath inside of him, one breath in which he can tell the police that it was me who did this to him.

When I fall asleep I end up dreaming about my wife, about Emily, and in my dream they are both alive. They talk to me, but what they say makes little sense, because in the dream I seem to be burying my family while they're still alive. Rachel Tyler appears—she's a younger version, one of the Rachel Tylers on display in the hallway of her parents' house. She accuses me of being a murderer, and in this world of dreams as well as outside of it that's exactly what I am.

When the alarm goes off it's two o'clock in the morning and it's raining. Daxter is curled up next to me, the first time he has done that in two years. I wonder if this means something. My house is cold and my mind is full of bad ideas. I get dressed and step out into the night.

CHAPTER FORTY-TWO

I throw a shovel into the back of my dad's car and park outside my house. I look up and down the street, searching for a taillight, then drive off in the direction of the cemetery, taking random lefts and rights to make sure no one is following. Nobody is. I need to get Alderman out of the ground before the others go digging for his wife. They're going to see the turned-over earth, they're going to know something has happened, but they're not going to know what. They may suspect—but they can't know. They'll see Alderman's blood on the coffin lid, so I'm going to have to do something about that too.

At the cemetery everything looks different, as though I'm still in the dream. The night is about as dark and wet as it can get in this city. There is an occasional sliver of pale light that breaks through and reflects off the windshield. It is completely still out here, and cold. I suspect if I tried digging deep into the ground to remove Sidney Alderman, it'd be like digging through quicksand.

I park out on the street two blocks away and walk back to the cemetery. Naked branches that look like skeletal remains reach out overhead and lock fingers above me as I enter the grounds. I slow down and stay hidden in the shadows of several oak trees along the sides of the road in case there are any police around. There doesn't seem to be anybody, but I go further onto the grounds before going back for the shovel, knowing I could only offer bad answers to questions about why I was carrying one.

Satisfied I'm alone, at least in the cemetery, I start to make my way to the church. I stay in the trees, getting close enough finally to see a patrol car parked outside with a sole officer inside. He's probably got the heater running to stay warm, and got a thermos of coffee as well. It's standard protocol to protect a crime scene this early on. I bet he's bored as hell. I stay in the same position, low to the ground, the cold making my knees and fingers hurt, and I spend ten minutes just watching. The rain beats on my jacket loudly, but not as loudly as it beats against the car. Occasionally a light comes on in the car from what I think might be a cell phone opening and closing. The guy's probably sending text messages to his wife or girlfriend, or both. Probably complaining about what a waste of time it is out here.

I need to return to the car, grab the shovel, and dig Alderman up. But now that I'm this close to the church, suddenly I have another, even stronger need—I have to know what's inside. I need to know if there are answers in there. And anyway, Alderman won't mind waiting another half an hour for the feel of the shovel.

I pass behind the trees and some graves, and circumnavigate my way to the back of the church. I hide for another five minutes, just watching and waiting to see if there is anybody else around. There isn't. The rain stays heavy and I'm pretty sure it's the reason the cop keeping an eye on the church is staying in his car and not patrolling around the perimeter every few minutes like he's been instructed to do.

The church is darker and colder-looking than normal, as though God has moved out and some malevolent presence has moved in. There are no lights on inside. The man who devoted his life to this place is lying on a slab in the morgue, maybe with his God, maybe alone.

I quickly make my way to the side door and I pause, waiting for either Schroder or Landry to step out of the darkness, or even Casey Horwell with her cameraman. Nobody does. There is police tape hanging in the lifeless air between poles that have been weighted on the ground. Police tape has been sealed along the framework. I try to pull it away without damaging it.

I pull out my keys and look at the one I got from Bruce Alderman. I look at it and I look at the lock on the door, and even though they don't look like they're going to match up, I still try jamming them together. It's useless. It could be for one of the other doors. I pull a lock-pick set from my pocket, hold a Maglite in my mouth, and go about working at the lock, nervous that the guy parked out front is going to pick this exact moment to come looking around. It turns out to be a simple enough pin-and-tumbler mechanism made more complicated than it ought to be by the cold and my nerves. It takes me almost ten minutes to make my way inside. The air is cold, the black void ahead of me unwelcoming, and when I close the door behind me all I have is my Maglite to keep whatever demons are in here at bay.

Before taking a step, I remove my jacket and shoes to avoid contaminating the scene with mud and water. I've entered the church corridor: to the left is the chapel and to the right, Father Julian's office. There is a basin of what I assume is holy water standing waist high next to me. The flashlight cuts a small arc through the inky darkness, but is swallowed up when I point it at the far wall of the chapel—I'm sure it's all but impossible to see it from outside. I run my hand along the top of the front pew where I sat last time I was here talking to Father Julian. It was when I was looking for Bruce Alderman. The following day I came back and we sat in his office and I was looking for Sidney Alderman.

I turn off the flashlight and stand in the darkness. There is something here, I'm sure of it. Something dark. Perhaps the church itself is angry. Bad things have happened here. Sins have been confessed and sins have been committed. The bricks and the mortar and the stained glass windows have every right to be angry. They've absorbed a lot of what's been said and seen over the years, and now that the keeper of secrets has gone all that sorrow and pain is starting to seep out.

I turn the flashlight back on and start looking around the chapel, not searching for anything in particular. The only eyes watching me are those of the icons pinned on or hanging from the walls, created in colored glass and woven fabrics and tapestries. Jesus feeding the poor. Jesus turning water into wine. Jesus dying for our sins. Did Father Julian die for his sins? For mine?

There are a few evidence markers placed variously around the floor. Whatever they indicated has been photographed, picked up, and is now gone. There are no blood splatters. No muddy footprints. The other night, did Father Julian's killer make his way into the church using the same means? Did he come through the front door, allowed entrance by the priest?

Through a side door? Did he come at night, or had he been here all day?

Did they know each other?

I rest my soaked jacket and shoes behind the first pew so I don't leave water everywhere and head down to Father Julian's office. It's a tangle of books and papers and clutter strewed around the room—not from any type of struggle, but as though he was trying to find something in a hurry. Or perhaps the police were, and this is the aftermath of their search. This is the kind of thing I miss most about being on the force: losing the opportunity to see the crime scene in its original form. There are more evidence markers, yellow plastic disks with black numbers printed on them. Fingerprint powder, small plastic bags, plastic vials, cotton swabs. Somebody must be figuring the maid will take care of it all.

I roll Father Julian's chair away from his desk and sit down behind it, then splay my hands on the table. I can't feel the grain of the wood because I'm wearing latex gloves, but the desk feels solid, cold, as though it could last a thousand years. A sudden memory of my family comes to me. I'm at the beach with Bridget and Emily. We're building a sand castle; my daughter's face is full of smiles and freckles, her blond hair shoved out at sharp angles by the Elmo cap pulled down over her head. The edges of the ocean are moving forward, the water reaching the moat we have dug, the walls of the castle only minutes away from falling into the sea.

It's okay, Daddy, my daughter says, and she stops digging, understanding the futile nature of what she is trying to save. *We can always come back next weekend. We got forever more days to build another one.*

I take my hands away from the desk, and the memory disappears. I don't try chasing it.

I open the desk drawers one at a time, but all of them are empty. I pull them out completely and check underneath them—again, there's nothing there. I put them back and start flicking through the books on Father Julian's desk, hoping something might fall out from between the pages. Nothing does. No doubt somebody else has done this already. I search under the desk, but there's nothing.

I make my way around the room, unsure of what I'm looking for. I open Bibles and books, novels and how-to guides, flicking through them and finding nothing then putting them back. I remember two months ago when I came in here and how everything looked back then, like nothing was quite in place, like somebody had come through and moved everything slightly. Was Father Julian looking for something back then? In this instance it doesn't look like Father Julian was the one who made this mess. The Father Julian I knew never would have allowed his office to get like this. There are holes in the plaster walls obviously formed by fists. There are other holes down lower, kick marks made by somebody becoming increasingly frustrated. Drafts of cold air come through them. The books pulled from the shelves have been torn down and tossed on the ground, discarded into piles. Some of the pages and covers have been ripped away. Did whoever did this find what he was looking for?

I step out of the office and carry on through to the rectory. The beam on my flashlight is getting weaker, and I have the feeling that if it goes out completely the demons surrounding me will get a firm hold. Jesus looks down, probably in judgment, maybe wondering what in the hell a guy like me is doing in a place like this. *Well, Jesus, I'm trying to make compensation. I'm trying to repent. That's what you want, right?*

I stop the flashlight on the floor where the dead priest lay while I stood outside two nights ago worrying about being caught. I crouch down by the dried blood. I close my eyes and think about the series of photographs that Schroder and Landry showed me. Father Julian was lying on his back, his head twisted to the side. Closer photos showed gashes in the back of his head from the impact of the hammer. I don't know how many times he was hit, but it was more than once. Perhaps the first blow killed him. At the very least it would have dropped him to his knees. I figure he ended up dead face down, but was rolled onto his back. I try to imagine the thirty seconds before that. Did Julian know his killer was there—if so, why would he turn his back on him?

The tongue had to have been cut out after he was dead. It's not the kind of thing you can do to a man unless you've got him bound, and even then it'd be a struggle. The photographs didn't show any evidence of that, nor of any defensive wounds on Julian's hands. I look up and point the flashlight at the ceiling. There are lines of blood up there, cast off from the swinging hammer.

I stand up. Father Julian's tongue wasn't cut out to frame me: that's why it wasn't dumped in my house with the hammer. It was cut out not as a message, but from anger. Father Julian wouldn't tell his killer something he needed to know. That made him angry. That's why there are holes in the walls even in the lounge of the rectory. What was he looking for?

The entire death scene is horrible under the focused beam of a halogen bulb: it looks yellowish, like a faded newspaper article. Everything in here looks old too, like it all came out of a 1960s catalog. My immediate thought is that it can't be a fun lifestyle being a priest. Everything you own has to be old and outdated. It's a lifestyle that doesn't rely on monetary possessions, but on scripture and love and peace. In Father Julian's case, perhaps a little too much love if it turns out he is Bruce Alderman's father.

The rectory is as messy as the office. Papers and books everywhere. Furniture has been tipped up, the sofa and cushions torn open. The bedroom isn't any better. The mattress has been pulled from the bed and sliced up, every drawer pulled out and tipped over, a clutter of clothes and toiletries spewed across the floor. In the bathroom the medicine cabinet is empty. So is the space beneath the sink. I head back into the bedroom. There are framed photographs on the drawers—some have been tipped down, some have cracked glass. I don't recognize anyone in them except Father Julian and Bruce Alderman. Most of the others in the pictures are wearing cassocks.

I pull up the corner of the carpet in the bedroom then, and it's a case of like father like son. There is an envelope beneath it. I wonder who came up with the idea first—Bruce or Father Julian—and then I make room for the possibility it was a genetic link.

The envelope is full of photographs, fifteen, maybe twenty of them. Most are of babies; there are a few of young children and a couple in their teenage years. I recognize Bruce Alderman. The photos were taken when he wasn't looking at the camera, as if he didn't know the photographer was there. In most of the shots he is isolated, alone. But these images are out of context. They don't mean anything by themselves.

It's hard to know how many children I'm looking at here; the ages and faces seem to change to a point where I can't tell if a six-month-old baby is the same six-year-old or sixteen-year-old. There are sixteen photos in total. It's obvious the age of the photographs changes by the quality and condition of the paper they've been printed on, and by the clothes the kids are wearing. Some pictures look thirty years old, some look like they may only be a few. It's impossible to know whether Father Julian took them or was sent them. Other than the photos of Bruce, all the others are taken closer up—indoor shots of Christmas presents being opened, of birthdays, happy moments caught in time.

I pull the carpet up further, then start lifting it in other areas of the rectory before returning to the office and doing the same thing there. Nothing. These photographs, these children—is this the secret Father Julian died for?

I head back down the corridor. I've been here over an hour and Alderman is still waiting for me. I pass Father Julian's office. When I was here a month ago he apologized for the mess. He'd obviously been looking for something. I squeeze my eyes shut and try to focus. Something here is falling into place. I can see the edges of it, forming, forming . . . and I think of the key that Bruce Alderman gave me. No numbers, no markings. Did that key belong to Father Julian? Is that what he was looking for?

Suddenly the door I used to enter the church opens up, then closes. The muffled sound of a voice drifts down the corridor toward me, followed by high-squawking radio chatter. I duck down behind Father Julian's desk and turn off my flashlight. There is more radio chatter; I hear the word *backup*; and I know the officer parked outside has asked for it because for some reason he's decided to do his job and walk around the building and he's found the security tape over the door has been tampered with.

I move to the side of the desk so I can see into the corridor. The beam of a flashlight is bouncing from the floor to the walls. It's getting brighter. I pull back just as the officer reaches the office. The light hits the wall behind the desk.

It moves over it and then moves on. He takes a step into the room and then takes a step back out of it. He carries on to the next room. I figure I have about two minutes to get the hell out of here.

I get out from under the desk and move to the door. My feet are silent on the cold floor. I listen to the officer making his way further along the corridor. Then I look around the door frame. He's further down the corridor toward the rectory. He goes around a corner, and as soon as he's gone I start back toward the chapel for my clothes. I reach the end of the corridor. A second flashlight, this one moving around the pews, suddenly moves across the room and hits my body. I look away before it can hit my face.

"You! Hey, you! Stop!"

But I do the opposite. I turn and run toward the exit.

CHAPTER FORTY-THREE

I'm out of shape. I can feel it in the first few strides. My socks slide on the floor and the chase is almost over before it begins. I can hear the officer behind me, and a moment later the first one I saw appears at the other end of the corridor, running toward me. I pull the door; it opens into the corridor and blocks the path of at least one of my pursuers. Then I grab the basin of holy water and throw it in the opposite direction. It clatters on the ground without hitting anybody, but a moment later there's a sliding sound and then the man behind me yells "Shit!" as he slips and falls. It forces his partner to slow down. I keep running.

I hit the line of trees as the two men burst from the building behind me. I change direction and keep running, not slowing when my feet crash into tree roots or get punctured by pieces of bark and acorns and stones. I can hear them following me, closing the distance. I make a left and a right, and keep making them. I can see the beams of their flashlights falling on me, on trees around me, but then they appear less frequently. The rain is pouring down heavily, drowning out all sounds of pursuit. I keep running, altering direction through the trees. Suddenly I'm out of the trees, heading across the cemetery between gravestones and graves. I have no idea where I am, and the best I can hope for is that a cemetery at this time of night in this kind of weather is a hard place in which to follow anybody.

A car comes toward me from the road and I duck down behind a gravestone. It passes me by. There is yelling and confusion. I look out and see one of the officers is only a few meters away. He comes toward me and I duck back down. He passes me and keeps going. He's making quick ground. I crawl toward another grave and then another, staying hidden for a few more seconds. I look back up—the officers are now twenty meters away. I stand up and run deeper into the cemetery. My feet sink slightly into the grass. Another car travels along the road and I have to hide again. The cold air makes it harder for me to breathe, and I start sucking down oxygen in deep lungfuls that burn and make me dizzy. I hide behind a tall grave marker and look back in the direction I've come from. I can see flashlights moving around the trees and graves not far from me. I'm unsure now of what direction to run.

I stay low and move further away, putting more grass and graves and meters between me and the flashlights. More patrol cars arrive—I can see their headlights, hear doors banging. I reach another cluster of trees and rest for thirty seconds or so. My feet are aching and probably bleeding, but I don't want to look. I check back in what I believe, though am not certain, is the direction of the church. I panic for a moment about whether my wallet or keys are in the jacket I left behind, and I quickly check. My keys are in my pants pocket, and my wallet—I remember now—is still at home. I stick with the direction I was heading. I'm aware of more cars arriving, and rest for a few more seconds behind another grave marker to watch the show. Their pooling location shows me where the church is. There are no sirens sounding, but there are plenty of flashing blue and red lights from patrol cars through the trees and from others moving through the cemetery grounds. I keep running. And running. I think about the extra weight Schroder told me I'd put on, and I can feel every kilogram of it slowing me down. The contours of the land change. I head up and then down and then up again, hitting slight slopes that feel steeper than they really are, and they soon make it difficult to see anything behind me. I reach another section of the cemetery, but still have no idea where I am. I forge ahead, trespassing over the dead. I keep looking back. No more light. No more patrol cars. Not that I can see. More trees ahead of me, another stretch of graves. I burst through another patch of bushes and grass, then suddenly I'm at a fence line. I want to scale it, but I can't, not yet, not for a few more moments, not until my heart rate slows some and my body is convinced enough to keep going.

The fence backs onto somebody's house, an old clapboard home with a huge gap between the house and the garage. I drop down into the backyard and I run for the gap. There is no other fence. I reach the road and look left and right. I know where I am. There is a bus stop a few meters away from me. I walk down to it and then decide it's a bad place to be waiting. I cross the road and sit down behind a hedge. I take some slow, deep breaths in an effort to bring my heart rate back to normal.

I start back toward the car, ready to duck down behind a

tree or a bush or whatever else I can find at the first sign of any other cars or people. Ten minutes later I'm heading along the same road as the cemetery. I can see lights and commotion way up ahead, but the car is a good two blocks short of it. I unlock it and duck into the driver's seat, traipsing mud and leaves and blood into the car floor. I set the envelope of photographs on the passenger seat. It's been a bit bent out of shape, but is mostly dry except for two of the corners. I start the engine, but leave the lights off until I've rounded the first corner. I think about the shovel in the trunk and I figure tonight wasn't the best night to go digging anyway. Besides, there's something unnerving in the thought of returning Dad's car to him after it's been used to drive a corpse around. That hadn't been on the agenda when I borrowed it.

By the time I get home I'm bordering on exhaustion, though I don't feel tired. It's sensory overload. Without the benefit of alcohol to keep things running smoothly, without sleep, I know I'm going to crash and burn.

I take a quick shower and check my banged-up feet. They're grazed, but not as bad as I'd expected. Then I take the pictures from the damp envelope and separate them so they can dry out. I don't look at them closely. Not right now. I can't. But I can't leave them out either in case Landry or Schroder show up. I wipe them dry with a hand towel, then put them into a fresh envelope and throw out the old one. In the corner of my bedroom I lift up the carpet, figuring that since it worked so well for Alderman and Julian, it's got to work well for me too.

I hit my bed and fall asleep without even willing it.

CHAPTER FORTY-FOUR

Nobody comes to my house during the night. I reckon the police will have narrowed down last night's visitor to the church to one of three people—me, the killer, or a reporter. They'll have found my jacket and my shoes, but even if they recognize them there's nothing on them to say they're mine, only DNA, and that'll take weeks to arrive. Landry and Schroder will undoubtedly be thinking of coming to talk to me; they'll be wondering if they can bluff me into admitting I went into the church, though they'll know they can't. I know the game. And anyway, all I have to say is the same person who planted the murder weapon in my garage also planted my clothes to try to complete the frame job, and that's also what I'll be saying in two months' time when they get DNA from hair follicles caught in my jacket. Landry will have gone through all of this, hitting it from all sorts of different angles, without coming up with one that will help him cement a case against me. I'm betting that in the end he'll know his argument and he'll know my argument, and he'll know that mine is stronger.

Of course all of this is moot if I can't get back into the cemetery and dig Alderman up before Monday.

The overnight rain has stopped and for the moment the clouds are mainly dispersed. I open up the curtains and dump my sopping clothes into the washing machine. It seems that getting messed up at night is becoming a habit. Then I make coffee, wondering at what point in the human evolution coffee became such an important ingredient, and I figure if nothing else in this world, no matter what happens in the future, coffee will sure as hell be around a lot longer than religion. I carry the photographs I've pulled back out from under the carpet into my office. I go through them all again, but recognize only Bruce among the various boys and girls. Then I turn them over. They all have names and dates on the back. Just first names. The dates go back twenty-four years. I start flicking through them, the names rushing out at me from the past month, the names connecting the dots.

I put the photos down. I stand up and start to walk around my office, my breath quickening. Excitement is starting to build, the kind of excitement I haven't felt in a long time, not since working homicides in my previous life, not since the thrill of feeling things coming together and knowing you're heading for the finish line.

There are five girls in these pictures. Four of them share names with the dead girls who've been found. I have no idea where the fifth girl is, but I have a first name. Deborah. There are three boys too: Bruce, Simon, and Jeremy. I have no idea where Simon and Jeremy are either.

I go back to Rachel's photo and turn it over. I remember the other photos I've seen of her on the wall of her parents' house. Then suddenly I'm back in Father Julian's office. *Bruce was like a son to me*, he's telling me. Like a son. Were all these people like sons and daughters to Father Julian? I think they were. I remember looking at the pictures of the missing girls a month ago and thinking how similar they were, how their killer had a type. I was right and wrong. His type wasn't based on characteristics the girls shared, or body type or age. It was based on who these people were. It was based on genetics. These people were targeted specifically because of who they are. Brothers and sisters. All of the victims, including Bruce, are related.

CHAPTER FORTY-FIVE

The house looks a little tidier than the last time I was here. I figure their lives are no longer on hold. The news they'd been dreading has arrived, and though they're struggling with it, they're starting to move forward.

"I don't know whether to thank you or hate you," Patricia Tyler says, and she really seems to be trying hard to make up her mind.

"Can I come in? Please, it's important."

"I don't know," she says. "The truth is I hardly know what to think anymore."

I pull out the photograph from Father Julian's collection. The rest are in the envelope, tucked inside my jacket pocket. I hand it over. I know immediately that she recognizes it. Her knuckles turn white as she holds it ever tighter.

"Where did you get this?" she asks, though I'm pretty sure she already knows.

"Please, can I come inside?"

She takes a step back for me to move in, and leads me down the hallway.

"Michael isn't here," she says, then pauses. "Thankfully."

The photographs on the wall are all the same as the last time I was here, but I see them a little differently now. Michael Tyler, who is holding her hand when she is maybe five years old, doesn't appear in any earlier photographs.

We sit down in the lounge. Patricia Tyler offers me a drink and I tell her I'd like some water. She gets up and returns a minute later, carrying two glasses. She sets them down carefully on a pair of coasters and I ask the question I came here to ask.

"You're right," she says. "It all seems like a lifetime ago. Longer, when I think about it really hard. Rachel was four when I met Michael and six when we got married. It was like starting a new life. I could only hope that Michael would one day look at Rachel as if she was his own." She takes a sip of water. "He did see her that way too. He loved her, and the past years—well, they're killing him as much as they're killing me."

"And Father Julian, he was Rachel's biological father," I say, and it isn't a question.

"It's been over twenty years, and you're the first person to ever ask me about him." She looks back down at the photograph. "I remember this moment," she says. "It was the day Rachel turned two. I was leaving work early. My mother would look after Rachel while I was at work. She made a cake and we had a party, but Rachel didn't understand the occasion."

I remember a similar party for my own daughter. I remember getting carried away and buying too many gifts. Emily was excited tearing them open, but her concentration would drift from her new toy to the wrapping paper the toy had come in, and she would run around the room as if she was on a sugar high while friends and family watched and laughed and played with her. She would have five more birthdays. Rachel Tyler had seventeen more.

"This moment," she says, and she twists the photo toward me for the briefest of seconds. Rachel is sitting in the corner of a room with her head resting on her knees, her arms wrapped around her legs, and her eyes either half-open or half-closed. "It was at the end of the day. I was getting ready to take her back home and she didn't want to go. She wanted to stay with my mother, because she thought that it meant there would be more presents tomorrow."

She pauses, and I have the feeling her mind is traveling down a path of a possibility not taken. She's thinking that if she'd left her daughter at her mother's house on that day nearly twenty years ago, Rachel would still be alive.

"I don't even know why I took the photo," she says. "I mean, I remember taking it, and I remember asking her to smile, but I don't really know why I went about it. I'd already taken lots that day. I sent it to Father Julian. He'd asked for one. This, this is all about Father Julian, isn't it? You having this photo. You took it from him. And he's dead and Rachel's dead and there's something to that, isn't there? That's why you're here."

"What happened after you had the baby?"

"Things were already in motion before Rachel was born. We both knew I could never have an abortion. He wouldn't allow it, and anyway, it wasn't something I would have considered. I also knew he couldn't be with me. I was going to be a single mother, but it wasn't going to be the end of the world.

I had to give up work for the first year and a half. Stewart told me he would support me. We set up bank accounts. Once I got married, Stewart didn't have to pay as much, but he did keep paying. I never asked him for anything more, and he never asked to see Rachel."

I think about this for a few moments, sure that there is something else here. If Julian did father those other children, was he paying child support to all of them? If so, how did he get the money? I keep the conversation moving along, but make a mental note to come back to this.

"Did Rachel know?" I ask.

"When she was old enough she figured out Michael wasn't her real dad. She asked who her father was, but I never told her." She takes a drink. "I could really do with something stronger. Can I get you something?"

"Water's fine," I say, and I take a sip to show just how fine it is.

"I guess water's fine for me too. I know how it sounds, getting pregnant by a priest of all people, but, well, I don't regret it. Things were different back then. Father Julian . . . Huh, it sounds so funny when I call him that, doesn't it? The father of my child, and here I am calling him Father Julian instead of Stewart. I wonder if that means anything."

"I don't know."

"Look at me, I'm starting to ramble."

"No, please, it's all important."

"Back then . . . Stewart," she says, managing to use Father Julian's first name, "was a young man, and he was very, very striking. Almost insanely handsome. I think women were going to church just to see him, not to hear what he had to say. He had this—well, this magnetism—and it was more than just his looks. Everybody liked him; he was very charming, very likeable. But he was also lonely, really lonely, and seemingly vulnerable, and somehow that made him even more appealing. One day that loneliness became too much for him, for me, and we, we . . . Well, you know the rest. Anyway, he would always be quiet after we . . . you know, after we were together in that way. He was intense too, and even though he knew he was making a mistake, neither of us could help ourselves. He would tell me that when he was around me it was like somebody else was taking over, like he was a different man. I think he was a good man trapped in the wrong profession."

"Did you ever tell him that?"

She smiles again. "More than once. But he said the priesthood was a calling, that he could help people, that he could do more good with a collar than without one. It was hard to watch. He was so dedicated to the church, it pained him every time we were together. In the end, I finished it, I had to. I didn't want to, but what choice did I have? It was tearing him apart. A month after we stopped seeing each other, I found out I was pregnant."

"What happened when you told him?"

"He wanted to do the right thing, only the right thing didn't fall in line with his big picture of right things. It was like every day he was fighting a personal war within himself. I think that war was there his entire life. He was never going to leave the priesthood to be with me, and he couldn't stay being a priest if others found out. So we both agreed to keep it quiet. I also stopped going to church." She dabs her knuckles into the bottoms of her eyes and pulls away some tears before taking another sip of water.

"Did Michael know?"

"He knew. I had to tell him. Can you imagine if he hadn't known? Every day he would wonder. He would think maybe

I was sleeping with so many people that I didn't know who Rachel's dad was. I told him, and he wasn't angry or disappointed. He was relieved, for some reason. I'm not sure why exactly. I think maybe knowing a priest had got me pregnant was much better than thinking I'd slept with some drug addict or criminal. Purer, or something. If that makes sense."

It does, in a weird kind of way. "Did you keep in touch with Father Julian?"

"In the beginning, of course, but after I met Michael I didn't really want to involve Stewart in my life anymore. He seemed to understand. Then the day Rachel turned sixteen he stopped the payments and I didn't ask him why, because I knew. Sixteen was the cutoff date. I never saw him over those years. If it wasn't for my mother, well . . ."

"He presided over your mother's funeral?"

"My mother had continued to go to his church. It's what she would have wanted."

"Your mother didn't know who the father was?"

"I refused to tell her."

"So Father Julian, he saw Rachel that day?"

She takes another sip of water, and when she pulls the glass back she seems to be studying the edge, looking for some microscopic flaw.

"He saw her. Then a week later she goes missing. That's the connection, isn't it? That's why you're here. If I had told Rachel he was her father, would things be different now? Is that the reason she's dead? Because I took her to my mother's funeral?"

I know what answer she wants to hear, but I can't offer it to her.

"Do you know if Father Julian ever had any other children?" I ask.

"It's my fault," she says, and she starts to cry.

I clutch my glass of water, unsure whether to sit next to her, whether to put a hand on her shoulder and try to comfort her. "None of this is your fault," I say, and it sounds generic because that's exactly what it is. "But please, this is important. Did Father Julian have any other children?"

She leans back and stares at me. Tears are streaking her makeup. "Other children? I . . . I never really thought about it. He could have, I suppose. But I doubt it."

"How did he get the money to send you?"

"I . . . I don't know. But Father Julian is . . . I mean *was* a good man. He would have done what it took."

I pull the rest of the photographs out of my pocket and hand them over to her. "There are names on the back," I say.

She looks through them, but doesn't recognize any of them.

"There is no way these can all be his children," she says, but I think she knows there is a way. I think she can see the resemblances too.

"These payments he made to you, they were credited directly into your account?"

"Of course. It was the only way."

"Do you still have any of the statements?"

"I . . . I suppose I do," she says, and I'm sure she does. I'm sure Patricia Tyler is the sort never to have thrown away anything from the last thirty years.

"Would you mind finding me one?"

"Why?"

"Because if I can get his bank account number, then if he did father any other children I can find their names."

"Do you think . . ." She pauses, unwilling or unsure how to continue. "Do you think all these girls who died . . . Do you really think they're related?"

I hold her gaze. She stares right at me and I tell her yes. She pulls her hand to her mouth as if to hold it closed from whatever she wants to say next.

"Then you already know who these girls are," she says. "They've been identified."

"Not all of them."

"What?"

"There are five girls in these pictures."

"Five? Oh," she says, and she gets it immediately. She gets that there is one more girl out there who I need to find. "I know where the bank statements are," she says, and she disappears for a few minutes before returning with one from five years ago.

"It's the last payment he made," she tells me.

I look at the statement. It doesn't have Julian's name on it. Just his account number, along with the word *Rachel*.

"Can I take this?" I ask.

"Of course."

I finish off my water and she walks me to the door. "The police, are they close to finding who killed him?" she asks.

"They're getting there."

"But you're getting there quicker, aren't you."

"Yes."

"Can you promise me something?" she asks.

"I'll do my best," I say, already knowing what she is going to ask.

"Promise me you'll find him before something happens to that other girl. Promise me that when you find him, you'll make him pay for what he has done. For Rachel. For the others. For all of us. Make him pay. Promise me you'll make it so he can never hurt another girl ever again."

CHAPTER FORTY-SIX

"What the hell do you want?"

"Your help," I say.

"You've got to be kidding."

It's still early Saturday morning. I should have called Landry or Schroder, but instead I've driven to the hospital. I need to work my own way, especially if I'm to get the opportunity to dig Sidney Alderman out of his wife's grave. There's no way I can do that if I'm in custody answering questions about how I know what I know.

Visiting hours on a Saturday morning mean the corridors are full of disoriented-looking family members and friends. The air has the sickly smell of disinfectant and vomit, but you get used to it pretty quick. Emma's father pushes me in the chest with his knuckle and I fall back a few steps. I don't put up a fight. He advances toward me. A few people look over, but no one does anything. "I should have killed you," he says.

"There's still plenty of time for that," I say, holding my hands up in surrender. "At least listen to me before you get kicked out of the hospital for assault."

"You're the Goddamn reason we're in here," he says. "They'd kick you out and give me a medal."

"Maybe you should hear me out," I say. "I have some interesting things to say. You are my lawyer, remember. You signed me out. That means it's your job to talk to me. If not, I'll go to your firm and find another lawyer. I'll tell them all about you. All about that trip we took."

"Fuck you."

"You didn't think it through, did you? I'm your responsibility until that court date has come and gone. See, you figured I'd be dead by then and it wouldn't matter. But now it does. Help me out and I change lawyers. Nobody has to know what happened."

"Go to hell."

"Think about it. Calm down and think about it."

He takes a step back and stands in the doorway of the ward. He looks at his daughter. She's awake and hooked up to a bunch of machines. There is a TV going. She glances from the TV to her father. Then his wife, an attractive blond woman dressed perhaps a little too formally for a hospital, looks at me too. She knows something is going on, but doesn't know what. There is no recognition. If there was she'd start screaming. She'd claw out my eyes. My lawyer turns back toward me.

"What do you want?"

I explain what I want, and the whole time he shakes his head.

"Impossible," he finally says.

"I thought lawyers thrived on the impossible."

"We thrive on sure things."

"But you make more money on the impossible."

"No judge will sign off on it," he says.

"That's the point, right? You don't need one to. Just get the template for me and I can do the rest. Then you don't hear from me again. Look, nothing is going to happen. I'm never going to tell anybody where I got it from."

"No," he says.

"No?"

"That's right," he says. "I go to my boss and explain what I did to you, and he understands. He'll tell me he would have done the same thing."

"And maybe I go to the papers and tell them about you. Even if they don't believe me, it still puts your name in disrepute. People might sympathize with you, they might even relate, they'll probably wish you'd pulled the trigger, but that'll be on their mind every time they're passing you over in preference for another lawyer."

"Won't happen. People will love me for it," he says.

"I think you have a great misunderstanding of what people love. You prepared to take that risk?"

He looks back at his wife. She's looking a little concerned, but I bet she doesn't know about the field trip her husband took me on. My lawyer planned on killing me. He didn't succeed, and I'm here to pull him deeper into the world he stepped foot in. Only I'm also giving him an exit. He just needs to see that—and, being a lawyer, I figure he will.

"Just the template," he says.

"That's all."

"And where am I supposed to get this from?"

"See, that's the thing. You must know people. I'm sure you can make it happen."

"It'll take an hour."

"I've got time."

I head upstairs to the cafeteria and order some coffee and a couple of chicken and egg salad rolls. There are a few newspapers lying around. There is nothing in the front-page photo of Father Julian to suggest that he was living a secret life. There is a stock quote from somebody high up in the police: "We are following up on leads, but can't release any further details at this time." They have a murder weapon and no suspect. There is another article a few pages in. It details Father Julian's history. He was assigned to the church thirty years ago. He was born in Wellington to a middle-class family, he excelled academically at school, he joined the priesthood at twenty-one. His mother died twenty-five years ago, his father is still alive. There are facts and figures that would be thrown out of whack if I were to tell them Father Julian fathered all those children.

I read through the rest of the newspaper, but don't get to the end before Donovan Green is back. He pulls out the seat opposite me, seems about to sit down, then changes his mind. He doesn't want to sit with a guy like me. He reaches into his jacket pocket and pulls out an envelope. He sets it on the table and keeps two fingers on it.

"We're done now, right?" he asks.

"That depends."

"On?"

"On whether that's a Christmas card in there or what I asked for."

He slides it across. I open it up and take a look at the court order. I've seen them before and know it's the real thing.

"I don't ever want to see you again," he says.

"For what it's worth, I'm sorry."

"Yeah. Lawyers hear it all the time, right? Everybody's sorry after the event."

I don't answer him. He stares at me for a few more seconds, and I can tell he's thinking about how life would be different for him right now if he'd killed me.

"Worse," I say.

"What?"

"It'd be worse. Trust me. You did the right thing."

He nods, seeming to understand, then turns and walks away. I push the newspaper aside, finish my lunch, and head down to the car.

CHAPTER FORTY-SEVEN

The traffic out near the nursing home increases a little on weekends, but it's not like visiting hours at the hospital. The hospital is a temporary thing. Relatives and friends don't mind making the visit because they only have to go a few times. Out here it's permanent. The visits don't fit in as often as they ought to in the schedule of day-to-day life. The nursing home is too depressing, even with its brightly colored artwork and flowers. There's no covering up the pain and misery here.

I sit with my wife and hold her warm hand. She looks out at the rain, but doesn't see it. It's hard to imagine that a person doesn't look forward to certain types of weather. Sun, rain, storms: they don't even register.

"Things are getting better," I tell her. "I've stopped drinking, but it's hard, I'll admit that. It's hard to describe. Without drinking I feel like a part of me is missing. I feel like I need to have one more just to say good-bye to it," I say, and I picture the one remaining glass in the back of my fridge. "One more won't hurt, right? Just to say good-bye. I think of you all the time. I wish things were different, but I want you to know that you're helping me get through this. You're the reason I'm getting my life back on track."

I tell her this, but I don't tell her that it's only been a day. Maybe in a week my speech will be different. Maybe I will be able to take that drink to say good-bye and not get pulled into the abyss. Maybe.

Back downstairs, Carol Hamilton is behind the desk.

"It's good that you're starting to come back," she says.

"I miss her."

"I know you do. It's an awful situation, and it's worse for you than it is for her. I just wish there was more I could do."

"I know. I make the same wish every day."

She doesn't answer, and I let the silence fall down around us like a shroud, letting us think our own thoughts on how life could be different.

"I hate to ask," I say, snapping her out of it, "but have you got a computer I can quickly borrow? And a photocopier?"

"I . . . umm . . ."

"It will only take me a minute or two. I promise."

"That's fine, Theo. Follow me."

She leads me into an office that has more photos of family and drawings from children on the walls than anything else. There are so many personal items that it's easy to see the people who work here need to stay grounded to a different kind of reality, one where the bad things that happen in life haven't extended to their own families. I'm about to play around with the computer and photocopier when I spot a manual typewriter. I can't remember the last time I saw one.

"One of the nurses," Carol says, "is still very old school." She doesn't explain any further and she doesn't need to.

I wind the court order into the typewriter, and type in the priest's name and location of the bank in the provided space. Then I sign it with some unidentifiable scribble. Carol Hamilton watches me the entire time, but doesn't ask what I'm doing. She doesn't point out that I've gone over the two minutes I promised her I'd be. When I'm done, I thank her for her time, and she does something different for once—she puts one hand on my shoulder and, with the other, grabs my hand and tells me not to give up hope. I'm not sure whether she means for Bridget or myself.

I already have the car started and in gear when she comes out the doors and waves me down.

"It doesn't mean anything," she says, "and you need to understand that. But it's still something you should see."

"What is it?"

"Come with me," she says, and I kill the engine and follow her back inside and upstairs.

My wife is still sitting by the window, staring out at the rain. Carol stays in the doorway as I walk into the room. Bridget is in the exact same position as earlier, and at first I'm not so sure what it is that Carol wants me to see, but then I see it. Bridget is clutching a photograph of our daughter. At some point since I walked out of here she has stood up and made her way over to the bedside drawers and picked up the photo frame. I think about the photographs of the dead girls in my pocket, and it seems like an omen: that of all days for her to have somehow taken this photograph it has to be this day. She is holding it against her, the frame pressing into her breasts, the image of Emily facing the window as though Bridget is trying to share the view. I want to read more into it, I want to believe this is more than just one of her automated responses, and I study her face for something—a tear, a flicker of emotion—but there is nothing. Still, it is the first time she has ever picked something up and brought it back to her chair. At least it's the first time I know of—it could be she does this at night and puts the pictures back in the morning. I don't know, but I like the idea that in the dead hours of the night she gets out of bed and reaches for Emily. It's sad, it's depressing, but it's the sort of hook that I can come along and hang some hope on.

I sit down next to her and I rest my head on her shoulder, and I hug her and tears slide from my eyes and soak into her gown, and I pray to the God I want to believe in but can't that Bridget will tell me that things are okay, that she will stroke the back of my head and comfort me.

But she doesn't. When I look back at her face it's just as it was moments before. But my hope stays firmly on the hook I placed it on. I stay with her for a while—I'm not sure how long exactly—an hour, maybe two. At some point Carol Hamilton walks away. I see her on my way back out and she smiles, but she doesn't say anything. I guess she is too frightened to offer me hope that she doesn't think is there.

When I get back outside it's raining hard. I drive home and change into some fresh clothes, even ironing a shirt and a pair of pants pulled from the dryer. My look could be the difference between getting the information I need and getting busted.

Back in town I can't find a parking space and have to settle for one six blocks away from the bank. A few years ago and this place would have been closed on a Saturday afternoon; now hardly anything closes. I look at my watch and check the opening hours on the door. The bank shuts in less than twenty minutes. I've timed things perfectly.

The security guard gives me a strange look, and I realize it's because I've taken two steps inside and come to a complete stop. I walk over to him. He seems unsure what to do. I pull out my ID, which I haven't used in more than two years. I used to have a badge that went along with it, but that got handed back. The ID has the word *Void* stamped across the side of it, but I cover it with my finger and let the guard look at it for about a second before I put it away.

"I seen you on TV," he says. "Didn't realize you were still a cop."

"Technically I'm not, but I'm working for them. That's why I still have the ID," I say, hoping it makes some kind of sense.

"Didn't know there was a *technically* when it comes to working for the police."

I give him the *What are you gonna do* stare. "Nothing is how it should be these days," I say. "All I know is the pay is better on this side of *technically* than on the other side of *actually*."

He shrugs, as if he doesn't seem to care one way or the other. I guess he doesn't. At twelve bucks an hour, why would he?

"I have a court order to access a customer's account," I say. "Can you point me in the direction of somebody to talk to?"

"Sure," he says, and he brushes a hand over the side of his head where a corner flap of his toupee is sticking up. He leads me to an open office door and knocks on it. A woman in her midthirties stands up from behind her desk and comes over. "There's a guy here who wants to access an account," he says, and she looks at him a little blankly because accessing accounts is what people come here to do. But then he adds, "He has a court order."

"Oh. Well, it's a little more complicated than that," she says, looking me up and down. "Hey, haven't I seen you on TV?"

"Probably. Can we talk in here?"

"Of course," she says, and she looks at the security guard with a dismissive gesture. He doesn't seem to react one way or the other, he just walks away, but when he gets near the main entrance he looks a little more vigilant now that a former law-enforcement officer is around.

She closes her office door and sits behind her desk. There's a name plaque on the front of it. *Erica.* On the wall there's an aerial shot of Christchurch that doesn't show the true emotion of the city, and a couple of photographs, one of which shows Erica standing next to a man who looks vaguely familiar, probably somebody from one of the numerous banking ads on TV.

"So, what's this all about, Detective . . ."

"Tate," I say, and I don't bother to correct her assumption that I'm still with the force. The business card I was going to give her stays in my hand, and the chances of coming out of here with what I want have just increased.

"I have an account number here," I say, and I slide the bank statement over to her. I have underlined Father Julian's account number. I also slide her over the court order. The judge's name on the top of it is as made up as his signature.

The thing with court orders is a lot can come down to the timing of the delivery. Erica picks it up, and then she does exactly what I expect her to do—she glances at her watch. I've seen it a dozen times at the end of the working day when we've shown up with one of these orders: it was often the time we'd aim for. The other thing is that people don't know what to do with them. They look at them, but they don't know how to react because most people have never seen one before. They've seen them get delivered on TV and they figure that what happens on TV is probably the thing that happens in real life. They suddenly feel like the order has just taken away all their rights of refusal and they don't argue it. They only ever fight it if they have something to hide.

Erica reads it thoroughly. In the location area the words printed are "to access any and all available accounts of the account holder" and after that I've typed out the account number.

"This is one of your bank account numbers, isn't it?" I ask.

"It is. Is this part of a criminal investigation?"

"I'm not at liberty to say," I say, and I figure she wasn't expecting anything less.

"I need to call my boss about the order," she tells me.

"No problem."

"I'll probably need to fax it to him."

"I don't mind waiting."

She checks the time again. "Give me a minute."

"Take your time," I say.

She leaves me in her office, and I'm not sure whether it'll be her or the police who come back in. I keep glancing at my watch, and each time I think I should just get up and go, cut my losses before Landry or Schroder arrives.

"The account is in the name of John Paul," she says when she returns. I figure the court order got faxed to her boss and not much further. Maybe to their law firm, but it's probably the kind of firm that charges too much to be on retainer on the weekend, so it's sitting in a fax tray somewhere. I've seen it dozens of times. She's not giving me a lot, just a few details. She doesn't see how it can hurt. She sits back down behind her desk. "Like the pope," she adds.

"How long has it been active?"

She twists the computer monitor to face her. "Twenty-four years."

"I need printouts of payments."

"Okay," she says. "It'll take a few minutes."

"No problem."

She taps away at her keyboard, then leans back. I don't hear a printer going anywhere.

"Did John Paul have any other accounts set up? Or was it just this one?" I ask.

"Just this one. But . . ." She stops, then looks back down at the court order.

"What?"

"When he set up the account, he also set up a safe-deposit box."

"A safe-deposit box? Here?"

"It's even at this branch," she says.

"Can I access it?"

"The court order doesn't say you can."

"Listen, Erica, this is very, very important."

She seems unsure of what to do.

"This safe-deposit box—did John Paul gain access to it with a key?" I ask.

"Of course. That's how everybody opens them."

"When was the last time he accessed it?"

She looks at her monitor. "Ten weeks ago."

"How many keys were issued?"

"Just the one."

"Can you tell me if this is it?" I reach into my pocket and drag out my keys. I twist the one Bruce Alderman gave me off the ring and hand it over to her.

"Sure. This is for one of our boxes, though I can't tell you if it's specifically for John Paul's box. We don't label the keys for a reason, you know, in case they get lost and people try to use them."

I stand up. "I need you to take me to it."

"What?" She looks at her watch again, then rests the key on the desk in front of her. "I don't know—I'll have to check with my boss."

"Okay, do what you need to do. But you essentially just said that whoever has the key can gain access to the box, that's why you don't label them. If you want, though, I can get the court order amended—that's fine too. I can get the judge to sign it and be back here in . . ." I glance at my watch, "an hour and a half. Two hours tops."

"Two hours?"

"Yeah. That's what it'll take."

She gives it only a few seconds' thought. "Okay. Since you have the key I don't see any problem. The room is this way."

And she picks up the key, and I follow her out of her office.

CHAPTER FORTY-EIGHT

Most of the safe-deposit boxes are a little bigger than a phone book, but there are perhaps a dozen or so that are two to three times bigger. There are three walls full of them, each numbered. Erica approaches them slowly, as if still reluctant to be doing this, but then she looks at her watch and remembers that it's time to leave and Saturday night is waiting. She puts the key into one of the bigger boxes, twists it, opens the door, and pulls out a metal tray from within. She sits it down on the table, then points out three small rooms off to the side.

"There's privacy in there. Take your time," she says, sounding as if she doesn't want me to take my time, but to get in and out of there in under a minute. I intend to help her out there.

The room doesn't have much legroom. I can reach out and touch both walls at the same time without stretching. I put the tray on the table and open it.

Audio tapes are stacked side to side, the small microcassettes that take up less room. They are all labeled with numbers. I pull a large plastic evidence bag out of my pocket and start filling it up. There is also an accountant's notebook, and I flick it open to see bunches of names and dates and figures before I throw that into the evidence bag as well. The box is now empty. I leave it on the table and I step out of the cubicle and find Erica is back. She looks at the evidence bag, but says nothing. I've closed over the seal and signed it so it all looks more official. She hands me the cardboard box she has filled with the printed bank statements.

She walks with me to the front door. The security guard is waiting for me. "I always wanted to be a cop," he says. "Would've done it too, but I have a banged-up knee that stopped me." It's a story heard from plenty of security guards over the years. It might have been a banged-up knee, or it could have been fear or lack of motivation, or he failed the psych test.

The bank is almost empty now. The security cameras in the ceiling have captured my image from a dozen different angles and I know this is going to come back and really bite me in the ass. But that's for another day. Maybe the same day they dig Sidney Alderman up. And today things are going well. Today my wife hugged a photo of my daughter and I hit a lead that could take me straight to Rachel's killer. When you get those kinds of leads, you don't slow down for anything.

As the guard unlocks the door to let me out, Erica starts to turn away.

"Just one more thing," I ask her, and she turns back. She seems about to glance at her watch again, but pulls herself out of the movement. "The photograph behind your desk, there's you and another guy—he looks around fifty, maybe sixty. He seems familiar."

"He was the bank manager here for many years," she says. "You would have seen him around if you ever came in here."

"Was?" I ask, and I'm starting to figure out who it is.

"Henry died a couple of years ago," she says.

"Henry Martins."

"That's right. You knew him?"

"I went swimming with him once."

Outside, the rain is still thick and heavy, and so is the traffic. I pass a guy scraping chewing gum off the sidewalks and depositing his collections into a plastic bucket. He's wearing a T-shirt that has a picture of the Easter Bunny up on a crucifix. It says *Jesus had a stunt double*, and I wonder how Father Julian would have reacted to seeing it. Another guy sniffing glue is leaning up against a bike rack watching the guy. I guess Saturday brings the crazies out a little earlier.

I get past them and run through the rain to my car.

CHAPTER FORTY-NINE

I'm anxious to listen to the tapes, but I have no way of playing them. I dump the contents of the evidence bag on the passenger seat. There are perhaps forty tapes inside it. I open the accounts book and see it's a log of some kind. The dates seem to match up with dates scrawled across the sides of the microcassettes. I start looking through the bank statements. There are over two hundred and fifty of them, one for each month. I figure Erica must have had a few printers going to get them all done in the small amount of time she had. The statements are full of random amounts and dates and names. I look in vain for Henry Martins's name, but what seemed like a random connection between Rachel Tyler and Henry Martins suddenly seems a lot less random.

I toss everything back into the bag and pull away from the curb.

I hit the mall and again struggle to find a parking space.

Late Saturday afternoon and it seems nobody in this city has anything better to do than come out shopping an hour before the mall closes. At the electronics store the only thing they have in stock for recording conversations is digital, but they suggest another couple of shops to try. I finally find what I'm looking for.

"Last one in stock," the guy tells me. "Hardly anyone uses them anymore. Even secretaries use digital."

"I have a thing for old technology."

I get back to my father's car only to find that a shopping cart has strayed from the flock and smacked into the back bumper, creating a small dent that I know my dad will spot around the time I'm turning the car into their driveway. This is the reason, he'll tell me, he didn't want to lend me the car in the first place. If he realizes that I'm driving without a license, then that will confirm it. If we can put a man on the moon, surely the digital age will reach a point where shopping carts can guide their way back into the supermarket by themselves.

I load fresh batteries into the tape recorder and pick a tape at random. I've been pretty certain about what to expect, and when I push play my suspicions are confirmed after just a few seconds of hissing.

"Forgive me, Father, for I have sinned."

"How long has it been since your last confession?"

Father Julian's voice is deep and clear. It makes me shiver to hear a dead man's voice, and I feel sick to know he was violating all of the people on these tapes. The other voice could be anybody. It's a male. Could be twenty years old. Could be eighty. I pause the tape. I have to. I have to sit in silence and let what has happened sink in. I have to prepare myself to hear the things that I'm going to hear. It makes me feel like I'm complicit in some way just by listening. I press play.

"I've done it again."

"Done what again?"

I look at the names Julian has neatly written into his log. The confessional is supposed to be completely anonymous, but I suspect the reality is that it's not. I think at minimum the priest has a good idea who they're talking to because it's likely to be somebody from their congregation.

"Cheated. On my wife. I know it's wrong, Father, but the problem is I can't help it. It's like another person takes over. It's like I know what I'm doing is wrong, but at the time I can't consider the consequences."

"Maybe you do consider them but choose to ignore them."

"I don't know. Maybe that's true. It would explain a lot."

I push the stop button and fast forward the tape for a while. When I push play I hear Father Julian's voice.

". . . to realize you are hurting more than just yourself."

"I know, I know." It's a woman's voice. *"It's just that, well, sometimes I can't help it. It's like a different person takes over."*

"Perhaps you should look at it from another . . ."

I push stop. Is this everybody's excuse? That they aren't responsible for anything in their lives? That their actions are justifiable because another person takes over?

"I'm a different person when it happens. I'm no longer me," Quentin James told me as he stood by the grave he had dug, waiting for me to forgive him.

Was that my excuse too?

Maybe. But I don't think so. I wasn't switching between personae. Alcohol made Quentin James the man he was, and he would live with a foot in each of those worlds, existing as two separate men. I'm different. Quentin James made me into a different kind of man, and there's no going back from that. There is only one Theodore Tate.

When I get home my body is exhausted, but my mind is still racing with excitement: it's a weird combination that makes me want to sleep, but at the same time pace the room. I don't get to do either, because walking from the driveway to my house I'm brought to a stop by Casey Horwell and her cameraman. I don't see a van anywhere, and assume they must have been camped out in a dark red sedan parked opposite. Again Horwell is wearing enough makeup to look like the media whore she is. I can see the thin lines and cracks in the foundation. She smells like stale coffee. I lower the bag of tapes and statements and hold it to my side, out of sight of the camera.

"Mr. Tate," she says, getting into my face. "It hasn't taken you long to get behind the wheel of a car since losing your license. You manage this, *and* you're a suspect in the murder of Father Julian. Your friends in the department you seem exceedingly proud of must really be working overtime to keep you out of jail."

"I thought reporters liked asking questions, not giving statements," I say, immediately wishing I was saying nothing.

"Actually we do both."

"Just not accurately."

I start to move around her, but she sidesteps into my way. She probably wants me to push her, and that's exactly what I feel like doing. I want to grab her by the arm and escort her off my property, but then I change my mind and go with a different tactic.

"Would you care to tell us how the murder weapon came to be found in your garage?" she asks.

"What murder weapon?" I ask.

"The hammer."

"What hammer?" I ask.

"The one that killed Father Julian."

"Who's Father Julian?" I ask.

She frowns a little, unsure of where I'm going with this. "The man whose church you have been parked outside of for the last four weeks."

"What church?"

The frown becomes a deeper crease and breaks a line into her makeup. "Is this a game to you?"

"What game?"

"People are showing up dead and you're the only commonality."

"What's a commonality?"

The creases deepen. Her smirk fades, quickly replaced by her annoyance, and beneath the surface of her makeup a different Casey Horwell is simmering.

"Where is Sidney Alderman?" she asks.

"What's an Alderman?"

She turns to her cameraman. "That's it," she says, and the camera is lowered.

"You're finished," she says. "We got you on tape driving into the street, and that makes you look bad."

"You think that's the best you can do?" I ask.

"Actually no. You haven't seen the best I can do, but you will. Come on, Phil," she says, turning to her cameraman, "let's go."

"Wait," I say.

She turns back toward me. She gives me such a dark look I'm sure she's trying to cut me open with it. "What for?" she asks.

"Your source. Who is it?"

"Are you that stupid? You think I'm going to tell you?"

"Just tell me this," I say. "Is it a cop?"

"I'm not telling you anything."

"Is it a cop?" I ask, and this time I yell it at her.

She takes a step back, and the cameraman swings his camera back up and starts to film me again.

"I suggest you back down, Tate."

"And I suggest you think about what you've got yourself into," I say. "This source of yours, if it's not a cop, then who can it be, huh? Who else can possibly have fed you all that bullshit about the murder weapon, huh? There's only one possibility. You're being played, Horwell, and you're too stupid to know it, and when you figure it out you'll be too arrogant to admit it. But you're responsible for anything that happens now, you get that? If you keep that name to yourself and it turns out to be the guy who killed those girls, and he kills again, then that's on you. You get that? You keep your mouth shut and don't go to the police, you're as good as helping him."

"Fuck you," she says. "You don't know a damn thing. You're some washed-up private detective who thinks he can do what the hell he wants and get away with it, just because his daughter got herself killed. You think you're the only person in the world to have lost somebody? You think her death is going to keep people feeling sympathetic toward you even after all of this? You're the one who's arrogant and stupid, Tate. Your career is over and I'm going to make sure of it. You're a piece of shit murderer who isn't going to keep getting away with it. And you're going to see me every single day of your trial and I'm going to expose you to the world as the man you really are."

I feel like jumping on her and slapping her until she gives up the name of her source, but that's not going to happen, especially with the cameraman standing here probably hoping I do. I just have to trust that the tapes and the statements will tell me what she won't.

I move past her and get inside and shut the door on the

world. I stand in the hallway, my heart rate up, feeling angry at her and also angry at myself for letting her get to me. I go into my office and sit down, but I can't focus on anything. I leave the tapes and the bank statements on my desk and I head out to the lounge. I switch on the CD player and turn the music up and walk around my kitchen, opening up cupboards looking for something to eat, wanting to do something to calm myself down, to find a distraction. I open the fridge, and there it is, the final glass waiting for me, full of liquid that can, for a brief moment, make me feel better.

I close the fridge door. Instead I make myself some coffee. I need something to calm me down, and I decide coffee isn't it, and I let it sit on my counter and watch it go cold. The anger starts to fade. I do what I can to push Casey Horwell from my thoughts, and when she is far enough in the background I go back to the office and sit down with the bank statements.

I reckon the original statements would have changed color and style as the bank updated its logo and even its name from time to time, but the printouts all look identical. I start adding up the amounts, comparing them against the logs Father Julian kept. Over the years he has taken in almost one hundred and fifty thousand dollars in deposits. He has made the exact same amount in withdrawals. The deposits are from the people on the tapes who didn't know their *Bless me, Father, for I have sinneds* weren't the first steps up to salvation, but steps down into Father Julian's world. The logs go back twenty-four years. So do the bank statements.

The logs and statements and tapes all add up to blackmail. There really isn't any other way to see it. Over the course of twenty-four years Father Julian blackmailed more than a hundred people. The amounts are different, and this probably reflects two things—the amount the victim was earning, and the amount the victim had to lose if his or her secret was found out. Maybe those being blackmailed never knew who had their secret. Could be they suspected, but people with secrets might be paranoid enough to believe someone more than just their priest knows. For almost a quarter of a century Father Julian played with fire. He must have known it would eventually burn him. Or perhaps it burned him the entire time. He was taking the money and using it to put out smaller fires.

In the end the fire got him. He recorded somebody who wasn't willing to pay, and that somebody knew I was following the priest and would be an easy target to frame. It wouldn't have been hard. Just flick on the TV and there I was, covered in blood one night and accused of murdering the caretaker, and two months later accused of stalking the priest.

But that's only a theory. And if that's the way it went down, then Father Julian's death wasn't related to the girls dying. Still, it would be a hell of a coincidence, although one that is entirely possible. Does that coincidence allow for the fact Henry Martins was the manager of the bank where Father Julian kept his tapes?

Julian must have selected his victims carefully, blackmailing only those he knew were non-threatening, those who for a price could have it all go away. He never tried to blackmail me, but I'm sure he recorded the session. Maybe he was scared of what I would do to him if he tried. I'd already confessed to one murder. He knew I was capable of another.

The anger kicks in and suddenly I wish Father Julian was still alive just so I could do something to him—I don't know what exactly, surely not the kind of Quentin James something, and I try not to let my mind drift there. I'd hurt him. Hurt him a lot. The bastard refused to tell me about the confessions he had heard from the man who killed those girls—and, what's worse, he must have known who those girls were. He found within himself the ability to blackmail people, to break the confessional vow he had with God in order to make money, but he couldn't bring himself to save those girls. How could a man with such mixed-up priorities live with himself?

Maybe blackmailing was still a step away from actually revealing the sins he'd heard in secret. Could be he never shared any of the confessions, and never planned to. Does that mean he wasn't breaking the confessional seal? I figure it's a technical question that could only be answered by a man caught up in the dilemma it poses.

I wonder if he knew the fire was coming for him. Part of me thinks he did, part of me is sure he accepted it.

I go through the logs and bank statements, looking at the payments Father Julian was making. He doesn't pay anybody for longer than sixteen years, but he pays some of them for less. Some considerably less. Most of the names are here, but not all of the people in the photographs are, and the number of names suggests there are more children out there than Father Julian had photos for. And there could be more children out there who aren't on these lists—children Father Julian fathered and was unable to take responsibility for. I wonder which names line up with the Simon and Jeremy I found on the backs of the photographs, and suspect I'm only a few phone calls from finding out.

These are Father Julian's child payments for the children he had in secret. The question is how many people could have known? I don't know, but I'm pretty certain Henry Martins did.

CHAPTER FIFTY

The logs are chronological and well detailed, and there are far more confessors here than there are victims of Father Julian's blackmailing. Before going any further, I head back two years into the dates and I find my name. Seeing it there brings everything into focus, as though any doubts I've had, or wanted to have, are peeled away, exposing the reality and grounding me to it. I find the correct tape. I put it into the machine, not sure that I'm prepared to hear myself from so long ago, not prepared to hear the man I used to be. I cue it up to the time stamp Julian listed. I'm not sure, either, where I stand on my belief of God, or where I stood on the matter two years ago. Part of me didn't believe in God, another part hated Him, and a third made me sit inside that confessional booth with the need to tell somebody what I'd done. Since then I have learned to live with my own secrets.

I catch the last few seconds of somebody else's confession,

there are a few moments of silence, and then my voice. It
sounds different. It sounds emotional, which comes as a surprise. At the time I thought I was completely detached.

"Bless me, Father, for I have sinned."

I close my eyes, and for a moment I'm back there, back in
the confessional, dirt beneath my fingernails and a shovel in
the trunk of my car. The gun I used was stripped down and
buried out in the forest too. Father Julian's voice plays from
the tape and at the same time I remember his words, voicing
them in my mind a moment before I hear them. He sounds
calm. We could have been talking about anything, and at the
time I remember being curious about what might have been
the worst confession he'd ever heard. Was mine going to be it?
Or would mine be tame? And if Father Julian was listening to
the confessions of cold-blooded killers, why in the hell wasn't
he doing something about it?

*"What does it make you, Father, when you commit a sin and
feel nothing?"*

"I think that—"

*"Does it make me human? Am I still a man, Father Julian, or
am I a monster?"*

"The fact you are here answers your question," he said. *"However, what you do next also counts."*

"I'm not going to the police."

"You need—"

"He killed her, Father," I say. *"He killed her and he probably
would have killed others."*

"That doesn't make it right."

"But it doesn't make it wrong either."

I press stop and the voices shut off. If I could go back in
time, would I do the same thing again? I don't know. I think
of Patricia Tyler and her request of a promise—*Make him*

pay, she told me. *Make it so he can never hurt another girl ever again.*

I eject the tape and start unspooling the thread, not needing—or more accurately not wanting—to hear the rest of what I had to say. I can learn nothing from it. All it can do is make me hurt.

I carry the tape outside and touch a match to it. It shrinks and melts and the recorded memory burns away. Father Julian never blackmailed me and I figure he never blackmailed anybody else who was confessing to murder. It would have been too dangerous for him. I think of him coming around to my house. I think of him sitting on the porch with me as we spoke about my wife. He knew of the anger building up inside of me. After my confession he never came around again.

I sit back down inside. I start drumming my fingers, and then I go back into the list of names. I scroll through them, looking for something else, and soon I find Sidney Alderman's name. I check the date. It's a week after his wife died. I hunt out the tape and cue it up, interested in what he has to say, hoping he is going to say something that will help me.

"*I guess you would call it a sin,*" Alderman says. His words are slurred. He's been drinking. "*Does that make us even?*"

"*Have you been drinking?*"

"*Drinking? Yeah, and why the hell not? She's gone. I need something to keep me company.*"

"*You still have your son.*"

"*My son? You mean your son, don't you?*"

There is a pause that stretches out long enough for me to think the rest of the tape is going to be blank, but then Father Julian's voice cuts back across the speaker and the conversation continues.

"*She told you,*" Julian says.

"Part of me always knew. Or at least suspected."

"I'm sorry, Sidney."

"That's it? You don't want to give me an excuse? You don't want to tell me you accidentally fucked my wife and got her pregnant?"

"Please, Sidney, I didn't mean anything to happen."

I press stop. Just what kind of man was Father Julian? How many marriages did he end? This man, this man who would come and see me, who would tell me everything was going to be okay, who would tell me everything was part of God's plan. What kind of man was he? I press play. Both men are dead, one because of me, and perhaps the other because of me too. The two ghosts of Recent Past carry on talking. Neither could know they would end up sharing more than just Lucy Alderman, that they would share a similar fate.

"Yeah, well I didn't mean anything to happen either," Sidney Alderman says.

"What are you talking about?"

"Bruce . . . He's, well, he's different now. I see him differently. He's not my son and I don't know what to do about it. One thing I do know is, I don't want you anywhere near him."

"Are you going to leave?"

"Leave? No. I'm not going to leave. See the thing, Father," he says, almost spitting out the word *Father,* *"is this. She's dead because of you. And I want you to know that. I'm going to be here every day for the rest of my life and you're going to see me around, and you're going to remember."*

"What do you mean she's dead because of me?"

"Come on, Father. You can figure it out. You read the papers, right? That guy who killed her, he said she stepped out from nowhere. Well that ain't quite true. She was pushed out from nowhere."

Silence for a few seconds. Not just from the tape, but from my house. I can't hear anything. I realize I'm holding my breath.

"You pushed her?" Father Julian asks.

"I hated her. She lied to me. She cheated on me. She kept the same fucking lie all those years. Were you still screwing her, Father?"

"You killed her?"

"You can't do anything about it except see my face every day. I want that guilt to kill you. It's killing me. Does that make us even?"

"I . . . I don't . . ."

"I thought it would make me happy," Alderman says, *"but the funny thing is, it doesn't. In fact I feel worse. I love her so much. I blame you, and I want to kill you, but I don't have the courage."*

"Sidney, you need to—"

"Don't tell me what I need to do! You know, I even bought a gun. I was going to use it on her and then on you. But I can't. What happened to Lucy, well, that will hurt you more than what I could ever do."

"What about Bruce?"

"Don't you dare tell him any of this. Any of it."

I press the stop button. The caretaker's grief is ten years old, but it still sounds fresh. Two months ago he told me he always thought about what I'd done after my daughter was killed and wished he'd had the courage to do the same thing to the person who killed his wife.

I think about what he did and I wonder if it justifies what I did to him. I wonder if there is some symmetry there—him lying on top of the coffin of the woman he loved, the woman who betrayed him, the woman he killed.

I decide that it does. At the very least it makes me feel better. It makes me look up from the bottom of the abyss. There is a way out of this.

I eject the tape, put it back into the plastic cover and set it aside. I go through the rest of the log, looking for names that will stick out, knowing there has to be something here though I can't think what. That's part of the problem: all I've been doing is thinking, and suddenly I'm hitting a wall. There's an answer somewhere in this list of names, it's in these tapes, but I'm so involved in it all that I can't see anything for what it is.

What am I missing?

I get up and walk out of the room. I leave it all behind me—the names, the numbers, the tapes, and the dates, knowing that I need to clear my head so I can at least . . .

The dates!

Of course!

I head back into the room and I look at the time line I've created. If the killer confessed, then presumably he did so on the same day or in the days immediately following the girls' disappearances. The first date I look at is the day Henry Martins was buried. The log says there was a confession that night. The log says the confession was made by Paul Peters. I find the corresponding tape and jam it into the machine. I wind it forward. Suddenly I feel more apprehensive about what I'm about to hear than I did of the other two confessions. This could be the recording of a man who did nothing more than steal his neighbor's apples, or it could be the confession of a monster. I press play.

It's the monster.

CHAPTER FIFTY-ONE

"I know who you are." The voice sounds a little familiar, but I can't place it.

"Do you have something to confess?"

"You killed her, you know."

"What are you talking about?" Father Julian's voice has a rushed quality, as if he has just entered the confessional after running from the rectory.

"As if you strangled her yourself. What you do in life has consequences, wouldn't you say, Father?"

"Yes, of course, but what you're talking about doesn't make sense."

"All our actions have consequences, don't they, Father. For all of us."

"We need to be aware and responsible for our actions, yes, that's true."

"Even you, Father?"

A pause, and I can imagine Father Julian looking confused right here. *"Do you have something to say?"*

"Are there others?"

"Others?" Father Julian asks. So now he's looking confused and shaking his head. *"I don't know what you're talking about."*

"Other children. Like me. Are there others like me."

"We're all children of God, no matter what our actions," Julian says.

"I'm not talking about God."

"I don't understand."

"I'm talking about you, Father Julian. I'm talking about your children. Are there more of us?"

"Oh my God," Father Julian says, and now he's no longer shaking his head. Instead he has a hand up to his mouth. All the confusion is slipping away. I imagine this moment was very real for him. As real a moment as any other.

"See, you do understand. Your actions have consequences, Father. Or should I say Dad?"

"I . . . I don't know who you are."

"Would you like to know?"

"Of course! Of course I would!"

"I'm the man who just killed your daughter, Father. Her name was Rachel Tyler. She died slowly, Dad. She was my sister, and she died slowly."

"No," Father Julian says, the word coming out in a whisper, and I can hear the pain in his voice. I know that pain. I think I even said the same thing when I picked up the phone to learn Emily was dead and my wife gone forever.

"I told her about you. She never knew her dad, but in the moments before she died I told her. She knew everything she wanted to know and then more than she could handle. Do you think that knowledge comforted her?"

"I . . . I . . ."

"You what, Father? You don't know? You don't know what to say? How do you think I felt, finding out who I was? How do you think it felt being abandoned?"

"Please, please, don't . . ."

"Don't what? You don't even know what to do, do you, Father? You feel helpless. Do you suddenly feel as though God has abandoned you? I know all about abandonment. You feel helpless and that's exactly how Rachel felt in those last moments. Tell me, Father, do you still want to do something good for her?"

Father Julian doesn't answer. I can hear his breathing. It sounds louder than it ought to be on a tape recorder with such a small speaker. The vocals are tinny, but that breathing is deep, like a wounded whale.

"You can't kill her," Julian says at last, but it's such a ludicrous thing to say to a man who has already committed the act. *"Please, please, tell me this is wrong."*

"Bury her," the killer says.

"What?"

"I'm giving you a chance, Dad. You can bury her and you can pray over her. You can visit her as often as you want—something you never did while she was alive."

"This is madness," Father Julian says.

"What other choice do you have? I have kept her for you to bury. She is here, at your church. You cannot go to the police, because you can't afford your parish to know she was your daughter. Or that you have others."

"I have no other children."

"You have me. All you can do now is bury her and pray and maybe we'll talk about it next time."

"Next time?"

But the man doesn't answer. The confessional door opens

then closes. Father Julian cries out for the man to wait: there are footsteps, then nothing. A few seconds later the tape goes quiet, and ten seconds after that a new voice comes through the speaker, confessing to an attraction to somebody who isn't his wife.

I rewind the tape and listen through it again. The words of Rachel's killer are chilling and form knots in my stomach. Hearing them again is almost enough to take me there, to be inside that confessional booth. I wonder where Rachel's body was left, whether she was placed on a pew or dumped on the doorstep. I picture Father Julian cradling her, part of him wanting to call the police, a greater part not wanting his secrets exposed. He was a coward who could not betray the confessional, a coward who asked Bruce, his son, to bury the girls and to bury the truth.

I check the log and find the date the second girl went missing. I start forwarding through the corresponding tape, going through snippets of dialogue until I hear the same voice. I rewind it a bit and find the beginning of the conversation.

"You lied to me, Father."

"I lied to you how, my son?" Father Julian asks.

"My son? That's very accurate, isn't it."

"Oh my God."

I pause the tape and check the time stamp against the log. This time Father Julian has written down Luke Matthews. Last time it was Paul Peters. I check off the rest of the dates and find more names that stick out: John Philips and Matthew Simons. Four names that are mixtures of names of the apostles. Father Julian never wrote down his son's real name. Did he not know it? Was it a son he paid child support to? Or one he completely abandoned?

"I knew there were others. And now Julie is the second."

"What have you done?" Father Julian asks.

"Did you know her?"

"What have you done?" Father Julian repeats.

"You probably never saw her, did you."

"No."

"Then thank me. You can give her the same burial you gave her sister. My sister."

Father Julian starts to cry. His sobs through the tape are the hardest things I've ever had to listen to.

I press pause and go into the kitchen. I grab the drink out of the fridge. I need it. I get it up to my mouth and the fluid touches my lips, then I throw it into the sink. I make some coffee. Suddenly I don't want to go back into my office. I don't want to listen to the rest of the conversation. I just want to burn the tapes and drive to the nearest liquor store and immerse myself in the bourbon that has kept me so numb for the last month. I look into the sink, but none of what I just poured in there is left. Father Julian's sobs have brought tears to my eyes. I close them and the tears break away and run down the sides of my face. I am almost with him as he listens. I know how he feels hearing for the first time his daughter is dead. I went through it once. He has gone through it twice. Did he go through it more than twice? I think he did. I think he went through it four times. Did it get easier or harder? Did it age him, did it break him, did it make him deny his God, or make his faith stronger? He could not break the confessional vow. Even when there was a pattern and he knew what was happening, he did not break it. He could break it to black-mail adulterers, but not to save his children. What twisted morals Father Julian had, but then churches are full of people preaching one thing and practicing another. Every day he must have struggled with the man he was. Perhaps he didn't want to struggle anymore. He hadn't been to his safe-deposit box in the eight weeks before he died. He knew the key was missing, and maybe he knew Bruce took it. Maybe he even figured out that it had been given to me. I think he knew that in some way this was coming to an end. I think he stood with his back to the man who would kill him, and he waited for it to happen.

I don't touch the coffee. I leave it on the counter and walk back to the office.

"*You can pray over them, Father. You can pray at the same time.*"

"*How did you know she was your sister?*"

"*Perhaps God can tell you.*"

The confession ends. I find the third one, and match the time stamp to John Philips.

"*Why are you doing this?*" Father Julian asks as his son tells him he has met another of his sisters. "*What did they do to you?*"

"*It's what they could have done.*"

"*Why any of this? Why come here and tell me?*"

"*Because you're the only family I have.*"

I keep listening. The dialogue is similar to the others. Father Julian's sobs are just as loud. A name comes up. Jessica Shanks. She was the third girl to have gone missing and the oldest. She was the one Father Julian started paying for in the beginning, five years before Rachel was born.

I stop the tape and find the last confession.

"*They are all dead now, Father.*"

"*I don't want you coming back here.*"

"*All of the sisters. You can see them whenever you like. Do you now finally take the time to visit them?*"

"*I want you to leave.*"

"Am I right?"

"What?" Father Julian asks.

"There are no more, are there."

"No."

"If you're lying to me, Father, I will find out."

"I know."

"And I won't be happy."

"I'm not lying," Father Julian says.

"If you are lying, Father, I will do two things. I will find the girls and I will kill them. I will make them suffer. Do you want to know what the second thing is?"

"No," Father Julian says, but there is no doubt he's about to find out.

"I'm going to come back here, Dad, and what I'm going to do is cut out your tongue so you can never lie to me ever again."

CHAPTER FIFTY-TWO

It's about as official as it can get. The dead girls are Father Julian's daughters. Their killer is Father Julian's son. I look down at the photographs of Jeremy and Simon and Bruce. Then I look at the photograph of the fifth girl, Deborah. Could be she is dead already, dead and buried and never found, or it could be she is living in another city in another part of the world, oceans and landscapes away from all of this.

Father Julian's logs show who he was recording and blackmailing, but they don't show how many children he had. The bank statements don't show that either. There aren't any Aldermans in these statements for a start. There isn't enough information to know how many women Father Julian used his position to take advantage of.

There are seven names on the bank statements. Four of them belong to the families of the dead girls. Of the three left, two might be for Simon and Jeremy, and one might be for Deborah, or it could be for different children I don't know about. All I can do is hope the photographs match up with the bank statements.

I have three first names—Jeremy, Simon, and Deborah—and three last names from the bank statements. I grab a phone book and start matching the names up, hoping for a hit, and when the first one comes I end up speaking to Mrs. Leigh Carmel. I identify myself and she quickly asks what it's about, and there is a hesitancy in her voice that suggests she thinks I'm about to try and sell her something. I tell her I'm trying to track down her son, figuring I have a two-to-one chance it's a son rather than a daughter, and I'm correct.

"What's he done now?" she asks.

"I just need to talk to him. It's important."

"He's always done something," she says. "That's always been the problem with Jeremy. Why don't you speak to his probation officer? They seem to have a closer relationship than we've ever had."

She gives me the number, and I hang up and call the probation officer straightaway, a guy by the name of Austin Bracken. Bracken doesn't sound thrilled to hear from me.

"You know that ain't the kind of information I can give out over the phone," he says. "Not to a private investigator."

"How about I give you my number and he can call me?"

"We're not in this business to forward messages," he says.

"Okay, okay, let me think a minute. Right, can you tell me where he was two years ago? Was he in jail?"

"Two years ago? Yeah. He was in jail then. He's been in for a four-year stretch. Got let out two months ago," he says, which means Carmel was in jail when Rachel Tyler was killed.

"What'd he do?"

"It's public record," he says. "Look it up."

I thank him for his time and cross Jeremy Carmel off my list. It leaves me with two first names and two last names that could match up either way.

My next hit comes a few calls later, when a woman answers the phone and I ask for Simon.

"Who?"

"Sorry, I mean Deborah. I'm trying to get hold of her."

"Well, so are we. We haven't seen her since yesterday. Can I ask who's calling?"

Her words make me tighten my grip on the phone. I tell her who I am and that I'm a private investigator.

"Investigating what?" she asks. "Has something happened to Deborah? Is she in trouble? Is that why we haven't heard from her?"

"No, it's nothing like that," I say, hoping my words are true.

"Then what?"

"I just need to get hold of her. It's important."

"I don't like the way you sound," she says, and I realize my grip is so tight on the phone my knuckles have turned white. "You make it sound like she's in danger."

I decide to go with the truth. "She might be. Please, you have to help me out here, I need to—"

"What kind of danger? Tell me! What's happened to my daughter?"

I ignore her question and push on. It's the only way, otherwise I could end up spending two hours on the phone with her. "Do you know if she was seeing anybody?"

"Is this some kind of joke? Has somebody put you up to this? I'm calling the police."

"Wait, wait just a second. Does Deborah know who her real father is?"

The woman says nothing, and I don't jab her with another

question, just ride the silence out, knowing her shock at the question may turn to anger or denial.

"Who are you?" she asks.

"I've already told you," I answer.

"What is it you're trying to ask? Tell me."

"Is her real father Stewart Julian?"

Again a pause. "Where's my daughter? What aren't you telling me?"

"Please, is Father Julian Deborah's real father?"

"How is this important?" she asks.

"It's important because it will help me find Deborah."

"I'm phoning the police."

"Good, I want you to, but first tell me. Father Julian was murdered because he was protecting secrets. They were his own secrets. Was he Deborah's father?"

I realize I'm overloading her with way too much information. At any second she might shut down. She doesn't answer. "Was he—"

"Yes," she says. "He was."

"Did he have any other children?"

"Other children? I . . . I guess I've never really thought about it. I suppose it's possible, just like anything is possible. But I doubt it."

"Okay, I'm going to look for Deborah. I want you to call the police and tell them she's missing. But first I want you to tell me where she lives and give me her number."

I write the details down, and try calling Deborah immediately after I've hung up. She doesn't answer. I leave a message.

That leaves me with Simon Nichols. He is the last person in the photos, the last person to be paid for in the bank statements. I think about what that means, and decide it stacks the odds in favor of him being the killer. I suck in a few deep

breaths. I never would have thought when I woke up this
morning that by the end of the day I would have the name of
the man who killed those poor girls.

There are a few people with that name and initials in the
phone book. I call them all, but get nowhere, which I find frus-
trating—I'm so close now. But then I'm able to track down his
mother, who answers on the tenth ring, just before I hang up.

"I'm trying to get hold of Simon," I say.

"Simon?" she says. "Um, can I ask who's calling?"

"My name is Theodore Tate. I'm a private investigator."

"What is this about?"

It's about Simon being a serial killer. It's about Simon being
a monster. It's about Simon killing his father then trying to
frame me for murder. I don't say any of this. Instead I say what
I already had scripted in my mind. "I just have a few questions
for him, just some routine stuff that might really help me out
on a case."

She doesn't answer at first, then there are some soft sounds
and I get the idea she is crying. Before she can say anything,
I get another idea—I know what she's about to tell me.

"You're about a year too late," she says, and suddenly I
know that not only is her son dead, that he was murdered.
I just know it.

And I'm right.

"It was about a year ago," she says, then tells me that Simon
was stabbed to death in his own home. "The police haven't
caught the . . . the guy, not . . ." She can't finish.

Her sobs remind me of how Julian sounded when he was
listening to the confessions of his daughters' killer. I hear her
cries, but all I can do is think about how empty my suspect
pool is, and I now have absolutely no idea how to find the
other brother who has killed so many.

CHAPTER FIFTY-THREE

I stare at the photographs of the girls as if somehow they're going to rearrange themselves and reveal an answer. I look at Simon, dead now, one more unsolved murder in a city with dozens of murders. The killer's signature is different for his sisters and brother. I wonder whether he'd have killed Jeremy too, whether the desire is there, or whether he even knows of the other brother. He certainly knew about Bruce. What relationship did they have for Bruce to be safe? Bruce's last words about dignity echo in my thoughts, making me shiver. Between Bruce and Father Julian, they thought they were giving the girls some dignity, a burial place where they could be prayed over and looked after. But what of those they took from the coffins and discarded into the water? What of their dignity?

I keep starting to reach for something different, to move it from one place to another, to shift about the bank statements and the logs, hoping, hoping . . . but there is nothing. I look at my watch. Saturday is shifting along quickly. And Deborah Lovatt is in danger.

I head back out to the car. The mud I splashed through it last night has dried. Dad would have a heart attack if he saw it. I dial the cell phone and try for Schroder, but he doesn't answer. I hang up and dial back and get the same result. I leave a message, then decide to call Landry.

"Tate, you just don't know when to let go," he says.

"I might have something for you."

"Really? I have something for you. You left your jacket and shoes at the church last night."

"What are you talking about?"

"Good one, Tate, but you know what? I'm not even going to get into it. We both know you were there and we both know that I can't prove it. So how about you do me a favor and stay the hell away from me."

"Look, Landry, this is important, okay? Real important. Did you find a tape recorder at the church?"

"A tape recorder? What the hell are you on about?"

"Did you find one or not?"

"What? What are you on about? No, there was no tape recorder."

"Okay," I tell him. "I can help you find who killed those girls."

"No, no you can't, Tate. This isn't your case. You're not even—"

"Trust me," I tell him, "and hear me out. Just listen to me, okay? Then you can ignore me or hang up on me or whatever, but at least hear me out. It's important."

"Okay," he says. "I'm listening."

"Where are you?"

"What does it matter?"

"I need you to go to the church," I tell him.

"Why?"

"Because you missed something."

"Missed what?" he asks. "This tape recorder?"

"I'll tell you when you get there."

"Come on, Tate, stop playing games. It's too damn late for your bullshit. I'm tired."

"Just call me back when you get there, okay? I promise you won't regret this."

I hang up on him before he can reply.

I drive to Deborah Lovatt's house, and can tell immediately that nobody is home. Her mother said she lived with two roommates. If they're around the same age as Deborah, then they'll be out in town drinking or at the movies somewhere. I get out of the car and walk around, but nothing stands out as being wrong. No busted doors. No broken windows. I leave a card wedged in the door so it hangs over the keyhole. I leave a note on the back saying it's urgent I speak to Deborah. Deborah's mother will have called the police, but the way things work in this city, that doesn't mean help is coming soon.

Traffic is thick on the way back to town, full of people all looking for somewhere better to be. Lined up at the lights, I can hear the stereo in the car behind me, the *thump thump thump* making the chassis of my car vibrate. I can see movement in my rearview mirror—occupants of the car are treating the ride into town as a party. The girl in the passenger seat can't be any more than fifteen, and she's chugging away at a beer.

My cell phone rings and I answer it. The music from the other car drowns out Landry's voice. I push my cell phone harder against my ear.

". . . do now?"

"What?" I ask.

The light turns green. The guy behind me toots his horn even though it's been less than a second. I move through the intersection and pull over. There's a guy dressed like Jesus sitting on the side of the road. He's biting into an egg carton. He looks up at me, his bloodshot eyes locking onto mine, and I realize he's at the end of the road I'll be driving along if I decide that maybe the drinking is for me after all.

"You there, Tate?"

"Give me a second."

There are toots and yells and waves as the car behind me passes. I pull away from the curb and drive further up the road to find another place to park away from Egg Carton Guy.

"Okay, go ahead."

"You're really testing my patience, Tate. I'm at the church, so what do I do now?"

"Head down to the confessional booths."

"Why?"

"Just do it."

"Okay, okay. You know it sounds like you're driving?"

"Well, I'm not," I tell him.

"Yeah. Okay, I'm at the booths. Now what?"

"Open them up."

"What am I looking for?"

"Check Father Julian's side. Check the roof. The back wall. Just check all of it."

"Check it for what? This tape recorder you're telling me about? You think Father Julian was making secret recordings?"

"Just do it."

"There's nothing in here."

"Yes there is," I tell him. "Tap the wall or something."

"Tap it? You think there's a false panel?"

"Yeah I do."

He starts tapping the walls. The small knocks carry through his cell phone. "This is a Goddamn waste of . . ."

He doesn't follow it up, and I know what he's found. There's silence for five seconds. Then he comes back on the line.

"How the hell do you know about this?" he asks.

"Father Julian was recording the confessions. He was blackmailing people." I look in the mirror and see Egg Carton Guy walking toward me. The mirror makes him appear closer than he actually is. "Since you hadn't found it already, I reasoned the tape recorder was hidden. What better place to hide it?"

"That's why you were following him? Fuck, Tate, why couldn't you have told us? You sure as hell could have saved us a lot of work and a lot of pain. And finding out this way, man—it doesn't look good. It looks like you put it there when you broke in last night."

"I didn't break in. All I knew was the tape recorder had to be there somewhere, and anyway, I only just found out. Look, Julian recorded his killer, right? He knows who killed those girls. Is there a tape in the machine?"

"Yeah."

"Then listen to it. Could be the night Father Julian died, if he took a confession first. It could be the last voice you hear on that tape is his killer."

"You need to come down to the station, Tate."

Egg Carton Guy stretches out the bottom of his shirt and starts using it to wipe down the side window of my car, my father's car. Egg Carton Guy moves his shirt in circular motions, but it isn't the kind of detailing my dad would have in mind. I roll the window an inch and hand him a couple of dollars. He says something, but I don't quite hear him, then he wanders away.

"Tate? You still with me?" Landry asks.

"Play the tape."

"I'll play the tape when I'm done with you."

"Maybe Julian referred to him by name." I say. "Maybe he did that because he knew what might be coming up."

"I'm sending somebody to pick you up."

"I'm not even home."

"How can that be? You've lost your license. You out walking?"

"Besides, you've got something more important to take care of," I tell him.

"Yeah? You got somewhere else for me to go?"

"There's another girl."

"What is it with you? Everywhere you go people are showing up dead, or never showing up again."

"She may not be dead," I tell him. "But you need to find her."

"Tell me."

I lay it out for him. Not all of it, but most of it. And not all of it truthfully. I tell him about the photographs of Father Julian's children, telling him Bruce gave them to me, but that I only just figured out the connection. I tell him how four of the girls are dead and there is still one out there. I tell him about the key Bruce left for me, and the tapes that I found, along with the log.

"You have got to be kidding me," he says when I'm done. "You know you're in for a world of shit now, right? Going into that bank like that? You should have just called me."

"There wasn't time, and like I said, I had a key," I say, not mentioning the court order. That will come later.

"You've been holding out on me for the last two months, slowing down my investigation, and you're telling me there wasn't time?"

"Hey, it's not my fault I'm ahead of you. And you should be thanking me. Most of what you have is because of me. If anything, I've sped up your investigation."

"Fuck you, Tate. DNA would have told us those girls were related. We'd have figured out the rest."

"Yeah, maybe you would have, maybe not, but you wouldn't even be looking yet. Not until those results came in."

"I'm coming to your house. Now. I want you to be there, okay? I'm coming to get all this stuff. And we're going to have a nice long chat, just the two of us."

He hangs up before I can debate the issue.

I drive back home and have barely gone inside when Landry pulls up. He looks furious. He has an edge to him that makes me wonder how many times he's looked into the abyss.

"Where are they?" he asks. "The tapes?"

"You first. You listen to the one you found in the confessional?"

"Yeah. I did. There's nothing on it of any use. Fact is, none of these tapes are going to be any good. You know we can't use them. Even if it was us who found them. Can you imagine the kind of shit storm we'll have if the public ever finds out about them? There are going to be lots of confessions of people cheating on their husbands and wives, cheating with their taxes, cheating in all the possible ways the human race can cheat. There'll be more too. Who the hell knows whether the sanctity of the confessional extends to a tape recording? Or is it limited only to the priest?"

"So you're going to keep them quiet."

"We'll listen to them, that's for sure, but I don't imagine we're going to be making any arrests from them. And if our killer is on these tapes—"

"He is."

"Then we gotta find a way of working around it. We mention these things and we're handing him a defense."

I lead him into my office and hand over the log.

"Money comes in from blackmailing," he says, "and money goes out for the kids. Looks like our Father Julian was a busy man. It's probably a miracle he lasted as long as he did without anybody finding out."

"Miracles are in his line of work," I point out.

"Maybe not in the end."

"I think Henry Martins knew."

"What?"

I fill in the Martins connection. He absorbs it, but like me he doesn't know what to make of it.

"His body was too decomposed from the water," he says. "There was no way to get any toxicology from him. No way to tell if he was murdered."

"What about the new husband? The one who started all of this?"

"Who?"

"The one who died and made you want to dig up Henry Martins."

He starts to pile the tapes into the evidence bag. "His death was accidental. Turns out he was being exposed to some toxin through his job that he shouldn't have been exposed to. I don't know, it wasn't my case. Lead paint or something. It was fairly prolonged. Weird how it's all led to this."

Weird. I'm not so sure that's the right word for it, but it'll do for now. It's getting close to eleven o'clock, and suddenly I feel exhausted. All I want to do is get Landry out of my house so I can go to bed.

"Was this his? It looks new," he says, picking up the small tape recorder.

"I just bought it today. I have a receipt."

"Yeah, well, I'm taking it. Consider it your first step in cooperating with the police. Enough of those small steps might go a long way to helping you out, Tate. What've we got now—and I don't mean the drunk-driving charges. We've got breaking and entering—"

"No you don't."

"We've got interfering with a criminal investigation. We've got—"

"Look, I get the point, okay?"

He picks up the photographs. "This them?"

"Yeah."

He says nothing for a few seconds, and then, "I really should be taking you in."

"Look, Landry, I'm about to crash here, okay? I'm beat. And I've told you everything I know, and I've given you everything I have. Go and do your job and figure out who this maniac is before he kills Deborah Lovatt."

"The fifth girl."

"Yeah. The fifth girl."

"Okay, Tate. For once I believe you. But I still gotta take you in."

"Look, if you take me in, then what? You're going to want to listen to all those tapes first, and you're going to want to run down everything I've told you about. So all you're going to do is sit me in an interrogation room for twelve hours before you even speak to me. It's pointless. Let me stay here, let me get some sleep, and if you want me tomorrow you'll know where to find me."

He doesn't answer, but he slowly nods.

I walk to the front door with him, and as angry as he is at me I'm pretty sure that if he'd been the one two years ago to decide not to exhume Henry Martins, then he'd be the one now needing to find justice for those dead girls.

I listen to him drive off.

My head hits the pillow, and I think I might even have slept for about two minutes before my cell phone rings.

"Why do I feel like I've just been played?" Landry asks.

I don't answer him.

He carries on. "I pressed play on that tape recorder of yours to get a preview of what was to come."

"And?"

"And what? It was up to Sidney Alderman. He was confessing about killing his wife. I guess that's the one you wanted me to hear first, and it means you knew I was going to take your tape recorder. You knew I'd listen to it. Why?" he asks.

"Makes you wonder what he was capable of, right? Guy like that, makes you wonder."

"Good night, Tate."

"Good night, Landry."

I hang up and turn off my cell phone, satisfied that the police no longer have any reason to dig Mrs. Alderman out of the ground.

CHAPTER FIFTY-FOUR

At first I'm not sure where I am. I wake up feeling exhausted and confused, and then it comes rushing back to me—not just the last day, but the last two years. These moments are the worst. Sometimes I can wake up and for the first two or three seconds everything is okay—I'm going to roll over and Bridget is going to be there and Emily is going to be in the lounge watching TV. Then those two seconds pass and the reality kicks in and it hurts all over again, the pain as intense in those moments as it was two years ago.

I get out of bed, still feeling groggy. I turn on my cell phone and find a message waiting. It's Landry. I figure if I don't ring him back real soon he's likely to show up. I carry the phone through to my office and sit down on my desk. For the second time within days everything I've built up has been taken away. All I have left are the newspaper stories I printed out at the library, along with the new time line I was making and some notes. I look at the articles with the pictures of the girls, and all I can think about is their killer's confession. These young women are looking to me to find them justice. There is still hope for them. It's a different kind of hope, but I promise not to abandon them.

I phone Landry back.

"You're holding out on me, Tate."

"I told you everything I know."

"But you didn't give me everything you have."

"What are you talking about?"

"The tapes," he says. "We're one short. According to the log Father Julian kept, you're on it."

"Yeah, well, I was. And that was a confession between me and my priest. Try and sound as angry as you want, Landry, but you know there's no way in hell I'd let you have that tape."

"Because of what was on it? The date suggests it was around when Quentin James went missing. The timing suggests a whole lot of things, Tate."

"What do you want, Landry? You gotta be ringing me for more than just this."

"When was the last time you saw Casey Horwell?"

"What? I don't know. Why?"

"Come on, when?"

"Yesterday. She blindsided me at my house. She had a bunch of accusations she wanted to share."

"And that's it?"

"Yeah, that's it. Why? Should I be turning on the news and seeing the story? You know she's bullshit. Most of what she—"

"She's missing," he says, interrupting me.

"Missing?"

"Yeah. Nobody has seen her in twelve hours."

"That doesn't constitute being missing," I say. "She's probably just sleeping off a hangover somewhere."

"Maybe. But you don't sound upset about it."

"Upset? Why would I be upset? You think something has happened to her?"

"Her producer said that last night Casey contacted her. She said she had a lead she was going to follow up, and it involved you. And her cameraman said you threatened her. Did she come back and see you last night?"

"You were here last night. Did you see her?"

"After I left."

"I turned my phone off and went to bed. That's it. I never heard from her. And I didn't threaten her. I warned her about her source. Somebody was feeding her information about the case. And there's a good chance it's the same somebody who framed me for murder. Don't you think it's possible he wanted to tie up one more loose end? After all, that's what he's doing, right? He got rid of Father Julian, he's after his last sister, and Horwell got herself caught up in all of that because she was too arrogant to see she was being played."

"Maybe."

"It's more than just a maybe. You need to find out who her source was."

"Her producer didn't know. Either that or she wouldn't tell me."

"It's the same guy who was on the tape. You can feel it, right? You feel it the same way I feel it. You *know* that's what happened."

"Okay, I'll check it out," he says. "But here's what I need you to do. You need to stay the hell away from everybody today, okay? Everybody."

"What about Deborah Lovatt? You need to find her."

"I know, but the simple truth is that we don't know she's missing yet."

"What? Are you kidding me?"

"No, I'm not kidding you," he says.

"She's been gone longer than Horwell."

"Before you get too bent out of shape, Tate, we are looking for her. And the best thing you can do right now is stay out of the way."

He hangs up.

I sit out on the deck, trying to put some distance—even if it's only thirty minutes and fifteen meters away—between me and my notes. For some reason everything I'm learning is becoming white noise. I can't focus on any one thought, and I can't remember the last time I felt this way. I would have been working a homicide. It would have been years ago. My life was different and I was different. The names that come from the tapes, the bank statements, the burials—there are facts here that for the moment aren't facts at all, but shapes floating around in the back of my mind with nowhere to fit, each piece swirling just a little too far out of reach. I try thinking about something else, but it only makes the images move faster, and there's nothing I can do to stop them.

I head down to the office and I stare at the girls and I try filtering through everything again, looking for something that doesn't seem to be here. Most of all I look at Rachel. In a way she is the one I think about the most. She is the one I saw stuffed into that coffin with the dirty diamond ring next to her hand. Hers is the pain I think about the most. I hold her picture and study her features, and the white noise I was hearing earlier starts to disappear.

If Rachel was the only girl to have been killed I'd be looking at the case in an entirely different way. But she wasn't.

What she was, though, was the first. I think about this. I try to strip the case back to the basics. The day Rachel went to her grandmother's funeral was the day all of this began. Her trip to the graveyard was the catalyst for everything that followed. Something must have happened that day.

I call Mrs. Tyler and she doesn't sound upset to hear from me. If anything, she sounds glad I'm calling. At some point in the last twenty-four hours it seems she's come to terms with a lot of things, and she senses the momentum and wants to be a part of it.

"The day of your mother's funeral," I say, "was there anything different? Anything out of the ordinary happen?"

She thinks about it, but can't come up with anything. "I don't even know what I should be trying to remember."

"Did anybody approach Rachel? Or you? It's my guess that somebody recognized her that day. Maybe they questioned her about it."

"If they did, she never told me."

I look at the other girls, and then I hide their pictures and details away and try to forget about them for the moment, focusing only on Rachel. Everything comes back to her and, more importantly, back to that day. If somebody did approach her, it could have been Father Julian, or Bruce or Sidney Alderman. The grudge Sidney Alderman had against Father Julian for sleeping with his wife makes him a likely candidate. Could be Sidney knew a lot more about Julian than the priest ever expected. Could be Sidney knew other women who got pregnant too.

"When you were going to Father Julian's church," I say, "back in the beginning, do you remember any other women who were pregnant?"

"Umm . . . No, not that I can think of."

"Anybody with a really young child?"

"Umm, yeah, there was one. There's Fiona Chandler."

"Was she married?"

"No. She used to be, but her husband left her before the baby was born. It was an awful thing to do. She never spoke about him, and she married again a few years later."

"Tell me about her husbands."

"I don't know anything about the first one. Like I said, she never spoke of him. Her second husband, Alec, he was very nice. But one day ten years ago he just got up and collapsed on the floor. It was a heart attack. She never married again, it was very sad. Well, still is very sad. Why—why are you asking me this?"

I don't answer. I give her a few seconds, and she gets there by herself.

"Oh my God," she gasps. "Are you, are you saying that . . . that Stewart, that he got Fiona pregnant too? Was it his baby?"

"It's possible."

"Oh no, oh no." She starts to cry.

"I need to get hold of her."

"You . . . you don't understand," she says. "You have no idea."

"What are you talking about?"

Her sobs start to grow louder. "You . . . Oh my God," she says, and it's all she can say over and over as the words intermix with tears and sobs. In the end she barely manages to compose herself enough to carry on. "You need to know something," she says. "I don't even know how to say it, but . . . but you need to know."

"Tell me."

And she does, and suddenly I understand everything.

CHAPTER FIFTY-FIVE

It comes back to Henry Martins. I asked Patricia Tyler eight weeks ago if she knew the name, and she didn't. If only she had, if only she'd known the name of Fiona Chandler's husband, the one who left her, then most of this could have been avoided. There was never any reason to suspect a link between the dead girl and the man who owned the coffin she was dumped into. Nothing links the others—it was just a matter of putting girls into the ground and using the coffins of those who had just died, making the digging easier. I've spent those eight weeks making death and making misery, but now things are going to change. Henry Martins was Fiona Chandler's first husband. He left her when Father Julian got her pregnant. He moved into a different world from her, he met another woman, he fell in love with a woman who wouldn't cheat on him, and he had a family. Twenty something years later I stood by his grave and watched his coffin get pulled from the dirt.

"Hey, hey, you can't come in here!"

The answers have come crashing down on me and the white noise is back. There are images and words screaming from every corner of my mind, and this is the way it sometimes gets when an investigation is coming to a close, the way it gets when the adrenaline is rushing and the high that comes is only an arrest away. Only this time my hands are shaking and I feel like a fool, so the high may not arrive.

I've just broken a dozen road rules getting here. The rain is pouring down, hitting the roof with the sound of land mines. I push my way into the hallway. If Henry Martins hadn't found out about his wife's affair, if he hadn't left her and had raised the boy as his own, then none of this would be happening. The girls, the priest, the Alderman family, even good old Henry himself—they'd probably all still be alive. For the briefest of moments I wonder if there would be other ripple effects if those people were still around, whether one of them could have crossed paths with my wife or with Quentin James two years ago and delayed one of them for the ten seconds it would have taken to prevent the accident.

"Hey, you deaf? You can't come in here."

"Where is he?" I ask.

"What?"

"Maybe you're the one who's deaf. Where the hell is he?"

"He's gone, man."

I push Studly against the wall. He's added a couple of piercings to the collection since I last saw him. I feel like pushing him right through the wall and strangling the skinny little bastard, but the anger I feel isn't toward him, it's toward myself for having been so easily deceived. It's toward David for being the one to have deceived me. Two months ago his pain was so raw, so unbearable, so believable. How the hell did I fall for such an act? Even as a cop I would have missed it. As did the other cops who spoke to him.

"Gone? Where?"

"He moved out. A few days ago. And he owes me rent."

I let Studly go. He pushes himself off the hallway wall and puffs his chest out, trying to look a lot tougher than he is, trying to look as though he let me start manhandling him.

"Where'd he go?"

"How the fuck would I know?" he asks, sounding tougher now that I've let him go.

I shove him into the wall again, and make my way down to David's bedroom. Last time I was here the place looked like a bomb had gone off. The furniture is still here, but everything else has gone.

"He told me to keep it," Studly says, "but bro, that stuff ain't worth shit."

"He ever bring other women here?"

"No. He's never been with anybody since—well, since Rachel went missing."

"She's not missing anymore."

"Yeah, he told me."

I look around the bedroom, but there's nothing here to help. I tip the bed up. I search through bedside drawers. I pull the corner of the carpet away on the chance this hidey-hole is more genetic than I first thought, but there's nothing there.

"Dude, you're destroying the place."

"You sure he's not seeing anybody else?"

Studly shrugs. "Man, I'm not his mother."

"Well, hopefully she'll know more than you."

"I doubt it. He hasn't spoken to her since Rachel went missing. Far as I can tell, he hates her. Man, really fucking hates her."

"I wonder why," I say, but I already know.

"Yeah," he says, trying to sound as if he knows too, but he has no idea. Nobody could.

"When did he go?" I ask.

"I told you, man—a few days ago."

"When exactly? Tuesday? Wednesday? Thursday?"

"I don't know."

"You don't know?"

"Man, I don't even know what today is."

I push past him again and start going through the rest of the house.

"Hey, man, you can't go through everything," he protests.

"Then tell me where he is."

"I don't know."

"He's your friend, right?"

"He owes me rent," he says.

"Then you owe him nothing. Take a guess. Where do you think he's going?"

"I remember him saying something about meeting a woman. He had a date. But it was a weird date. I remember that."

"If it was weird enough to stick out, why the hell can't you remember the details?"

"I was, man, you know . . . I was kind of, well, in a different state."

"You were stoned."

"Best as I remember, yeah."

"You get her name?" I ask.

"Nah. Maybe. I don't know."

"Could it have been Deborah?"

"Sure, it easily could have. But it just as easily could have been Susan. Or Nicola."

"That's real helpful."

Studly shrugs. "That's all I know, man. Hey, you find him you tell him he owes me rent, okay?"

"Look, this is important," I say, and I hand him one of my business cards. "You remember something, you give me a call."

"Yeah, whatever," he says, and he screws the card into his pocket. I figure in five minutes he'll forget it's even there.

"Okay, let's do this your way," I say. "Got some scissors?"

"Fuck you, man."

"I'm not going to cut you. If I wanted to do something fun I'd just shoot you. Now, scissors? Come on, *dude*, hurry up."

He heads into the kitchen and shows back up a few seconds later. I reach into my pocket and pull out the money my mother gave me. I count out two one-hundred-dollar notes. I cut the scissors across them, separating the notes into halves. I hand him a half from each note, along with the scissors, and I pocket the other two halves.

"What the hell am I supposed to do with these?"

"They'll help you think. You gotta come up with something useful and I'll give you the rest."

CHAPTER FIFTY-SIX

I sit in my car, but don't drive anywhere. I think about Rachel Tyler, and I think about David Harding, and I wonder who felt the most revulsion when they found out the truth. For the years they were dating, there is no way David or Rachel could have known they were brother and sister. As they shared the same bed, as they held each other in the night, as they spoke of dreams and fears, there was no way they could have known.

Rachel & David forever.

That's what was inscribed on the ring.

Then somehow David found out. The truth made him sick. It would make anybody sick, and it would make anybody angry too. I wonder if he ever knew that type of reaction was within him, that depth of anger. Did he blame her? Did he blame himself? Or just Father Julian? David has his own abyss, and maybe he didn't even know it, not until that day. He killed Rachel because he could not handle the fact his sister was his lover. Most men would have felt the anger, the embarrassment, the pain, but what is the normal reaction? To move on, to try and forget about it? To never talk about it, to bury those memories and emotions as deep as they can be buried, and then never mention them again? Or find a shrink, to admit it wasn't their fault, to process it, and process it to the point where it becomes just one of those things, like missing the deadline on your tax return or spilling red wine on the carpet.

David's rage took him beyond Rachel Tyler and to other girls he had never met, then it led him to kill Father Julian and to planting the murder weapon in my house. He chose me because he saw me on the news, but the thing about David was he was caught in the student world—a world where he slept in every day and missed the news report the morning following my car accident. He didn't know to move the murder weapon back out of my garage.

I start driving away from the house. Other possibilities start to filter their way through my thoughts as I drive to Fiona Chandler's house.

"I never told him who his father was," Fiona Chandler tells me while I stand on her doorstep.

"So your maiden name is . . ."

"Harding," she says. "Then it became Martins, and now it's Chandler. Some good names and bad memories."

She invites me in out of the rain and we stand in her hallway with the door open. She sucks in a deep lungful of cigarette smoke, then blows it into the air, aiming for outside. It forms a small cloud as it hugs the cold air and slowly moves toward me.

"How did David react when you told him about his father?"

"I never told him, not the complete truth. He thinks Henry Martins is his father. He doesn't know about Father Julian."

"I'm pretty sure he does."

"That's impossible. David was already angry for a lot of reasons. He didn't have the easiest of lives. He was abandoned by two men he never knew. I didn't need to tell him everything, so I only ever told him about Henry. I told him that Henry left me when I was pregnant, but I never told him that Henry wasn't his father. He asked if Henry made child support payments. Henry didn't, and even though Father Julian offered to, I didn't want his money. He had ruined my life, and I never wanted anything to do with him. So all David knew was he had a dad who wanted nothing to do with him and wouldn't help support him."

"Why'd you keep going to the church if you wanted nothing to do with Father Julian?"

She shrugs. "I know it doesn't make sense. It's just that, well, I kept thinking he'd leave the church behind to be with me. But he didn't."

"And you never told Patricia of your affair with Father Julian?"

"It wasn't the sort of thing you went around telling," she says. "Perhaps these days, but not back then."

"Did David find Henry? Talk to him?"

"He wanted to. And that just made him angrier."

"What do you mean?"

"It happened the same week I told David about him. Just one of those things, I guess. He wanted to visit Henry and talk to him because he thought Henry was his dad. He wanted to confront him, I suppose, but he never got the chance. Henry died that same week. It was an awful coincidence, and I guess David felt abandoned all over again."

"So when was the last time you saw him?"

"I went to Patricia's mother's funeral. David came along, of course. David and Rachel met when they were kids through Patricia and me. It was one of those relationships you could see coming up before it ever started. Anyway, it was a few days after that I think Rachel disappeared. It was around the same time Henry died—I can't remember exactly the details. I'd call David, but he'd never want to speak to me. After a while he stopped taking the calls. Time just kind of went by after that. To be honest I don't really know what happened. The shock and the loss, I guess, but that's when family should become closer, right?"

She stares at me for some kind of confirmation, and I slowly nod.

"Except he was losing people—he lost Rachel, he lost a dad he thought he was about to meet. Yet these things seemed to rip us apart. Believe me, I tried. I really did. But there's only so much you can do. David, well, he had his own life. He was in control of it and I couldn't change his decision. Can you believe that? I did the best I could, but in the end it wasn't good enough and his anger toward being abandoned became anger against me, and, well . . . well, I should have told him sooner. If I had told him when he was a small boy, maybe he would still think of me as his mother and not some . . . I don't know, monster or whore or incubator or whatever it is he thinks I am."

My cell phone starts ringing.

"I should take this," I say, and pull the phone out of my pocket. "It's important."

I take a few steps back from the doorway and flip open the phone. I don't recognize the number. "Hello?"

"Yeah, man, it's Oliver."

"Who?"

"Oliver. You were just at my house?"

"Oliver? Oh, Studly," I say.

"What?"

"Nothing."

"I got something for you."

"Yeah, money does the memory wonders, right?"

"How do I know I'll get it?" he asks.

"Do I look like the kind of guy who would lie to you?"

"Honestly, man, you look like a guy capable of anything."

"Then maybe you should think about that and tell me what you remembered."

"Okay, okay, dude, but you gotta gimme the other halves of those notes, man."

"I guarantee it. Now tell me."

"I want them now."

"No, the only thing you want now is to not piss me off."

"Okay, okay. Look, David said something weird the other day. I mean, it might not mean anything, right, but this girl he was seeing. Like I said, he only just met her, right? So to me it seems a little odd he'd say that."

"You haven't told me what he said."

"Oh, yeah, man, you're right. Shit. My point is, who takes a person they've just met to a funeral? That's what he said. He said he was taking her to a funeral on Sunday, but that's weird, right? You don't have funerals on Sunday. Anyway, that's where he's going to be tomorrow, though I don't know what funeral."

"It's Sunday today."

"It is? Oh, shit, man, that's awesome! Do I still get my money?"

"No, because nobody gets buried on a Sunday."

"Shit, man, that's why it sounded so weird to me. But that's what he said."

"Then you're wrong. Unless . . ." I look up at Fiona Harding. "I gotta go," I say, the message for both her and Studly.

I tuck the cell phone into my pocket and sprint to my car.

CHAPTER FIFTY-SEVEN

"Why can't I get hold of Schroder?" I ask.

"He's busy, Tate," Landry says. "He's got his own case he's working on. I was about to call you anyway. Where are you?"

"He did it," I say. "David Harding killed Henry Martins first. Then Rachel. Then the others."

"What the hell? Are you drinking?"

"He did it, Landry. He absolutely did it. He found Henry Martins and confronted him about leaving, and when he learned the truth, when he learned from Martins that his real father was Father Julian, he used that university education of his and killed him, but first he got the list of names. Martins knew about Julian's bank accounts. That's how Martins found out Julian was having those affairs. It might even be why he started to suspect his own wife. He knew the list of names and he gave them to David before he died."

"Where are you?"

"Listen to me, Landry. David Harding—"

"No, you listen to me. Where the hell are you?"

The city is dark now. The cloud cover is thick, but the occasional flash of sky comes through and shows a quarter moon or a few stars before shrouding back up. Sunday night is kicking in, and Christchurch is getting ready to watch primetime TV before falling asleep and starting the week all over again.

"Answer me, Tate. Where the hell are you?"

"I'm out and about."

"I told you to stay the hell out of the way. Where's Horwell?"

"What?"

"She just phoned her producer a few minutes ago. You're in some deep shit."

"What?"

"You need to come into the station."

I pull the car over and cut the ignition. "What the hell is going on, Landry?"

"Horwell made the call. Somehow she got to her cell phone. She says you abducted her and you're going to kill her. She said everything she suspected about you was true, and you found out. She said she had proof you killed Quentin James and Sidney Alderman, and also Father Julian. And she gave us a location."

"That's bullshit."

"Come down to the station," he says.

"Have you found Deborah Lovatt?"

"Stop making things harder for yourself."

"It's David Harding. He's doing all of this."

"You're wrong about Harding. I have a good bullshit meter, Tate, and Harding didn't even make a blip on it."

"That's because the guy's a sociopath," I say. "It was an act. Come on, Landry, you need to trust me."

I pull back out and start driving fast. I steer around a corner a little too quickly and my dad's car fishtails. I drop the cell phone while I gain control of the car.

"What the hell?" Landry asks when I pick the phone back up. "Where are you going?"

"When is Father Julian getting buried?" I ask him.

"What? He got buried today."

"Nobody gets buried on a Sunday."

"Yeah, well, God or somebody made an exception. It was all part of the service. It was Julian's church, so it made sense somehow to have the funeral today. Look, Tate, you need to calm down and think about what you're doing. You hurt Horwell, and you're—"

"I don't have her, Landry. You're being used, don't you get that?"

"Used? Explain that to me?"

"Figure it out yourself. Look, I'm on my way to find Deborah Lovatt. I know where she is. She's—"

"She's at home, Tate. She spent the weekend with her boyfriend, and she left her cell phone behind. She's home and we've spoken to her."

"What?"

"Whatever is going on, Tate, is going on inside your head. Now listen to me, you need to . . ."

But I'm not listening to him. Deborah is at home? It doesn't make sense.

". . . some serious shit," he says.

"What?"

"I said—"

"It doesn't matter. I gotta go," I say. I hang up. A moment later my phone starts ringing. I put it on mute and ignore it.

If Deborah Lovatt is fine, then who is David meeting today?

The cemetery is like a magnetic pull. It's so strong that even if I drove all night in the other direction somehow I'd end up arriving back here. The entire graveyard is one huge shadow. My headlights fight back the darkness as I drive into it. There are no police cars parked anywhere and I figure that's all part of David Harding's plan. The night of the funeral of a murder victim, the police normally have the grave under surveillance. It's standard procedure, because killers often like to come back. But not tonight. David Harding has led them all away in a different direction, probably about as far away as he can get them from the cemetery. He's using Casey Horwell and me as bait, and it's working.

The sky is overcast, no slivers of moonlight, and as I start to run to the church the rain begins again as if to cleanse the night. I think about how that conversation between David and Henry went, and decide it would have started badly and only got worse. I can only assume he was David's first kill. I wonder what he thought, how he felt, and I wonder if in that we are similar. I felt nothing after killing Quentin James. I certainly felt no desire to do it again, even though I have done. I wonder if killing Henry Martins was like scratching an itch for David, or whether it was an experience that created an urge.

I reach the church. There is nobody around. No cars. No sign of life. But eight hours ago things were different. Eight hours ago all the crime scene tape was pulled away from the chapel and the pews were full of people. Father Julian came back to the church one final time for one final service. Friends and family and his parishioners prayed over him. They sang, they shed tears and told stories, and they put tokens and photos on his coffin. Some would have felt relief. None of them truly knew the man they were burying.

I make my way inside the same way I did the other night, and walk through the chapel and to the front of the church, my flashlight leading the way. The place still feels like it has a presence—maybe it's Father Julian. I scan through the registry and find it's already been updated with the Sunday funeral of the priest. I study the map of the grounds and figure out the location.

I carry the small Maglite with me as I walk among the dead, and the images of what happens in horror movies when people like me walk through places like this suddenly seem real. Hands digging up through the ground, the rotting dead back to some semblance of life with bony fingers as they claw their way from the dirt that has kept them captive. I shake the images away and they're replaced with David Harding, a man far scarier and far more real.

It takes me ten minutes to reach the other side of the cemetery. Running through the gravestones and the trees is like running around in a maze. There could be a dozen other people in here and I'd completely miss them. Given the amount of time I've spent in the cemetery lately I ought to know the place like my own backyard, because that's what it's become. Maybe if I started drinking it'd all come back to me. The rain starts to ease up again, and the soft ground sucks at my feet. When I get to the section of plots I want, I don't even know for sure that I'm in the right place. Everything looks the same.

I start scanning the headstones. Names and dates start flashing by as I begin running between them, hardly slowing down as the flashlight lights up the inscriptions. Birthdays, death days, messages from the dead, from the living, beloved by all, by some, by few—they blend into one as I move between them, my feet threatening to slip on the grass with every step. I start looking for freshly turned earth.

There are thousands of graves out here. But only one of interest.

It doesn't take long to understand that I'm lost. Dark trees and dark graves, and nothing to help me get my bearings. Even when I start to backtrack my steps, I don't know where they are. The grave I want could be anywhere. The church could be anywhere.

Then the world rushes up as my feet drop away, and suddenly I'm falling. Six feet down to be precise. I get my arms halfway up my body, but not all the way, and my face hits the opposite edge of the grave wall; my head snaps back, my shoulder smacks into the edge of the coffin lid, one leg goes into the coffin, and the other is shunted against the dirt wall. For a few moments I can't move as the darkness settles in around me. I have no idea what has happened. The world has gone dark and my mind is spinning.

Slowly this land six feet down from the rest of the world shifts into place and it isn't pretty. I can feel a hand beneath me, pressing into my chest. My face is wedged up against the side of the coffin. I manage to roll onto my side, and suddenly the light appears again as my body shifts off of the flashlight. I pick it up.

I'm the only person in the grave. The coffin is open, the pink lining clean except for a sprinkling of dirt, and the entire thing is wet. And blurry. The entire coffin is blurry, and when I hold my hand out ahead of me and point the flashlight at it I see both hand and flashlight are blurry too. I reach up and touch my forehead, and my fingers come away wet with blood.

I grab the edge of the coffin to try to pull myself up, but my hand slides across it and I slip back. I kill the flashlight and let the darkness settle over me, and for a moment I have fallen far deeper than the depth of the coffin, and into another world that light or life has never touched. I listen to the night, but can't hear a thing—not at first—then I begin to make out a soft murmuring. It disappears, and I begin to convince myself it was only the wind when it starts again. I turn the flashlight back on for a second to orientate myself, then I make my way to the end of the coffin and step onto it, balancing myself by pushing my hands into the damp walls of the grave. I think about Sidney Alderman, and then I think about all the policemen and policewomen I've known over the years, and all the cops in movies and TV and books who say they never believe in coincidences. I think of Quentin James and I think of the man I became. I think all those cops who don't believe in coincidences need to live a little more.

I reach up and brace my arms over the ground and kick at the cold wall of dirt as I make my way up. Every day above ground is a good day, so the saying goes, and suddenly I know whoever came up with that got it dead right. I listen for the sound again, but can't hear anything. I point the flashlight at the temporary gravestone and highlight Father Julian's name. There are no other inscriptions—they're being saved for the real gravestone.

There's a mound of dirt piled up about a meter away from the coffin. A large tombstone ahead of it must have blocked my view of it before. I stay low to the ground and look around, but all I can see are dark shadows across a landscape of black. I creep a few gravestones along, then squat down. I reach into my pocket for my phone, only to find that it's been busted in the fall. Maybe God is trying to tell me something about cell phones.

I drop down to my knees and I listen as hard as I can. I close my eyes and wait, and after a few seconds the noise returns—just briefly, but it's enough for me to get a fix on the direction.

I move a short distance away from the grave.

I take the flashlight out of my pocket. There is a dark shape on the ground. I crouch and turn on the flashlight. A girl, perhaps in her late teens or early twenties, is naked, her skin scuffed up with mud. Her hands are bound behind her, her ankles bound too. The same duct tape binding her has also been placed across her mouth. The rain has swept the blood from a cut in her shoulder over her chest. She is shaking. Her face is so pale she looks as though her body has been completely exsanguinated. Her dark eyes are wide with fright as she stares at me. She tries to pull away. All she can see is the flashlight, and I realize she thinks I'm the one who did this to her. I have no idea who she is, what sister she could be. I turn off the light and take off my jacket to put over her, and then the sound of a car comes crashing through the silence.

CHAPTER FIFTY-EIGHT

"Don't worry, I'm going to get you out of here, okay?"

The flashlight is still off, so I can't tell whether she looks as though she believes me or not. But I'm sure her mind will grip tight to the *or not* bit when I tell her what's going to happen next. I have put my jacket back on.

"I'm going to leave you tied up, okay?"

She starts whimpering.

"I need him to think he's here alone with you."

The headlights wash toward me, and I duck down on the other side of the gravestone to where the girl is lying. The car comes to a stop, and I figure David has just dumped Father Julian in the lake. David is following the same routine, even though he didn't start it.

"Don't let him know, okay? If he lets you speak, don't tell him. You have to be calm. I'm a police officer, I'm going to help you get through this, but you have to trust me. You're going to be okay, I promise."

The lights are no longer pointing in my direction, but rather at the grave I fell into. David keeps them on, but shuts off the engine. He steps out of the vehicle and crosses the path of the beams, and I can see he's dressed completely in black. Maybe he's mourning his father. There is another change that has taken place since the last time I saw him, but then I realize it isn't a change at all, that the man I am looking at is the David Harding he has been for the last two years since he found out the woman he loved was his sister. The man I saw two months ago was the impostor, the grieving David Harding who stared at the ring and who looked like his heart had just been torn open. I move out from behind the stone and duck behind another one five graves away.

He looks out over the graveyard and I wonder if he's look-ing for me. He pauses when his eyes come to rest on the girl. There is enough ambient light for him to see her. He shrugs his shoulders back as if to get rid of a crick in the middle of his back, then walks forward. He isn't holding anything in his hands. When he reaches her he crouches down.

"This isn't your fault," he says. "Really there is only one person to blame, but if it makes you feel any better, he's taken responsibility for his actions."

The girl murmurs. There is enough light to see the absolute fear in her face. Enough light to see it's not the girl from the photographs—it's not Deborah. Her hair is tangled up and sticking to her cheeks. David reaches forward and brushes it aside.

"You're probably wondering how I can be doing this," he says, "and sometimes I wonder the same thing. I think about it a lot, you know. Ever since Rachel. She was your sister too. I think how things might have been different, but you know what? They're not different, are they? They're exactly as they are."

He grabs her arms and starts dragging her toward the grave. She slides easily over the wet ground. I still have no idea who this girl is.

She tries pulling away from him, but she's too weak, too cold, and probably in too much shock to be able to fight him. He gets her next to the grave. He lays her alongside the hole and crouches over her.

I start circling around the edge of the light toward him.

The girl's murmurs grow louder.

"Sshh," he says, "sshh. It's going to be okay now. It's going to be okay. Things are going to be easier for you than the others."

He unzips his jacket and takes it off. He undoes his belt and pulls it from his waist. He undoes the button and the fly, and starts to lower his jeans.

He hears my footsteps as I run toward him. He looks over his shoulder, but he can't move because his pants are halfway down his legs, and when I hit him he's in no position to defend himself. We fly into the grave and he lands heavily on the coffin with me on top of him, just like it was with Sidney Alderman. There is a loud cracking sound of bone breaking, but if it's mine I can't feel anything.

It's not dark down here like it was last time, and I've a better idea of the geography of the place now, so I'm able to right myself before he does. I pull him up by the front of his shirt and swing my fist at him as hard as I can, and this time the sound of breaking bone comes from my hand as it connects with the side of his face. He falls backward, and I start to shake my hand, unsure of how many fingers I've just busted.

I get to my feet and back away.

David Harding lies unconscious, his arm twisted on a strange angle and his face lolled into the corner of the coffin.

I make my way out of the ground the same way I did last time, only a little slower now and in a lot more pain. The girl is staring at me. There is a small blood spot in her left eye, perhaps from a burst blood vessel. I pull the tape from her mouth and she sucks in a deep breath. I grab my keys and try using the longest one to cut through the duct tape around her wrists, but it won't make a start.

"Wh-where is . . . is he?" she asks, her teeth chattering and her eyes darting back and forth like a wired-up junkie's.

"It's okay," I say.

"That's . . . that's what he said."

I try picking at the edge of the tape, but my fingers are too cold on one hand and busted up on the other.

"What's your name?" I ask.

"Stacey."

"Listen to me, Stacey, it's going to be okay. My name is Theo and I'm here to help you. You just have to wait here for a few seconds."

"No, no, don't leave."

"I'll be ten seconds."

"Please."

It hurts to ignore her cry, but I do it. I open the door to David's car and pop open the glove box. I find a pocketknife in there that makes fast work of the duct tape.

She sits up and folds her arms in front of her.

"Okay, Stacey, here's what I want you to do. We're going to get you to your feet and into the car," I say, taking off my jacket. "It's dry and warm in there," I say as I wrap the jacket around her, "and I want you to drive away from here. You know how to drive, right?"

"Where do I go?"

"I want you to drive home. Then call the police."

"Okay."

I help her into the car. She tightens the jacket around her when she sits down. I lean in and start it.

"Drive carefully, Stacey. You're in a state of shock, you need to be careful. Do you think you can drive?"

"Yes."

"Are you sure?"

"There's another woman."

"Where is she?"

"He made her make a phone call. He made her lie about where we were."

"Where is she, Stacey?"

She starts to cry. "I was so scared. I couldn't help her. I wanted to, but I couldn't. I couldn't do anything."

"Where is she?"

"He put her into the water. He tied something around her legs and she couldn't swim with all that weight. She just sank. She sank real fast. It was so . . ."

She doesn't finish the sentence.

"Put your seat belt on, Stacey."

"Okay." She answers as if on automatic now. "Do you have a cell phone? I can call the police."

"Not on me. If you don't think you can drive, then wait at the exit from the graveyard."

"What way is that?"

"Turn around and go back the way he came. You'll see where to go soon enough."

"Okay."

"And Stacey?"

"Yes."

"Take your time. There's no hurry now. I have a promise to keep."

CHAPTER FIFTY-NINE

There has to be a shovel around here somewhere, but I can't see it. I don't want to spend long looking for it, and after about a minute I figure that's long enough. The night is quiet except for the wind swirling around the trees and the rain slapping on the ground.

I shine the flashlight into the grave, and David is lying there in the same position I left him.

"Hey, hey, David, wake up. Hey!"

I pick up handfuls of dirt and start throwing them at his face, hoping they'll bring him around, but they don't. My hand is aching from the punch I threw. I throw more dirt at David. He groans. He looks half-asleep as he tries to roll over inside the coffin. Things get a little awkward for him, and he reaches up to his face and a moment later opens his eyes.

Everything must flood back to him, because now he sits up straight. His arm is on a funny angle and he stares at it with a confused look. He seems to understand what has happened just as the pain hits him. His face tightens up as he tries to cradle his bad arm with his good.

"What the fuck?" he says.

"Remember me?" I ask.

He looks up at me, and I point the flashlight at myself so he can get a good look.

"Hey, look, mister, I don't want any trouble here," David says, as if I'm the one causing trouble and he just happens to be in the wrong place at the wrong time.

"Cut the bullshit, David. You're not fooling me twice."

"I don't even know who you are," he says, and two months ago he might have been able to act his way out of any situation. But right here, right now in this moment, the mask he wears to fit into and be a part of normal society doesn't cover his eyes.

"You know who I am," I tell him.

"And what if I do?"

"If you do, then you know you're in serious trouble right about now."

"So what, you're going to kill me now? Is that your plan?" he asks.

"You know I really haven't decided yet. That's about as truthful as I can get. See, the last eight weeks have been kind of tough on me. Hell, the last two years. I'm trying to weigh everything up, and I just don't know."

"Fuck you." He gets to his feet and starts looking around, probably trying to figure out if he can climb out before I get to him. I wonder how he got Father Julian out. He doesn't look strong enough to have lifted that much weight. I point the flashlight at the ground and pick out drag marks across the grass. He probably tied a rope around the body and towed it with his car. Maybe he towed him all the way to the lake.

"Tell me why," I say.

"Get me out of here, man. My arm is killing me."

"Talk to me."

"No."

"Come on, tell me why," I say. "Was it because you liked fucking your sisters?" I ask, trying to shock him.

He doesn't answer. Just looks up at me.

"That's why you raped them all, right? Because you loved it."

"How can you know anything about anything?" he asks.

"I heard the tapes, David. I know you enjoyed it."

"It's so simple for you, isn't it?" he says, and here is the calm David again. And perhaps the real one lives in both worlds—good and bad, light and dark—a man who balances his life between creating an illusion and playing a monster. "It's simple to stand up there and look down on me, judging me, because you're not the one with a head full of disgusting memories, you're not the one who—"

"You're a sick boy who acted out," I say. "That's the bit I understand. Rachel didn't deserve what you did to her, not by any means, but I can at least figure out why. What I can't figure out is why the others? Why kill them?"

"Why not?"

He reaches his hand out to the ground above the grave and I step toward it. He pulls it away without the need for me to crush his fingers.

"When you were here two years ago for Rachel's grandmother's funeral, what happened? Who spoke to her?"

"It wasn't her."

"To you? Somebody spoke to you? Was it Sidney Alderman?"

"Just some old drunk who smelled like he hadn't showered

in about a month. I told him to fuck off. You want to know what he told me?"

"What?"

"He said, 'How does it feel fucking your sister, David? Is she juicy?' I pushed him away and he just laughed at me, like he was somehow proud of it. I took a swing at him and knocked him to the ground. He stopped laughing then, but he wasn't finished. He said, 'Do you know who your dad is? Do you know who her dad is? Look it up, boy, look it up. And do something about it.' I walked away from the guy, but his words, man, they just kept following me. It wasn't because the guy knew who I was, it was something else. I found out the following day who my father was."

"Henry Martins told you."

He starts to laugh. "That old bastard was just as bad as the others. He told me all about Father Julian, and told me I wasn't the only one. That priest had been sleeping with his parishioners for years. I asked him about Patricia Tyler. He knew, man! He fucking knew her. I went back to the cemetery. Bruce was my brother. The old man, he was messed up with drink, but Bruce was okay. A bit nervous, but okay. And the closest thing I had to family."

"What about your mother?" I ask.

"You're kidding, right? If she hadn't been whoring around back then, none of this would have happened. I'd have had a normal life."

"You wouldn't have even existed."

He shrugs, like it doesn't matter.

"When you were alone at the funeral, how did Sidney Alderman know who you were?"

"How should I know? I guess he recognized my mother, and later I had all the proof I needed."

"You told Rachel who her dad was, and took her to see him, didn't you."

"She confronted him and he admitted it. I waited outside for her. When she told me, I felt like I'd been hit in the stomach with a sledgehammer. I dropped to my knees and just threw up. When she tried to comfort me I pulled away. I didn't want to be anywhere near her. I told her to leave me alone, but she wanted to talk. Thing is, she couldn't when I had my hands crushing her throat. The life had gone out of her, and still I couldn't let go. You probably think that's bullshit. You think that it was my plan to kill her if that old drunk was right about what he said, but it wasn't. There was no plan. We were still in the cemetery when it happened. I could even see the church."

The rain is starting to get heavier and I wonder if it's pooling inside the coffin or soaking into the wood. I have both hands jammed in my pockets—my right one is starting to throb painfully—so I start pacing around the grave. David keeps turning in the coffin so he can keep looking up at me.

"And the others?" I ask.

"What about them?"

"Why'd you kill them?"

"They were my sisters. I figured if it could happen once, it could happen again."

"You're full of shit. You'd already killed Henry Martins, which means you already knew the truth before driving Rachel to speak to Father Julian. That means you thought about it pretty hard. It means the knowledge of you being with your sister grew like a cancer inside your brain and the only way you could cut it out was to kill Rachel. You took her to see Father Julian knowing that she wouldn't be seeing anybody else ever again afterward. Once you knew who those other

girls were, there was no chance of accidentally dating one of them. You were killing them because you enjoyed it. What about the girl tonight? She's not even one of your sisters, is she? You just can't stop yourself."

He shrugs. "So what does it matter?"

"Because you were talking to her like she was. It just goes to show how fucked in the head you really are. But why me? Why try and frame me for Father Julian?"

"You killed my brother."

"He killed himself."

I think about Patricia Tyler's last words to me, the promise she wanted me to make. The last month has been full of broken promises. I think of the man I once was, the man I became when I was drinking, the man in between, and the man I am now. Which one of them is the real me? I could keep talking until the police arrive, or take him into the station myself. That would earn me some credit. They'll lock David up and there's enough evidence to put him away for a long time, but a long time in this justice system is only ten or fifteen years. Is that really justice? He won't even be forty when he comes out. I doubt that would sound like justice to any of the girls. Or to Patricia Tyler. Can this sick kid be redeemed in ten years? Is redemption even possible?

"We're going to the police," I say.

"Fuck that."

"It's the only option."

He goes quiet as he thinks about it. "Okay, but you're going to have to help me out of here. My arm's broken."

"Don't try anything."

"I won't."

I close my eyes. I think of Emily. I think of all the dead girls. I think of a promise I made. I crouch down and lower my hand. He grabs it and pulls me down, and I fall, just as I have been falling since the day I drove Quentin James out into the woods. I let it happen, and I knew it would happen, and when I land on top of him my face doesn't register the surprise he was hoping to see. His plan, his only plan, to pull me in and crack my head into the coffin or break my neck, hasn't worked. He can see that now, and he can see his mistake.

The blood floods out over my hand. It's warm and sticky and thick, and I hate the feel of it. When I pull it away from him, I leave the pocketknife I took from his car in his chest. He reaches down to it and pulls it out as if he's just been stung by something, then looks at it as if he has no idea what it is. He stares at me, his face pale and streaked with blood and tears. His mouth opens and closes, but he can't say anything; his mouth forms an O, but nothing comes out. This lonely boy who learned who he was and made the rest of the world pay for it. He breathes heavily until the breaths become softer and softer. The knife falls from his hand.

He sinks back down as he dies in front of me. I wipe my hand across the soggy lining of the coffin before pulling myself out. I sit on the ground and lean against the gravestone, and I watch the sky, looking for a break in the clouds, hoping for a break in the rain, wishing more than anything that I could have a drink right about now.

I'm not sure how much time passes before the police arrive, but I'm still sitting here when they do. Three days sober, and more positive than ever that I now know exactly who I am.

ACKNOWLEDGMENTS

This US version is a little different from the version that came out in NZ back in 2008—it's been a little tweaked and a little improved and is around five or six thousand words longer. I have a really cool team of people to thank for looking after the books—the team at Atria. I would like to start out by thanking Judith Curr, Mellony Torres, Emily Bestler, Janice Fryer, Lisa Keim, Daniella Wexler, Isolde Sauer, Anne Spieth, and Gillian Cowin. And, of course, my editor Sarah Branham, who has made this book sharper and better than the original, and to whom I'm eternally grateful and lucky to have in my corner.

I'm also eternally grateful to have the best agent in the world looking after me—Jane Gregory of Gregory & Company. Jane has been changing my life in great ways over the last few years. Working with Jane and also doing a fantastic job are Claire Morris and Linden Sheriff. Then there's

Stephanie Glencross, who is, without a doubt, one of the most talented editors I've ever worked with. I'm a lucky man to have her looking after me too.

And, of course, thanks again to all of you who have enjoyed the books, to those of you who send encouraging emails, have sent cool messages on Facebook, for showing up at book signings—you guys are the reason I do what I do and, I've said it before and I'll say it again, you guys are the reason I keep trying to make bad things happen (but only in the books . . . I promise).